"You want to preach? I'll give you five minutes. Explain it to me, Father. How can an American side with Germans against his own country, and in good conscience?"

Fr. Viktor read faces around the stark, smoky office. At best his countrymen deemed him misguided; at worst they suspected him a minion of evil incarnate. Beyond the expectancy that permeated this murky room he felt a deeper silence, the sensation of a million dead listening from the edge of Eternity, all wondering why one Bavarian village should be spared the cup they had been forced to drink in one unfathomable swallow. And yet, a bright conviction lined every thought crossing his mind: *My cause is righteous.* The priest drew a breath and prayed that Americans would listen . . .

THE SOWER of BLACK FIELD

Inspired by the True Story of an American in Nazi Germany

KATHERINE KOCH

ISBN 979-8-9876299-1-8
Library of Congress Catalog Card Number: 2024913051

The Sower of Black Field is a work of fiction. Where real people, events, establishments, organizations, or locales appear, they are used fictitiously. All other elements of the novel are drawn from the author's imagination.

For Ed Pancoast,
the movable piece in the Framework who
brought this unknown story to the Koch family.

PRAISE FOR *THE SOWER OF BLACK FIELD*

"A compelling exploration of faith and resistance in the face of oppression."
　　　✓ GET IT —*Kirkus Reviews*

"Faith in God, and the testing of that faith, is interwoven throughout the novel . . . A picture emerges of people caught up in a conflict not of their making, resisting as they can from its evils, and finding strength in the courageous example of their pastor."
　　　—*Chanticleer Book Reviews,* "BEST BOOK," 5 STARS!

"*The Sower of Black Field* is a beautifully-told and compelling story of a man who defies seemingly insurmountable odds, guided by the belief that faith and goodness win in the end . . . Katherine Koch has done us a great service by unfolding the story of Father Viktor Koch, C.P., a true hero whose courage helped save a German town from certain retribution and ruin. *The Sower of Black Field* inspired me and gave me hope in humanity."
　　　—*Father Edward L. Beck, C.P.,*
　Faith and Religion Media Commentator, author, playwright

"An extraordinary achievement. Koch takes the complexities, drama, and contradictions of World War II, and brings them to life in one small German town on the brink of disaster . . . Somehow an American priest and his community find a way to turn a potentially deadly punishment into a soul-searching, redemptive act of faith and resilience."
　　　—*Dr. Christopher E. Mauriello, author of* Forced Confrontation:
　The Politics of Dead Bodies in Germany at the End of WWII

Table of Contents

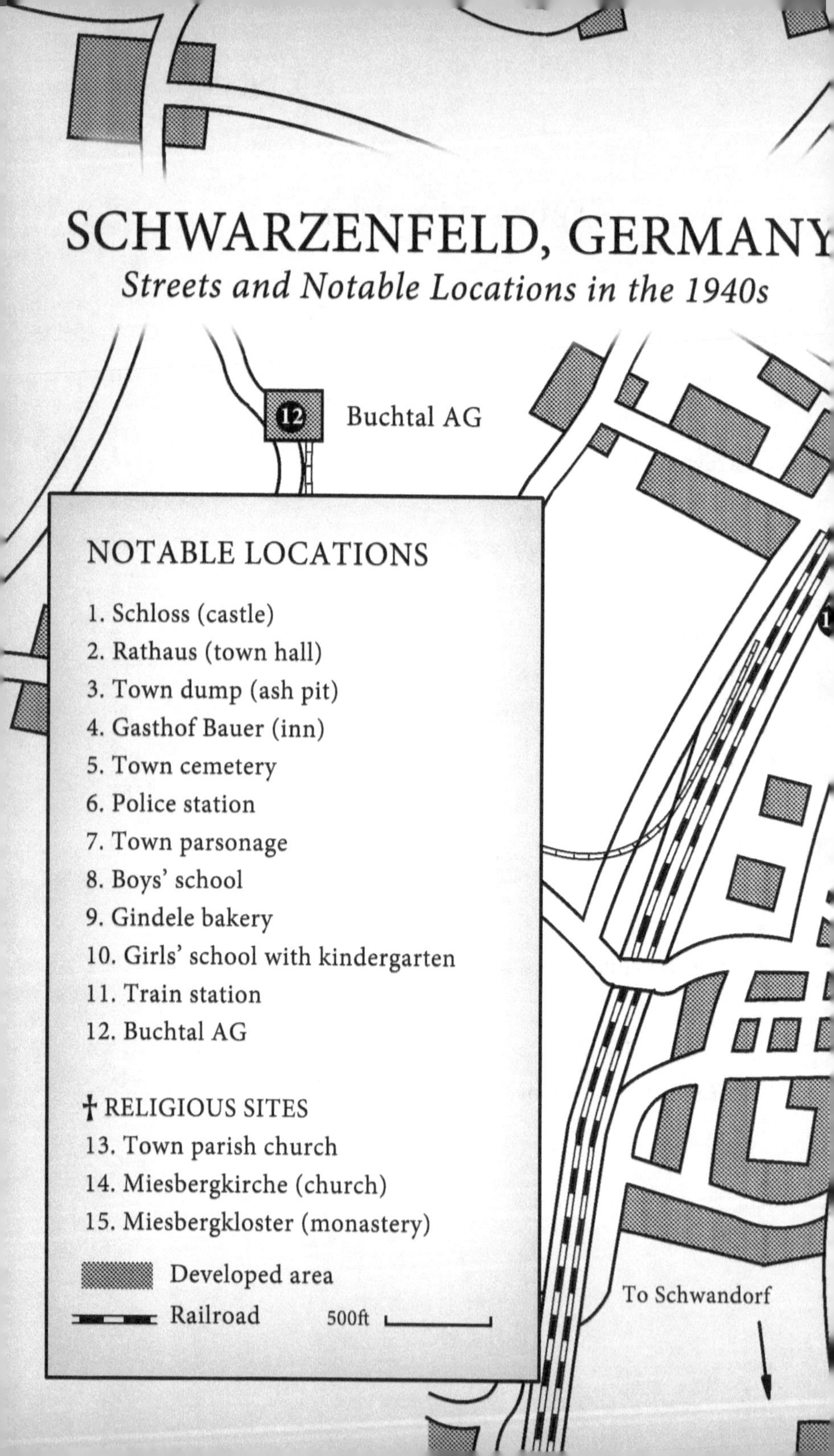

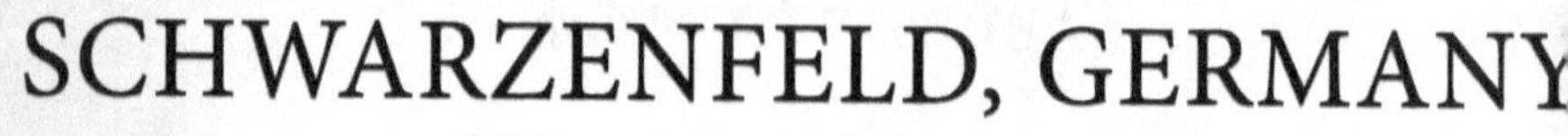

SCHWARZENFELD, GERMANY
Streets and Notable Locations in the 1940s

12 Buchtal AG

NOTABLE LOCATIONS

1. Schloss (castle)
2. Rathaus (town hall)
3. Town dump (ash pit)
4. Gasthof Bauer (inn)
5. Town cemetery
6. Police station
7. Town parsonage
8. Boys' school
9. Gindele bakery
10. Girls' school with kindergarten
11. Train station
12. Buchtal AG

✝ RELIGIOUS SITES
13. Town parish church
14. Miesbergkirche (church)
15. Miesbergkloster (monastery)

Developed area
Railroad   500ft

To Schwandorf

Naab River
Naab River
Naab River Bridge
Miesbergallee
Bahnhofstrasse
Hauptstrasse
Ambergerstrasse
14
15
6
8
10
9
7
1
13
2
5
4
3

THE BAVARIAN OBERPFALZ
Within Germany, April 1941
Bavaria
Bayreuth
Flossenbürg
Nürnberg
Amberg
Schwarzenfeld
Schwandorf
Bavarian Oberpfalz
Regensburg
GERMANY
Oberpfalz
Bavaria
Annexed territory in Lithuania
Annexed territory in Czechoslov
Annexed territory of Austria
20mi

TO THE READER

The Sower of Black Field recounts historical events that transpired in Schwarzenfeld, Germany, between 1941 and 1945, as witnessed by American missionary Fr. Viktor Koch, C.P., and his followers.

Readers who are familiar with this history will encounter elements not found in German or Passionist chronicles. Names of select historical figures have been intentionally changed, and characters based on real people have been added for thematic relevance. I used fiction to fill in details long forgotten by eyewitnesses, and to heighten dramatic tension in certain scenes. In this novel I have also included an afterword titled, 'Author in the Confessional,' which highlights points where I applied creative license. For those who are interested in bare-bone facts, an annotated historical account exists on the website www.viktorkoch.com.

Sharp-eyed readers will note that German nouns are handled differently from conventions found in English grammar manuals. I have chosen to honor capitalization rules for these words according to their native language.

Last—and perhaps not least—American readers may wonder how to pronounce Fr. Viktor's surname: *Koch*. It is always articulated the same way in Germany, but it has many phonetic variations in the States. *Koch* is the German word for *cook*, and Fr. Viktor's parents adopted this pronunciation after immigrating to American shores.

—K.K.

INTRODUCTION

Schwarzenfeld is a backwater village nestled in the rambling, pine-covered hills of southeast Germany. To an observer in the 1940s, it is a typical Bavarian farm town. The houses are austere plaster, topped by red-tiled roofs. A stately, white-walled castle broods overhead like a relic from a bygone age, its presence whispering of a history that stretches back to the medieval era. Only a far-flung train station hints at a connection to modern times. For centuries, two sharp gray steeples have dominated the skyline—one belonging to a rococo parish church, the other to a hilltop shrine—and both stand as a testament to the Catholic fervor that burns deep in Bavarian culture. Months have passed since a car rolled along the dirt-paved roads, for automobiles are a rarity here. A pedestrian ambling along Schwarzenfeld's main thoroughfare, the Hauptstrasse, is far more likely to encounter a cattle herd lazing about the street, or farmers hauling their wares by wagon. However, one fact makes this nondescript village the most remarkable place in the Third Reich: in this town, Germans have given their loyalty to an American.

This U.S. citizen is Fr. Viktor Koch, C.P., a missionary and Pennsylvania native who left America to found a new province for his religious order, the Passionists. All members of this monastic community have vowed to sow a novel doctrine—they declare suffering the great and terrible equalizer of humanity, uniting every soul on earth regardless of nation, race, or creed. Intuition tells Fr. Viktor that Germany, the vanquished aggressor of World War I, needs this far-reaching message more than any other country. He is a foreigner by birth, but not by culture or language. A son of German immigrants, he speaks fluent *Hochdeutsch* with a round, downy American accent.

Appointed to lead the new European province, he departs for Bavaria in 1922, at age fifty. From the start he proves his mettle. Accompanied by Fr. Valentin Lenherd, C.P., his closest friend and fellow Passionist, he bears witness to the turmoil that wracks his ancestral homeland. Inflation and unemployment ravage the country like twin plagues. Not even a bucketful of German marks can buy a loaf of bread. The Weimar government forbids new religious orders from opening institutions in Germany, condemning the Passionist mission to failure, but Fr. Viktor is undeterred. At times like this, he is apt to quote his favorite adage: "God provides." Instead of conceding defeat, he wheels and deals with Bavarian cardinals, holds whirlwind fundraisers in America, and opens two monasteries—one in Munich, Germany, and a second in Maria Schutz, Austria. He relishes each victory over the German government, celebrating every triumph with a fine cigar.

In 1933, when he visits Schwarzenfeld and decides to build a new monastery beside the Miesbergkirche, the hilltop shrine overlooking their town, the population hails him as a hero. He has $200,000 in U.S. funds at his disposal—enough to hire every able-bodied laborer in the impoverished village, plus tradesmen scouring the countryside for work. Thus, as Adolf Hitler beguiles a desperate nation with economic miracles, the devout Catholics of Schwarzenfeld find an American priest ushering them from poverty into plenty. They reverently call Fr. Viktor "our Provinsche," a moniker derived from his official title, provincial.

When the winds of oppression and war sweep through Europe once again, Fr. Viktor struggles to ignore grim predictions made by Fr. Stanislaus Grennan, his superior in America: *the German province will prove to be a total failure.* In 1937, the Nazis close his monastery in Munich. Gestapo agents begin hunting down foreign missionaries and drive them from European shores, including American Passionists who joined the German mission. Through sheer coincidence, Fr. Viktor finds a legal loophole that prevents his own deportation. After the first panzers rage across Poland's border, German priests of military age receive call-up notices from the *Wehrmacht*. A province forty-one members strong drops to thirteen overnight. The most devastating event occurs in February 1941: Fr. Valentin Lenherd, his comrade through tribulation, dies of cancer. Fr. Viktor barely has time to grieve before the next threat unfolds.

By April 1941, Hitler's persecution of the German Catholic Church is entering a new phase. Nazi authorities have confiscated monasteries throughout Bavaria, evicting their inhabitants and reallocating the facilities for secular purposes. One organization that benefits from these mass appropriations is the *National-sozialistische Volkswohlfahrt* (NSV), the public welfare department charged with the task of opening rest houses, military hospitals, and shelters for German citizens fleeing cities plagued by air raids. In Schwandorf, a town six miles south of Schwarzenfeld, NSV office director Wilhelm Seiz receives orders from the State to house one hundred children evacuated from Hamburg. Searching the

Oberpfalz, his attention falls upon a spacious residence that suits his needs perfectly. Confiscating this building is not a straightforward matter: a foreigner owns the mortgage, and an international scandal might erupt if the occupants refuse to leave peacefully, but the fires of Seiz's determination are stoked. Though he is only a minor official, he has cultivated connections in the party. He will stop at nothing until the property falls into NSV hands.

The building he wants to acquire is Fr. Viktor's monastery in Schwarzenfeld, the Miesbergkloster.

JESU XPI
PASSIO

CHAPTER ONE

THE AMERICAN PROVINSCHE

APRIL 9, 1941

The car, a black and silver-trimmed Mercedes, rumbled out of the hills like thunder from a cloudless sky. Stillness gripped the Bavarian village of Schwarzenfeld. Field hands plowing a lush expanse of farmland stood bloodless, breathless, haunted, watching it pass. Townswomen drew aside curtains and furtively peered outside. They whispered among themselves. *Look there. Do you see it? Has someone been denounced? Is it the Gestapo, do you think? Someone is in trouble, that is clear enough. Who?* The harbinger rushed across an iron bridge spanning the Naab River. It roared between knots of white plaster houses and scattered a cattle herd lumbering along Schwarzenfeld's main road, the Hauptstrasse. Then, to the dismay of all who watched, it slowed. The Mercedes veered onto a tree-lined alley and clambered up the Miesberg, a grassy hill that loomed protectively over their town.

An idyllic sun-gold church and monastery crowned the mountain. Fr. Viktor Koch, C.P., hastened from the churchyard where he had prayed a rosary at the grave of Fr. Valentin Lenherd. He shaded ice-blue eyes from the morning sun and shivered. "Well, this doesn't bode well," the sixty-seven-year-old missionary said to himself in English, his native tongue. The government had confiscated privately-owned cars for the war effort two years ago, forcing civilians to travel on foot or by train. In this remote corner of the Oberpfalz, only gendarmes, secret state police, and political officials enjoyed the privilege of automobiles, and if they rolled up to his door in one, it meant the Reich deemed their mission important enough to deprive German troops of a gasoline ration.

The Mercedes skulked through his courtyard gate. It prowled within the shadow of a plaster wall that circled his church and cloister. His face cold and stern, Fr. Viktor tucked his arms beneath a long black mantle. He longed to flee into the mystic peace of his hilltop monastery, the Miesbergkloster, but thought better of it. Men arriving in a Mercedes would insist upon speaking to the pater provincial.

Car doors opened and slammed shut. A lone pair of boots approached in a brisk cadence.

"Heil Hitler."

"Herr *Amtsleiter* Seiz," Fr. Viktor said. "*Gruess Gott*—God greet you." He considered himself fortunate: in this part of Bavaria, fervent Catholics outnumbered National Socialists four to one, and even devout party members grudgingly permitted him to return a greeting in God's name. His oiled and ticking mind shifted gears into *Hochdeutsch*. He had learned High German from his mother and father, both immigrants who escaped serfdom in their native fatherland to begin life anew on American shores.

"What brings you out here to Schwarzenfeld, Herr Amtsleiter?"

"You have an important guest," Seiz explained. "That man you see over there, the one getting out of the car. That is *Gauleiter* Fritz Wächtler. He is here from Bayreuth, and we have arranged for him to stop at the Miesberg."

"You brought the Gauleiter here?" Fr. Viktor said. The political office was comparable to that of an American state governor. His visitors were German officials, not Gestapo. Still, he felt no inclination to relax. "And what have we done to deserve this honor?"

"Gauleiter Wächtler would like to inspect your monastery," Seiz announced.

"Weren't you here for that last week?" The provincial looked at him sidelong. "I didn't like it then, and I sure don't like it now. Why are you doing it again?"

"The Gauleiter wishes to see the Miesbergkloster himself."

"Really? I can't imagine why a Gauleiter would be interested in a monastery." Fr. Viktor studied Seiz. The Amtsleiter—a county-level office director—was in his early forties. He wore a meticulous brown uniform and a matching cap that bore silver banding and an eagle insignia below its peaked crown. The hat's brim cast a shadow over his sharp nose and fair, clean-cut features, shading sapphire eyes that gleamed with fierce purpose. Meeting that cold jewel stare, the provincial pulled his mantle closer, tighter.

"Look, this is Holy Week and I have to join my community for prayer. Come back another time."

"But I have orders to show Gauleiter Wächtler around the Miesbergkloster this morning."

Seiz plucked a paper from his breast pocket. The letter bore Wächtler's signature along with an inevitable stamp, an eagle wrapping its talons around a wreathed swastika.

"Apparently you do," Fr. Viktor muttered.

"We will not be an inconvenience to you, Pater. Go attend your prayer service, we can find our own way around the building."

Fr. Viktor's skeptical gaze bounded from the party member's satisfied smile to the paper fluttering in his hand. "It seems I have no choice in the matter."

"I see we have an understanding," Seiz said amicably.

Fr. Viktor plodded up a staircase leading to the monastery door while Seiz beckoned the two men who had emerged from the car. The hawkish gathering struck Fr. Viktor as an odd assemblage of party leadership. Behind Seiz stood *Bürgermeister* Georg Braun, the mayor of Schwarzenfeld. The man wore a gold-fringed swastika button on his lapel, confirming that he had been a party faithful since the day Hitler announced his revolution in a Munich beer hall. Gauleiter Wächtler, a stern-lipped, silver-haired man, loomed beside the mayor like a roiling thunderhead.

Silence stretched after introductions. Three party members waited for Fr. Viktor to open the door of this monastery, his haven. "*Meine Herren*, welcome to the Miesbergkloster," he greeted warily. "If you'll follow me . . ."

———

Heaving open an arched wooden door and stepping aside for his visitors, Fr. Viktor squinted into a dimly lit vestibule. Impatiently waiting for his eyes to adjust, he flinched at black shapes, the figures of four monks from his depleted community. His brethren shuffled along, all gray or graying, the oldest bow-backed by age. They gawked at swastika armbands and swung to him, shaken, wide-eyed. He waved them away.

Fr. Paul Böhminghaus rushed down a wooden staircase. The middle-aged Austrian lingered until he caught Fr. Viktor's eye, then receded into a shadow haunting the doorway. Last week he had transferred from the community at Maria Schutz to the one in Schwarzenfeld, succeeding Fr. Valentin as rector of this monastery.

Paul. The provincial reflected. The death of his dear friend Fr. Valentin had torn a hole in his soul, and when he needed a listening ear or a steady presence by his side, he invariably found Fr. Paul standing at earnest attention.

The Austrian priest joined him and peered over the gold wire rim of his spectacles. "Do you know who that is, Viktor?"

"It's the Gauleiter."

"Do you see the crimson collar patches on his coat? He is a leader of the Reich. A man like that reports directly to people like Himmler and Göring. What is he doing here?"

"Seiz brought him," Fr. Viktor said.

"But why would he bring such a high-ranking official here to the Miesbergkloster?"

"He's up to something. Whatever the party wants, it must be real important."

"A Gauleiter." Fr. Paul drew in a hissing breath. "I fear this may be it, *mein Freund.* You may not be lighting any more cigars in celebration."

Gauleiter Wächtler glared as the two priests exchanged conspiratorial whispers. Fr. Viktor smiled back affably. "Seiz told me to join our brethren for prayer. Plainly, he doesn't want us meddling in his affairs. Not that I'm asking for an invitation." He jerked his head toward the corridor.

"Come on, Paul. Let's meddle."

"May the dear Lord be with us." The Austrian priest crossed himself and followed.

Fr. Viktor proceeded in a leisurely stroll behind their visitors. Seiz led Gauleiter Wächtler and Bürgermeister Braun into the residence wing, his arm curling around a sheaf of detailed notes he had written during his previous tour. Three brown uniforms towered starkly against stucco walls of tranquil white; sharp footfalls invaded the hallowed silence. "Herr Gauleiter, allow me to present the Miesbergkloster," the NSV director announced, his smooth baritone voice echoing along the hall. "This building has exactly twenty-five monastic cells, one refectory, one kitchen, three recreation rooms, three bathrooms, two parlors, one choir room, and one library. Only six residents are here now, but this place can accommodate more people than that. It is a woefully inefficient use of space, as you can plainly see."

A series of arched wooden doors stretched along their left and right. Seiz opened one and stepped aside for the German governor and the mayor. "The sleeping rooms are comparable to what you see here," Seiz continued. "Four by six meters in space. They are all sparingly furnished. A chair, a desk, a bed." He pursed his lips at the room's only embellishment, a wooden crucifix. "The facilities are very modern, with cold *and* hot running water—in every room! This amenity is rarely found in the countryside."

Fr. Viktor hovered outside the doorway, his eyes sliding right to trade looks with Fr. Paul.

"This is an inspection?"

Blinded by Seiz's machinations, he relied upon powers of observation that fastened on minutiae. The Gauleiter flipped light switches on and off, on and off, testing light fixtures. Braun opened and shut windows, admiring the quality of their construction. The next time Fr. Viktor wrote his father superior in Pittsburgh, he would decline from mentioning this visit. He loathed the prospect of reading another letter enumerating the reasons why his mission in Germany amounted to a fool's errand.

His attention narrowed upon Gauleiter Wächtler. Lips curled in disgust, the German governor waved toward a crucifix. "Are those things in *every* room?"

"The crosses will be taken down." Seiz swept back into the corridor, passing both priests without venturing eye contact.

Fr. Paul pinched and adjusted his spectacles. "Why should these people decide what we do in our monastery?"

"Indeed." The provincial glared at the back of Seiz's dark, sleekly groomed head. *Inspection?* He mulled. *Oh, you devil.*

"This monastery was constructed eight years ago?" Gauleiter Wächtler's gravel voice boomed along the corridor.

Seiz whirled on his heel.

"That's right." Fr. Viktor followed an impulse to assert himself as master of the house. "Not even gold can buy this monastery," he said, glancing in Seiz's direction. "There's too much love in it. Its very foundations are a symbol of the friendship our religious community shares with the people of Schwarzenfeld."

"Eight years ago." Gauleiter Wächtler fingered swastika medals pinned to his tunic. "At that time, our Führer was just beginning to get Germany back in order."

"Yes, those were such desperate days," Fr. Viktor agreed. The Depression had depleted America, yet its impact back home paled in comparison to the destitution that had coursed through Germany. The pain had called him and Fr. Valentin to this land. They were Passionists: in a suffering face they beheld the visage of Christ.

"And how did the party let you build a monastery when the Catholic Church is forbidden from opening new institutions here?" the Gauleiter asked.

"How?" Fr. Viktor rubbed his chin, reflecting. "Back when we were in the planning stages, there was a slight misunderstanding.

The party knew we had a construction project, but somehow—and I really have no idea how it happened—it escaped their attention that we were building a *monastery*. They thought we were building a residence house." The provincial cringed at the memory. "They nearly shut us down—until we reminded them that Herr Hitler made it mandatory for German men to find employment after the Depression. So many people needed work, and in a place this small, well, opportunities were hard to find."

"Pater Provincial Koch hired every unemployed laborer in Schwarzenfeld and the surrounding areas to build this monastery," Fr. Paul interjected with reverence. "He rescued this entire town from poverty."

"The unemployment rate in the Oberpfalz was nil compared to the rest of Germany. The party had to let us finish construction." Fr. Viktor grinned, remembering the lovely cigar he had enjoyed after the incident. An American adage shot through his mind: *fight fire with fire.* In his experience, that logic worked for the Reich. The survival of his province depended upon it.

Gauleiter Wächtler grunted, though he also smiled faintly. Fr. Viktor interpreted the sound as a contemptuous laugh.

"So, you put bread and meat on many tables," the German governor observed. "That would explain why you are popular in these parts . . . Provinsche." Wächtler swiveled back toward Seiz, who shot a glare in Fr. Viktor's direction before swaggering off to conduct an "inspection" of the monastery kitchen.

Provinsche. Fr. Viktor found the moniker endearing, but parishioners never used it in his presence. The Germans considered it rude to address a revered figure by his nickname, and he knew enough to perceive the governor's use of it as a slight. Fr. Viktor quelled a compulsion to make a pithy remark about "der Hitler."

———

The Gauleiter's tour stretched into an hour-long visit. Fr. Viktor followed the procession through a methodically selected chain of rooms, including a kitchen redolent with the aromas of coffee and eggs that his German brethren proudly scrambled in "American style," a second-floor vestibule decked with Marian statuettes that elicited another scowl from Gauleiter Wächtler, and a recreation room that Seiz recommended for office space.

At length the tour ended at the Miesbergkloster veranda, where their visitors stopped to admire a stunning panorama. Fr. Viktor tugged his mantle closer and stepped outside, reveling in mild spring sunlight. Cumulous clouds billowed overhead. Their shadows slid lazily over a rolling landscape studded by church steeples, quaint Bavarian homesteads, and the Naab River's meandering silver line. Oh, he loved this place. Even when she lay shrouded in the grays of early spring, the Oberpfalz entranced him. More than that, Germany exuded a sense of age that stirred his blood. The Miesbergkirche, the hilltop pilgrimage church towering beside his monastery, had been constructed two centuries ago, and by European standards, she was still a child. Schwarzenfeld's founders had established the riverside village back in the year 1015. *This town is 926 years old!* The thought staggered him.

"Look at our visitors," he said to Fr. Paul. "They see the beauty of nature, and the bones of time. Yet they feel no awe for the Creator who made it."

Fr. Paul meditated. "Perhaps one must allow the Presence to exist within oneself first, before he can rejoice in His blessings."

"True."

"These men. That Gauleiter especially."

"What about them?"

"When you look into their eyes, Viktor, what do you see?"

"Mm. That *stare*," he muttered. "Sometimes I wonder if the party doesn't appoint leaders based on that alone."

A breezy silence stretched for a moment. "The light of the body is the eye," Fr. Paul quoted, his serene voice drifting across a gulf of contemplation. "If therefore thine eye be single, thy whole body shall be full of light. But if thine eye be evil, thy whole body shall be full of darkness. If therefore the light that is in thee be darkness, how great is that darkness!"

"Matthew six, verses twenty-two and twenty-three," Fr. Viktor said. "I always liked that one."

"I have been looking for that light in the eyes of these men," the Austrian mused. "It disturbs me greatly to see it so dim—even non-existent."

Fr. Viktor thought of bowed heads and rosary beads, the devotion of parishioners kneeling in the pews of his church. *Keep that light kindled in this dark land. Amen, Lord—but what do I do about these men?*

His visitors loitered around a slender railing that overlooked the monastery's freshly tilled gardens. Gauleiter Wächtler peered southeast, where red-tiled rooftops sprouted in dense clusters at the Miesberg's base.

"Small town," the German governor commented.

"And it is quiet," Seiz pointed out eagerly, his neck craned to evaluate Wächtler's reactions. "It is far from the air-raids."

The Gauleiter's iron gaze gravitated in Fr. Viktor's direction. "You may have German heritage, Provinsche," he said, peering down his long nose, "and your *Hochdeutsch* is impeccable, but you were not born in this country. Your accent is as clear as day."

"Yes. I was born in America."

"What part?" Wächtler interrogated.

"I was born in the north, in a state called Pennsylvania. I come from the city of Sharon, if you want to know. It's a coal and steel town, and not much bigger than Schwarzenfeld."

The Gauleiter drew back in dismay. "But why are you here? It is against the law for a foreigner to preach to German citizens."

"Oh, I have dual citizenship," Fr. Viktor assured. "I'm an American *and* a German."

"You have papers to prove this?"

"Of course."

Fr. Viktor briefly summarized his mission to found a branch of the Passionist Order in Germany and Austria. He noted Seiz nervously flicking a lighter, his hand shielding a cigarette from the wind. "We have another monastery in the Austrian Alps, and it turns out I lived there just long enough to meet the residency requirement for Austrian citizenship. Because of the annexation into Germany, any Austrian citizen is automatically a citizen of the Reich. Do you want to see my papers? It's no problem. They're in my office, I can go get them."

"Hm." The Gauleiter's eyes dropped to a black and white medal pinned to Fr. Viktor's cassock. "You Jesuits," he muttered.

"We are *Passionists*, Herr Gauleiter," Fr. Paul corrected, his pride in their order overcoming the dread inspired by crimson collar patches. "We are monks of the Passionist Order. Did you see the symbol that we all wear on our robes?" Hastening from the veranda's colonnaded recess, he pointed to the medal upon his chest. *Jesu XPI Passio.* The letters and three nails lay inscribed within a heart, and the heart itself was crowned by a cross.

Fr. Viktor smiled; his friend intended no disrespect to Jesuits. Each religious harbored a stalwart devotion for his order. Gauleiter

Wächtler deigned to glance at Fr. Paul's medal before turning back to the galloping panorama of the Oberpfalz.

"Well, now that the tour is over," Fr. Viktor said, maintaining a neutral tone, "why don't you tell us why we've had the honor of this visit today?"

Intuition told him that this question might trigger a decisive moment for the men in his presence. Observing from the veranda's shadows, Frs. Viktor and Paul watched Seiz position himself in Gauleiter Wächtler's line of sight and pause in anticipation. The NSV director tapped ashes off his cigarette. Fr. Viktor's nose twitched at the dry, faintly sour scent of Turkish tobacco. Gauleiter Wächtler strolled several paces while considering the monastery's sunlit edifice. At last, his grizzled head bobbed in satisfaction. *Yes*, Fr. Viktor thought. *Something has been settled.* Their decision made, the guests proceeded to stroll about the monastery grounds. The provincial beckoned to Seiz, who eyed him shrewdly. He lingered.

"Either the Reich is changing its procedures, which I sincerely doubt," Fr. Viktor said, "or this was no inspection."

Elation lighting his features, Seiz exhaled a triumphant plume of smoke. "You always were a clever man, Pater."

"You want to meet before church?"

"Why?"

"Confession. I hear it's good for the soul."

The party member laughed. "I put my faith in Germany."

"Of course you do."

"All right. Let me explain what is going on, and fortunately, we have no need for a confessional." Seiz took a long drag from the cigarette, mustering himself.

"The State is taking possession of this building, your monastery. The church and sacristies will remain under your control."

He gestured toward the cemetery. "Your province co-founder, Pater Valentin Lenherd, died last month. Your novices were drafted into our army. Your American brethren have been sent back home. Except for the two of you, and four German nationals too old for military service, this building is practically empty. The NSV can put it to better use, namely, as a boarding school to protect German children living in cities threatened by air raids. You have a monastery in Austria that accommodates twenty-five people, and at this time it houses only seven. You will transfer your belongings from this monastery to that one, and leave this building to us. In fact," Seiz considered his watch, all business, "I am sorry to tell you this, but you don't have much time to evacuate. The Gauleiter wants this monastery in our hands by noon tomorrow."

Fr. Paul recoiled. "Noon tomorrow?"

"I suggest you start packing."

"A boarding school?" Fr. Viktor said.

"Yes, a boarding school," Seiz confirmed. "Do you see, Pater? Do you finally see? As I have tried to tell you many times before, our intentions are charitable."

The provincial glanced at a swastika band clutching a brown sleeve. "Right," he murmured. "And the children you house here. What will they learn?"

The party member frowned. "Well, they will learn the history of our people, of course. And why they should be proud of their German heritage. The girls will learn the domestic skills that are needed to run a household and raise children. Like your Church, the Reich approves of large German families. Boys will learn the meaning of duty and—"

"And what about religion?" Fr. Viktor broke in.

"Excuse me?"

"Can we teach them more than blood and soil? Will you let us look after their spiritual welfare, and explain how we are all bound together by the pain of the human condition?"

"Can you—" Seiz flinched. He flicked ashes from the cigarette. "Pater. As I have told you already, my concern is charity. I care only that these children have food on their plates and a roof over their heads, and what they learn is . . . that is up to the Reich. I have no say in that matter."

"I see." Fr. Viktor leaned against the railing, his elbow resting upon an upraised knee. He mustered himself, trusting to faith.

"Well, Herr Amtsleiter, I'm sorry to say you've been wasting the Gauleiter's valuable time here today."

"Wasting it?" Seiz said. "How?"

"You can't take over this monastery, *mein Herr*. We have orders from the cardinal of Munich to stay."

The party member flicked ashes again. "Faulhaber?"

"I see you've heard of him." Fr. Viktor suppressed a smile: every National Socialist in Bavaria knew Cardinal Michael von Faulhaber. A vehement critic of the Reich, Faulhaber was notorious for delivering pungent homilies from the pulpit of St. Michael's Cathedral in Munich. "Cardinal Faulhaber and I go way back," he continued while the party member studied the shine of his boots. "It's no secret that the Reich has been confiscating monasteries left and right. His office is negotiating with the Interior Ministry about this matter. Of course, we share your concern for the children. I know you're a persistent man, I'm sure you'll find a place for them."

Seiz watched him steadily. "You would put your orders above the welfare of German children?"

Fr. Viktor blew a sharp sigh. "Look, I sympathize with your problem, but I've taken a vow of poverty. I don't own this building.

It belongs to our order. The mortgage is owned by the provincial of our mother province in America. You want to buy it? You have to call him."

"You misunderstand, Pater. The Gauleiter is involved now. I don't have to call anyone to acquire your monastery."

In his peripheral vision, Fr. Viktor noted Fr. Paul glancing back and forth.

"Okay, fine." The provincial tugged his leather belt, drawing himself up. "Go ahead. Throw us out and see what happens. Our American mother province will hear about it, that's for sure. And the next time Faulhaber visits Rome, the Vatican will get a real earful about the Reich kicking us out on Holy Thursday. Holy Week, of all times! Now, what do you think the pope will say about your Führer after *that*? Honestly, Herr Amtsleiter." He leaned closer, his eyes narrowing. "And aside from the terrific scandal you'll cause over this matter, I'm sure you'll make quite an impression on the large Catholic population living in this region. I doubt you'll find them in a very generous mood the next time you send the Hitler Youth around to collect donations for the Winter Charity drive."

The party despised public relations flaps, especially ones that rippled into international consciousness. His jaw flexing, Seiz lifted his head and puffed on a cigarette smoked down to a nub. "There are negotiations, you said?"

"Mm-hmm."

"With the Interior Ministry in Munich."

"That's right."

"I will inquire about these orders."

"Yeah, you do that."

"Perhaps Gauleiter Wächtler will extend your deadline."

"Perhaps."

"Heil Hitler." The party member flung his cigarette into the garden and stalked off. After turning to shoot a glacial stare at Fr. Viktor, he slammed the fence gate behind him.

Fr. Viktor frowned at the cigarette releasing spires of smoke from an asparagus patch. Standing in breathy silence, Fr. Paul watched the Mercedes roll down the hillside with a sulky rumble. "Viktor?" The Austrian ruffled his thinning shock of gray-brown hair. "*Mein Freund?*"

". . . Oh, for Pete's sake. Orders from the Gauleiter. Noon on Thursday? Party charity my foot!" Fr. Viktor trudged down a short flight of concrete stairs and lumbered through tilled soil. "Steal our monastery and sell it to the Reich—that's your idea of charity? If you think you're using my monastery to indoctrinate children, well, you've got another thing coming. Go 'Heil Hitler' at someone else's doorstep!" He stooped, retrieving the cigarette. "Yes, Paul?"

"Correct me if I am mistaken. Nothing has been settled with these negotiations. How do you know that Cardinal Faulhaber will prevent the Reich from taking this monastery?"

Fr. Viktor shrugged. "I'm working in the Framework," he said, using his favorite term for the Lord's plan. "God provides. Who am I to argue with His mysterious ways?"

"Naturally. But the Amtsleiter may return. If he forces the issue by involving the police, we will be resisting the State itself. Those disputes usually end in the party's favor."

"Have faith!" Fr. Viktor said heartily. He pitched the cigarette toward blue sky and rolling hills. "Seiz doesn't have a prayer's chance against Faulhaber. I'll phone his representative and make him aware of this situation. But first, why don't we celebrate today's victory with a good cigar?"

CHAPTER TWO

SORROWFUL FRIDAY

APRIL 11, 1941

In the wet, miserable dawn they lined up.

At 7:30 a.m., while roosters crowed a raucous greeting to the new day, all the old men and sullen housewives who still bore red stamps on their ration cards ventured outside. Gripping windblown hats and shawls, they slogged, dour faced, through a cavernous street that was the Hauptstrasse, past sheer-faced buildings that towered ghostlike in the sodden murk of morning, until at last they reached a row of houses where merchants ran shops from street-level parlors. The customer line snaked outside a gray homestead that loomed above the Bahnhofstrasse street corner. Alive with hunger and writhing impatience, it coiled around a narrow entrance fringed with ivy. A wrought iron sign creaked gently, gently in the gray rain. Its flared Gothic letters read *Bäckerei Gindele.*

Scale by scale, its movement stirring bells above the Gindele Bakery's arched doorway, the serpentine line crept into a white stucco room stripped of furnishings. It curled gratefully within the parlor's dry warmth, then pounced upon two women who bustled behind an oak table that functioned as a serving counter. The first customer drew a button-popping breath, reveling in the rich, hearty scent of bread rising in an oven.

"Awful weather today." Fingering a swastika pin on his coat lapel, he turned to fellow customers. "And what was I saying? Oh, yes. Our campaigns have been a tremendous success so far. We took Paris without resistance. Yes. Every town our army passes through, they are waving white flags and surrendering. Our men opened soup kitchens and shelters for the French. Yes! At our Führer's order." The man's voice swooped high and low in worshipful tones. "Well, I believe I see his reasoning. The humanitarian effort will ensure a successful occupation of the country. My wife and I went to see a film in Amberg last Tuesday. They showed it all in a newsreel."

His attention drifted to a worker behind the serving counter. Slim and fair as wheat, she smoothed trembling hands over a black dress and reached for the sack he had brought for his bread.

"Heil Hitler, Frau Heidl. Your husband died in France, yes?"

Frau Helene Heidl looked up.

"Heil Hitler," she said, the words catching in her throat like dust. "Yes. He died in Dunkirk last June."

The man removed his hat. "*Kopf hoch!* He died for the Führer."

Helene felt no compulsion to lift her head high as he had suggested. Custom required her to wear mourning garb for another two months, though the color she wore did not matter, for death was final and infinite. In her heart, every garment she wore would always be a resolute black.

The thirty-two-year-old widow struggled to function. The snaking line. The bread. She considered this customer who prattled about newsreels. He was a native Berliner, the retired headmaster of Schwarzenfeld's primary school, and he greeted everyone in Hitler's name. Frau Maria Gindele, the house mistress at Helene's side, reached for the man's ration booklet and snipped away one red stamp. She invariably honored Bavarian tradition, giving patrons a sweet *"Gruess Gott"* in a buttercream voice, but she was such a benign creature that the party faithful never troubled her over salutations. Helene always returned the greeting offered to her. The widow thought it a safe and practical approach.

Oak floorboards creaked beneath a heavy tread; the bakery owner emerged from the kitchen behind her. Herr Norbert Gindele, a robust, dark-haired man nine years Helene's senior, carried a board laden with bread. She rushed to assist.

The baker wiped a towel over his glistening brow and tugged his collar. "We are all suffocating in that kitchen," he reported in a chipper tone, "but our troops are bearing the hardship with splendid courage, I must say. Another batch will be out soon."

When he flashed a charming grin, Norbert reminded Helene of American film star Clark Gable, only with lighter brow lines and a sharp widow's peak. She smiled and shook her head, thinking of his "troops."

"Ah, Herr Gindele! Heil Hitler."

Norbert had moved toward the kitchen. He halted the instant the headmaster greeted him. *"Gruess Gott,"* he responded, his tone a challenge.

The headmaster regarded him with a speculative gaze. "You fought in France. Yes?"

"Yes. Poland also."

Helene's aquamarine eyes darted toward Maria. The baker's wife twirled an upraised hand, a signal to pack their customer's bread in a hurry.

"Ah, wonderful!" the headmaster said. "I was telling my friends here about a newsreel they are showing in Amberg, about France."

"Is that so." Norbert looked toward the kitchen.

"Oh, yes! It reminds me of my younger days in the first Great War." The headmaster slid his palms together, itching for a rifle. "I would not mind taking another shot at the French!"

Norbert directed a cold, level gaze at the man. "My regiment had a few skirmishes with them. Not everyone agrees with the New Order, it would seem."

Helene plucked a loaf and shook her burned fingers. "Here you are." She thrust the bread sack back at their customer. "Have a good day!"

"Oh, I do wish they would find a way to show these films in our town!" Instead of departing, the headmaster loitered at the counter. "Why, it would do a lot of good to motivate people in these parts. One wonders if these farm people have any concern at all beyond their own fields. Do you not agree, Herr Gindele? When I go to the next party meeting, I will propose it. The films are inspiring, I say. Simply inspiring!"

"Inspiring?" Norbert's head snapped up.

"Oh, yes. Very much so."

"Hah!" The baker snorted. "The man is inspired."

"Norbert, do check the bread that you put in the oven," Maria prompted quickly.

"Yes," the headmaster agreed, "I have taken enough of your time already. Before I go, let me salute one of our fine men who secured great victories in France and Poland. Heil Hitler!"

The headmaster jerked his arm up with the zeal of a man attending a party rally. Helene froze. Tension broadened through the parlor, a silence broken only by the sound of Norbert twisting a towel in his hands.

"Let me tell you something that I believe, *mein Herr*," he said in a slow, crisp voice. "Something that I believe very fervently after spending one year on the front lines."

The headmaster lowered his arm. "And what is that?"

"Norbert!" Helene hissed.

The line shifted while customers moved for a better view. Norbert squinted a baleful eye and rested an elbow on the serving counter. "One day," he gritted, "I am certain that Germany will rue this *inspiring* war that Hitler is spreading across Europe!"

The baker stormed into his kitchen before their customer could aggravate him further by departing in Hitler's name. Given the look on his face Helene suspected that he would have spit on the floor, if he weren't in his own establishment.

The headmaster scowled. "See if I get my bread from this bakery anymore—"

The bell swallowed his words. It spasmed on its hook, ringing, fading, a gray stir of motion, dying. Then silence. Customers traded looks in dismay.

Maria crossed herself, touching her forehead, chest, and left and right shoulder. "Oh, Leni. I pray Norbert will not be sent to the front again. Or arrested."

"I thought you were going to talk to him."

"I have put it in the Lord's hands," Maria said. "He will carry us through."

Helene flinched. "Well, yes," she stammered, "trusting in the Lord, that is fine, of course, but we need Norbert here—"

Maria's serene eyes met hers and she fell silent. Customers crowded the counter. *Better stop talking*, the widow thought. It was far from prudent, speaking one's mind in public.

"Can you manage by yourself for a few minutes?' Helene said. "I will talk to him."

Maria sighed at the widow's black dress. "Oh, you poor dear. You must feel so beset by troubles. Yes, I can manage for a moment. Do go ahead."

The baker's wife gave her an angel's smile and reached for the ration card of their next customer.

———

Helene clomped away on thick-heeled shoes. "Prayers, dear Maria," she muttered. "One cannot put all of one's hope in prayer." The widow knew. She had learned the hard way.

Her gaze swept the crowded parlor until it settled on a wall adorned by a crucifix, the symbol of a God that sustained her through misery. During the Depression she had toiled as a maid for a wealthy Freiherr in Regensburg. Every day she had smuggled his meat scraps home in an apron to feed Klaus, her eldest son, only a toddler at the time, while her husband Nikolaus traipsed the Oberpfalz in search of work. Every day, she had prayed for him. Weary and desperate, Nikolaus stopped in his native Schwarzenfeld, and in this dirt-road village he stumbled upon a miracle: the American Provinsche's decision to build a monastery rescued them all from poverty. They moved to Schwarzenfeld, and she gave birth to a second son, Hans. When war sundered their family again, she relied upon prayer to endure daily war reports, rationed food, and a cold, lonely bed. She had fervently clung to a belief that Nikolaus would come home. Then Bürgermeister Braun strode up to their house on a blustery morning, delivering heartbreak with a death card . . .

The kitchen door groaned open before Helene. Palpable heat flushed sweat from her cheeks; the scent of hot-ember pine mingled with the aroma of sweetly toasted dough.

"Norbert?" She edged past a table spanning the kitchen's length. Youthful faces swung in her direction: Norbert's troops. Schwarzenfeld's schools closed on *Karfreitag*—Sorrowful Friday—yet the morning promised no respite for Norbert and Maria's children. They worked, all five, their assistance a dire necessity to keep the bakery running efficiently. Their son and three eldest daughters sliced and rolled dough. The youngest girl touched her tongue to her upper lip and focused with a child's determination, pasting red customer stamps to reports for the Reich Office of Nutrition. Party officials used those grid-marked papers to calculate supplies that the bakery used, and no one else could spare the time for such drudgery.

"Norbert?" Helene called again. She caught a glimpse of the baker in the oven room, his face outlined in a molten glow.

"Leni!" Norbert greeted, all charm again. He suggested with authority that one of the children assist their mother, and his eldest daughter departed without a word. *Good*, Helene thought. The man knew that she intended to talk. Norbert and Maria were natives of Baden-Württemberg. Both of their families had settled in Schwarzenfeld eight years ago. As fellow outsiders to a small Bavarian village that branded anyone born outside its borders as *Fremde*, foreigners—German or otherwise—they all became fast friends. Helene followed Norbert into a prim sitting room.

"What you did was unwise, you know."

He closed the kitchen door behind them. He was a striking man, handsome, fiercely moral, a devout Catholic.

"It may not have been the wise thing to do, Leni. But it was the *right* thing to do."

"But you know what the party does with people who speak against the war! What do you expect Braun will do to you?"

"He will resort to vexations, I should think."

Helene's jaw dropped. "Vexations."

"Our Bürgermeister is not a fool. If he takes a baker from his shop, he knows he will upset the food supply. Empty bellies make for poor morale." The baker shrugged, looking away. "I just have to be mindful. I cannot push him too far."

"Oh, Norbert." Helene plunked into a parlor chair. "Listen to me for one moment, I beg you. Will you listen, please?"

She let silence stretch. He leaned against the wall, not looking at her, but he was listening.

"Can you imagine what will happen if you are taken? Responsibility for this bakery will fall on my shoulders, and Maria's shoulders. Look at me, I am in black!" He didn't, but she pushed onward. "Can you imagine Maria and I raising our children, running our households, serving customers, and baking enough bread to feed all of these people who depend upon us? Exactly how many loaves do you bake in a day? Twenty dozen?"

He nodded mutely at the estimate.

"That is 240 loaves. How would Maria and I manage that? All the other bakers in this town are working from 5:00 a.m. to midnight already, just like you. They cannot make more bread to support the customers that would leave this shop empty-handed." She watched him pace, hands on his hips. "If you were not needed to manage a bakery, then why did they bring a good soldier home from the front? Explain this to me, please!"

"Because this soldier is a little old for all that marching," he snapped back. "And, I was no soldier to begin with. I am no great loss to the *Wehrmacht*."

Helene reined herself. Norbert stood with a long, vacant look, a wan figure in a gray room. He cracked open a window, then eased himself into a chair beside her.

"Leni," he said gently again. "I am not insensitive to your fears. But I cannot help but rage against anyone who supports this war."

"Why?" she demanded.

"There is so much that I have not told you because . . ." He gestured at her black garb. "But perhaps now, if we are being open with each other?"

"Honestly, when have I ever *not* spoken my mind?"

"Oh, yes," the baker chuckled to her relief, "God knows! This is what makes you such a dear friend. And Nikolaus also. He was the best of men, God rest his soul."

Norbert crossed himself. Helene breathed slowly, her gaze falling to a tassel-fringed rug. Grief was like a loose thread. She felt a desperate unraveling within, hearing Nikolaus' death mentioned a second time today.

"If only," her friend clawed the air, then clapped large, muscular hands upon his knees. "If only you understood the way things are at the front. The way they *really* are."

The widow leaned forward in interest.

Norbert brooded. "In France, it was like the headmaster said. Our men are ordered to conduct themselves with honor. They operate soup kitchens, even for enemy civilians. But Poland . . ." He turned, checking the kitchen door, then he faced her again and lowered his voice. He didn't want his children to overhear. "Poland was another world. No one was distributing soup bowls there. In my division we had an SS regiment assigned with us. The *Leibstandarte*: Hitler's elite. One time we came upon a village full of partisans."

"Partisans?" Helene asked.

"Militants. Armed—loyal to Poland. A comrade of mine said that the SS were herding partisans in barns. Not just men. There were women, children, even infants. That seemed strange. We went to watch. We were close enough to see, but far enough to avoid being seen. The SS—" he drew a breath, his face contorted in the strain of revealing the unthinkable.

"What did they do?" Helene whispered.

"They locked the barns where these people were gathered. They set fire to them. Every night, Leni. I try to sleep, but I can still hear their screams."

Norbert's brown eyes loomed like fevered wells of memory. Helene pulled a hand to her mouth and looked away.

"Have you ever seen things that make you turn cold inside? Things that make you feel stained with blood, consumed by sin, just for having stood there, watching them? *That* is war, Leni. Not the things they show in those newsreels."

"*Ach, Gott,*" she breathed.

"Salute that? Glorify that? *Nein.* I refuse to do so! God never meant for a creature to treat another so savagely."

"No."

"I just hate the way these party devils go on. The godless fools! 'Inspired by war.'" Norbert seethed in disgust.

A chill wind blew through whisper-white curtains and Helene shivered at an appalling awareness of death. For a moment she wished that she had remained with Maria. But a mission had driven her here. What was it?

The parlor. Our customers.

A vision of the line coiled around her, its grip suffocating.

"Norbert." Helene smoothed blond wisps behind her ear. In the emphatic silence, her voice sounded hollow and forlorn.

"I understand you hating this war. It has stolen Nikolaus away from me completely. They buried him on unmarked ground in Dunkirk. I have no memorial where I can mourn him. Often I wonder, 'Where is God?' I cannot fathom why He forsakes us during our darkest moments." She braced herself for reproach from her devout friend. Norbert faced the window and said nothing.

"It all seems hopeless, Norbert. I know that. But we must be practical." Helene swung a pointing finger. "In that parlor, there are women and children depending on you to feed them. Don't tell me this is not important to you!"

She heard her words marching in impassioned steps, yet somehow they faltered before they could reach the man before her. He just stared outside and entrenched himself in blood-soaked memories of war. The widow stopped talking.

She understood why Maria left him alone.

A clap of thunder echoed from somewhere in the house. Helene twisted around to listen. She paled as a voice trumpeted from the parlor: "Herr Gindele!"

Norbert grunted. "Looks like our headmaster wasted no time denouncing me."

"Herr Gindele!"

The baker flung open the sitting room door. Helene followed him through the kitchen, past his wide-eyed children, and into the parlor. She recoiled from the glowering visage of Karl Dobler, Schwarzenfeld's chief of police. Officers in blue-green uniforms swarmed behind him.

"What the devil do you want?" Norbert demanded.

"You will come with us for questioning."

Maria rushed to Norbert's side. "Officer Dobler," she greeted. "*Gruess Gott.* Is there a problem?"

The Gindele children poured from the kitchen and crowded Helene. The youngest cowered against her, and the widow rested a palm upon her braided head.

"Frau Gindele." Officer Dobler raised his arm in a zealous Hitler salute. "It seems your husband has caused no end of trouble since he returned home from the front last month. We have had a complaint against him. It is the third one this week." The police chief scowled at Norbert.

"It is a misunderstanding, I assure you," Maria pleaded, her palms open and beseeching. "He cannot leave. Please! There is so much baking to do—and look at all these customers!"

Officer Dobler remained impassive. "He is coming with us."

Helene drew a breath and prepared to protest, but stopped, knowing that she would accomplish nothing. The police chief's swift arrival stunned her. He had never responded this quickly to a denouncement. A policeman reached for Norbert's arm. He ripped it away. "I know the way to your station. It is only a block away. You people love to make such a show of this." Customers stepped aside for him, gawking. He peered across a silent parlor toward his children and wife. Maria crossed herself and buried her face in shaky hands. Helene stood mute and helpless as Officer Dobler escorted him through the front door.

Maria fled to the kitchen and helped her children finish the day's batches while Helene served customers on her own. The bakery closed at noon. Norbert had failed to return. The widow trudged home, despair drenching her like a thick, lashing rain.

———

At 1:00 p.m. Helene crept into the Miesbergkirche sanctuary for Mass. Singing drifted from the balcony above, a melancholy hymn performed a cappella by the St. Barbara Boys Choir. She remembered a time before war swept Schwarzenfeld's men away, when rich tenor, baritone, and bass voices had filled the sanctuary.

The widow genuflected beside the third pew, occupying an aisle seat where Hans, her seven-year-old son, could easily see her. He served as an altar boy. There he was, holding a crucifix aloft and leading the procession as it made its way down the aisle. His chestnut hair parted in the middle, curling away from a satin forehead. He bore a stunning resemblance to his father. Last year, Klaus had led the procession. Helene heaved a sigh of regret. This year her eldest would spend the afternoon at a junior Hitler Youth troop meeting.

She searched the sanctuary and found Maria clutching a rosary, praying fervently. Her son and four daughters held vigil at her side. Still no sign of Norbert.

Karfreitag. Sorrowful Friday.

The Passionist paters held a special prayer service on this day. Fourteen elegantly painted plaques ringed the church walls, each depicting scenes of Jesus suffering during His Passion. *Jesus is condemned. Jesus carries His cross. Jesus falls . . .* Frs. Viktor and Paul paused near each painting—a Station of the Cross—leading prayers, guiding meditation. Helene tried to follow along, but the crucifixion seemed so ancient, and too many troubles plagued her mind.

Nikolaus. Norbert. Klaus. The customer line. Each thought pierced her like a nail burrowing through flesh.

While the congregation prayed, Helene retreated into herself, deep into flesh and blood and black mourning garb, all her hope entombed in a sepulchre of despair.

"Today we remember the suffering of Christ on Sorrowful Friday. Or 'Good Friday,' as we call it where I come from."

The American Provinsche. His accent entranced her. It was a grammatically correct river of *Hochdeutsch* that lacked the throaty inflections of native speakers. As it flowed through the sanctuary, she felt its unique cadence sweeping her back into a living realm. Fr. Viktor usually donned gold-threaded vestments for a sermon, but not today. Following Passionist custom on *Karfreitag* he remained robed in a monk's habit, a crucifix tucked in his leather belt.

"When I contemplate the meaning of this day, I think back to a Sunday morning when I was a boy, oh, about fifteen years of age." He absently stroked a bible on the church's gold and marble lectern. "A missionary visited our parish church in Sharon. On one morning, he delivered a sermon like the one I'm giving today. My family and I went to Mass every Sunday, so much of what he said, well, we had heard it before." The Provinsche shrugged. "But then he said something *different*. Something striking. 'The Passion of our Lord did not end on Calvary,' he said."

A pause.

Helene's attention shifted from a statue of the Virgin Mary to the American priest.

"In fact, the Passion is going on right now."

Fr. Viktor's lips quirked up at the edges. The sower allowed time for parishioners to absorb the seeds of new ideas. "'The old man is turning senile.' I'm sure that's what you're thinking." People in the pews traded looks. "No! It's true. In fact, I'll prove it." He pointed toward a life-size carving of Christ affixed to the church wall. "Look upon that crucifix there, and ask yourself what you see. If it's simply Jesus on the cross, you need to look deeper."

The high ceiling amplified creaks from old pews and the gray murmur of bodies shifting, chins lifting, heads turning. Struggling beneath the burden of sorrow, Helene raised her head and focused on a crown of thorns.

"Today, if you're scourged by grief," Fr. Viktor said, his words sending a shudder through the widow, "if you're pierced by fear and oppression, if your burdens are so heavy that you stumble beneath their weight, then look *there*, and realize what you're seeing." He continued in a deep, haunting timbre:

"In your darkest sufferings, *you* are the Crucified Christ. His Passion is still going on through you, through me. Through all who are in pain. In every moment of human suffering, He is present."

The third reminder of loss tore at Helene. Out poured the pain she had struggled to contain today, all the fears, the sorrows, the wet, stinging memory of words she could not bear to hear. *Frau Heidl, it is my duty to inform you . . .*

Her tears snared Hans' attention. At the altar boy's pew, his chestnut head bobbed back and forth, straining to see her. Helene bit back grief and mustered a smile.

"My friends," the Provinsche continued from the glimmering altar, his attention briefly resting upon Helene, "today on Sorrowful Friday, we must stop seeing ourselves as individuals with solitary problems. No matter who you are, whether you're rich or poor, whether you have love in your heart or bitter hatred, whether you are a devout Catholic or you don't believe in God at all, we're connected, all of us—and on an intimate level. We're united by the reality of suffering. No one can escape it. And if we can accept that Christ is present in suffering, then we are each a cell in one sacred body. Christ Himself affirms this. 'Whatever you do to the least of my brethren, you do also to Me.' Think about that, what it means . . ."

The river voice slowed with eddies of caution. Helene glanced toward a rear pew and searched for Officer Dobler. He wasn't there, but he had sent other policemen in his stead. Even in the Miesberg-kirche one minded one's words, and it was clear what the Provinsche left unsaid. She envisioned Poles thrashing in a burning barn and felt herself turn numb.

"Today, as you find yourself uplifted upon your cross, I'm sure a question comes to mind. A question that Christ Himself posed. At the height of His agony, Jesus cried out, 'Father, why have You forsaken Me?'"

Fumbling through her purse for a kerchief, Helene looked up.

"It's a profound question. Let's examine it in light of today's revelations. It's obvious that we have free will. We can choose to intervene in suffering—or we can walk on, pretending not to notice. If what I've said is true, if the Holy Spirit inhabits each of us, was it really the Father who watched in silence as Jesus suffered? Or was it the world?" The provincial's gaze traveled the church. "Today, as we find ourselves crucified by grief, by fear, by war, is it God who seems to forsake us . . . *or is it we who forsake one another?*"

Helene flinched and then drew her head back. A pensive silence washed through the sanctuary as parishioners sank into contemplation. The sower's seeds were taking root.

Fr. Viktor continued thundering at his pulpit. "To those of you living a Passion today, I say this: soldier through the pain! Every sorrow you bear is a golden stone on the path to Heaven. Today, let us make a solemn vow to each other. Let us promise to forsake *no one.* Let us move to help all who bear crosses: the sick, the grieving, the dying—*all* who are neglected and alone. In the presence of a suffering man, *we will see Christ staring through his eyes*, and reach out!" The provincial broke into a radiant smile. "My friends, let us pray for the courage to live our faith." He thrust the crucifix above his head with stirring vigor. "Let us live by the cross!"

———

Fr. Viktor finished his homily at 3:00 p.m. Helene waited for Hans to emerge from the altar boys' sacristy while parishioners loitered about the courtyard and chatted.

Alone in the sanctuary, the widow mulled. Born and raised a Catholic, she had absorbed decades of liturgy, years of doctrine, and Fr. Viktor's ministry differed from everything she had heard in Germany. *How is it different?* Her brow knit in deliberation. Many of the pastors she had known preached scripture in such baroque fashion, but a Passionist spoke clearly and consistently about the human condition. He made suffering and reconciliation a topic of meditation for monk and parishioner alike. It was an oddity that he preached in Schwarzenfeld at all, Helene reflected: Reich law forbade foreigners from ministering to Germans. According to the town grapevine, Braun had scoured Fr. Viktor's papers for even the slightest flaw, but every "i" had been dotted, every "t" crossed. He rightfully claimed citizenship in the Third Reich.

Is it God who seems to forsake us . . . or is it we who forsake one another? Helene mulled.

She pulled a kneeler and folded her arms upon the pew ahead. It wrenched her, trying to reconcile God with a universe where the love of her life lay buried in unmarked ground. But *this* vision, this reminder that evil was a worldly phenomenon that even Christ could not escape. Yes, she could relate to that God through the common ground of loneliness and sorrow that pierced the soul. He had been victimized like Nikolaus and the Poles in burning barns. The concept went down like a dose of quinine, but she could wince at the bitterness and start to heal.

Voices echoed from a sunny church vestibule.

"They accused me of listening to the BBC. 'Ridiculous!' I told them, 'My wife gave away our radio last week.'"

"Heavens," a woman rebuked mildly. "I had no choice. It was for your own good!"

"I need no radio to know the truth. I have seen it. We are not liberators, we are *butchers!* How will God judge me—"

Helene shot up from the pew. "Norbert?"

A figure roved at the church door, gesticulating. Motion fluttered in the courtyard. That was Maria. When her husband vented, she always rushed her children out of earshot. If they found occasion to repeat their father's words in public, the results would be disastrous.

"Norbert! Oh, thank God." Helene stood breathless at the vestibule door.

He nodded wearily. "Don't worry, Leni. Dobler tried to break me. I am not broken yet."

Helene's eyes adjusted to sunlight in the marble vestibule. "Norbert," she gasped. Exhaustion bruised his eyes. He paced back and forth, restless, tormented; his black hair stood shocked and unkempt, as if he had gripped at his locks in frustration. It dawned upon the widow that she had interrupted a serious conversation. She debated whether to leave until Maria slumped at her husband's declaration. Helene drew an arm around her.

Their attention shifted to an old American priest swathed in black. Fr. Viktor rested a hand on Norbert's shoulder in a paternal gesture. "Herr Gindele, my friend." He addressed his parishioners formally, yet warmth flowed in his voice. "Your remorse tells me that God is alive within you. That's what He'll judge."

The baker peered up. "I am going mad. I must do something to fight them, Pater."

"Yes, you must." The provincial stared beneath his brows. "But consider this: unless the party embraces free speech, the voice of one man—as strong and heartfelt as it may be—will be silenced quickly." Norbert hung his head. "You want to fight back and accomplish something? You've got to find another way to do this."

The baker looked up. "What way, Pater?"

"Fight them here." He tapped a fist against the heart-shaped medal pinned to his cassock. "Fight them with faith."

"Faith?"

"Faith." Fr. Viktor affirmed. "It's the most powerful weapon we could possibly have. They want us to worship Hitler, but we have our own God, and the power of a worldwide organization behind us. They find *that* more threatening than any of your outbursts, I assure you. Don't go out of your way to provoke them. The more Catholics we have *outside* of jail, resisting them by living a life of faith and conscience, the better. And God provides ways for us to fight back, even without engaging them in verbal battles. We talked about this before. Remember?"

The baker nodded, considering. He looked up to the priest like a son offering obedience to a beloved father.

"Yes, Pater. I will do as you say."

"Go in peace," the old man said.

The Gindeles departed. Helene wilted in relief. At last, she had been released from the smothering grip of responsibility for that customer line. *Our American Provinsche.* She looked up in veneration, absorbing the oak-like presence, the hearty smile in a weathered face, the lucid blue gaze that read the secrets in one's soul. When he spoke, every Catholic in Schwarzenfeld said 'yes, Pater,' without hesitation. To him they lugged their crosses up this hill, all their squabbles, their sins, their bitter tears, and no matter how heavy their burdens were, he accepted every one, never bending or breaking beneath their weight. During the darkest moment of their lives, he had put bread and meat on every table. For that he would always have their loyalty.

"Frau Heidl," Fr. Viktor greeted gently. "Preaching the Passion tends to stir deep emotions. Are you all right?"

"Oh, I am fine," she said. "Your sermons touch upon things that are real and relevant. But that is the point, yes?"

He squinted into a cloud-dappled sky. "If I thought there was anything more real or relevant in this world, I wouldn't be here." He beamed, and Helene swore she had never seen anyone more at peace. The old man looked down again, reading her shrewdly.

"How's Klaus?"

The widow bowed her head. Fr. Viktor saw one's pain, all right. "Grieving," she said. "He is still grieving. He was so close to Nikolaus."

Together they strolled into the sunlit courtyard. "Klaus is going through things," Helene said. "He will not tell me what, but I know they must be horrible. I *feel* his suffering in the way that a mother does. You understand?" The Provinsche nodded. "I am desperate to intervene. Desperate! He keeps refusing to let me."

"I was a son, once. Seems like ages ago." Fr. Viktor grinned, the parchment skin by his eyes crinkling deeply. "Society—in Germany, and America also—puts pressure upon boys to show strength. Klaus probably realizes that his peers will respect him more if he accomplishes it on his own, and children, well . . . even *they* can be cruel."

He paused thoughtfully in the shade of a spring maple. "Klaus may not say it—he may feel awkward, trying to express the sentiment—but you are his rock. Whatever he's suffering through, he can endure it because he knows he has your love and support. As his mother, you have a bond with him."

Helene briefly closed her eyes.

"Yes."

"Let him know that you're here for him," the old man advised softly. "Through that bond, you can give him your strength."

"I will try."

"And let him know that the church doors are always open. *Always*. I'm praying for him, and waiting for the day when he walks through them again."

Helene nodded. "Yes, Pater. *Danke schön*."

Small feet trotted up. "There you are, Hans!" Fr. Viktor exclaimed. "You did a splendid job during Mass today. Take good care of your mother."

The boy soaked up praise. Helene stroked his hair. "Oh, he does! He really does. Without my boys, I would be lost."

CHAPTER THREE

A SON OF GERMANY

April 15, 1941

"*Eins . . . zwei . . . drei . . . los!*"

Klaus Heidl slinked through a grassy thicket. Thorns snagged his shirt. The eleven-year-old gulped cold air, inspecting himself. He wore the black uniform of a *Jungvolk*—a junior Hitler Youth. A jagged white *Sieg* rune branded his sleeve. Blue cords gripped his willow-thin arm. *Good.* They remained tightly fastened.

Satisfied that his blue armband was secure, he crawled onward. Coolness squished between his fingers. Water soaked his knees, chilling the skin beneath. Mutti would groan when he returned home. She always made such a fuss when he tottered into the kitchen with muddy clothes, but a soldier invading enemy territory always crawled on his belly, and if a muck pool yawned before him, well, he just steeled himself and slid right through. Mothers didn't understand this sort of thing.

Leaves rustled. He turned. Three soldiers, all boys his age, crawled close behind. Blue cords bound their arms as well. The enemy had already killed one man from their platoon. Klaus poked his sandy blond head above windswept grasses and searched for their dead troop mate. The boy hunkered on a log, plainly bored, his sleeve stripped of cords. The rules condemned him to watch the rest of their war game from a distance.

A uniformed figure staggered through the thicket. Klaus froze. Another Jungvolk boy traipsed by, searching the grasses. Red cords fluttered from his arm.

"Attack!" Klaus screeched.

Blue troops pounced. Boyish howls shattered the forest peace. Their enemy turned and ran at a fist-clenching pace.

The red trooper was thirteen. A pillar of lean muscle, he towered above the blue team. Klaus had devised a strategy, a good one, he believed, though its success depended upon finding a red soldier stupid enough to wander from his encampment. Three slim boys hugged the enemy's tree-trunk legs and pulled on thick, ropy arms. "Hold him still, hold him!" Klaus gripped crimson cords and flung them above his head. "Yea! We killed him!"

The victory prompted breathy smiles from his teammates.

The red soldier rolled away, his hand clutching bruised ribs. With a sly cackle, he bared white teeth at them.

"What are you laughing at?" a blue trooper demanded.

"Hey!"

Four red soldiers pounced from a ring of pines. They had anticipated Klaus' strategy and sacrificed one of their own, luring his team into the open.

"Retreat! Retreat!" Klaus howled. His troop mates backed away, wheeling, stopping short. Arms flung them to the ground.

Grunts, wails, and curses pierced the sky. Frightened sparrows shot from their perches. Enemies waved blue cords like trophies, but dead men fought back. They kicked. They thrashed. They punched. Red-banded giants tumbled to the ground.

A body thudded on top of Klaus. "My arm!" Pain seared his right shoulder, a white-hot current. Strong hands wrenched his elbow. Blue cords tore away, though Klaus ceased to care.

The pain! It hurts!

Their troop leader sauntered over, observing. At fourteen, he was their eldest member. He burst into convulsive laughter as younger boys doubled up in pain.

"Come on, give it right back to him, Heinz. Don't just lay there and take it. What kind of punch is that, Werner? My little sister hits harder than that. Hit him! Harder! I want to see bruises!"

The Miesbergkirche bell tower rang out the time: 15:00 hours, 3:00 p.m. The troop leader sighed and hoisted himself upright.

"All right. Break it up, break it up! This war game is over. Get into formation."

They regrouped into a line, all ten boys, red and blue, their full Jungvolk troop. Klaus heard the whisper of approaching footsteps on grass. He lifted his chin and stared straight ahead.

"Only one enemy kill," the troop leader sneered at him. "And all of your men lost. Your father is a war hero, Klaus. What would he think of you, when you have led a platoon three times without a single victory?"

Klaus breathed, licked dry lips. "But . . . you make up the teams. You always make us fight boys who are bigger and stronger than us. It's not fair."

"What did you say?"

He swallowed hard. "Nothing."

Hands clasped behind his back, the troop leader paced up and down the line like an army commander. Sunlight glinted off the silver dagger he wore on his belt.

"What are you, a Mama's boy? Yes, of course I pit you against stronger members. A good leader beats out weakness until there is nothing left but muscle and an iron will. As our Führer commands, we Hitler Youth are cruel and brutal and built for domination. I will make you all slim and swift as greyhounds, tough as leather, and strong as Krupp steel!"

"Heil Hitler," a trooper muttered.

Klaus gaped at his troop mate. The leader wheeled on the boy. Klaus snapped his head forward again.

"You will say that with respect for our Führer. Salute!"

Klaus jerked as their leader slapped the trooper.

"What a sloppy salute. Do it again! And hail the Führer!" Veins pulsed in their leader's neck. His ivory face flushed crimson.

"Heil Hitler!" The trooper bawled. Blood streamed from his right nostril.

"Again!"

"Heil Hitler!"

A smack. "Again! I will not tolerate a sloppy salute."

"Heil . . ." A sob.

The troop leader forced the boy to salute ten times. He then ordered him to run ten laps around the wooded clearing, despite the fact that his nose spewed a river of blood. Klaus and his troop mates exchanged glances. They ached to report what they endured, but as a rule, Jungvolk leaders tolerated no meddling by adults. "'German youth shall be taught by youth,'" he had reminded them, quoting Hitler, and only a dimwit kid failed to pick up on the warning: if they dared to snitch on him, he would just beat them harder.

Klaus watched the bleeding trooper huffing and puffing along. He massaged a twisted right arm and prayed that no one would make him salute. Especially his troop leader.

———

On Tuesday after the midday meal a knock summoned Klaus to the front door. He recognized his fellow trooper, the miserable bleeder. In a whipped voice the boy droned orders from their troop leader.

Mutti licked her thumb and arranged Klaus' hair. Her touch stirred an impulse to wallow in his hurts and apologize for making her fret so much. His poor mother. She staggered home from the Gindele bakery six days a week and wilted into a chair at the kitchen table, her head resting upon folded arms. After hours of cooking and cleaning, she scrubbed mud stains from his uniform until it looked crisp and fresh again. *I am sorry, Mutti.* He teetered on the verge of whimpering the words, then his leader's admonishment roared through memory.

What are you, a Mama's boy?

Klaus plunged outside and scampered along country roads to his destination.

"The Rathaus." He withered before Schwarzenfeld's town hall, a beige plaster house with white trimming. Swastika banners flapped from ivy-fringed windows. Klaus tested his right arm, lifting it level to his shoulder. "Ah! Ow." It dropped back to his side. "Oh. Not good. This is not good." A town hall swarmed with important men who expected salutes. A failure to execute it flawlessly would reflect upon his troop leader.

I will make this a game.

Klaus envisioned himself decked in the gray-green fatigues of a soldier embarking upon a perilous assignment. He summoned a mental image of his captain: thin lips, a sharp nose, stone-strong features. That face belonged to no one in particular, though by a peculiar coincidence it vaguely resembled his father. Klaus preferred imaginary leaders. They *never* struck subordinates. They dispensed praise, kindness, and discipline—when necessary—in perfect balance. A good leader reminded him of Papa.

His imaginary captain barked orders. "Your mission, *Leutnant* Heidl, is to infiltrate enemy headquarters and avoid contact with officers, troop leaders, Bürgermeisters, or any important men. If you fail in this mission, you will reveal your secret to the ruin of us all. Remember. The fate of your country depends upon you!"

Pressed to invent an army classification for himself, Klaus settled on Leutnant, the rank Papa held. His imaginary captain always reminded him that these assignments determined whether Germany triumphed over her enemies or suffered crippling defeat. By Klaus' count he had saved the fatherland thirty-three times since Papa left for Poland.

"Here we go. Mission thirty-four."

A corridor swallowed him. He crept along, his back thrown hard against a wood-paneled wall. The lonely clap of his hob-nailed boots echoed in shadows.

He was alone.

The clickety-click of a typewriter drifted from an open door. Klaus tip-toed into a white plaster room occupied by Bürgermeister Braun's secretary. Schwarzenfeld's Hitler Youth branch lacked its own office, so this station served as a drop-off point for collection materials. Every week the party sent his troop around town, the purpose varying from scrap metal drives for the German army to collections for charitable causes. Shiny red coin canisters stood lined up on a table. That meant his troop collected for charity today.

"Heil Hitler." Klaus snatched a can, grabbed a wooden box of gifts to give contributors, then darted away.

Immersed in her typing, the secretary muttered a greeting. Under different circumstances he would remind this lazy adult to salute properly, though today he let it slide.

Ha! Good work, Leutnant Heidl.

He heard rumbling at the town hall's entrance.

"Oh, no." Klaus scurried into a corner. The secretary watched her door. Boots. Boots. Boots. Given their ominous rhythm, Klaus expected an army to march in at any moment.

A figure swept into the room and Klaus lowered the collection can he had clutched to his chest. So it wasn't an army, just one party officer followed by two staff members. The second he gusted into view, the boy's jaw dropped. Political leaders in Schwarzenfeld were gray and fat, and when they wore mud-brown uniforms he thought they resembled round, lumbering potatoes. This man differed from them entirely. His troop leader's description of the German ideal shot through his mind: slim and swift as a greyhound, tough as leather, and strong as Krupp steel. *So that is what it looks like.* Klaus was entranced. The leather-tough man strode into Bürgermeister Braun's office and shut the door behind him.

"Who is that?" Klaus breathed.

One of the officer's staff members eased into a seat with the grace of a bird finding a perch. She wore the prim blazer of the National Socialist Women's organization. "Don't you know your local political leaders?"

She had spoken in *Hochdeutsch* rather than the local dialect. As a rule, one used proper High German in government offices. "I know most of them," Klaus said, following suit. "But I have never seen him before."

"I suppose that is not surprising. He comes to these parts so rarely. That is Herr Amtsleiter Seiz. He is the People's Welfare director for three districts, including yours. You know all that collecting you boys do for charity? That is for his department."

"He is a charity worker?" Klaus' chin jerked back. "Huh. He walks like a general on a battlefield."

The woman's hazel eyes twinkled. "He is here today on official business for the Gauleiter," she confided. "It is a matter of great importance."

The boy brightened. "Ooh!"

What a delicious bit of information. He swept that nugget of intelligence into a mental file. His imaginary captain just ate up stuff like that.

Klaus strode outside and blew a windy sigh. A Mercedes sat parked on the curb of the dirt road. "Stage one complete." He had almost blown it back there when that officer flashed out of nowhere. "Seiz, Seiz, Seiz. Herr Amtsleiter Seiz." The name sounded sharp, like a scythe whispering through wheat.

Klaus' imagination soared while he pondered the mission that brought Herr Amtsleiter to Schwarzenfeld. *Official business— for a Gauleiter!* It oozed intrigue.

Klaus stepped smartly up the Hauptstrasse. Following routine for a collection, he stood on the street corner and waved his can. A farmer fished coins from his pocket, and the boy offered him a little army figurine from his wooden box.

While on duty, he briefed his imaginary captain and asked for an assignment with the Fourth Panzer Division. This meant he could fight with Papa. His father served in one of the first squadrons to cross the Polish border when war broke out. After the invasion, radios and newspapers had proudly declared victory for Germany. "What is it like in a panzer, Papa?" Klaus asked when he had returned home on furlough. The boy imagined it: a reek of fuel so pungent his nose curled. The sway of motion in an iron cage. Creaking. Always creaking. A motor droning so loud that its vibrations rattled his cheeks and lips. How did Papa demonstrate that? Oh, right. Klaus imitated to enhance his mental vision. "Pop pop pop pop . . ."

Footsteps. "Oh. Hello down there."

Mortified, he flinched up. He had tottered around like a wind-up toy and collided with a postal worker.

The man shot him an odd look, then grinned broadly under a white mustache. "My apologies. Do you need help with those?"

Klaus frowned. "Huh?"

The postman pointed. Figurines lay scattered at his feet. He had spilled the box of gifts intended for donors.

"Oh. No. I will pick them up," Klaus said.

The postman tipped his cap, bidding him *Gruess Gott* rather than hailing Hitler. Klaus ignored it. The old man shuffled up to a gray homestead behind them, the Gindele house.

The boy knelt, picking up figurines. "Ugh! What a mess." His movements slowed and a realization made him shiver: he felt like a colossus hunkering over the aftermath of a terrible battle. Thirty wooden figures lay silent and motionless, one face-down in the mud, another still clutching a rifle. Gray-green paint covered their little wooden bodies. That meant they belonged to the German army.

His gaze settled upon a soldier lying isolated on the roadside and his awareness of the world slid away. The figure looked like a man dying alone.

A knot burned in Klaus' throat. He cradled the soldier gently in his palm and slid him into the trinket box with his comrades— placing him face-up, so he looked alive. "Stupid," he chastened himself, but he could not bear the thought of soldiers dying, not even little wooden ones.

Klaus watched the postal worker amble up to Herr Gindele's house. An ivy-fringed door opened to reveal a bright, beaming Frau Maria Gindele. She vanished into the hall and her son appeared. He pinched a telegram between hesitant fingers. The postman strolled off to the next house. Klaus rubbed a fist in his eye and continued scooping up the spilled figurines.

Shouts began wafting from the house like the aroma of fresh-baked bread.

Klaus looked up. Curiosity smoldered in his mind.

I am a spy.

He flung the last soldier into his wooden box and dove into the turf behind the Gindele house. He doubted that real German spies squirmed through grass and dirt, though it struck him as an adventurous prospect. While creeping into position, he reflected on intelligence gathered thus far. Fact: after the war swept able-bodied men to the front lines, Schwarzenfeld's post office hired Hitler Youth troopers to expand their depleted work force. Fact: veteran postal workers still delivered one piece of registered mail: army call-up notices. Fact: according to Mutti—another agent deemed trustworthy by their government—Herr Gindele fired up the bakery's ovens each morning at 5:00 a.m. sharp, and sweltering heat drove the house's inhabitants to open windows.

Klaus stopped crawling. Throaty voices were muffled at first, but they grew louder. Clearer. The spy drew slender legs to his chest. Hunkered behind a neighbor's fence, he squinted toward a kitchen window and strained to hear words above clanging pans.

"I will not have it!"

"I must go."

"I can say that I need you in the bakery. Tomorrow I am going to that Rathaus—"

"You will have to manage without me, Father. They have called me up. I must go!"

Delighted by this ill-gotten nugget of information, Klaus giggled. He cupped a hand over his mouth and struggled for calm.

Norbert and Maria Gindele's son paced behind sheer curtains. "This town is full of women who have sons my age fighting on the front. You know how those old hens talk. I can hear them clucking now. 'My boy is risking his life for the Führer, and there is Norbert Gindele's son staying at home safe and sound like a coward, because his father's bakery is so important.' I will never be able to leave this house without hanging my head in shame!"

"*Mein Gott!*" his father roared. "What do you think it is like on a battlefield? It is a despicable carnival of death. Do you remember what happened to Herr Heidl in Dunkirk, or have you forgotten about that already?"

"Father!"

"You could be the next one to get shot up, and for what? To be a hero? To die gloriously for the Führer? I have seen men die, boy. It is not glorious. It is *senseless!*"

"This is not about heroism, or glory, Father. I have to go. Don't you understand? There is nothing you can—"

"No! I will not send my son to die in a madman's war!"

"Good heavens!" Frau Gindele admonished. "Will you keep your voices down?" She slammed the windowpane shut.

Klaus flinched at a sharp *thwack.*

Voices stopped.

The boy strained to breathe. Herr Gindele's words shot him back into a cold granite reality where he was a runt in a Hitler Youth troop and war had ripped Papa away to a dark, infinite place beyond his reach.

Klaus tottered down the Hauptstrasse. "Shot . . . shot up. *Mein Papa*. All shot up." He stumbled. He staggered around farm wagons. He broke into a run. He fled faster, faster, trying to outrun an inferno raging within. How *stupid*, this notion that dying was glorious! The boys in his Hitler Youth troop thought they knew death. To them death meant sitting bored on a log with an arm bare of cords while everybody else rollicked about, but Klaus knew better. Death was a mouth, a fat, monstrous mouth that devoured everything: childhood freedom. Laughter. His mother's happiness. The will to smile and hum and sing. Worst of all, it swallowed what he wanted most: the deep, quivery joy of feeling Papa stroke his hair and hearing him trumpet, *Good boy! I am proud of you.* The terrible mouth kept eating and eating until his heart felt so empty that Klaus wondered why it still beat.

Klaus reached the Naab River's stony embankment. He collapsed. Grief poured over his face in torrents.

The Miesbergkirche's bell tolled from a distant hilltop. His soul used to soar when he heard its clatter. Now he belted out a long, lonely wail. It only reminded him that he had prayed every day for Papa's return and his father would never come home.

An hour later, Klaus blinked at tree shadows growing long in the late afternoon sun. He looked down. Crystal waters reflected a mournful face, the aquamarine eyes squinting through slits.

He pulled himself up and shook his collection can. Five coins rattled pathetically in its tinny hollow. A whole regiment of soldiers still inhabited his trinket box. Hastening toward the Rathaus, he checked a clock on the steeple of the town's rococo parish church.

"4:00?" He gasped. "I should have been back an hour ago!" By this time, the rest of his troop had finished their collections and returned cans heavy with coins.

He raced to Schwarzenfeld's town hall. The front door. It refused to budge! "No, no. Oh, no!" He howled, pulling harder, then groaned in relief. It swung open. The mayor's secretary had not locked the doors, not yet. After returning this stupid can he intended to run home, curl up in his room, and lay in solitude until night washed over him.

"There you are! Where have you been? I have waited here for a whole half hour! I have to count our collections and report them, you know."

His teenage overlord. The boy stood seething in the office, his face a blast of Nordic cold.

Klaus went numb.

"Sorry." He had always returned his materials promptly, so he knew little of the procedure that followed a collection.

His troop leader shoved him in the chest, making him totter backward. "Hey. Are you forgetting something?"

Klaus hoisted a gaze heavy with misery. He shifted his can under an achy arm and offered his best salute. His troop leader scowled at him.

"What are you doing? You don't use your left arm to salute. You use your right arm!"

Desperation seized him. *My mission. I blew it.* Just when he thought this day had reached its lowest point of pain and failure, he shuddered at the sound of deeper trouble approaching. Boots. Boots. Boots. Their rumbling shook the hall. Men strode into the secretary's office, not just one, but three: Bürgermeister Braun, Officer Dobler, and Herr Amtsleiter Seiz.

A hand gripped his injured arm.

"Ah!" he squealed.

"What is the matter with you?" The troop leader demanded. "Have I not taught you how to salute officers?"

Bürgermeister Braun stroked a swastika pin on his lapel. Officer Dobler snorted. Herr Amtsleiter Seiz stopped giving orders to his secretary and turned around.

"Do you think your father would be proud of a salute like that?" the troop leader barked. "Your father sees you, you know. The dead are with us in spirit and they see everything. Salute!"

He flung Klaus' arm high above his head, wrenching a wail from him.

"THAT IS ENOUGH!"

The troop leader's grip went slack. Both boys cowered from the officer who stood glowering at them: Herr Amtsleiter Seiz.

"Sorry, Herr Amtsleiter," the teenager stammered, "I don't know what—he is—I trained him properly, I don't know why—"

"What is your name? Are you the leader of his troop?"

Silence clutched the room. Nothing good followed questions like those. Klaus slid a look at his Jungvolk leader. The boy's ivory face turned a shade paler. Instead of protesting adult intrusion, the teenage overlord blurted answers and then bolted when the man dismissed him. He forgot to depart in Hitler's name.

Klaus fought sickness. Daring to peek up, he felt his heart stop. Herr Amtsleiter Seiz stared hard beneath his brow.

"You there. *Komm mit mir.*"

———

Klaus reeled into the maw of the hallway. A tall silhouette thundered ahead of him. Herr Amtsleiter Seiz never paused, nor did he look back to check that Klaus had followed his lead; he took it on faith. The boy struggled on wobbly feet, left, right, left, right, straining to keep up with him. Seiz walked even faster than before. *Herr Amtsleiter is furious,* the boy thought. *He is furious that I cannot salute right and he is going to kill me!*

Seiz halted near a door. Klaus tottered into a room that smelled of ersatz coffee and aged wood. It was dark and murky, except for the window to his left. Sunlight poured in golden shafts. He mustered all the strength that remained in his withering body.

"Heil—"

"Do you need a doctor to look at that arm?"

Klaus let it swing limp at his side. He shook his head and balled his hands up to stop them from shaking.

"What is your name?"

"K-Klaus. Klaus Heidl, Herr Amtsleiter."

"Klaus Heidl." Seiz repeated his name as if etching it into memory. Klaus shuddered in the dark-light room and braced himself for the worst.

On the fringes of awareness he heard rustling. Before his eyes, a blur of brown fabric resolved into the charity worker crouching on his haunches. He removed his cap to get a clear view of the child before him. Klaus flinched at intelligent, clean-shaven features bathed half in light, half in shadow; the sharpest blue eyes he had ever seen looked straight into his own. He looked away.

"Your troop leader mentioned your father. He died fighting on the front?"

Klaus moved his lips, but his voice refused to work.

"Hm?"

He sniffled. "Yea."

"He died for the fatherland. We should honor his sacrifice."

The boy twitched a shoulder.

"You don't feel the same way? Why not?"

Klaus' brow knit. He had said nothing. *How can he tell what I think?* It dawned upon him that the answers formed right on his face and Herr Amtsleiter was reading every crease. "I just—I don't know," Klaus whimpered. "It is stupid."

"What is?"

"Just . . . everything."

"Who told you that?"

Klaus strained to control shuddering features. *Shot up . . . madman's war.* Mutti always spent the night pacing, wondering what would happen if Officer Dobler arrested Herr Gindele. The thought of bringing hardship upon her made him sick.

"It is foolish to repeat what you heard, young man." Seiz spoke softly, his voice still sharp with authority. "There are terrible consequences for saying such things."

A fitful glimmer seized Klaus' attention. Herr Amtsleiter wore an oval badge on the left breast pocket of his uniform. A German army helmet protruded above two crossed swords, and an oak wreath circled both symbols. Klaus knew what the badge's silver plating meant. It indicated that the man before him had suffered at least three wounds in armed combat.

The boy lifted a trembling finger. "That pin."

"What?"

"They gave my papa one of those. Only his had a swastika on the helmet."

If Seiz intended to pull a chain of denouncements from him, Klaus doubted he would stop to acknowledge a child's observation. To his astonishment, the charity worker glanced down.

"The wound badge?" Seiz said. "Well, of course. They added the swastika when the second Great War started."

"You were in the first Great War?"

"Yes."

Klaus lifted his head, his fear giving way to fascination. "What happened to you?"

In the back of his mind, he imagined Mutti chiding him for asking personal questions, yet the charity worker showed no sign of irritation. Instead he smiled, and despite the fact that they stood inside a government building, he dropped from *Hochdeutsch* into the ease of their local dialect. Klaus relaxed. Herr Amtsleiter Seiz wouldn't act this genial if he intended to kill him.

"When one is young, one gets many fanciful ideas running through his head. You know what I mean?" Seiz grinned, the skin by his eyes creasing. Klaus nodded. "I was only sixteen. Germany was losing the first war, and I was going to be a hero. I was too young to fight, but the situation at the Western Front was so grim that no one cared. They marched us out with a bare minimum of training. I took two shots to the thigh, here and here, and another that nearly shattered a rib." Seiz pressed a point three centimeters below the badge, then sighed. "After surviving such a harsh lesson, one stops reveling in dreams."

The boy gnawed his lip. "What was it like?"

"What?"

"Getting shot."

"Getting shot?" The charity worker scratched his chin. "It happens so fast that one notices very little at first. I suppose it was like the sting that one might feel if he is hit very hard with a small stone. The real pain doesn't begin until a few seconds later."

Klaus let that knowledge trickle into visions of Papa's death. Hitler's portrait adorned a darkened wall. The Führer's stern image turned all hot and blurry.

The charity worker quickly pointed at another pin on his lapel. "Here. What about this one? Do you know what this is?"

"Um. It's, ah." Klaus sniffled thickly. "Yea. That is one of those pins people get when they give money to the winter charity."

"Yes, but I meant the pin itself."

"Oh." He squeezed tears away. "It looks like a shield, I guess."

Seiz pulled two chairs from the conference table and moved them into the light. He eased down, unfastening the shield pin. "Of all the mementos we distribute in the NSV, this is my favorite. One must give ten Reichsmarks to get a pin this nice, and that is difficult with a war going on. But this pin represents much more than the concept of sacrifice. Come, have a seat."

Klaus scraped wetness from his cheeks. His troop leader would slap him for crying, but his tears didn't faze Herr Amtsleiter. The charity worker dropped the pin into his smaller hand. His calming presence and the faint odor of Turkish tobacco on his breath reminded Klaus strongly of Papa.

"The design of this shield is Teutonic in origin," Seiz told him. "Do you know who they were, the Teutons?"

Klaus blinked up at the half-lit face. He shook his head.

"They were one of the Aryan tribes that migrated across Europe long ago," Seiz explained. "They were fierce warriors. The Roman legions even feared them. In addition to sacrifice, this shield reminds me of the heritage that we Germans have, and the love that roots us to this land. No one with German blood can stand on this soil and fail to feel that bond. It is *ancient*. Think about it: every Heidl that came before you—your father, your grandfather, great grandfather, *his* great grandfather—every one of your ancestors over the last thousand years was born here, raised here, fell in love, had children, and died here. All on this soil."

"A thousand years." Klaus tried to wrap his mind around that. To him, eleven years seemed an eternity. "That is a long time."

"It is a very long time," the charity worker agreed. "Most of all, this shield represents protection. We are protecting everything that our ancestors fought for, and died for. And that would be us. Our generation. Our people—"

"The People's Community," Klaus said with him. Seiz spoke those words with a hushed wonder that entranced the boy.

"Exactly. One nation of unified spirit. We are bound together into a greater whole, one that lives together, suffers together, and rejoices in the promise of our common fate. Does this sound like nonsense to you?"

Klaus smoothed a thumb over the pin. "No."

"Then your father is a hero because he was willing to give his life for our fatherland, and for everything he loved. That includes you, your mother. Do you have brothers or sisters?"

"A little brother."

"Your brother also." The charity worker shifted, facing him directly, and his body turned fully into golden sunlight. He spoke in a tone that resonated with Klaus' sorrow.

"When a soldier dies, he leaves behind loved ones who grieve. Your troop leader would tell you that one should ignore one's pain. I say that confronting it, as you are now—this takes more courage." He considered the boy for a long moment. Set against the dark of the room, his clean-cut visage looked gentle and luminous. "Be proud of your father, Klaus. He would be proud of his son."

"Really?" Klaus felt his brow crimping. "You *really* think he would be proud of me?"

"Yes. If I were him, I would be."

For the first time in a year, a genuine smile warmed the boy's face. He pondered the shield in his palm and marveled. "You get all that meaning, just from this little pin?"

"Mm-hmm."

"I understand why it is your favorite." He handed it back, but the charity worker shook his head.

"No. I want you to keep it."

"But I gave you no money."

Seiz plucked the pin from Klaus' hand and lightly tugged the collar of his Jungvolk uniform. "Perhaps not. But still, I think you have sacrificed enough to deserve it."

Klaus' jaw slackened. He reached up, enchanted by cool metal beneath his fingertips.

"*Danke schön,*" he breathed.

A knock resounded from the shadowy door. Braun's secretary leaned into the room. "Herr Amtsleiter? Herr Bürgermeister has made the arrangements that you requested."

"Perfect. *Vielen Dank.*"

Seiz rose and slipped his cap on with one smooth motion. Klaus leapt from his seat with such enthusiasm that his hobnailed shoes smacked the oak floorboards and he twitched in shock. Seiz laughed, nodded approval.

"Duty calls. Now then. Wipe those tears, and pull yourself together. If that arm does not heal in a few days, you get a doctor to look at it. That is an order, young man."

"Yes, sir!" Klaus said. "*Jawohl.*"

Herr Amtsleiter regarded him shrewdly. Klaus felt a fresh rise of panic. He braced himself for questions about the loudmouth baker who had spoken against the war.

"That troop leader of yours," Seiz said instead. "He is quite the 'little Caesar,' hm?"

Klaus released the breath he had been holding. He started to speak. He stopped and simply tipped up his face, letting Herr Amtsleiter read his expression. The Hitler Youth despised interference from adults, but it occurred to Klaus that complaints from a party office director might be taken seriously. Not only that, but Seiz had witnessed the troop leader's cruelty with his own eyes.

Relief soaked into the boy's aching heart. He could honestly say that he hadn't snitched. His teenage overlord had condemned himself with his own actions.

"*Gehen wir,*" Seiz commanded. "Let's go."

He departed from the conference room as if plunging toward tasks that required swift action. Klaus cursed his inability to salute properly. He had encountered few leaders who deserved salutes, but Herr Amtsleiter had earned one from him today. The charity worker had even neglected to interrogate him about Herr Gindele.

Footsteps. Klaus focused on the sound the way he would concentrate on drumbeats during a Jungvolk parade: *left, left . . . left right left.* He pushed his string-bean legs faster, farther, harder, but lagged behind whenever he matched Seiz's rhythm. Just when he began to despair, the wind at his side understood him and the long, deliberate stride he labored to emulate measured itself. As they walked together, Klaus' heart leapt. His face crimped again, not in grief, but chest-popping pride. He followed Herr Amtsleiter's example and lifted his head high. Bürgermeister Braun stepped aside for the charity worker and the eleven-year-old strutting at his side like an attaché from the Jungvolk. Klaus was ridiculously young to hold such a position, he knew, but no one would dare to mention that in Herr Amtsleiter's presence.

They reached the Rathaus door. Klaus stood silent and rooted while NSV personnel vanished into a gleaming Mercedes. Seiz was swiftness and thunder, and Klaus was a flag stirred and longing for another chance to flutter in his breeze. He had been lucky, he realized, for amid the wind he perceived a tempest reined under tight control. The boy pitied enemies who stood before that onrushing storm.

CHAPTER FOUR

SWASTIKAS OVER THE MIESBERG

APRIL 16, 1941

At 6:00 p.m., the Miesbergkloster's doorbell erupted with insistent ringing. Fr. Viktor glanced up from the refectory table where the Passionist community had gathered for their evening meal. A rotund brother cheerfully bade the gathering to continue their repast and shuffled off to greet their callers. He bustled back moments later, his hands wringing.

"Pater? Pater Viktor?"

"What is it, Bernard?"

"There are men at the door. Men in party uniform."

Fr. Paul shifted around. "Who?"

"The ah, the Bürgermeister, Pater," Br. Bernard said. "And also that welfare officer. The one who was here last week."

"Seiz." Fr. Viktor squinted at movement in the vestibule beyond. A chill washed through him: he counted more than two people. The clinking of forks and plates subsided and his fellow religious sank into leaden silence.

"And Pater," Br. Bernard added, "they brought the police!"

Fr. Viktor met Fr. Paul's sudden gaze.

"Paul, come with me. The rest of you stay here."

Br. Bernard stood in the doorway while party officials amassed in the vestibule. "*Entschuldigung,*" Fr. Paul said. "Excuse me." His soft voice jolted the poor brother. Bernard stepped back, allowing room. Fr. Viktor touched his shoulder, calming him, though cold premonition seeped into his own bloodstream. The ancient instincts flared to life. These days, no one survived long in Germany without them. A week ago, Cardinal Faulhaber's representative at the Interior Ministry had effused assurances. *Yes, Pater Koch. The cardinal and I are certain—quite certain—that the foreign aspect of this case will deny the Reich ownership of your monastery. I shall keep you apprised. Do expect a call from me.* Last week's parade of sermons churned through memory like a river, and in surfacing for breath, he realized that the call had never come.

"Good evening, *meine Herren,*" the provincial greeted crisply.

"Have you packed yet, Pater?" Seiz asked.

"Packed for what?"

Seiz withdrew from light into full shadow, his swagger telling Fr. Viktor precisely who had organized this swastika-banded siege force invading his vestibule. Officer Dobler accompanied him. The police chief brought five armed gendarmes—one a Catholic furrowing his brow in sorrow. A company of NSV volunteers snaked back to the door. *And Seiz.* The party member lurked at the rear, content to let local officials take over.

Bürgermeister Braun stepped forward. His voice thundered in the vestibule. "Gauleiter Wächtler granted you an extension for

Holy Week. Your time has expired. You have one hour to pack your possessions and leave the property."

"But Herr Bürgermeister," Fr. Paul hastened, "surely you know of the command that Cardinal Faulhaber gave to us. He has ordered us to remain in our—"

"You have a telephone here, do you not?" Braun said.

Fr. Viktor looked back to find his brethren crowding the refectory door, their faces drawn, anxious. Faulhaber's name ceased to deter the party. *What's happened?* He wondered. *What's changed?* He struggled to think of an obscure law he might play like a card in this dangerous game, though only a fool bandied words with the party faithful.

"Yes, we do," he confirmed.

"Good. Then I suggest that you call the Interior Ministry at once and discuss your orders with the cardinal's representative."

Fr. Viktor shot a glare in Seiz's direction. The party member stared at the floor, aware of his attention, his bitterness, making a point to look elsewhere. The provincial turned away slowly and plodded to the phone.

"I am sorry, Pater Koch." The voice on the other end quivered to the heights of apology, though he barely heard it above the anger howling within. "Gauleiter Wächtler's office became involved in these negotiations. I was not expecting that, I do not know who prompted them to become involved, or—well, perhaps it could have been the Reich Welfare Organization. The State is bringing children from the cities to rural areas for their protection, and your monastery is ideal because of the modern features, you see. Their representatives simply refuse to accept 'no' for an answer."

Fr. Viktor's shoulders slumped. "So that's it? They own the monastery?"

"No. The mortgage on your Miesbergkloster is owned by your mother province, so the building is, by lawful authority, American property. Foreign ownership requires the State to purchase the monastery in order to gain complete control, Pater Koch."

A breath hissed through his gritted teeth. He paced as far as the phone cord permitted. "We are *not* selling. I hope you made that clear to them."

"Yes, of course we told them. But the building is on German soil. The party can legally demand the right to its use."

"They can?"

"Yes, I fear this is so. For that right, they have consented to pay rent each month. The bill will be paid by the NSV."

Fr. Viktor kneaded a temple. "All right. They want to open a school here? Fine. We'll keep a few rooms and stay out of sight."

"I proposed this already, Pater. It was not satisfactory."

"But still, it is *our* monastery," Fr. Viktor said. "Right?"

"That is correct."

"But if it's our property, why do we have to leave?"

"You can try to resist, Pater. But if you do, then you and your brethren will be penalized. I am very sorry."

Faulhaber's representative braided a list of legalities with condolences. Fr. Viktor struggled to hear him above the rush of his blood. He needed the German Catholic Church to engage the State on his behalf. For years he had hoped that her leaders would unite, speaking with the power of an institution, condemning religious oppression that raged like a wildfire in Germany, yet the Reich was secularizing another monastery and the ranks above watched in silence. A bleak, windy sensation swept through him, the lonely feeling of being left to the mercy of a hostile regime. A voice on the phone probed for signs of life. "Yes." His voice felt brittle. "Right.

The packing. We'll get started." Faulhaber ordered compliance with the Reich, and Fr. Viktor had vowed obedience to the Church.

The phone receiver slid from his grasp and clattered into place.

Fr. Paul met his gaze. He expected to find rebuke in the Austrian's features, but the round face conveyed no reproach, only sadness and acceptance of circumstances beyond their control.

Footsteps clapped in the hallway. Seiz breezed by, engrossed in the task before him. Volunteers marched behind. He had the air of a blameless cog in the machine, one who just followed orders. Fr. Viktor grunted, head shaking.

Bürgermeister Braun stalked into the room. His swastika pin gleamed on the lapel of his mud-brown party uniform. Officer Dobler skulked behind him. "Temporary living arrangements have been secured for you and your brethren," Braun announced. "After you remove your belongings from the property, you will report to the town parsonage and remain there until you can move to your monastery in Austria. And as for you, Pater Koch. I suggest that you return to America." The mayor gave him an up-down look. "And take your foreign doctrine with you."

Hot obstinacy boiled into Fr. Viktor's veins. "But we have a church to run in this town. How are we going to manage that from Austria, or America?"

"That is your problem, Pater, not ours."

"I can take this to Rome," he challenged.

"And I can throw you in prison," Dobler said.

Fr. Viktor stared.

Braun calmly flipped back a sleeve, consulting a watch. "The time is exactly 6:15 in the afternoon. You have one hour to leave, not a minute more. We want the furniture kept, all the beds, sheets, tables, desks. They will be useful for the children."

"That's preposterous. How do you expect us to clear out a monastery in one hour?" Fr. Viktor demanded.

Braun grinned coldly, cheerily. "Do you doubt the charity of us National Socialists, Pater? The NSV will assist you and your brethren." He snorted at a crucifix hanging on the wall. "Don't forget to take those crosses."

———

Frs. Viktor and Paul broke the news to four priests and brothers crowding the refectory door. The provincial watched their expressions shift from open-mouthed dismay to acquiescence, then finally to grim resolve. Meditating upon this fresh misfortune, a brother quoted the book of Job: "The Lord gave, and the Lord hath taken away; blessed be the name of the Lord." Fr. Viktor admired his fellow monks. He could not accept loss with such serenity, not under circumstances like this.

A desperate restlessness still blew through him. Instinct drove him to entrench, to resist—but only if a higher power willed it. *Lord. What is Your will?* His brethren dispersed and started packing. He rubbed his brow, not knowing what to do.

A fist rapped on the monastery door, jolting him. Opening it slowly, he spotted horse-drawn wagons pulling into the courtyard.

Wagons?

A head moved into view. Dark hair tumbled over a sharp widow's peak. "Herr Gindele," Fr. Viktor greeted. "What are you doing here?"

"*Gruess Gott.*" The baker leaned close. "It seems I have visited the police station so often that I have made friends there." He smiled wryly. "About an hour ago, a gendarme stopped by the bakery and told us what was going to happen. Herr Gietl and Herr Obendorfer have come with me. Can we help you?"

Fr. Viktor touched the medal on his chest and felt his heart pounding. "Can you . . . ? Of course you can help! Thank you for coming." He reflected: *the light of the body is the eye.* In Norbert he beheld radiance, the gleam of a righteous soul responding to pain. *So, we haven't been forsaken after all.* He swung the door wider. "What's all this?"

"What is—oh." Norbert pointed toward the wagons and the mountain of cargo they carried. "The crates, you mean? Yes. Those are from the bakery. I thought they would be perfect for packing."

"Yes, they will. You sure got enough of them, from the looks of it. Thank you."

"Oh. Look at that." The baker inspected his black jacket and scraped at flour dusting a sleeve. "Maria and Leni did not have much time to clean them. I apologize."

"No, my friend. No need to—"

"Before I forget! Do you have a place to store your belongings? The Obendorfers and the Gietls are offering their barns to you. Would you like to use them?"

Fr. Viktor watched Norbert soberly, reading the flustered air, the jittery hands scraping flour from black fabric. He shoved aside his own cross for a moment. "I heard about your son," he said gently. "I'm so sorry."

"You heard. Well, I see the rumor mill has lost none of its steam. People in this town talk endlessly about me and my family. How dull their own lives must be." The baker hung his head, heaving a sigh as heavy as his heart. "We fought bitterly. No matter what I say, it does not matter. No words of mine will change his mind. He is determined to go. Pater, this is too much for me. First they take my son. Now look what those *Schweinehunde* are doing!" He waved a claw toward the cars. "With you leaving, I am losing God when I need Him most."

"You'll never lose God, my friend," Fr. Viktor assured.

"Well, I am losing a father anyway."

The provincial rested a hand on Norbert's shoulder. "They say the Lord gives us only what we can handle. On days like this, even I wonder how we'll live up to His expectations."

Two sets of footsteps echoed from the monastery, one a serene and familiar murmur, the other a nerve-rattling thump. Norbert swiveled, beckoning Herr Gietl and Herr Obendorfer, but when he turned again he bared his teeth. Seiz edged through the door, absorbing the baker's mirthless grin in taunting silence.

"Be at peace, my friend!" Fr. Viktor hauled Norbert inside. "Nothing good will come of a dispute here. Paul?" Seiz stepped outside without incident and directed NSV volunteers.

"Herr Gindele," Fr. Paul beckoned. "*Kommen Sie, bitte.*"

"Pater?" a voice said.

The provincial kicked a doorstop into place and looked up. "Herr Obendorfer." The old farmer blinked away tears and offered him a packing crate.

"I do not know what I will do, Pater." Herr Obendorfer's voice squeaked like a wagon wheel. He buried his fleshy nose in a handkerchief. "The sowing. The harvest! You always sent your brethren to my fields when my sons went off to France. How will I manage forty acres of wheat by myself?" The farmer held up a hand, showing fingers with thick, inflamed joints. "And what will you do? Will you return to America?"

The farmer's laments trickled into Fr. Viktor's bloodstream. He had tended this town's needs in every way possible. *What will I do?* He peered out to the hills, feeling the wind inside, the desperation, but there were no answers.

The provincial struggled to find uplifting words for Herr Obendorfer and retreated to his room.

A wall clock ticked out fleeting minutes: 6:30 p.m. 6:31. 6:32. Fr. Viktor yanked drawers. As he packed, sorrows gusted in the dark of his mind: the sowing, the harvest. Sowers of God's word, banished. The NSV offered rent. Yeah, Seiz was definitely paying rent after this stunt. Fr. Viktor didn't need the NSV's money. The American mother province provided enough funds for him to cover expenses, which mainly consisted of payments on the monastery's mortgage. Even so, if he could compel the Reich to pay his bills and support the Church it despised, that suited him just fine.

Fr. Viktor stared at a folder labeled in English: Letters, 1925. He opened it delicately, like a wound. A letter from Fr. Stanislaus Grennan met his unwilling eyes.

"We regret the sad possibility of the German province proving to be a total failure," his father superior had written to Rome. "Like all Passionists we wish to see our congregation grow and spread, and we would be delighted to have a strong German province. But we are forced to admit that the prospects of this are very, very dark . . ."

The folder landed with a *thud* into the packing crate.

He hunted through files until he found a second document, one so crisp and fresh that the odor of ink made his nose itch. It declared his citizenship as Austrian. When he had taken his first trembling steps on European soil twenty years ago, he could not have foreseen himself opening a monastery in Austria, nor could he predict the political upheaval that forced her annexation into Germany. He could not have envisioned Hitler's terrifying rise to power, nor the decree that banished all foreign missionaries from German shores. If a higher power intended him to return home in failure, as Grennan supposed, then why did this certificate rest in his hands, granting the legal means for him to continue his ministry in the Third Reich? Why had these factors aligned, providing exactly what he needed before he knew its necessity?

Fr. Viktor lifted sunken eyes and gazed upon a crucifix. *But what lies ahead in the Framework? Is there a reason for me to stay in Germany, Lord, or is this my will only?* These "signs" might be nothing more than coincidence. He acknowledged that. And he felt a visceral bond with this land that eluded definition. Germany coursed through his veins and whispered in his marrow. When he spoke her tongue, he heard an echo of his ancestors speaking in the same language; standing upon the soil where they had lived and died he felt vibrations of their voices. If the compulsion of heritage rooted him here, then Grennan and Faulhaber were pulling him in the right direction after all. Perhaps a whole new mission awaited him in the States.

The clatter of a distant door disrupted his thoughts. Uniformed figures marched past his room. An official in a silver-banded cap issued orders.

"I want a count of all items left behind. Linens, dishes, soap, silverware, everything. Be quick, but accurate. If something cannot be used for the children, then pack it up and take it to the office. We will distribute it elsewhere."

Fr. Viktor packed the crucifix on his wall, gathered up his crate, and followed Seiz. "I suppose this is all going according to plan for you," he said.

Footsteps stopped. The party member stood swathed in shadow. He half-turned and looked at him through the corner of an eye. "If you cannot look beyond your problems to see the good that I am doing, Pater, then there is no point in discussing the matter."

"The *good* you're doing." Fr. Viktor's glance fell upon a swastika armband and his brow furrowed. "What good?"

"For the children," Seiz emphasized, turning to face him fully. "I cannot fathom why you want them to stay in dangerous places."

"You're sparing those children *physical* harm, that's true," Fr. Viktor agreed. "But you're turning a house of God into a den of indoctrination. I'll never agree to that."

Seiz prowled forward. "And what is so terrible about a system that has delivered Germany from poverty and defeat? What is so evil about teaching children to have pride in their nation, their people, their race?"

Fr. Viktor pondered a swastika on the sleeve and motivations that seemed both virtuous and sinister. A light flickered in Seiz's sapphire eyes, but the provincial did not know what to make of this man. It was impossible for him to say if grace inhabited this soul.

Seiz regarded him narrowly. "Here."

"What?"

"Your brethren missed one of these. Get rid of it." The party member held up a slim wooden crucifix, the kind that monks hung in their cells.

"Why not hang it in your office?" Fr. Viktor said sincerely. "Christ died to redeem you, too. A reminder won't do you harm."

Seiz scoffed and flung the cross into his packing box. He stalked down the residence hall and vanished around a corner.

Robes whispered at the provincial's side. Fr. Paul folded calm hands. "At least he had the decency not to throw it away," the Austrian priest said.

"Yeah, I suppose."

Glass clinked nearby. They looked up.

"Bernard. What are you doing?" Fr. Viktor asked.

Hunched and waddling, Br. Bernard emerged from the hall that led to the refectory. He lugged several bottles of Mass wine in a bulging apron. "*Vorsicht!*" Fr. Paul implored, "please be careful!" The Austrian priest relieved him of two bottles.

The brother nodded, red-faced, puffing. "This," he gasped, "is the last." His knuckles whitened around the apron's seams. "Please, Paters. You go ahead."

Fr. Viktor bounced his packing box and tried to make room for a bottle, but NSV attendants waved him on, eager to secure their claim upon the monastery. Panicked jiggling echoed behind him. He caressed stucco walls, feeling wrenched by this parting, but there was no time to grieve, or think. He reached for the door. "Bernard? Hang in there. You okay?"

He winced at the shriek of shattering glass.

"What was that?" Seiz bellowed from the hall.

Fr. Viktor heard boots racing toward the vestibule. He glanced up at the ceiling, sharing a stoic moment with the Almighty, then turned to absorb calamity. Cap crushed in hand, Seiz backed away from a pool of wine and a bottle still gurgling out its contents. Poor Bernard held up a torn apron. He turned in disbelief to Fr. Paul. The Austrian pulled a hand to his mouth.

Fr. Viktor nudged glass with his boot. "Bernard?"

"Yes, Pater?"

"How many bottles was that?"

"Well, eh, I did not stop to count, Pater. But, I think . . ." The brother tapped a fingernail against his teeth. "It might have been eight bottles."

"Eight? Well." Fr. Viktor aimed a good-natured smile at Seiz. "Here's something for your list, Herr Amtsleiter: eight bottles of wine, courtesy of our German-Austrian Passionist Province. That might not be an exact count, but I doubt it matters anymore."

NSV volunteers convulsed in laughter. Seiz snapped his head over his shoulder. "Clean this up. Now!" Then he glowered at the Passionists.

Good thing the man isn't carrying a gun, Fr. Viktor thought. *Thanks be to God.*

"Come on, let's go."

Fr. Viktor opened the monastery door and led his brethren outside. Dusk fell thick over the mountain like a funeral shroud. Squinting through shadows, he watched parishioners bustle about the courtyard, perhaps fifty people. NSV volunteers lugged boxes of robes to the courtyard and flung them into crates. Fr. Viktor watched farmers collect a box tenderly, with reverence, and hoist it upon a wagon that would deliver it into Herr Obendorfer's safekeeping. The sight moved him. A Catholic gendarme stood back as Officer Dobler mounted a swastika flag upon the courtyard gate. He turned to the priests and apologized on behalf of the police. Fr. Viktor thought of Herr Obendorfer's teary, gray-flecked eyes.

The sowing, Pater.

He recalled a parable where Christ spoke of a sower and compared souls to patches of earth receiving God's Word.

"A sower went out to sow. As he sowed, some seeds fell along the wayside, and the birds devoured them. Some seeds fell upon thorns, and the thorns choked them. Still others fell on good soil, and they brought forth fruit, some thirtyfold, some sixtyfold, some hundredfold." Fr. Viktor watched the setting sun bathe farmland in a golden haze. *Schwarzenfeld*, he pondered. In English, the name translated into *Black Field*. The founders had named this riverside town after the fertile loam that nourished their crops. A smile broke over his weathered features. "Good patches of lush soil. That's what these people are. But the thorns are proliferating in Germany, and the fowl are ravenous." Every farmer in Schwarzenfeld would assure him that a viable crop required daily maintenance, and conscience was a delicate flower to grow.

Fr. Viktor lifted his gaze heavenward, where clouds marched across a twilit sky. Soft winds rustled maple trees. They carried the scent of rain, an impending storm. "What will become of this harvest if we leave?"

———

"*If* we leave?" Fr. Paul said.

Huddled alone in the Miesbergkirche flower sacristy, Fr. Viktor looked up to find his fellow religious standing open-mouthed in the doorway. Fifteen crates of holiday ornaments cramped the dark and dusty room. The provincial began rummaging for a candle.

"Paul. Do you see what's happening out there? It's clear that we're enemies of the party, and the Reich demands absolute loyalty from its citizens. But the people out there are responding to pain. They're following *our* doctrine."

"This is inevitable, Viktor. At the risk of being overheard—" Fr. Paul leaned back to check a dark, somnolent church, then he continued in a whisper. "When you had this monastery constructed, you saved these people from poverty. Naturally they feel more loyalty to you than to the Reich itself."

"Granted, the situation is . . . *unique.*" Finding the candle, Fr. Viktor mounted it in a brass holder forgotten since Christmas and lit the wick. "But, if the Passionist message has any chance of taking root in German soil, this is the place to make it happen. I won't abandon this mission."

"But Cardinal Faulhaber ordered us to leave."

"Well, not exactly."

"No?" Fr. Paul's eyebrows raised into sickles of curiosity. "What did he say, exactly?"

"He told us to cooperate with the State."

"But the State ordered us to leave."

"The Miesbergkloster. Not Germany."

Fr. Paul absorbed that. He nodded. "It will be difficult for us to remain in Germany without a monastery."

"You only need a monastery if you have a community. This is a matter of survival now, and we can maintain a foothold in Germany as long as we're running a church. You and our brethren will go to Austria. I'm staying here."

His fellow religious adjusted circular spectacles on a round face and struggled to see what the future held.

"If it is the will of God that the Passionists stay in Germany," the Austrian priest deliberated, "then I should remain with you."

"Why is that?"

Fr. Paul pulled up a crate and perched himself upon it. "I have been in Schwarzenfeld only two weeks. Surely it is not His will that I return to Austria after such a short time."

Fr. Viktor grinned. "God bless your courage, Paul."

"If we remain here, then we will need someplace to live."

"I'm thinking." The provincial rubbed a creaking knee. A spider crept up a wall stained by watermarks. It vanished into a wide ceiling hole. He slid into reverie.

"You know, Grennan always thought Valentin and I were out of our minds, trying to establish a province here in Germany. I can only imagine what the good old father superior will say about today, and I'm sure Valentin is rolling in his grave—rest in peace, my old friend." Fr. Viktor crossed himself. "I think of all I've seen in this country. The poverty after the first Great War. The humiliation." He scratched a long earlobe, reflecting. "I remember one time, I found a woman rummaging through trash cans behind our first mission house. I asked her what she was doing. 'My children are starving,' she told me, 'how else will I find food for them?' A thousand marks couldn't even buy a loaf of bread. The money was that worthless."

"Yes," Fr. Paul said. "I have heard many such stories."

"Back at that time, a few American dollars could buy a castle."

"Or hire a town to build a monastery."

"That, too." Fr. Viktor gazed at shadows flickering on dingy walls. "Suffering is the common thread that binds us all—but it must be processed spiritually. What is Hitler doing to the people of Germany? He's taking their pain, and twisting it for his own ends. In the history of humanity, we've proven that we're capable of the greatest evils when hate turns us blind to the pain of our fellows." He heaved a sigh, thinking of Norbert's stories of atrocities in Poland. "Germany *needs* Passionists, my friend. This town is providing the means to fulfill our mission—out of loyalty, yes, that is true. But these chains of coincidence don't just happen spontaneously. I believe that each link joins with the next *by design*. We must hold our ground, and have faith that we're in Schwarzenfeld for a reason."

Fr. Viktor rose, kneading stiff muscles in his back. He studied the sacristy. The decrepit, wedge-shaped room ran two meters wide at its broadest end, tapering toward a narrow door on his right.

Fr. Paul pointed at the ceiling hole. "What is up there, Viktor?"

"Hm?" Fr. Viktor looked up. "Oh. There's a room above this one. That was the door. It once had a staircase, but it was half-rotted when Valentin and I bought the property. We never had a chance to rebuild it." He paused, arms folded, thinking.

"Paul, I remember hearing that you were handy with tools. You were a carpenter, right?"

"Yes, a long time ago." The Austrian's brow creased. "Why do you ask?"

Fr. Viktor grinned.

"What would it take to make this sacristy livable?"

CHAPTER FIVE

THE YEAR OF THE MOTHERS' REVOLT

APRIL THROUGH SEPTEMBER 1941

Soon after Klaus joined the Jungvolk, Helene learned that Baldur von Schirach, the Reich leader of the Hitler Youth, assigned themes to years and imbued each with stirring purpose. He formulated his slogans to satisfy a child's hunger for adventure and foster national spirit among German youth. Herr von Schirach declared 1940 "The Year of Trial," which Helene considered fitting, and 1941 "The Year of Our Life, a Road to the Führer," though she felt no inclination to envision her destiny, or those of her boys, as a path to a leader who marched their father into death's embrace. Disgust compelled Helene to create themes of her own for Klaus and Hans. She suggested "The Year of Good Conduct" to deter boyish squabbles and "The Year of Achievement in School," perhaps lacking in the excitement von Schirach injected into his mottos, but at least they were wholesome in their intention.

Privately, Helene dubbed 1941 "The Year of Despair," a morose sentiment confirmed by Norbert's announcement of the monastery eviction, followed by a frantic rush to clean crates. The widow staggered along a melancholy road like the lone survivor of a bombing, uncertain of her destination and not caring, for she found it impossible to focus on anything except a certainty that she had forever lost a second father in her life. Fresh bereavement hung over her like a veil until the following morning when Norbert burst into the bakery kitchen. He had returned from 6:00 Mass at the Miesberg church.

"The Provinsche, Pater Paul. They are staying!"

"What?" Suspecting that his mind had cracked under the strain of recent events, Helene stopped to gape at him.

Norbert relayed plans that the Provinsche confided to him after Mass. Maria wilted into a chair. "They want to stay in the sacristies? Those dirty little rooms?" She wrinkled her nose. "Oh, certainly you misheard him."

Norbert lifted his head with a somber air. "I am repeating his words with fine accuracy, *mein Schatz*. As the Lord commands, I do not bear false witness against my neighbor." Hat pressed to his heart, he meditated, then amended, "Well, it is a transgression that I never commit with *family or friends*, at least."

"But Maria is right," the widow objected. "Those sacristies are hardly suitable, Norbert."

"I agree, but this is an act of resistance. It is courageous of them, I say!" Norbert explained Fr. Paul's plans to renovate the flower sacristy.

Helene washed her hands at the kitchen sink and clutched them dry on her apron. "If they make the sacristy habitable, that helps," she concurred. "If they stay, they would have the two rooms, inadequate as they are. There is that lavatory outside the church, I suppose. But to live properly, one must bathe, and cook food. How will they do that?"

Norbert nodded. "Yes, I mentioned this to Pater Viktor."

"What did he say?"

"What he always says. 'God provides.'"

Envisioning life in the sacristy's cold, miniscule confines, Maria hunched her shoulders. "But what about the men who drove them out, Norbert?"

"What of them?"

"Certainly they do not expect the paters to stay."

"True. But as usual, they have underestimated this town. Schwarzenfeld will never forsake its pater provincial."

A grandfather clock in the hall chimed seven low, melodious tones, a sound that normally prompted a flurry of activity in this kitchen, but the three of them continued trading glances with each other and ignoring raw dough. Maria fingered a crucifix necklace. Gossamer jingling fluttered across the quiet room.

"You know, perhaps the bathing problem could be solved easily enough. We could invite them to come here when they need to wash up."

Norbert considered. "Yes, they could do that."

"But they will have no kitchen," Maria continued. "I think it would be best if someone cooked their meals for them."

Helene perked up. "What about—"

The baker cocked an eyebrow, waiting. "Yes?"

"Well, if we are seriously giving thought to this," she said, "I think I know someone who might be willing to help."

After work, Helene breezed up the Hauptstrasse toward the Dirrigl home. The mistress of a boarding house, Frau Paula Dirrigl spent long hours cooking meals for eleven people, her family included. Helene found her leaning over a bubbling stove, stirring pots of broth and sauce while her maid scrubbed floors. Deafened by a childhood bout of scarlet fever, Frau Dirrigl had to watch Helene's lips to understand her. The widow explained that Frs. Viktor and Paul lacked a kitchen to cook their own food, and an ebullient smile washed over Frau Dirrigl's gentle face. She agreed to cook meals; her maid would secretly deliver them to the Miesberg-kirche. That resolved everything, except for the supplies required to refurbish the dilapidated sacristies. Norbert insisted upon ordering them for the paters.

"I will construct a staircase for access to the upper room, and install a radiator for heat during the winter," Fr. Paul explained during a visit to the Gindele house. "I believe that I can draw hot water from the monastery. After all, the NSV must run the boiler if they want the building to be habitable for the children. But this must be done quietly," he emphasized. "We do not want to raise suspicions. In this small town, it will take a miracle to keep our plans secret for very long."

Helene considered it ironic that an act of Hitler and not of God diverted attention from the paters' continued presence. On June 22, the night Frs. Viktor and Paul crept from the town parsonage and officially took up residence in the flower sacristy, radios throughout Germany tuned in to the *Deutschlandsender*, the national broadcasting network, and they all learned about the Führer's declaration of war against the Soviet Union. The airwaves trembled with speeches extolling Germany's holy struggle against an enemy that mercilessly slaughtered Christians. To Helene's irritation, Baldur von Schirach changed his theme for 1941 to "The Year of the Crusade Against Bolshevism."

By September, she doubted that Bürgermeister Braun and Officer Dobler had failed to notice Frau Dirrigl's maid traipsing up the Miesberg's slope with a basket under her shawl, but another consequence of war perturbed them far more than two priests entrenching themselves in a church. Locomotives rolled into Schwarzenfeld's train station. Out poured a flood of Russian *Fremdarbeiter*, POWs sent to assume the work of German men fighting on the front lines. As a rule these laborers lived in barracks that kept them strictly segregated from ethnic Germans, but concern for worker morale compelled one factory owner to dismiss other laws. Instead of providing board, he distributed ration stamps and turned his laborers loose. Under the watchful eye of police officers, Poles and Russians strolled freely into bakeries and meat markets and stepped into line with German customers. Their arrival triggered another event that defined 1941. Aside from being "The Year of Despair" and "The Year the Paters Stayed in Town," it also became "The Year We Met Zizi."

"*Brot, bitte?* Bread, please?"

Seated behind the bakery counter, Helene looked up. The lean voice stumbling through German belonged to a gangly creature holding a ration card in his fist.

Must be a new arrival, she reasoned. The man didn't know enough to bring a sack for his bread.

Maria reached for his rations. "Oh," she gasped.

"What is it?" Helene asked.

The widow watched her smooth out a clump of paper. Every ration card contained colored stamps—red for bread products, blue for meat, white for dairy—indicating the exact amounts that its owner could purchase in one week. It was Friday and the laborer's card contained only three white stamps.

"Bread?" Sunken eyes traveled from Maria's face to the card she held. Dark irises flicked anxiously in an oily visage. "Please?"

Helene studied him in glances: a red "R" badge sewn into his right sleeve. Long, narrow nose. Black hair, matted. Bony cheeks. Skin crinkling and drooping like melted candle wax. "Bread?" he pleaded. The widow flicked a glance downward. Black-nailed fingers twitched and fluttered on the countertop. She wrenched a bread board beyond his reach.

Oh, don't you try it, she thought. *I won't let you!*

Iron clinking drew Helene's attention. Her jaw dropped. Maria cradled the card in her lap and moved her scissors near a corner. The blades sliced invisible paper.

"Oh my God." The widow snapped her head forward. She checked the customer line for brown coats and swastika badges.

"Bread?" The laborer's eyes fixed on round, crisp loaves. "Bread, please?"

Maria smiled. "Yes, of course you will get your bread. Leni?"

"Um . . . all right," she said. "Here you are."

The laborer snatched her offering. He caught sight of Maria holding up his ration card, darted, recovered it, then he froze. The man stared at them in breathy silence.

Helene shifted in her chair.

A toothy grin flashed across the laborer's face. He pointed to his chest. It occurred to Helene that he was introducing himself. "Ziziswili," he repeated, "Ziziswili." She wondered if he had spoken his first name, or if that was his first and last name jumbled together.

A bony hand reached over the counter and hovered in midair. Helene drew a breath. Without anyone pausing to remember that Ziziswili was a Russian and Maria Gindele a German, the baker's wife introduced herself and shook his hand.

"Zizi, ah. Zizi what?" Maria stumbled over his name.

Zizi chuckled, as if she had worked out a clever nickname for him. He bowed, then scurried through the parlor door. The bell clattered cheerfully with his departure.

Helene released the breath she had held in a startled gust. "Oh, I cannot believe what just happened."

"What?" Maria asked.

"Well, he is a Russian."

"He is not just a Russian. That was Jesus."

Helene stared. "What?"

"Well, you go to church like I do. You have heard the Provinsche's sermons, just as I have." Maria smoothed her flowered dress and reached for the ration card of their next customer. "Christ is present in all who suffer. Those men are subjected to hard labor in the factories and they get such meager rations. We will not forsake them in their pain."

The widow leaned close. "Yes, but he might be a Bolshevik. Don't they *kill* Christians?" She drew back and winced.

"I admit I did not think about that." Maria mulled. "If he is, then perhaps it is all the more reason to show him why Christians should not be killed for their love of God."

Helene's gaze meandered across the parlor and settled upon a crucifix. Sunlight splashed the wall, causing its varnished surface to gleam. When did the Provinsche encourage them to envision Christ's face in a Slav—and a Bolshevik for heaven's sake? Memories of Fr. Viktor's Sorrowful Friday sermon drifted through her mind and she turned away quickly. Yes, by God, that's exactly what he had said. He commanded them to see Christ's face in all who suffered, all who were neglected and alone. Not just Germans. Not just Catholics. *Alle.*

Later that afternoon Helene wandered along the muddy street, stepping catlike around wagon ruts. "Oh, stop worrying," she muttered to herself. "Anyone would have reacted the way you did. Don't think another thing of it." Despite that self-assurance, the widow couldn't help feeling that she had erred. She reached her house, a white plaster cottage nestled three houses down from the Gindele bakery. As she prepared lunch, thoughts of scissors and sermons clouded her mind, making her pause in lengthy introspection. Then Klaus and Hans returned from their first day of school at the *Marktschule*. Klaus offered a "*Guten Tag*"—good day—before vanishing into his room. Hans stood in the kitchen and frowned at a crucifix hanging upon chicory blue walls.

Helene looked up. "What is it, *mein Kleiner?* Why do you look so sad today?"

"The cross is gone," Hans said.

"Gone?" She twisted around. "But it is there, child."

"No, Mutti," he piped, "not *that* cross. I meant the one in our classroom. Our teacher said we didn't need it anymore."

She flinched at him. "Your teacher said what?"

———

". . . I tell you. They attack our Church, they ban our feast days, they banish the good sisters from our schools and replace them with *Fanatiker*." Norbert spat the word as if he been holding a mouthful of rotten eggs. "They poison our children with their songs, their slogans. They throw the paters out of their monastery and cast them into the street. Now what do they do, those *Schweinehunde*? They tear crosses off the walls of every classroom in Germany! 'They are to be replaced with pictures suitable to the present time.' Bah!" The baker clenched his teeth. "What a flaming, stinking, rotting, vermin-covered heap of rubbish that is."

Helene pulled her lips into a tight "o" and watched him storm back and forth across the Gindele sitting room, his words as sharp as a swinging saber.

Rosary beads clinked from a doorway. Fr. Viktor nodded a greeting to the widow and another priest seated on her left, Dean Josef Spangler. He then pulled up a parlor chair, brooding, while his clear blue eyes followed Norbert. Water slickened his gray-flecked hair; he had just emerged from a bath. The paters arrived punctually for that purpose each Saturday after the bakery closed at noon. At the Provinsche's side, Fr. Paul meditated, his hands folded calmly in his lap.

Helene watched, amazed, while Maria glided past her husband without paying him the slightest attention. She then offered a cream torte to her guests and poured ersatz coffee into porcelain cups that bore hand-painted Alpine flowers. Fr. Viktor took Maria's hand in both of his and bestowed what Helene recognized as a weekly ritual of thanks.

"May the Lord bring a thousand blessings to you and your family for the kindness you've shown us, Frau Gindele," he told her.

Maria offered him a warm smile. "Pater," she said, her rich voice flowing serene amid her husband's litany, "you and your brethren helped us during a time of such desperation. I am thankful that He gave us a chance to return your generosity."

". . . I tell you," Norbert continued seething, "if the party does not put those crosses back, they will lose this war of theirs."

"Good God," Helene said, "do be careful, Norbert. One could end up in prison for suggesting such things!"

"Oh, I am not merely suggesting—" He raised a pointing finger. "Wait until you hear this. Maria, did you bring it up here? That letter?" The baker strode to a lamp table and clutched up a stack of letters.

"The one our Norbert sent?" she asked him. True to German custom, the eldest son in a German family bore his father's name.

"Yes." He flipped through envelopes. "Where is it?"

"Did you write him about the crosses?" Fr. Viktor asked.

Maria nodded. "I did. But much to my surprise, he knew about it already. He heard about it from men in his regiment."

"Ah! Here it is." Norbert waved a letter. "Here, Maria. Read that part to them. You know the one." He motioned, impatient.

"Yes, I know, I know. Come sit." She patted an empty space on a striped, blue-white settee. He plunked down, grunting, his arms folded in continued ire.

Maria unfolded paper with slow tenderness. "Yes. Here we are. 'Mother,'" she paused, clearing her throat:

Mother, I have heard shocking news from my comrades. Have they taken the crucifixes down from the schoolrooms in Schwarzenfeld? If it is true, then I hardly need to tell you how I feel about it, and I can imagine Father's reaction.

She aimed a good-natured look at her husband. An impish smile flashed over his face. "Yes, I am sure that he can," Helene said, head shaking. It occurred to her that Norbert Gindele reveled in his flights of righteous fury.

Maria continued in an earnest tone:

But I cannot begin to express to you what effect such news is having here on the front lines. Perhaps the best way to explain how we feel is to tell you what one other Catholic fellow in our regiment said when his wife wrote him about the crosses. He shot straight up from his seat and declared, 'Are we out here fighting a crusade against the

Bolsheviks in Russia for Bolsheviks in the fatherland?' Many of us felt betrayed, and some suggested—

Maria flipped the paper straight, faltering, "some suggested that every German soldier would have a curse hanging over his head as a result of this crucifix action."

"There, do you see!" Norbert cried. "The Reich needs no curse to lose battles. The failing morale of our men will do it for them."

"They have indeed made a grave miscalculation if they have not considered the faith of their own soldiers," Fr. Paul agreed.

"If your son heard this from comrades in the army," Fr. Viktor said, "then news must be traveling far and wide."

"News and more besides, I should think," a low voice rumbled. "Our soldiers on the front lines are not the only ones who are angry."

Helene turned her attention to Dean Josef Spangler, another priest and Gindele family friend. He had wreathed himself in pensive silence until that moment. He assisted in Mass at the town parish church and he had hosted the paters at his parsonage during the first three months of their eviction. Gathering in the Gindele sitting room for ersatz coffee, cake, and conversation had developed into a ritual for all of them. The dean had piercing sky-blue eyes, and he wore his snowy hair parted along the middle of his head. Helene thought it made him resemble a plumed white bird. He spoke softly, though his words boomed like notes from a trumpet. Norbert regarded him with probing intensity.

"What do you mean, Herr Dean?" the baker asked.

"Just this week," he said, "I was at a meeting of the diocese in Regensburg. I spoke to friends in the clergy, all from Bavarian villages. They have seen communities rising up in protest, or parents holding demonstrations outside schools and government offices."

"Protests?" Helene gasped. "Outside party offices?"

"Oh, yes," the dean confirmed. "They told this one story about a county southwest of us, in Parsberg. The parents in a town over there gathered outside a school building, and they demanded that the crosses be put back. One of the administrators told them to take the matter up with their Bürgermeister. So, this growing mob marched to his office. And then they learned that he was lately away on business—"

Norbert chuckled. "An excuse he made up after looking out the window, no doubt." He had returned to his charming self again.

"Perhaps," the dean said. "With no success there, they began marching on county-level party offices and went to the Kreisleiter. Well, he came out and started shouting, saying that he had nothing to do with this crucifix action, but everything he said was drowned out by their protests. Finally he told them, 'Those of you who do not want to hear what I have to say should leave,' and would you believe it?" Dean Spangler burst into throaty laughter and slapped his thigh. "The entire crowd promptly departed!"

"Have they put any crosses back?" Norbert asked.

"This is the odd thing," the dean mused. "In some districts they have been replaced, and in others they are still being taken down. It would seem that the party itself has no idea how to handle this scandal it has created."

Maria pressed a delicate hand to her cheek. "Oh, dear. They are probably filling every jail cell in Bavaria with protestors."

"I am not so certain," the dean said. "The protestors in these other towns are all women, and mostly mothers."

"With all the men at the front, that is virtually all that is left in Germany," Helene pointed out. "But why would that make any difference?"

"If the authorities start making mass arrests of mothers," Fr. Paul reasoned, "what will the State do with all their children?"

"Exactly," the dean agreed.

"We have got to do something!" Norbert erupted.

"Do what?" Maria asked.

"I say we do what they did in Parsberg: demonstrate outside the town hall and refuse to send our children to school until they put the crosses back."

His proposal wrenched Helene. "A demonstration?"

"'The voice of one man will be silenced quickly.' Remember?" He glanced in Fr. Viktor's direction. "But one hundred voices of women and mothers? They cannot silence *that* easily." His emphatic, black-brown eyes swept the sitting room. "Listen. Religion is more than scripture and worship. It has a vital function in society. Imagine a world without it: no influence compelling one to empathize with the agony of a suffering man. No parable to make one see that pain is a reality—even across the battle line. I was in Poland. I have seen what happens, and I tell you it sickens one's soul to see how *evil* a man will become, how quickly he descends into brutality." Norbert's lean, handsome face flushed with the heat of horrid memories. "Leni. I am not ignorant of the danger. But neither are the other Catholics in Bavaria, and look at them. They are rising up! If there was ever a time to fight back, it is now!"

"But civil disobedience is an extreme step, Norbert," Helene protested. "It is especially dangerous for you, after the trouble you have gotten yourself into already."

He scowled.

"Well, it is," she persisted. "And certainly the last thing Pater Viktor and Dean Spangler would advise us to do is run off and have ourselves a big, loud protest outside the Rathaus!"

"Well, I don't know about that," the baker said. "Our pater provincial comes from a country where revolution is considered to be a God-given right, yes?"

Fr. Viktor peered down into his coffee cup and smiled, as if he perceived their attention sliding in his direction without needing to see it.

"Yeah, that's true."

"And how would people protest in your native place of Pennsylvania?" Norbert prompted.

The widow shot a plaintive gaze at the old man, though he didn't see it. Immersed in thought, he rested his coffee cup upon its saucer. Finally, his shrewd blue eyes drifted up to engage Norbert.

"Germany isn't America, my friend," he advised softly.

"I know, Pater."

"What would we do." He propped his elbows upon his knees. "When we Americans want to make our voices heard, we protest peacefully, perhaps by circulating a petition, and presenting it to officials who might listen."

"A petition," Norbert said, turning thoughtful.

Dean Spangler interlaced his fingers. "'Freedom of speech.' This is what they would call it in America, yes?"

"Amen, Herr Dean." Fr. Viktor turned back to Norbert. "If Schwarzenfeld chooses to protest, I have one suggestion."

"Yes, Pater." Norbert slid forward, earnest, attentive.

"Whatever actions you encourage in this town, for your own safety, you must find a woman to lead them."

The baker's shoulders sank. "A woman?"

"A woman," Fr. Viktor confirmed.

"Yes, I do think this would be prudent," Fr. Paul chimed in agreement. "Frau Heidl is correct. It would be disastrous for this town if you were arrested."

Norbert gloomed toward a vase of wildflowers. Helene sank back in relief: their Provinsche had spoken.

"As long as someone in this town is doing something," the baker conceded, "yes, I can abide with that. Find a woman to lead it." He slid a glance toward his wife. "What about you?"

Maria flinched at the question. "But if I am involved, then the authorities would naturally assume that you are also."

"Yes," he allowed. "I suppose that is a point. Leni?"

"What?"

A grin leapt to his face.

Helene's jaw dropped. "No, Norbert. Oh, no!"

"Oh, yes, it would be perfect!" He smacked his hands together, then rested them on bouncing knees. "Imagine it. Here you are, the mother of two boys, the wife of a war hero who sacrificed his life for the Führer—!"

"Yes I am a widow," she shot back, "and I must think of Klaus and Hans. What if something happens to me? Nikolaus' parents are in their eighties, they cannot keep up with two active little boys! I cannot take such a risk."

Norbert looked at his wife, then back to Helene. "All right." He quickly recovered his chipper bearing. "There are other Catholic mothers in Schwarzenfeld. One way or another, we will find a way to make this happen."

———

The paters left at 4:00 p.m. to prepare for afternoon Mass at the Miesbergkirche. This prompted a general departure, complete with expressions of warm gratitude to their hosts.

Helene stepped outside and pulled a black shawl around her shoulders. Custom no longer required her to mourn, though wartime conditions afforded few opportunities to make or purchase clothes, and despair still followed her like a shadow. Two women trudged by, hugging baskets of sun-ripened apples from local orchards. Dull bells clanked. A farmer herded cows toward pastures along the Naab River. Schwarzenfeld bustled with the carnival energy of a farm town during harvest season. She slogged through, oblivious, pondering. Dean Spangler delivered sermons every Sunday from the town's beautiful rococo parish church. Officer Dobler attended his homilies to monitor the tune of his trumpet voice. *And Paters Viktor and Paul?* Their unique doctrine did kindle her, and she felt *moved* by Fr. Viktor's mission. The Provinsche believed in it so strongly that he suffered to live in a dingy flower sacristy. Yet in the secret sanctum of her heart, Helene despaired. She doubted their efforts would bear much fruit, given the realities of the Reich.

Helene tipped her head back, letting a breeze soothe her. She drank in the sight of a cerulean sky fringed by picturesque Bavarian houses. "*Lieber Gott.* Don't let anyone get into trouble over this. Especially Norbert."

Footfalls pounded behind her. Boyish howls echoed amid cowbells and the lowing of steers. A yelp startled her. Helene turned to discover upset baskets, women chasing spilled apples. A blur thudded against her.

"Oh!"

The Jungvolk trooper fled without offering an apology. "Ill-mannered child. What jackal of a mother raised you?" The widow stomped after him, ready to deliver a scathing lecture on proper manners, then a wave of recognition hit her. The child had a wiry little body, beanpole limbs, and a shock of sandy hair.

"Klaus!" she howled.

More feet hammered the ground. Behind her. She darted. A second Hitler Youth charged after her son like a raging bull.

"That is your mother?" the other trooper taunted. "Ha, look at the little mama's boy."

Klaus skidded in the dust. His face twisted into a mask of pure ferocity. His fist flew up to deliver a punch.

"Klaus!"

Helene's shriek rose above the street as blood sprayed in the afternoon sun. Two boys tumbled into a knot of kicks and grunts until farmers rushed over and tore them apart.

"Klaus? Klaus!" Helene rushed up, frantic. A farmer wrapped a muscled arm around her eldest. The boy wriggled, still rearing for a fight. A straw hat tumbled from the farmer's balding head; he winced, nodded an awkward greeting, then handed her son to her. She cringed, mortified.

"Klaus, what are you doing!" Helene demanded.

"He started it." Klaus sucked a knuckle.

"Well, I don't care who started it. Good God." She smacked dirt from his chest and legs. "Why is he fighting with you?"

"Because I killed him today." Klaus twisted around. "Ha! I got you good." They had emerged fresh from a war game.

The other Jungvolk boy struggled against the farmers who pulled him back. He glowered, lunged at Klaus in vain, then finally plodded home.

"Oh, look at you! You are a mess." Helene cupped her son's chin. Blood dripped from a delicate nostril. Welts marred a sweaty brow. Dirt streaked his face. A wave of sorrow washed away her anger: the child had been defending himself. "Those boys," she gritted. "I hate how they pick on smaller children!"

They stalked home. "But they always pick on smaller kids," Klaus said. "Our troop leader orders them to do it."

"Your troop leader? But I thought that horrid boy was gone!"

"Somebody got rid of *him* a long time ago." Klaus sniffled thickly through blood. "This new one is at least a little better."

"Well, I don't see how."

"He mixes up the platoons so older boys fight alongside younger ones. At least we all get a chance to win that way."

"But you still come home a mess! This hardly seems like an improvement to me." Their cottage loomed ahead like a haven from the mad world. Helene checked on Hans. He romped with neighbor boys in a back alley, yowling happily. She stomped up to a side door. "Klaus, get inside. Sit down. Sit!" Her finger shot toward a chair at the kitchen table. "My God, your nose! You are bleeding all over. Oh, I *hate* the Hitler Youth. If it was not compulsory, I would take you out in a second! I envy Norbert and Maria." They had a perfect excuse to keep their children from joining the organization: they needed their help to run the bakery.

Helene grabbed a rag. A faucet squealed at her touch. "Pinch your nose—the one side—like that. Breathe through the other nostril." She took a deep breath herself. The sight of a bleeding child electrified her with panic. "All right, hold still."

Klaus groaned, but he sat obediently as she wiped the red ribbon oozing down his face and throat. Aquamarine eyes shifted up to watch her, the brows arced in endearing pertness. Meeting that gaze, those clear and luminous eyes identical to her own, the young mother stood arrested. Oh, this sandy-haired imp. He could stop her heart with a smile. She caressed a cheek moistened by sweat, and he soaked up her touch the way the rag absorbed water and blood. Beneath this bruised shell, he was still the vibrant child she loved fiercely. Underneath it all, he would always be her boy.

A silver glint caught Helene's eye. "What is that?"

"Huh?"

"That thing on your collar."

Klaus reached up, touching a shield pin. "Oh, that. Someone gave it to me. Sometimes I wear it for luck during the war games."

"Oh? Who gave it to you?"

He plucked the rag from her and delicately tested his nose. It had stopped bleeding. "Some charity person at the Rathaus. He felt sorry for me."

"Why? What happened?"

Klaus shrugged.

Helene smoothed a thumb over the shield, admiring elegant tracery. The design was ancient, probably Nordic in origin. It was made of common tombac and quartz, yet its production required enough skill to make it worth a few Reichsmarks. "Well, clearly something happened, child. That is a nice trinket to be giving a Jungvolk boy. Did this happen today?"

Klaus flicked a glance up, lips pursed. "No, it was a long time ago. My old troop leader was just . . . doing and saying stupid things." He swung a leg, kicking air. "Then, this officer showed up and yelled at him. I told him about Papa. He told me to keep the pin. He said I had sacrificed enough to deserve it."

Helene teetered between gratitude and disquiet, wondering who had stopped to comfort her son. The man had business at the town hall. That told her all she needed to know about him. If he felt compelled to defend a weepy beanpole boy from a teenage overlord, his attitudes were either atypical for a party member, or her son endured treatment far worse than he let on. She knelt before Klaus and took his hands in hers.

"Dear boy, I am sorry for all you are going through. You are growing up in a world so harsh, it breaks my heart. It is not the way things have always been, nor is it the way they should be."

His eyes shifted away, but he was listening. Helene thought of the Provinsche, what he would say at this juncture. *We are all bonded by pain.* She stroked the backs of Klaus' hands with her thumbs.

"You know, child? As dark as things seem, it is still possible to find hope in this world. We are suffering together. All of us. That means something."

He bristled. "Mutti, I don't want to hear that."

"Hear what?"

"That religious stuff. It is nonsense."

"There was a time when I thought that also. But if one looks at it in a different way, it actually sounds practical—"

"Mutti. Do you want to know what one learns in the Hitler Youth? You want to know what is practical? This!"

Her son raised a fist and shook it in her face. She recoiled so abruptly that she tumbled back and thudded upon the floor.

"Klaus."

"When one is in the Jungvolk, Mutti, *this* is what matters. If the world is harsh, then one must be harsh also."

Helene flinched at the fist. Her vision went hazy as it shifted and refocused upon a nightmare sight, at gentle features warping in bitterness.

"Child. Your father would not approve of this talk."

"Papa is gone and there is a war going on. Our troop leader says it all the time: the Führer wants us to be a cruel, brutal youth. This is what makes sense. That is what I must be."

Helene stared at the fist, at the sweet face with a raw nostril, at a gaze so cold that her body froze and her mind went numb. At last, she remembered to breathe. "Your room. Your clothes. Go change those clothes." Above the blood-rush of a pounding heart, above the memory of Norbert railing about war and Poland and men blind to pain, she heard hobnail boots plod away slowly. *The Hitler Youth is compulsory. I want him out! But there is no way. Shaking fists. Brutal youth.* She reeled at one of the most horrid realizations a mother could have. *They are beating the humanity out of my son!* What light would make this child see where his leaders were taking him? What cause might compel all their children to question the course that the Reich had charted for their young lives?

Dazed and shaken, she looked to a delicate crucifix gracing the kitchen wall.

The following Monday Helene marched into the Gindele bakery with a new theme for 1941. Norbert straightened, his hands submerged in dough.

"All right." She smacked a paper on the work table. "Here is the essay for your petition. What is next?"

CHAPTER SIX

DAILY BATTLES

OCTOBER 1941

When his Hitler Youth leader summoned the troop at half-past two on a Thursday afternoon, Klaus scampered to his room and prepared for duty. At first he wriggled into his uniform, following normal habits. Inspecting himself in a mirror, he stroked a jagged white symbol sewn on his sleeve. The *Sieg* rune possessed mystical powers that assured victory for a German warrior, yet a fight loomed before Klaus, and it occurred to him that this insignia might spark enemy wrath. The boy fished a wool sweater from his closet.

"Camouflage: check."

Another idea occurred to him. He plucked a shield pin from his dresser drawer and held it to a window, watching sunlight glisten over its surface. He smiled at the memory of an officer in the Rathaus. "Good luck charm: check."

A strategy frothed and bubbled in his mind. He tip-toed into Mutti's room and found Papa's silver war wound medal. "Honor badge: check."

His gear complete, Klaus marched down the hallway and summoned a dutiful air while lifting the lid on a clothes basket. His brother's underwear and socks spilled out. "Ew." Nose pinched, he kicked them beneath a china closet, dumped his dirty clothes on top of a pile that gave off an obnoxious stench, then he engaged in a fruitless tussle with a lid that refused to shut. "That is strange." He recalled a time years ago when Mutti had caught a horrendous flu. Despite a raging fever and hacking cough, she had sponged her brow and scrubbed clothes until her knuckles bled. Even Papa's protests had failed to deter her from keeping up with chores. "Where is she?" In the parlor, bare hooks protruded from a rack where she normally draped her coat and scarf. "What is she doing?"

Outside, Klaus found his little brother kneeling in the alley behind their house, his lips moving in prayer. He was conducting a funeral for toy soldiers. Twig crosses adorned four earth mounds ringed with pebbles; wooden figures stood at attention. Hans peered up, bashful, dimples creasing his cheeks.

"Altar boy adjutant: check!"

A red can awaited him at the Rathaus. Klaus exchanged salutes with Bürgermeister Braun's secretary. "Equipment: check!"

His trinket box and collection can in hand, Klaus halted on the Hauptstrasse. Hans stood at attention beside him, awaiting orders. Sheer-faced houses lined the roadway, their stark white facades receding and welding together seamlessly. The sight reminded Klaus of armies forming ranks, the houses towering like soldiers, the men frozen in that breathless instant when gunners peered across a deadly space and slipped fingers around triggers. A German boy surveying his battleground, he felt the fight swelling in him. He pictured Erwin Rommel, revered general of Germany's Afrika Korps, lifting binoculars to his eyes and observing enemy tanks rolling against an arid expanse. Rommel's cunning strategies against British armored divisions earned him a nickname: *der Wüstenfuchs*, the Desert Fox.

I am Leutnant Heidl, the Homefront Fox!

Klaus blew a sigh through gathered lips. "Let the battle begin."

Under normal circumstances he would man a street corner and wave his collection can at people passing by, but desperate times called for desperate measures. His adjutant at his side, Leutnant Heidl poked a buzzer at the Dirrigl house, where he unleashed his door-to-door campaign. He selected his greeting with wily care.

"*Gruess Gott.* We are collecting for the Winter Help charity. Do you have money to donate for the poor?"

The Dirrigl family maid crossed her arms. Her milky features suddenly curdled.

"No one in our house is giving money to the party. Not until they put those crosses back in your school!"

The door slammed shut, jolting him. "But it is for charity!" Klaus cried.

They marched to the Gindele house. Leutnant Heidl planted firm hands on his hips and squinted at a gray house perched upon the Bahnhofstrasse street corner. He aimed Hans toward the door and gave him a shove.

"*Gruess Gott.*" His brother lifted the can in beseeching hands. "Please remember the poor. They have no food and no shelter, and that is really bad during the winter. God would want you to give money. Please?"

Frau Gindele mewed in sorrow. "Oh, you little angel. My heart aches for them, and I will remember them in my prayers. As much as it pains me, I must say no." The woman leaned close to offer a consoling whisper. "But, I am saving our donations. Do return when your teachers put the crosses back."

Leutnant Heidl slumped in dismay. "Frau Gindele said no—to an altar boy?" He watched Adjutant Hans plod back. "This is bad."

They ventured out to a farmstead on the town's fringes. A pert girl ogled his shield pin. Offering him a jaw-dropping ten Reichsmarks, she flashed a mischievous grin and padded off to pilfer money from her father's study. Klaus loitered, waiting, stroking metal gently with a finger. It pained him to part with his good luck charm, but Herr Amtsleiter Seiz needed donations to support those children he had put up in Pater Viktor's monastery. Surely he would appreciate money more than sentimental attachments to a trinket. It turned out that fate spared Klaus the sacrifice. A *hausfrau* stormed outside and buffeted him with a broom.

"You devils!" she squawked. He bolted, Hans howling behind him. "Open your bible, boys! 'Whoever causes these little ones who believe in Me to sin, it would be better for him if a millstone were hung about his neck and he were drowned in the depths of the sea!'" Her gnarled hands clutched a fence gate. "That is Matthew 18:6. You tell that to your schoolteachers, you hear?"

The battle raged on. Ten houses later, Leutnant Heidl hauled out his last weapon in desperation.

"Heil Hitler. We are collecting for the Winter Help charity. It is your duty to give money. My papa died for the Führer. See this?" He tugged at the wound badge pinned to his sweater. "He is a war hero who did his duty. He would want you to do your duty also."

The townsman, a party faithful who worked on Bürgermeister Braun's staff, offered a zealous salute. Once his eye dropped to the collection can his enthusiasm faded.

"You are the tenth Hitler Youth to come begging for money this week. I have given a donation already." The man presented a soldier figurine, a sure indication that he had offered a contribution to another collector.

"Would you give more for me, the son of a war hero?"

The party loyalist slammed his door shut.

Shaking his collection can, Klaus mourned a soundless stir of motion and wondered if the Desert Fox had ever suffered crippling defeats like this one. "Stupid cross!" He kicked pebbles and sent them rattling across the street.

"You are mad again," Hans groaned. "How come you are always mad?"

"I am not *always* mad. I am just mad right now."

"You are too always mad!" his brother protested. "And what did you do to make Mutti so upset? You two have been acting funny."

"I don't know," Klaus whined. "She is just fussing. You know how she gets." He looked away, his brow furrowed. He knew quite well what had happened. He had emerged fresh from a fight that day, his heart thumping hard, the blood rushing in his ears, and all the fiery statements from his instructors and Hitler Youth leaders just tumbled right out of him. *What is so terrible about repeating the things I hear from the people who teach me?* Certainly they would approve of his reaction. Yet the shock on Mutti's face made him feel bruised all over, as if he had been kicked from head to toe. Oh, this world confounded him so! At times like this he ached for Papa. A boy needed a steady presence to sit by his side and just listen, a guide who would sort out the mysteries of the world and praise him for the things he did properly, or speak in a stern tone when he needed discipline, then gently explain how he had erred. *Without Papa, how will I ever get things right?*

"I am sorry, Hans," Klaus said. "It is just this religious stuff. I don't understand why everybody is raising such a fuss."

"I understand why they are angry," his brother piped. "I want the cross back also."

"One can still see the cross at home, right? And one can see the cross in church. So, it is not in the classroom. Who cares?"

"The Provinsche says that God is everywhere. So, why should the cross not be everywhere also?"

Klaus swallowed hard. "God was not with Papa."

"He was too. Mutti said that God missed him so much, He just had to bring him back home to Heaven, is all."

Klaus sighed in exasperation. For a moment he remembered personal rituals devised after Papa left for war, private ceremonies performed nightly, in absolute secrecy, with faith so shiny and perfect that Heaven could not ignore them—if God existed.

"But what about all that stuff in the Bible? 'Ask and you shall receive.' We asked, and did we receive? No. That cross is just a decoration. It doesn't *mean* anything or help anybody."

"That is not true," Hans said. "It helps me."

"Oh, yea? How?"

"It helps me, because I think Jesus knows how I feel."

"Huh?" Klaus drew his chin back.

"When I see the cross, I see Jesus. He is all beaten and bloody and naked, almost, except for that cloth. Jesus had a really bad day a long time ago, so He knows what mine are like." Hans clapped a hand to his chest, exuding boyish dignity.

Klaus rolled his eyes. "All right, fine. But why does it matter if it is in a *classroom*?"

"Even in school, it is important to think about other people who are sad, or being bullied and all."

"You would not last long in a Jungvolk troop," Klaus muttered. "They would beat you up for caring about people who are too weak to help themselves."

"But if you believed that, then how come you are collecting for charity?" Hans asked.

"What do you mean?" Klaus said, turning defensive.

"Poor people have got lots of problems. Right? And charity means that you care, and you are helping them out. What would the Hitler Youth say about that?" Hans lifted his chin high.

Klaus flinched at the shiny red can.

"Hans. Go home."

———

Klaus groaned. "Jesus knows how I feel." The wooden soldiers rolling around in his trinket box had more sense than his brother.

The following morning, Friday, October 10, he trudged into ground zero: an austere, sweat-scented classroom in Schwarzenfeld's *Marktschule*—the town elementary school. Hitler's portrait glared above a slate blackboard. The coal pupils seemed to eerily follow Klaus as he padded across the room. Four white smudges reached beyond the framed picture, hinting that a crucifix once hung there. Klaus' gaze traveled over plaster walls he had always perceived as searing white, yet that phantom imprint revealed a fact that eluded him until now. That cross protected a clean place while time had imperceptibly turned the wall a dull shade of brown.

"Wood on a wall. That is all the cross is." Why did its absence in a classroom cause so much fuss in this riverside village?

Chuckles and howls reverberated around a cramped room. Twenty students suddenly fell silent and scrambled for seats behind oak benches. They barked a Hitler salute as their teacher bustled through the door.

"Boys, boys!" A sharp voice lashed at them. "You make such a ruckus, one would think this is a Jew school."

Herr Schmitt, the school headmaster, taught boys attending fourth-year classes in the *Marktschule.* When the Führer declared war against Russia, a ravenous increase in enlistments wrenched male instructors below age forty into the German army, hauling Schmitt from retirement. Their headmaster was an old shoe of a man. Spots and impossible crinkles lined his leathery skin, and scuffs of white hair glinted across his shiny head. Klaus dimly registered the remark about Jews. A native Berliner, his teacher referenced them often. Living in a Catholic farm village, Klaus had never met any Jews, and Mutti and Papa had never mentioned them. He failed to understand why Schmitt despised them so.

Creaky oak floorboards groaned beneath an approaching tread. A swarthy man loomed at the door. He bowed his head to avoid scraping his skull against its wooden frame. Klaus drew a breath at the sight of gleaming badges, knee-high boots, and an aqua-green uniform.

"Officer Dobler. Come in, come in!" Herr Schmitt exchanged salutes with him and gestured toward a seat in the front right corner. The police chief engulfed a wooden chair meant to accommodate a child. The sight elicited snickers from students. Officer Dobler scowled at them.

The headmaster peered above the wire rim of his spectacles. "Class, we have a visitor. You will be on your best behavior."

His bead-blue eyes surveyed them, though their instructor had no cause for concern. Only a dimwit misbehaved around a pillar of muscle like Officer Dobler.

"We will get to his business soon enough, but first, let us show our police chief how we start our day. Let us have a rousing report from the front lines!"

The war report! Klaus longed for updates from North Africa. They were a sumptuous platter for dreams of Papa surviving Dunkirk to join the *Deutsches Afrikakorps*, fighting under the Desert Fox. A man puffed his chest in button-popping pride when he followed a leader he loved, and Klaus wanted to envision Papa alive and happy.

"Our army has defeated the Communist enemy in Kiev!" Herr Schmitt's voice swooped grandly.

"Klaus?"

"Yea?"

"Where is Kiev? Point it out, please."

"Yes, sir."

He stalked up to a world map pinned upon the wall. Swastika flags improvised from sewing needles and scrap paper marked German victories; the most active fronts thrust east across Russia and plunged south past the Mediterranean, where Rommel fought the British in North Africa. Klaus obediently pointed out the Soviet city to classmates who yawned and propped cheeks against their fists. His eye dropped wistfully south. Herr Schmitt reported nothing from North Africa.

Mucus rumbled in a clearing throat. Officer Dobler observed him intently. "*Hallo,*" Klaus greeted with a sheepish grin. The officer merely stared at him. He scurried back to his bench.

What is he doing here?

"And why is our Führer fighting to get all this land for us?" Old Schmitt called upon students, carrying on business as usual.

"Living space for our people!" A classmate answered.

"Because other countries have colonies, and Germany got left out," another added.

"We did not just get 'left out,'" the headmaster retorted. "Our enemies insisted upon humiliating us. Our land and our colonies were stolen from us!"

He selected students to approach the map, and boyish fingers roamed around, straining to locate colonies wrestled away by the British, French, and Australians. The list struck Klaus as exotic: Tanganyika. Palau. Cameroon. South-West Africa. A hefty slice of New Guinea.* Where were these places? He was amazed. His mind pieced facts together in youthful context. The world was a schoolyard, and Germany was a willow-thin child fighting off bully nations. He pictured greedy hands groping for hats, shoes, socks, any possession capable of being torn away in mocking laughter. His attention shifted back to landmasses studded with swastika flags, and he felt a stir of pride in his country. Germany was no longer that playground weakling.

"Do you see all that he is doing for us, our Führer!" old Schmitt trumpeted. "How fortunate we are to have a leader who is restoring our nation to her full glory!"

The headmaster slid a furtive look at the police chief. Officer Dobler hunched in the corner with a spider's patience.

"You boys have heard the name of Herbert Norkus, correct? You know his story. Right?"

Klaus and his classmates nodded. The party had immortalized that name in stories and films, ensuring that every German child knew his tale.

"Let us see how well you remember. Who was Herbert Norkus? Someone tell us." Schmitt pointed to a pupil. The boy hauled himself up from a third-row bench and stealthily massaged a rump that was turning numb upon the unforgiving plank.

---

* The former colony of German East Africa included parts of present-day Burundi, Rwanda, and the mainland part of present Tanzania (formerly known as Tanganyika). South-West Africa corresponds to present-day Namibia. Germany's former territorial holdings on the island of New Guinea are part of the country of Papua New Guinea.

"Herbert Norkus was a Hitler Youth boy who lived in Berlin. He was in the troop that was led by Baldur von Schirach."

"And what were Norkus and his troop doing?" Schmitt pointed to another student.

"There was going to be a party meeting," the boy enthused. "They were going to talk about the Communists. And Norkus and his troop, they were secretly putting pamphlets in mailboxes, telling people about the meeting."

"And what happened then?"

"He was killed!"

"Tell us how!" Schmitt demanded.

Students turned to the storyteller. "A group of young Communists tracked them," he gushed. "And when they found them, they pulled out their knives, and they started stabbing everybody, right there in the street! There was blood *everywhere*!" Schmitt nodded in approval and bade him to continue. "Baldur von Schirach and all the others, they ran away, but Norkus was cornered. The Communists stabbed him—twice in the chest, three times in the back. And they cut off his lip, and sliced up his face, even!"

"Eew!" Students sang, enraptured by gore.

Klaus mourned over another story of death, the mouth that swallowed people whole, even children.

"Good, very good!" Herr Schmitt praised. Officer Dobler sat brooding at the floorboards. "Yes. There is even a film that tells his story—*Hitlerjunge Quex*. This village has no equipment to play films. What a shame. You boys would have enjoyed it. Ah!" The headmaster paused beside a world map studded with swastika flags.

"See here? Do you see our victories against Russia? There are Communists in Russia. If we had no leader to defend us from these savages, imagine what they would do to good boys like you. Can you imagine what they would do to your *families*?"

Down the hall, students in another class recited a poem of homage to the Führer. Klaus shivered.

"Given the good that he has done for Germany, it is appropriate that we honor our Führer and display his portrait right up there, in front of our classroom. Do you not agree?" Schmitt surveyed twenty pupils who offered him their undivided attention. The scuffed head nodded. "Yes. Our Führer deserves this honor. But some people in our town do not agree. They wish to display *crosses* instead! Let us talk about that cross. What does it teach? Pity for suffering. Right? Mercy for weakness. What ridiculous notions! Did the Communists have mercy for Herbert Norkus? Did our enemies have mercy for Germany after the first war? Do enemy soldiers have mercy for our men on the battlefield?"

Klaus drew a hand to his chest, clutching a wound unseen.

"*There is no such thing as mercy!*" Schmitt's voice had a strange tone, a razor sharpness. "Why, it does not exist in the natural world! Think about it. Does a spider have compassion for the fly in its web? Does a hungry hawk catch a mouse and stop to think about how it will suffer?" He shook his head. "In nature, a superior force does not act with compassionate intent. Doing so threatens its survival. And we, my students, we Germans are a part of nature! This is what you must learn in this classroom. Not fairy tales about *compassion*."

Klaus frowned. He recalled himself standing on a street corner, collecting donations on behalf of the NSV. It suddenly struck him as odd that a leather-tough party member like Herr Amtsleiter Seiz should concern himself with the poor.

"But, you boys are smart!" Schmitt declared. "You can tell what is truly best for our country. Now, we need you to be as brave as Norkus! We need you to do your duty." The tone of his voice made all twenty students stiffen to attention.

Officer Dobler straightened in the ridiculous chair.

"These people who want the crosses brought back. They are causing a great deal of trouble. We must learn who is behind this. Have you seen anything odd at home? Your mothers leaving at strange hours? Distributing papers, or signing them? Anyone?"

He waited.

"Anyone?"

Klaus looked to his classmates. They peered at darkened light fixtures and gazed out sunlit windows. Students down the hall stopped chanting patriotic poems of praise to Reich and Führer. Silence throbbed through the school.

Schmitt traded looks with the police chief. The headmaster smacked his large, leathery palms together, a habit that preceded announcements.

"*Achtung!* Attention! If each and every one of you proves your loyalty like Norkus—*each and every one*—I will dismiss class an hour early! How about that?"

Gasps rose in a breathy chorus. Klaus dimly heard squeals and hoots around the room. He was thinking of Mutti. He remembered her thumbs gently stroking his hands and her warm, throaty voice whispering his name.

"I came home yesterday and saw my mother signing a paper!" a classmate revealed.

Officer Dobler shot up from his seat. "Good! What did this 'paper' look like?"

"It had signatures on it."

"How did your mother get this paper?"

"A woman brought it to our house. I only caught a glimpse of her through the doorway, so I don't know for certain who she was. She had pale blond hair, big blue eyes."

"Why are you looking at Klaus? Klaus, you are very quiet."

"Huh?" He jerked to attention. The classmate who spoke was the boy he had decked on the street last week. The kid smirked.

"Have you noticed your mother doing anything odd, Klaus?" Schmitt queried.

At home, a basket spilled clothes. Wooden pegs stood bare from an empty coat rack. His mouth felt like a desert.

"No. Nothing."

"Remember what I said to the class. We cannot leave early, unless everyone reports everything he knows. What have you seen?"

Nineteen students groaned. A bench mate smacked a fist into an open palm, daring him to wreck their chances of escape from this stinking white cell.

"I have seen the boycott. All the Catholics in town are refusing to donate money." He mustered a wan smile. "How stupid, when there is all that talk in church about charity."

The headmaster squinted at him. "Your mother works at the Gindele bakery, yes? I have seen her. Light blond hair, big blue eyes just like yours."

Footsteps thudded toward Klaus. Slow. Like drums. Officer Dobler towered over him. Klaus shrank away. A rush swam through him, the same feeling he experienced during a war game when he crept near the woods and the mere snap of a twig sent him bolting. Truth pursued him, though he dare not turn to behold its terrible specter. Truth reached for him with groping claws. He moved a hand to his arm, protecting imagined cords.

What do I do?

His mind pounded. His heart raced. He remembered a shield pin glimmering in the half-light. Herr Amtsleiter had shielded him from harm.

He could not forsake his mother. He had to protect her.

"Other women in town have light blond hair and blue eyes," Klaus insisted. "Horst wasn't seeing my mother, I am sure of it. She would not cause trouble."

"Is your mother loyal to the Führer?"

"Everyone in my family is loyal to the Führer. My father died for Germany. He has a war wound badge."

Ice-ringed pupils fixated upon him. "Think of Norkus, Klaus." Herr Schmitt's voice seemed to skulk around him. "Think of your father. They were brave. You can be brave, too. I cannot release this class early unless every boy does his duty—including you."

"It is very strange that you have not seen these papers, when the rest of your classmates have mentioned them," Officer Dobler mused. "I think that someone is being very careful, and trying to hide them from you."

Klaus' jaw slackened.

"All right. I remember now."

"Good boy."

Klaus fled for shelter behind lies. "They were, um. They were at the Gindele house. Yea. I saw them there."

"You saw the papers at the Gindele house?"

His throat squeaked.

"What?" Officer Dobler cupped his ear.

"I saw them . . . on a table. Anyone could have put them there."

"Perhaps your mother did it. She works at the bakery."

Anger flared in him. "My mother works at the bakery, but these papers are not her fault. It is *Herr Gindele* who is doing it all. I am certain!"

He glared at his interrogators. Behind him, he heard creaks and pale movements. The headmaster looked up. He responded to an upraised hand.

"Herr Schmitt, can we leave early?" a classmate asked.

Schmitt turned to the police chief. "What do you say, Officer Dobler? Have these boys proven themselves loyal?"

The police chief studied Klaus with a cold mica gaze. He angled his head, considering. "Yes," he said at last. "They have done their duty."

———

Klaus burst from the school doors.

"Stupid cross. Stupid, stupid, *stupid* cross!"

Tolling thundered from a distant hilltop. It was noon. Shouts rippled below a feathery sky while his classmates reveled in a freedom that felt sickly sweet. He wanted to hunt down that miserable snitch who denounced Mutti, though he saw no sign of the boy. Anticipating his wrath, the trooper had fled. "I will get you later." He would settle a personal score during the next war game.

"Stupid." Klaus probed his sleeve. He shuddered at a bareness there, at cords of virtue stolen away. "Stupid, stupid, stupid!" But Mutti was safe. He had seen to that. Officer Dobler declared him loyal. Yes. He had wrenched her from harm's way, just as Herr Amtsleiter Seiz had rescued him from his Hitler Youth overlord. "Stupid cross." The boy fought nausea while contemplating what awaited Herr Gindele. "Stupid, *stupid* cross—"

A cloud of pale men with round, dark eyes strolled up the Bahnhofstrasse. Klaus noted "R" badges sewn into their clothes. He shrank away, wondering how many *Fremdarbeiter* in Schwarzenfeld were Communists.

His hob-nailed shoes pounded the ground. His eyes were flame. Hot breaths puffed from his nostrils. He would march into the kitchen and confess what he had done—what circumstances had forced upon him—before the stunned "o" of Mutti's face. She would bellow and fuss, but he would bellow louder and louder until she fell to her knees and vowed to stop . . . well, whatever she was doing. Their cottage loomed into view.

"Mutti!"

The front door hung ajar.

A hen waddled across the street, oblivious to the world and its troubles. Klaus licked dry lips. "Mutti. Are you home?"

He stumbled inside. He went numb.

The parlor was dark. Papers rustled across a wooden floor. He recognized his mother's writing. These were chore lists, the kind she compiled every day to keep herself on track. "Mutti?" Bounding into the kitchen, he found cabinets swung wide. The drawers were heaped upon the table, their contents spilling out. "Mutti!" Silence flowed thick and heavy through his house. In the bedroom he shared with Hans, dressers vomited clothes. "Where are you, Mutti?"

He bolted to her room. Her mattress. It spilled from her bed. Papa's shirts, trousers, and socks had been torn from a storage chest. His mother's dresses lay heaped beside a brassiere and a weird mess of white rags. And the clothes basket. Klaus stopped. The hallway basket. It gaped like a wicker busybody blabbing secrets about their upturned lives.

He grunted in fury and gave it a kick.

Calamity erupted outside. Klaus raced through the back door. His face crumpled. Blue-green uniforms buzzed around the Gindele bakery like mad bees swarming around a hive.

He plodded back to the *Marktschule* and awaited Hans. From there he fled to their grandparents' house across town. "What is wrong?" his brother pleaded. "Where is Mutti? Why are we going to Oma and Opa Heidl's? Klaus!" He couldn't answer. Talking hurt too much. The world was a backward, lopsided place today. He feared it would never be set right again.

———

At noon sharp, a foreman at the Buchtal ceramics factory signaled an end to the morning shift. Rations in hand, Polish and Russian *Fremdarbeiter* flooded Schwarzenfeld's streets. Like a wave, they washed into butcheries, farmer's markets, and bakery shops. The bells dangling above Norbert Gindele's parlor door announced customers with a delicate clatter, and Maria rushed into the kitchen to assist while Helene clipped stamps and distributed bread. The Gindele family's eldest daughters were due to return from school any moment, and the widow had to leave soon. Klaus and Hans would be wandering home in an hour.

Black-nailed hands pattered against the serving table. Helene looked up. A candle-wax face stretched in a listing grin.

"Zizi. *Gruess Gott.*"

"Bread." A ration booklet waved in his fist.

"You have stamps. Good." Helene plucked his offering, and glanced up to study him. "It is customary for one to bring a sack, you know. One does not carry his groceries in his hands."

The Russian rocked on his heels. Perhaps he intended to consume the entire loaf right now. She tried to explain the sensible notion of dividing bread into daily portions, but Zizi failed to understand. He continued demonstrating his mastery of a lone German word.

"Yes, yes." Helene carefully lifted a hot loaf. "Here is your bread, and your rations."

"Here."

"What now?"

"Here!" A ration book flapped in her direction again.

"What? Oh, heavens," she said. "*Na, na,* I have taken your stamps already!"

"For bread-bread. For bread . . . and bread. *Eins, zwei,* one, two. Bread one!" Bony hands fluttered in emphatic pantomime. Bells clattered and ten Poles wandered into the parlor, stepping into line. "Bread, bread!" Zizi grew plaintive. Helene was on the verge of calling Norbert and asking him to contend with this ridiculous little man. "Bread one. Bread one!"

"Oh," she said.

His intentions dawned upon her. He wanted to give her the stamps he couldn't provide a week ago, thus stripping Maria's gesture of its meaning.

"Um. No. You can keep that stamp." The widow pushed his booklet away.

"I keep?" Zizi pulled the stamps to his chest. "I keep." He paused in consideration. A hand hovered toward Helene.

"Ziziswili," he announced.

"Pardon?"

"Ziziswili."

Helene's shoulders rose and sank with a sigh. Blackness lined his nails. She wondered what dreadful manufacturing process stained skin in such a manner.

Memories of a fatherly countenance shot through her mind, and wise blue eyes prompted her to remember a message of tolerance and compassion, even for enemies.

Investing faith in an American priest, the German woman slipped her hand into that of a Russian and introduced herself.

"Ah!" Zizi burst, delighted. "Yelena."

"Um, no. It is 'Helene.' You understand? *Heh-lay-neh.*" If this foreigner insisted upon knowing her name he should pronounce it correctly, although he resisted every attempt to correct him. Bells clattered. The customer line coiled, impatient.

"All right," she capitulated. "Pleased to meet you, Zizi."

"Yelena! Ha ha ha!" Zizi chortled. He gripped his bread, remembered his card, then darted. "Yelena, Lena, Lena . . ." He sang her name as if gloating over a prize.

She clapped a hand to her brow, mortified.

The next customer strode up and Helene flung herself into work. It would have been better to accept Zizi's offer. The Reich Office of Nutrition scrutinized the stamps that she and Maria collected each day. It tallied customer demand, and allocated exact quantities of wheat, yeast, salt, and other ingredients—all measured down to the gram—that Norbert needed to meet his quotas. All things being equal, a discrepancy between supply and customer stamps should have prompted the Office of Nutrition to investigate. A devout Catholic who relied upon the goodwill of fellow parishioners, Norbert coaxed extra wheat from farmers who were steadfast friends, and asked a Catholic miller to grind secret gains. She had noted that the extra loaves produced from his bartering found their way, without fail, into the bags of Slavic *Fremdarbeiter* who trudged into the bakery without stamps.

Helene reflected upon Sorrowful Friday, when Norbert confided the atrocities he had witnessed in the East. Knowing the baker, this was likely an act of personal reconciliation for marching with an army that would commit such horrors.

The widow shook her head. *Yelena.*

Well, it was a pretty variation on her name.

A bread board whispered across the serving table. Norbert emerged from the kitchen. He shot a secretive smile her way. "So?"

"So, what?" she asked.

"How many do we have?"

Helene paused, scanning the customer line for swastika pins. "I think I counted 185 signatures. That is nearly every Catholic mother in Schwarzenfeld."

The baker stroked his mustache. "Very good. It is nearly time, I think. Soon, we deliver our 'package' to the Rathaus."

"I say we do it tomorrow."

"Tomorrow?" Norbert said. "That soon?"

"The longer we wait, the more nervous I become," Helene admitted. "We only give the party more chances to discover our—"

Bells. Footsteps. At the door. Helene's attention tore across the room to find Officer Dobler thundering up. A team of gendarmes surged behind him. The widow paled while he plucked papers from his crooked arm and laid them delicately, one at a time, without a word, upon the serving table. The essay. The signature sheets. She had stored them in her dresser, tucking them beneath the cloths she used to pad her underwear during periods. Her boys would never have occasion to peruse that drawer. The police felt no such qualms.

"Take Frau Heidl," he ordered. "And Herr Gindele as well. I have reason to believe he is a part of this also."

CHAPTER SEVEN

CHURCH AND STATE

OCTOBER 10, 1941

After reading his breviary at noon, Fr. Viktor heaved open the Miesbergkirche's wooden doors and let a breeze gust into the sanctuary. A pristine autumn sky stretched above him. He lifted a beaming face, reveling in the sight, then froze. Christ staggered across the church courtyard and gazed at him through the stricken visage of Maria Gindele.

He ushered her into a pew and spoke soothingly while her sobs thundered through the church. "Frau Gindele. All right. It's all right." When parishioners staggered up to him in this state, he longed to thrust formalities aside and address them by their first names, though he suppressed that impulse, realizing that it was thoroughly American. He was a servant of God, and cultural norms denied his German followers—even those he treasured as dear friends—a reciprocating privilege of calling him 'Viktor.'

Norbert and Helene's story poured out in a torrent. His followers rallied to a righteous cause, and the realization prompted a rush of pride. They had dared to push the Reich, but predictably, the Reich pushed back.

You're responsible for them, old man, he chastened himself. *You're the one who recommended this plan.*

"Officer Dobler," Maria wept. "He had the papers in his hands. The signatures, the essay. Norbert and Leni are in terrible trouble."

"We've seen your husband taken for questioning before, Frau Gindele," Fr. Viktor said gently. "Did Officer Dobler say he would release them?"

"Oh, Pater. He said that he will get foreign laborers to replace Norbert and Leni. He said I should expect to train them next week!"

"I see." The provincial brooded.

"I hope you will not think my faith weak, Pater," Maria said, her voice a warble. "The petition is a just cause. But I cannot think of anything but Norbert and Leni and that bakery. Training new bakers is not done in one day, and the laborers. They don't even speak German! With all the laborers in the factories, we have twice as many customers as we used to. I will fall behind. People will go without bread. Do you see?" Teary hazel eyes probed his. "I have my girls to raise. And the customer line." She sniffled. "Oh God! That customer line. It will all be on my shoulders, Pater . . . oh, those poor people. How will I ever . . . ?"

"All right. I understand." He grieved at the picture she painted. Bread served as a major staple of the German diet. The Reich's ration system prevented citizens from obtaining other foodstuffs to alleviate their hunger.

"Have you tried going to the Rathaus and explaining this to Bürgermeister Braun?"

"You mean, to confront him?" Maria recoiled. "Pater, he will order me to manage the bakery myself. I will say '*Ja*,' and walk out, even if this is impossible for me."

Her submission resulted from more than humility. In this country it was an expected response to authority. An American, he felt no such reservation.

"Are your daughters home from school?"

"Yes. They are running around the kitchen in a panic, there is a line outside the bakery. We are falling behind."

"I'm sure," he said. The girls could help manage the bakery, at least for a little while. "All right. Go back and take care of your customers and your daughters."

Maria blanched. "Are you going to approach Bürgermeister Braun yourself?"

"You let me handle this," Fr. Viktor said firmly. "Okay?"

"Yes, Pater." The woman sighed with relief as an onerous burden slipped from her shoulders. She departed.

Fr. Viktor debated what do to. A confrontation with Braun promised disaster. He had heard enough stories of clergy members engaging the party to their own undoing. He longed to call upon a cardinal or a bishop, but the loss of his monastery had taught him a searing lesson: he could not depend upon the German Catholic Church to unite against a hostile State and protect his parishioners.

Fr. Viktor felt a wave of panic. He breathed in, breathed out, restoring calm. He possessed granite faith tested by the rigors of a long life, and experience taught him that a higher power provided—in fact, had already provided—through His Framework. Christ Himself affirmed that notion: *Your Father knows what you need, ere you ask Him.* Over the past weeks and months, perhaps even years, that power guided him from one moment to the next, preparing him, and thus every kernel of knowledge gleaned before today, every acquaintance he made along the way served a purpose that would reveal itself in time.

He knew how to proceed: "Fight fire with fire." The success of this perilous maneuver depended upon finding a party member willing to strike a spark. "Fight fire . . ."

Voices sailed from his monastery. One hundred school girls from Hamburg occupied the Miesbergkloster. He rubbed his brow and struggled to concentrate while they sang a lovely paean to Hitler.

Footsteps. Fr. Paul rushed up the church aisle in bead-clinking strides. The Austrian priest had departed for a stroll ten minutes ago. He returned earlier than expected.

"Viktor, I saw Frau Heidl and Herr Gindele being taken to the police station. Also, I spoke with one of our friends in the gendarmerie." Fr. Paul drew a breath and hesitated.

"What did he say?" Fr. Viktor prompted.

"Bürgermeister Braun is determined to learn who put Frau Heidl up to this petition action. He suspects you and Herr Gindele."

The provincial imagined what Norbert and Helene endured at the police station. He pulled a moist palm down his face.

"Braun will rip them apart, Paul. I've got to help them."

"*Mein Freund,*" Fr. Paul said, "I fear that Herr Bürgermeister will order arrests, and not just two. You are a venerated leader and they are not eager to make a tense situation worse by arresting you unless they have proof of your involvement. But I suspect that they will come for you."

Fr. Viktor leaned against the church's side door. He watched twenty girls at play, darting in and out of view, chasing a ball across the courtyard. Two children waved at him, blissfully unaware that they would patter down to the refectory next week and find plates without bread.

Fragments of realization fit together and a solution struck him like a lightning bolt from the blue.

He leapt toward the flower sacristy. Robes whispered behind him. "Viktor," Fr. Paul said, "where are you going?"

"Schwandorf." The neighboring town lay six miles south of Schwarzenfeld. He decided to take a train.

"And what about Herr Gindele and Frau Heidl?"

"That's why I'm going to Schwandorf." He tore a black fedora and an overcoat from a wall hook. "Better say a prayer, Paul. Better yet, make it a rosary."

"Why is that?"

"I've got to pull the Lamb from a lion."

"The Lamb from—?" Fr. Paul adjusted his spectacles, considering. His jaw dropped. "If *that* is where you are going, then I doubt one rosary is enough."

"We're working in the Framework." The provincial clapped the arm of his fellow religious. "Have faith, my friend! God provides in mysterious ways."

———

At 3:00 p.m., Fr. Viktor trudged along cobblestone alleys sweeping him deep into the town of Schwandorf. Crimson flags rippled and flapped from sandstone windowsills; Hitler's likeness glowered from banners on the brick edifice of a government building. The provincial opened a door and stopped short, confronted with a six-foot depiction of Aryan motherhood guiding an infant's lips to her breast. White lettering beneath her cerulean dress implored German citizens to support the 'Mother and Child' program. A ridiculous compulsion made him tip his hat and murmur, "Good afternoon, Madam," in English.

He crossed himself and walked inside.

The room was cramped, yet immaculate, the air laced with ambient traces of typewriter ink, floor varnish, and perfume worn by women in his midst. Flowered scarves bobbed around him like a motley sea. The only man in the room, he felt alien here.

A sleek, dark-haired secretary turned from a filing cabinet and stopped short, eying him warily. Badges sewn into her black blazer identified her as a member of the *Frauenschaft*, the Reich association for German women. He had grown accustomed to her glacial reaction when he strode through this door each month. Tedious arrangements between Cardinal Faulhaber's office and the State required her to surrender six hundred Reichsmarks into his outstretched hand, though he had no intention of treading the path of normality today.

The provincial stepped into line behind a slip of a woman stroking an enormous belly. He tipped his head, reading the papers she was signing: medical forms, request for prenatal care in a party-sponsored rest home, registration for childcare classes. Two girls scampered across the room and hunkered down, moving the arms and legs of button-nosed dolls. Above their braided heads a black and white poster announced the 1934 winter charity drive. Fr. Viktor studied its imagery: a ragged woman and child huddled on a street corner, their faces upturned in awe as sturdy male arms reached out to them. "None shall hunger," Gothic letters assured, "none shall freeze." His gaze swept toward a poster depicting two men, one wearing Lederhosen, the other suited in party brown, both toiling to erect a structure that resembled a multidirectional sign post. "Public health, child protection, fighting poverty, assisting travelers, People's Community, protection of mothers," Fr. Viktor read, translating words inscribed within each sign. He ground his teeth. "These better be more than just slogans."

He scanned posters for swastikas and counted only one. A different insignia dominated the walls of this party office: an enigmatic rune formed from an N cradling an S, the latter reaching skyward through an uplifted V.

Space cleared at the front desk. Fr. Viktor requested a moment with the office director, but the secretary lifted her head, squared her shoulders, and ferociously defended his time. Her obstinacy drove him to drastic measures. He insisted upon collecting the NSV's October rent five days early—a matter requiring strict department approval. She pursed her ruby lips and rapped on a door bearing the director's name:

WILHELM SEIZ, AMTSLEITER.

Footfalls thundered from the private office. "It is not the fifteenth yet, Pater. Do all of you Americans find it impossible to follow schedules, or is this just your problem?"

Fr. Viktor turned to face a man in gray suit pants and a crisp white shirt, the party member he had last seen glowering over a wine pool in his monastery.

"I'll take your rent if you have it," he said to avoid a lie, "but that's not why I'm here. I have another matter to discuss with you."

"What matter?"

"I need your help."

Seiz stepped back as if the provincial had declared himself infected with plague. The NSV director surveyed him, his eyes narrowing in suspicion. "Whatever your problems are, I want no part in them. Take your money and leave."

He vanished into his private office.

"This trouble's coming your way, Herr Amtsleiter!" Fr. Viktor bellowed. The office door stopped a split-second in lieu of slamming shut. "It's coming. This is your chance to stop it."

Silence broadened in the waiting room. The door remained fixed in that near-closed state for a moment, then it creaked open. Seiz glared at him, and for good reason, he knew. They had gravely underestimated each other the last time their paths crossed, and neither of them intended to make that same mistake twice.

"I have serious problems on my hands already, Pater. Every Catholic in the area is boycotting party collections, including mine."

"If you don't hear what I have to say, a deficit in collections will be the least of your worries. Trust me on this."

The secretary leaned near Seiz and hissed the word *Polizei* just loud enough for Fr. Viktor to hear.

The party member's scowl leapt into a grin.

Fr. Viktor tensed, but there was no turning back. He could only plod ahead on this treacherous path.

"Hm. All right, it is," Seiz consulted a wristwatch, "3:25 in the afternoon. Check on us in exactly five minutes, Anna. If he fails to say anything that interests me, we will call the police and make sure they arrest this American agitator. Now then," he opened his office door, thoroughly amicable, "come in, Pater Koch."

———

"A petition?" Seiz said.

"Yes, a petition."

"I have worked in government offices for nine years. Do you know how many petitions I have heard of in that time?"

"None, I'm sure."

"A petition." The party member mused. "I ask myself, 'Where would German citizens get an *amerikanische* idea like that?'"

Fr. Viktor rolled his eyes.

"You told them to do it," Seiz surmised.

"No."

"But you knew that they would protest. You gave them your approval."

"What makes you say that?"

"I know how Germans obey their leaders, Pater, political and religious. If you had told them 'do nothing,' then you would not be here right now."

He shifted in a chair across from Seiz's desk and glanced out a window.

"You Americans. One would think with all the Germans that sailed across the Atlantic, you people would have a better understanding of authority and obedience."

"My parishioners stood up for a cause they believe in," Fr. Viktor countered. "They're upset about this order to remove the crosses, and from what I hear, so is the rest of Bavaria."

Seiz eased back into his seat and shot one of those stares that seemed to elevate him to a force of nature.

"So you come to the NSV for help. Yes, indeed you need help. Once the police interrogate your parishioners and get the incriminating evidence they seek, they will look everywhere for you. But you are correct: that dirt-road village of yours is not the only place where Catholics have protested this crucifix action. I hear that the Gestapo are being dispatched all over the Oberpfalz." Seiz nodded, taunting. "Oh, yes. They are interrogating people as well. They are hoping for denouncements, one would expect."

A habit gripped Fr. Viktor's throat. He avoided reaching up to loosen the collar, knowing what the gesture would betray to a man observing every draw of breath, every tic and flutter in his face.

"I imagine the party would love having one instance—just one—where it can be proven that a priest incited his parishioners. You are trying to hide. Is that why you are here?"

"Why would I hide *here*, of all places?"

"I should call the Gestapo and have them pick you up right this minute!"

Seiz pounced on his desk phone.

"Wait!" Fr. Viktor gripped the hand clenching the receiver. "Would you listen? I'm not here for my own sake."

"Then why are you here?"

"Because of all the party members I've met in Germany, you're the only one I know who empathizes with suffering. A lot of people will suffer over this business—a lot of German mothers and children!" Fr. Viktor said, emphasizing words he had read on the waiting room posters.

Seiz tore his hand away. "You should have considered that when you started talking about petitions. Do you think I am blind?"

Fr. Viktor had an opinion on that point, but decided not to annoy the party member in his effort to reach the charity worker.

"Hardly."

"I know all about you. You and Pater Böhminghaus are living in that rat hole of a sacristy. The town is supporting you, so I let the matter drop. You are fortunate that I have not called the police already and had you arrested for remaining on the property."

"I see that you stay informed," the provincial said without expression.

"And you insult me, if you think I cannot see your motives in this matter. We don't need to release your Catholic agitators to bake bread. *Fremdarbeiter* can replace them."

"Oh, come now. Do you really expect Frau Gindele to raise four children, train foreign laborers who don't speak German, oversee the production of two hundred loaves a day, and tend that customer line? She'll be doing all of it alone. Her assistant is the other woman who's being detained: Frau Helene Heidl—and she's got two boys of her own to care for." Fr. Viktor watched sapphire eyes dart away briefly, chasing thoughts.

"Mark my words: a lot of people will go without bread, likely for weeks. I don't have to remind you of those children you've put up in my monastery, they get their bread from the Gindele bakery, too." He paused to let facts trickle into Seiz's bloodstream. "And what about the German mothers who will walk away from the bakery empty-handed? They can depend on government handouts until this is resolved. Right? 'None shall hunger.'" He drove a stare back at the NSV director. "Who's going to support them, I wonder?"

He waited. A clock ticked on the wall.

"Of all the desperate ploys," Seiz said. "You have made another horrible mess, and you have the audacity to march in here and make me clean it up?"

Fr. Viktor shook his head, remembering spilled wine. "You know how Catholics feel about their faith."

"They should feel that way about the fatherland."

The provincial let serenity seep back into his words. "Look. We both know that Braun is a devout National Socialist. He won't stop to consider the suffering of women and children. But I know that you will."

The groan of a door disrupted them. Fr. Viktor checked a wall clock: 3:30 p.m. The secretary leaned inside. She addressed Seiz as Wilhelm. As a rule, the Germans reserved that level of familiarity for family, bed mates, and friends they held dear.

What a shocking lack of formality from a subordinate, the provincial thought.

The party member twisted a gold band on his ring finger and steadily watched Fr. Viktor, letting indecision stretch to whatever length amused him.

"I think . . . give me ten minutes more." He braided his reply with the same thread of intimacy. "Then we will turn him in to the police for sure."

Fr. Viktor swiveled back to face a man who sought complete domination over him. Wilhelm Seiz had decided to continue this parley. Pondering the prospect of arrest, the priest accepted that as a hopeful sign.

"You are a persistent man, Pater." Seiz rose and prowled the office. "When did you come to this country? 1920?"

"Twenty-two."

"Twenty-two, then." Seiz leaned against a bookcase. "So you know what it was like here after the first Great War, and during the Depression. Tell me. What has religion done for Germany? Did Christ rescue us from poverty? Was it God who delivered us from humiliation and defeat? And you." He squinted in accusation. "You come from America, the land of riches and plenty, and you preach to *us* about suffering? Look around this room."

Seiz pointed out ten wooden frames hanging upon white plaster walls.

"You will find pictures and letters from Germans who have come to the NSV for help. I assure you, Pater, they know more about suffering than you do."

Another jab. Seiz flung presumptions like darts. For a moment Fr. Viktor contemplated his childhood in Sharon, a period of searing bereavements and hardships that forced him to shoulder adult burdens by age seven. Their poignancy allowed him to challenge these piercing accusations. Instead he listened to the pain of another human being.

Seiz flicked dust from a picture of a mother cradling a child. "I myself spent four years living on the streets of Nürnberg," he revealed. "My father died on the front during the first war. I damn near ended up just like him. Then the Depression came. My mother and sister did inconceivable things to get food for us. When I could no longer tolerate the hunger, I wept in shame, thinking of what they had to endure so I could eat." Seiz's voice firmed. "It was National Socialism that saved this country. Not God. And I will never let another German suffer like that, not while I am in the NSV."

"I see." Fr. Viktor reflected on the mother he had once found behind a mission house in Munich, upturning garbage cans in a desperate search for food. The Depression had pounded America with economic hardships, but its effects all but devastated Germany. The country's obligations to pay war reparations had only compounded the agony. In Seiz's voice he heard pain festering without spiritual release, anguish twisted for dark purpose. Despite his own arguments against this man, he let a higher power speak through him in the tone of a concerned father.

"It grieves me to know the hell you've endured. I remember those days. I may not have suffered with you all, but even so. I felt the pain in my heart."

Seiz slid a guarded look at him. "Perhaps I will believe you on that point, Pater. When you built that monastery, you helped a lot of Germans in need. I have never forgotten."

"Then help me now," he continued in a disarming tone. "Talk to your contacts in the party. Please."

The charity worker stood head bowed, arms folded. After a long moment of deliberation, he leaned close and let his voice drop to a whisper.

"If your people wanted to protest, this petition was the most foolish thing they could have done. A list of names in the hands of the party is a dangerous thing."

"It's signed by German mothers," Fr. Viktor told him. "What can they do?"

Seiz peered at him. "These women have fathers and brothers and husbands, yes? The Gestapo *will* make use of this list. The party always punishes disobedience. Always."

Fr. Viktor searched for pretense in an earnest visage. He read only dire candor from a man who knew the Reich. A slow, cold tingling drained down his face.

"If I succeed in convincing Bürgermeister Braun to release your people, then do something for me," Seiz said.

"What?"

"You will give a sermon on charity. Convince the Catholics to stop this boycott against NSV collections."

The provincial ground his teeth. Seiz had likely planned this counter maneuver the moment they had trudged into his office. "I don't preach politics at my pulpit."

"I did not say 'preach politics,'" Seiz clarified without offense. "I asked you to support charity. I think we both believe in this concept, correct?"

Fr. Viktor pondered. They were engaged in a desperate gambit, and he could see no other recourse. "We do," he admitted.

Seiz accepted that as a sign of consent and reached for the phone. Silence stretched while switchboard operators established connections, but within moments he greeted the *Ortsgruppenleiter*, the highest party official in Schwarzenfeld. Seiz had befriended the man, Fr. Viktor gathered. Hauling his weary bones up from the chair, he stretched and listened to half a conversation in progress. Norbert and Helene remained in police custody.

"And what did they say? Yes. About Pater Koch." Seiz was watching him with sly amusement. "Was he held for questioning?

Why not? Well, where is he? You don't know." The charity worker picked at a fingernail. "No, I advise against wasting your time, I have a feeling he will show up eventually."

What a piece of work you are.

Fr. Viktor turned to the walls. For the first time since he had plodded into Seiz's office he relaxed enough to survey his surroundings. These letters and pictures intrigued him. Not a speck of dust felted their wooden frames. *Is Adolf here?* Small surprise. There he was. Hitler's likeness scowled above the charity worker's left shoulder.

A family portrait hung on the right wall. Fr. Viktor recognized that obstinate secretary: Seiz's wife. He laughed softly, head shaking. They had two young daughters.

The provincial moved on. He paused, realizing that he had craned his neck, contemplated, and then stepped over to another reflection point. He performed those same motions every day in the Miesbergkirche while meditating upon fourteen plaques, the Stations of the Cross depicting Christ in His Passion.

My God, I'm in a chapel.

He studied iconic imagery that burned deep into memory, the fragments of a different Passion Seiz held sacred: Schwandorf's poor lined up before a soup kitchen; German war orphans in a kindergarten, receiving medical care; images of haggard refugees in war-torn France, where Seiz had spent two months coordinating relief efforts with the German Red Cross; a letter from a mother in Hamburg. In a neat, spidery script, she lamented the nightly terror of bombing raids and praised the Schwandorf NSV for protecting her daughter in Schwarzenfeld's boarding school.

Fr. Viktor glanced sidelong at Seiz. A phone propped to his ear, the man steadily observed his reaction.

The provincial turned again to study years of humanitarian effort, keenly aware of Germanic names, Nordic faces, knowing that a malevolent doctrine lurked behind each frame, yet his shoulders sagged. At last he understood the meaning of that inscrutable NSV rune. *Charity in the hands of the Third Reich. The goodwill arm of an evil empire.* It amazed him that the NSV director could breathe, compressed as he was between extremes. Fr. Viktor longed to kick the mechanism keeping Seiz's wine and venom suspended in perfect equilibrium, disrupting its clockwork timing just enough to induce an imbalance that would sicken him. After vomiting up the poison he had ingested, perhaps he would reel to the engine and examine the half-corroded bolts and gaskets of his conscience. *Can this soul still be redeemed?* The sower pondered. What good might God yet accomplish through Wilhelm Seiz?

"Well, Pater. I assume that you are coming?"

He turned. The charity worker tugged a coat from a closet and paused with the air of a man about to speak. Instead he strolled out, leaving the office door swung open behind him.

———

They ambled up to a street corner outside the NSV office and awaited a car approved by Schwandorf's town party leader. Fr. Viktor feigned to watch cobblestone roads. Seiz stood at his side, impeccably dressed in a tailored gray suit and coat. He was a minor official, but he did his best to look the part. Surely, the charity worker knew he would end the boycott if everyone walked free: Fr. Viktor trusted that much. And yet, this man had a frightening talent for subterfuge.

Dear God, help me, the provincial thought. Seiz was a coin flipping end over end, and only the Almighty knew what side of him would land face-up.

"Learn anything new over the telephone, Herr Amtsleiter?"

"Not really," Seiz said. Fr. Viktor drew a breath, released it slowly. "Well, I suppose there was one thing. The Gindele bakery produces exactly 264 loaves per day. Earlier, you quoted 200."

"My mistake," Fr. Viktor said. Seiz had obtained figures from party records. In reality the number fluttered closer to 300, with secret loaves finding their way into the hands of Slavic laborers. This war had inflicted devastating wounds upon Norbert Gindele's psyche, and the baker opened himself, healing emotional pain through spiritual commitments to people disparaged by the Reich. It also provided a means to peacefully resist a regime he loathed beyond words.

Seiz plucked out a cigarette for himself and held out an offering; Fr. Viktor declined. He preferred cigars, and indulged in them only during times that called for celebration.

"You know, Pater." A lighter flicked. "I am sure I know what you think of National Socialism. But you see only half the picture."

"Yeah? How so?"

"Look around you. Do you see the man sweeping the street? And there. Look at those postal workers coming from the *Postamt*. They are civil servants, like myself. Well. There is *some* difference in class." Seiz scratched his lip with a thumbnail, his voice tinged with regret at his modest status in German society. "But the man who carries the mail has just as much value as the wealthy factory owner who receives his deliveries. And even the street sweeper can hold his head high if a landowner should step out of that bank there, on the corner. It is German blood that gives them their worth. Through blood we are elevated into a greater whole, where all Germans are equal. This is what National Socialism has given the German people that God cannot."

"The People's Community, you mean."

"Precisely," Seiz confirmed.

Fr. Viktor watched the post office's wrought iron sign sway in the breeze. He had always thought of National Socialism as an unfathomable political movement, its followers all people with an appetite for the obscene hatred that Hitler served up in a banquet, yet for the first time he gleaned more behind it, a complex social message that exalted even the most unremarkable citizen. And he could see it. He easily envisioned millions of Germans drinking that down, unquestioning. A man born and raised upon free soil, he gazed upon the bounty that Hitler laid out for them and saw what truly filled each bowl and cup.

"Back in the States we believe in that same thing: equality regardless of class," he began.

"Well, there we are," Seiz enthused.

"But it's a God-given right, regardless of race. Even in our own national history, we've learned that racial inequality leads to war. It almost tore our country in two." He watched Seiz squint down the street, blowing smoke in a long breath.

"And National Socialism may give Germans a sense of unity," he continued, "but God gives one that's far deeper. In the whole that is Him, there are no boundaries of race or country. All are equally deserving of charity."

"And where exactly was this 'greater whole of God' after the first war?" Seiz challenged. "You know how our enemies crushed us. Did any Good Samaritans feed us Germans, and heal our wounds?"

Fr. Viktor groped for words to shake this man.

"Tell me. If it pains you to see Germans suffering, how can you follow a leader who's pulled this country into another war?"

"You have asked a worthy question." Seiz adjusted a gray hat, considering. "As a priest, you have vowed obedience to the Catholic Church, correct?"

The provincial let the air seep from his lungs in a sigh of acquiescence. Blood-red banners rippled in a crisp breeze.

"When Cardinal Faulhaber ordered you to hand over the keys to your monastery, even if you did not agree—and I am certain that you did not—did you fail to give him your obedience?"

"Germany isn't the Church."

"And the Church is not Germany."

Fr. Viktor faced the charity worker, aware of the wind and the flags and a thump in his chest, his heart sick with understanding. Seiz's loyalty verged upon religious devotion.

"With all my soul, I pray for God to open your eyes. I pray He does it soon, before you fall too far from grace."

Seiz read him for a somber moment. Then he scoffed.

"Pray for yourself, Pater. You and your parishioners are the ones in grave danger here."

A black automobile rumbled into view: a police car. Fr. Viktor's pulse quickened as Seiz opened a door for him. The provincial noted a cigarette pinched between the charity worker's thumb and forefinger, in German fashion. It was still lit.

Seiz gestured affably, inviting him to take a seat; instead, Fr. Viktor strode around to the opposite door.

"Yeah, right. *You* get in this car first, Herr Amtsleiter, so I know you're really coming along."

Seiz laughed and stamped out the cigarette. "Take us to Schwarzenfeld," he ordered the driver. "The police station. *Schnell!*"

At Schwarzenfeld's police station they opened a door into pandemonium. Fr. Viktor's jaw slackened. "Oh my God." Denied a chance to demonstrate before administrators at the school, Catholic mothers flooded the hall and staged a protest. An old woman wheeled, a crucifix in hand. She demanded that Seiz hang it in her grandson's classroom or risk burning in Hell. The charity worker tossed a glance at Fr. Viktor, but he could only stand amazed. He processed life in flashes: a wood-paneled room. Chanting women. "Free Frau Heidl! Free Herrn Gindele! Keep God in our school!" Voices swelled in a deafening tide. Hobnail boots drummed along an oak floor; gendarmes beckoned Seiz.

The provincial watched all hope sail off in a slate gray blur, vanishing around a corner. He felt the Framework converging in a contest between the fates.

Amidst the din: "Viktor? Viktor!"

Paul. His fellow religious held vigil with Dean Spangler. They had emerged fresh from interrogations.

"Will he do it, Viktor?" Fr. Paul asked him in a rush. "Will the Amtsleiter intervene on our behalf, do you think?"

"Pray," he said. "If Seiz falls in line with the party, God help us."

Officer Dobler ushered Fr. Viktor along winding corridors into darkness. His greeting flung fuel onto fears kindled back in Schwandorf.

"It seems Herr Amtsleiter spoke correctly," the police chief said coldly, cheerily. "He predicted that you would show up, Pater."

Norbert and Helene slumped on benches in a holding cell that exuded all the ambiance of a bomb shelter. The baker clutched a ragged head, his fingers woven deep into black strands. "Herr Gindele," Fr. Viktor called softly. His parishioner gasped in relief. The provincial's attention swung to Helene.

"Oh, child."

He winced at a haggard face and aquamarine eyes wept raw. Flaxen hair spilled from a bun that long since ceased to serve its purpose. He eased down beside her.

"Four hours," she said, voice shaking. "They interrogated me this long, but asked only one question. 'Who put you up to this? Was it Herr Gindele or Pater Viktor?' I gave them the same answer."

"And what was that?"

"'I am a woman of my own mind. No one tells me what to do.'"

"I grieve for what you've been through," Fr. Viktor said. "Bless you for your courage, Frau Heidl." She wove a weary hand around his arm. He covered it with his own.

"Leni and I have gotten ourselves into the devil's kitchen," Norbert groaned. "I regret that you were pulled into this, Pater. But I am glad that you came."

Fr. Viktor mustered a smile. Back home in America, a man in a similar predicament claimed to find himself in hot water.

"You didn't think I'd let you face the wolves alone, did you? No, I just had to get some help first."

"Help?" Norbert asked. "From who?"

"Don't ask, you won't like the answer."

A sympathetic police officer gazed upon them in sorrow and hooked a crucifix upon a melancholy wall. Fr. Viktor nodded in gratitude. "Let us pray." Dry words scraped his sandpaper throat. "Our Father, who art in Heaven, hallowed be Thy name . . ." Back in America, one monk and a pious village could kindle a flame hot enough to bend the laws of a nation. A different reality reigned here. *So this is what it means to live in oppression,* the American brooded. If this gambit failed, they would wind up in Gestapo custody by morning. *And my parishioners?* The Secret Police would have a list of names. They would observe them, hound them, make examples of them and stun all of Bavaria into submission. He saw it all with chilling clarity. His voice joined Norbert's and Helene's in fervent appeal. Their fate depended upon wine and venom balanced to a nicety. "Lead us not into temptation, but deliver us from evil—"

The creak of a door broke through prayer.

"What?" Norbert said.

"We are free?" Helene cried.

"Yes." The sympathetic officer had returned. His smile struck them as surreal. "It seems that we have no reason to arrest you!"

"What!" The baker shot to his feet. "Those *Schweinehunde* spent four hours tormenting us, now they say they had no reason?"

Fr. Viktor hoisted a red-veined gaze toward a stark ceiling. "Holy Moses." Against all odds, God had found a way to provide. Gendarmes ushered them from their holding cell, and as he reeled toward freedom with Norbert and Helene, the moment of incandescent joy faded.

The Reich always punishes disobedience, Seiz had warned.

"This isn't over," he realized. "What about the petition?"

He stiffened, hearing the gasp of tearing paper.

Gendarmes led them back to the hall where townswomen clustered around Bürgermeister Braun. The mayor clutched paper, his teeth bared. Dismay ripped from the crowd.

"This petition," he grunted, "never existed. As long as I am Bürgermeister," he clenched his jaw, pulling, "the crosses stay down. Anyone who protests will be sent to prison!"

All around the station hall, heads swung toward Fr. Viktor. He spread his hands in peace. It was a defeat, but he prayed to look back one day and find that God had somehow worked through this turn of events.

Protests receded in an ebbing tide.

Seiz strolled over and studied the provincial fixedly, not to intimidate him for once, but to check for comprehension of the logic that justified this outcome. Fr. Viktor nodded.

"What is that party devil doing here?" Norbert gritted.

Seiz lunged. "You keep your head down and your mouth shut, dammit! All three of you barely escaped a prison sentence." The baker bristled until Fr. Viktor touched his shoulder. Seiz pulled away. "You must return home. Your bakery is behind on its quotas, and thanks to that boycott, I have no handouts to provide." He stopped short. "And Germany's sons need their mothers. Especially sons without a father."

Helene tucked wheat-colored tendrils behind her ear and then blinked at a pin on Seiz's lapel. The two locked gazes. Plainly, they shared an understanding. Fr. Viktor shifted back to Seiz and stood arrested by the sight of mercy in chains, the face of a charity worker who would deplete himself to alleviate the pain of others, though he reserved that wine for a chosen few.

"Frau Heidl," Seiz greeted gently, formally. "The NSV provides rest homes through the 'Mother and Child' program. If you would like a week to recover from this unfortunate affair," he cringed, studying her bloodshot eyes, "we can send a volunteer to perform your chores at home, and care for your two boys while you are away. Party membership is required for a privilege like this, normally, but with the permission of the Amtsleiter, a German citizen would be permitted, and I would be happy to grant it." He waited with an encouraging air.

Helene glanced at the pin. "That is kind of you, *mein Herr.* But I cannot leave Norbert and Maria to manage that bakery. I will be fine. My sons and I look after each other."

Seiz smiled. "Your eldest is a wonderful boy." He slipped on his hat and paused, fixing Fr. Viktor with a stare that reminded him of his expectations. "*Auf Wiedersehen,*" he said, sparing everyone the aggravation of Hitler's name.

"Go in peace, Herr Seiz," the provincial replied.

Seiz read him narrowly. He had always addressed him by his party title before. The charity worker pursed his lips and departed.

"Pater, why bother reaching out to him?" Norbert objected, recognizing the fatherly tone. "That devil is beyond hope."

"There are thorns in his heart for sure," Fr. Viktor agreed. "But there's still good ground to be found beneath."

Norbert looked sidelong at him, then shook his head.

"Be careful, Pater. One could get one's hands cut, trying to pull those brambles out."

"We'll see about that." The provincial watched Helene tug her blond locks free and finger hair clips in pensive silence. "Do you know Herr Seiz?"

"Not personally, no," she whispered. "But I have seen that pin he had on his lapel. He gave one to Klaus."

He pondered that. "Hm."

The Miesbergkirche steeple chimed out a new hour: 6:00 p.m. Spent by the day's events, Fr. Viktor trudged from Schwarzenfeld's police station with Fr. Paul and Dean Spangler. His fellow clergymen reveled in their freedom while he contemplated Sunday's sermon. *Charity*. The Germans called it *Nächstenliebe*, "neighbor-love." Doctrine proclaimed it the highest of three theological virtues—charity, faith, and hope—each so sacred that they were infused into a soul only by the hand of God.

Fr. Viktor perceived divine intention whispering in the silver night, speaking of a mission to be fulfilled, and a tragedy to be averted—God's greatest virtue, choked by thorns. The sower said a prayer for Wilhelm Seiz. *Pray for thine enemies.* He considered praying for Hitler, then shook his head. He would leave that one to Cardinal Faulhaber.

CHAPTER EIGHT

CHANGES IN THE FRAMEWORK

1941 TO 1944

The news broke in Schwarzenfeld on a Thursday afternoon, but Frs. Viktor and Paul learned it first in the Gindeles' sitting room during their usual Saturday visit. For her husband's safety, Maria refused to allow a radio in the house, so they depended upon newspaper reports to glean details. Dean Spangler arrived with a week's worth of the *Mittelbayerische Zeitung* tucked beneath his arm, and amid a weighted silence, he read aloud to the grim gathering. Fr. Viktor registered fragments: Japanese planes attacking American soil. Thousands of his countrymen dead, a harbor in ruins. In the wake of bloodshed Hitler stood jut-jawed before the Reichstag and painted President Franklin D. Roosevelt as a madman in league with international Jewry.

"'Two hours before our Führer began his address," the dean read in a faltering voice, "Reich Foreign Minister Joachim von

Ribbentrop delivered an official letter to the American *Charge d'Affaires* in Berlin. Diplomatic relations have been severed. It is now a fact: the German Reich is in a state of war with the United States of America.'"

He folded the newspaper in his lap. Outside, snowflakes swirled thick from a leaden December sky.

"Madness!" Norbert pounded the wall, jolting the room's occupants. "This is absolute madness. Is it not enough that our men are fighting Russia and North Africa and most of Europe? Now they must fight America also?" He hissed in disgust. "May God protect my son on the battlefield."

Dean Spangler leaned his plumed head back to face the baker. "Japan is our ally," he pointed out. "Perhaps it was the Japanese attack on America that forced this decision. Though I have always suspected it was only a matter of time before the United States became drawn into the war."

"Pater?" Helene said softly.

Fr. Viktor bowed his head over folded arms. The moment he had heard *Amerika* and *der Krieg* occurring in the same sentence he retreated into memories of home. He had last visited Sharon seven years ago, and since that time his nephews, all boys with missing incisors, had sprung into men of fighting age. His gaze traveled over the sitting room, the faces in his midst, the untouched apple strudel on a lace-draped table, a gray afternoon looming outside. He would always remember where he was today, how the world looked. Fr. Paul and Dean Spangler radiated compassion while Helene and the Gindeles eyed him like kin fretting over a venerable patriarch. And they were family, he realized. They were sons, daughters, and brothers in faith, and their presence felt just as sacred and binding as the company of his own blood.

"So," he rasped, "it's happened. America is entering the war. I suppose it was inevitable, as Dean Spangler said. Though, I prayed they would stay out of it."

"Our countries may be at war, Pater," Norbert said solemnly. "But you are no enemy. You are a father to us."

He peered up. "I know. None of you are an enemy to me."

"You are not leaving Germany, are you, Pater?" Helene asked, her eyes widening at the prospect.

"No," he assured. "It would be dangerous to return home now, and I have no intention of going anywhere else. War or not, there's still a mission to fulfill."

Maria served strudel and a contemplative pall settled over the parlor. War declarations had dampened all enthusiasm for the conversation they so frequently enjoyed.

While they ate, Fr. Viktor's attention drifted and settled upon Helene. She picked at the dessert on her plate and stared at the rug with such intensity that he could feel a question building.

"Pater," she said at last, her voice a wisp of sound in the room, "you prayed that America would not enter the war, yes?"

"I did," he confirmed.

"Do you think that God did not hear you?"

He finished his strudel. "No, not at all."

"But why did it go unanswered, then? Your prayer, I mean. It is perfectly reasonable to pray for peace in one's homeland. What would it have hurt for Him to fulfill it?" Helene set her strudel aside on a lamp table, the dessert half-eaten.

Her face gave it all away. She leapt upon this event to confront him in the desert of shattered hope, and it was a place he knew intimately. Around the room, forks clinked against plates and attention collectively slid his way.

"Well, I suppose I've learned to look at it in a different way," he said. "It's true the thing I prayed for didn't happen: America will now suffer in this war."

Dean Spangler gloomed at headlines on newspapers. "Free will on earth has intervened, it would seem."

"Free will is a great and terrible gift," Fr. Viktor agreed. He squinted, reflecting upon a youth fraught with pain. "But still, I've been through enough in this life to know that God's will isn't absent from the picture. Even at this moment, though all looks bleak, He's searching for ways to intercede."

"How?" Helene asked.

"He'll work through the Framework."

"The Framework." Helene's brow furrowed. "I think I have heard you mention this before. Yes?"

Fr. Paul drained a final drop of ersatz coffee from his cup. "God's Framework," he mused. "Every Passionist who has sought the pater provincial's wisdom is familiar with this theory."

Helene moved her chair across the tassel-fringed rug and sat face to face with Fr. Viktor. She clasped her hands primly in her lap. "Tell us, Pater. What is the Framework?"

Dean Spangler stopped flapping newspapers. Norbert and Maria leaned closer, perched at the edge of the blue-white settee. Fr. Viktor felt a slow smile creep over his face. Amid the silence, he heard snow whisper against the window. "What is the Framework? It's God's plan. But it's not a *plan* the way we think of it. It's a dynamic thing that is very much alive." He smoothed a finger over his freshly shaven chin, pondering the best way to describe it.

"See, I think time has no meaning where God is concerned. Past. Present. Future? Those are concepts that *we* limited beings need to navigate the Framework. But He sees the infinite fabric of time. He knows everything that may ever occur, with all possible outcomes. Those are paths of the Framework, you see—all events, their potential effects—all woven together." Fr. Viktor interlaced his weathered fingers to emphasize the idea. Helene nodded, intrigued.

"We're all born into the Framework with gifts, convictions, a calling. A sense of direction that guides us on the journey of life. But even He can only hope we reach the destination He intends."

"Because of things like the war?" Helene asked.

"The war—or more basically, free will."

Norbert stroked his mustache. "Free will."

Fr. Viktor nodded. "When we're faced with a decision, we can follow a righteous path—the one God would ask us to walk. Or, we can take another path we think is better, for whatever reason, even a destructive one against His will. We have that freedom. Who knows? Maybe this liberty is *necessary* for the world to function as it should."

"Perhaps," the dean boomed in a low voice.

The provincial angled his head in contemplation. "And it's not just our own choices that impact us. The decisions of others help and hinder us on the journey as well. I think the Framework is like a cosmic chess game to Him. Every piece has a mind of its own. Some move against His will, and others move with it. When a soul is in pain . . . when human choice causes a critical part of the Framework to fail, who can He move to ease the suffering, or set things right?"

Helene settled back in her chair. "And how is one to know, or see God's will at work in one's life?"

"Personally, I sense Him in the *good* of the world," Fr. Viktor enthused. "In the unexpected kindness of a stranger, in the love of family. In people who help us, uplift us during moments of sorrow."

"You are saying that He is working through us," Helene said in hushed revelation. "Through our acts of love and good will."

"Right. Want an example? Take the Miesbergkloster. Paul and I believe it's God's will that we sow the message of the Passion here in Germany. Free will got in the way of that, of course, when the party took the monastery. And when all seemed lost, look what happened." The provincial's fond smile swept the sitting room. "He provided for us through you people, and the mission was saved."

"Ohh," Maria sighed, touching her heart.

"So, if free will prevents God from working one way," Helene reasoned, her eyes narrowed in thought, "then He moves different people, and works through them—if they are willing. Therefore, it is not God who forsakes us. No. It is *we who forsake one another.*"

"Precisely," Fr. Viktor confirmed.

Helene watched snow swirl outside. The provincial read melancholy reflections in her face and felt a deep flow of sympathy.

"Even though free will is running rampant in this world, Frau Heidl—and that's clear in the headlines—a higher Power is working through it in ways we can neither see nor expect. That's why it's vital for us to see Christ in all who suffer. When we intervene—even if it's just the simplest gesture—we *heal* a part of the Framework. We open a path for Him to reach souls in need, and set things right."

"But what if something cannot be set right, Pater?" the widow asked. "What if no path will undo an evil that has been done?"

"Then you have golden stones paving your path to Heaven," he concluded with gentle assurance. "If you've suffered pain that can't be undone, you're beloved in His eyes."

———

The fact of war plunged like a stone into the pools of Fr. Viktor's mind, but an innocent question rippled his thoughts long after he left the Gindele parlor. A reflection of Helene's gold-wheat features clarified before him, her voice laced with endearing vulnerability.

You are not leaving Germany, are you, Pater?

He felt again the sensation of being anchored to German soil. There was a sacred nature to this sentiment. War declarations imbued it with new holiness: *love thine enemy.*

"I've got a mission," his intuition said. "That's why I'm here." Surely God worked through him to fulfill a purpose, one He would reveal in His own time.

Every month Fr. Viktor maintained a ritual of traveling to Schwandorf to collect rent from the NSV. On one sweltering August day in 1943, he trudged from the train station and stopped short. Farm wagons rolled past government offices, an unusual sight. Their wheels creaked beneath the weight of human cargo. Languid arms drooped over carriages, and faces around him bore the raw, weather-beaten look of nomads. "Gypsies?" he presumed. Yet fair-skinned women and children surrounded him, and Germanic voices swirled in a din that filled the cobblestone streets. The dialects they spoke were rarely heard in Bavaria.

Fr. Viktor ambled up to Seiz's office and discovered vagrants loitering around the rune-marked doorway. Shoulders bumped him while he edged inside. He breathed shallow against the stench of wanderers who had staggered for days in the summer heat. A child whined; looking down, he discovered a wild-haired boy gnawing on a crust of bread and scrambling out of his path. *How many people?* He counted: one, two, . . . thirty-three drifters crowded Seiz's office. The dismal sight reminded him of the staggering destitution he and Fr. Valentin witnessed in the aftermath of the first Great War.

"Looks like the shelter we ran back in '22," he murmured to himself. "Except it's staffed by party members instead of nuns."

Frau Seiz distributed clothing and milk bottles to mothers cradling infants. Fr. Viktor wished her *"Guten Tag"*—good day.

"Who are all these people?" he asked.

"Pater Koch. *Guten Tag.*" She greeted him by name, and out of courtesy she avoided any mention of Hitler. Her icy manner had thawed after the boycott ended. "They are *Flüchtlinge*," she explained. "German refugees."

"German refugees? From where?"

"They come from the north to escape the bombing. In the cities, bombs are falling like hail, they say. Those English! It seems the Tommies are determined to reduce this country to ashes." Frau Seiz pursed ruby lips, as if suddenly remembering admonitions to mind her tongue around him. He doubted that she thought much about Germany's own aggression. "Here in the countryside, it is the task of the NSV to find food and shelter for these people. But there are hundreds coming to us in need, Pater. Hundreds! I don't know what the party expects Wilhelm to do." She shook her head at a ragged mother breastfeeding an infant.

The provincial looked around, absorbing the stoicism of people left only with the clothes on their backs. "Hundreds." He doubted Seiz could resolve this with evictions. "Well, I'm sure that monastery will be useful to you."

"The monastery? Yes. Ah . . ." Frau Seiz tugged the neckline of a flowered dress, fanning herself. She eyed him sidelong. "You are here for the rent?"

"Right."

"Wilhelm is there, at the desk."

"Oh." Fr. Viktor twisted around. "Shall I get it from him?"

No answer. He turned back and caught a glimpse of her cooing to children, fleeing his company as fast as possible. The provincial mulled over a severed conversation. "Hm."

Refugees stepped aside, allowing him room. "Good day," he bid Seiz. An upraised palm bade him to wait. The charity worker held a phone receiver to his ear and murmured affirmatively as a voice spoke on the other end. A map of the Oberpfalz sprawled over his desk. Fr. Viktor glanced at numbers jotted around Nabburg and Burglengenfeld, two *Landkreise*—counties—where Seiz managed NSV operations. The notes detailed incoming refugees. Observers spotted one hundred drifters wandering along western roads, Fr. Viktor gathered. An estimated two hundred surged down from the north. Fifty more trickled up from a flooded district to the south. Only the eastern roads remained clear.

Fr. Viktor then looked up to study Seiz himself. The charity worker fixated upon tasks at hand with his usual lancelike intensity, although shadows bruised the fine tissues beneath his eyes, giving a cavernous look to the hollows, and the contours of his face—already worn lean by a hot-blooded temperament—were pinched and sunken. His fingers twitched in yearning for a cigarette, a luxury denied by wartime shortages on the German home front. The provincial recalled pictures and letters adorning office walls and felt a rush of concern for a wayward son. Priesthood was a sacred privilege, demanding patience, sacrifice, and at times a Herculean strength to forgive.

The phone clattered down.

"This rent payment I give you today is the last that you will receive from the NSV," Seiz announced.

Fr. Viktor nodded at suspicions fulfilling themselves. He watched a refugee girl rocking herself in forlorn comfort. "Low funds? If it's the money—"

"Funds are low, yes. But this is not the problem."

"What's wrong, Herr Seiz?"

That earned him a glinting look. "I call you by your title, Pater, and you should address me by mine—especially when you are in my office." He turned to a locked box, voice lowered. "I am not one of your parishioners."

"I know." Fr. Viktor deemed the surname an acceptable mode of address and shoved the matter aside. "What's wrong?"

"I have received orders to surrender the monastery keys to the authorities."

Unforeseen hope bloomed like a flower. "You mean the party's giving it back to me?"

"*Nein.*" A lid whipped open, the latches clattering. "The Reich has decided that your Miesbergkloster is needed for matters of greater importance than a school. I have been ordered to evacuate the building at once."

"And what 'matters of greater importance' would that be?" Fr. Viktor asked.

Seiz shot him a look, as if he had posed a ridiculous question.

"Who gave this order?" the priest prodded.

"The Gauleiter," the charity worker breezed. "New tenants will arrive on the first of October. I expect they will approach you about your rent." He licked a thumb. Bills flapped at his touch. "*Drei, vier, fünf . . .*"

"Who's moving in?"

"*Sechshundert.*" Seiz smacked six hundred Reichsmarks on the desk. "I have no idea. The State has not seen fit to inform me."

Fr. Viktor looked around at refugees in need of housing. He ground his teeth at the thought of party organizations occupying his monastery, though it dawned upon him that the Reich might use it to serve a purpose far more sinister than a National Socialist boarding school.

"Listen," he said, leaning over the desk, "let me and Paul back into that monastery. I'll talk with Faulhaber, you talk to Wächtler. I

have no objection to sheltering refugees: no one is being indoctri-
nated. And if you tell Wächtler you have a crisis—"

"The State is aware of this situation already."

"Well, it's American property. It seems to me like I should
have some say—"

"These orders are clear, and they will be followed precisely!"
Seiz snapped irritably. "That is the end of this discussion."

Fr. Viktor flinched. *That's what Gauleiter Wächtler told him,*
he discerned. Seiz had likely pulled on every connection that helped
him confiscate the monastery, but this time the war superseded
all pursuits on the home front, and Seiz obeyed orders without
question. Germany was his church. The provincial shook his head.
The choices of souls hell-bent upon destruction were accumulating
in the Framework, and he and Seiz could only stagger along paths
winding deep in the Reich's oppressive shadow. His attention fell to
the map. He studied numbers forming a halo around county lines.
With a pang he remembered the rosaries he had prayed for Allied
victory, and he shivered at a vision: if his hopes came to pass, Hitler
would refuse to surrender. The man would fling Germany from
one shattering defeat to the next faster than Party Welfare could
stitch up the country's wounds and mop up the blood.

"Could you use another pair of hands?" he asked.

"For what, Pater?"

"To help with your refugees."

"The Catholic Church is strictly forbidden from performing
charitable functions in Germany," Seiz droned, focused on the map.
"At the order of the Führer, the NSV has responsibility for all efforts.
There are no exceptions."

Fr. Viktor watched him knead a stiff neck. "I know how you
feel, Herr Seiz."

The charity worker clicked his tongue in irritation.

"I ran welfare houses after the first Great War," Fr. Viktor confided, "and I too had a superior who turned a deaf ear to all my troubles. Under conditions like these, charity is a vise. You internalize everyone else's misery until it agonizes you to hear another sad story, but you just keep giving, and giving, and when you're empty you drive yourself even harder to give more. Take it from one who knows. You need to take care of yourself. If you keep this up, you'll get the life pinched out of you."

Seiz stared at his map, as if envisioning the miserable horde staggering to his door. The charity worker heaved the heaviest sigh that Fr. Viktor had ever heard.

"Listen," the provincial urged softly. "I've vowed obedience to the Church, but even I take matters into my own hands, when necessary. Let me help."

Seiz gathered himself. His haggard features shifted into hardness. "Our business with your monastery is over. Heil Hitler."

A stare slid away, knifelike. He vanished behind the resolute thump of his office door.

Fr. Viktor flicked his eyes heavenward. A woman bumped him. She gasped apologies in an exotic German dialect. He heard deep, pitiful sobs and stood lost in thought, watching the lonely refugee girl continue to rock herself back and forth.

Crisp bills crinkled in his palm. He recalled that the Province bank account contained ample funds to cover his expenses, and this rent arrangement merely asserted his ownership over the monastery. It served no other purpose.

He furtively slid money between books at the front desk and stepped back into simmering streets, eerily aware of Christ engaging him through the eyes of desperate wanderers.

"What a fate it is, Lord, praying for victory while tasting the sufferings of the enemy," he said. "I wish You'd do this for more people than me."

On October 1, trucks lumbered up the Miesberg's slope under the cloak of night. Fr. Viktor froze, hearing a faint *rum-rum-rum* echoing beyond the chapel where he and Fr. Paul chanted Matins, the midnight devotion observed by Passionists. Without a word they crept past shadowy pews, their robes swishing, rosary beads rattling, until they reached a side door in the church sanctuary. Together they peered out toward a monastery that stood stark and haunted, transformed by the hour.

Four trucks lumbered into view and halted in the courtyard. Metal sheaths covered their headlights, turning them black, except for bright slivers that permitted drivers to navigate a land darkened for war. The narrow bars of light rendered a menacing aspect to the vehicles invading American property.

Figures stepped out and they lifted their arms, betraying the crimson flash of armbands. Fr. Viktor hissed through gritted teeth.

"My eyes aren't what they used to be. What do you see?"

Fr. Paul adjusted his spectacles. "They are carrying something."

"Can you see what?"

"Boxes. There are many wooden crates, it seems. But I cannot tell what they—wait."

"What?"

"They are opening one box to inspect the contents. It seems to be a glass tube. Not a chemistry tube. Much larger than that, I think. Yes, those are vacuum tubes." Fr. Paul looked up in dismay. "Who is the party moving into our monastery?"

"I don't know," Fr. Viktor said. "But I like this far less than the boarding school."

———

After the shriek of Nikolaus' death, Helene likened her faith to a vase perched upon her kitchen windowsill. Clear as diamonds, it caught the sunlight and dazzled her with its brilliance, yet given one tragedy, one grave misfortune in life, that crystal revealed its fragility, tumbling against a stone world and shattering into pieces. Although she would grit her teeth and muster the strength to fit shards together slowly, tediously, common sense told her that the glass would remain forever fractured, incapable of holding any belief of substance.

While pondering Fr. Viktor's Framework theory, the widow perceived herself fingering slivers of faith and examining them critically. Primal forces corrupted good men, twisting them into predators and victims. Leaders preached to masses that clamored for blood. Armies raged amid the inferno of war, and Heaven stretched above it all, pristine and blue and unperturbed. These insights had once shattered her belief in God—until the Provinsche revealed his take on the world and its woes. Every flutter of revulsion she felt for this war, every instance when she passed bread to Zizi and Maria pretended to snip stamps, took on such meaning that it stunned her. God far exceeded her naïve conceptions of Him, and if she had fragile faith, the sooner it shattered, the better, for it was not faith at all, but a garish vessel filled with her own emptiness.

And the Provinsche. His theory amazed her. The old man had known despair and doubt: she recognized the signs. This Framework concept arose from a need to reconcile evil with the existence of a good, loving God. What had happened to him back in America? What life experiences led him to this epiphany? Helene longed to ask, yet always refrained. She revered the old man. It seemed disrespectful to prod him with personal questions.

Preparing for church the following Sunday, she fished a crucifix pendant from her dresser and vowed to wear it as a sign: her faith was no longer glass, but tempered steel.

"Work through me to accomplish good, if You can," she whispered to a cross on the wall. "Today I surrender myself to You completely. I will be a movable piece in Your Framework."

But free will, the widow mused. It was indeed a great and terrible gift. It granted each heart the liberty to live in grace—or open a dark door into disaster. Such was the case in July, 1944. No one in the Gindele sitting room could have foreseen free will aligning against a tranquil soul in their circle of friends.

Helene reflected. The arrival of the Miesbergkloster's new tenants set events in motion. Last October she sat transfixed with Dean Spangler and the Gindeles, listening to Frs. Viktor and Paul describe their observations through the vestibule windows.

"They're from Berlin," Fr. Viktor revealed. "They say they're part of a 'Continental European Research Institute for East Areas.' Whatever that is. Their director visited us the morning after they showed up." The provincial rubbed a knobby knee. "I'd kick them out in a heartbeat, if I could."

"What are they doing?" Helene asked. But Fr. Viktor only shook his head.

Norbert paced the sitting room. "They must be working on something for the war effort. That much is obvious. A weapon? Who knows. And they are doing it in a monastery!"

"It must be ideal for them," the dean rumbled grimly. "Here in the countryside, their work is far less likely to be destroyed by a bombing run."

Fr. Viktor tugged at a long earlobe. "Yeah. But, it's American property, and we're staying in that sacristy. I'm not letting the Reich drive us out."

His gaze hardened to granite strength. On the matter of his Miesbergkloster, their Provinsche had a mountain will and they knew he would never budge.

Another thread of free will wove deep into life's tapestry: *Der Krieg.* Once a nightmare confined to newspaper headlines, radio broadcasts, and letters drifting home from sons, fathers, and lovers, the war marched straight into the home front. On a blustery April afternoon in 1944—the Year of the Refugees—Helene halted on the street and watched a line of ragged-looking Germans snake along the road. Sullen women sheltered in alleys between houses. A child ducked beneath her mother's coat. They all watched Helene, their faces drawn, hungry, dripping in the gray rain while she trudged by, feeling privileged to have a house. She offered pleasantries that were met with uneasy silence. Her dialect confused them.

"Frau Heidl?"

Schwarzenfeld's lead party official lurked on her doorstep. Social workers hovered at his side, dressed in rain-soaked blazers.

"Open your door," the party officer demanded.

"Yes, *mein Herr.*" The widow complied while he beckoned to people in line.

"What is happening?" Helene's jaw dropped as a mother, grandmother, and three boys filed into her house with the air of guests slogging in after a tedious journey. The refugees flung coats upon wall pegs and unlatched suitcases. They made themselves at home in her parlor. "Who are these people?" Still agape, Helene listened to a social worker explain wartime pressures. Faced with a crisis of staggering proportions, Party Welfare issued orders requiring homeowners in the countryside to quarter refugees in spare rooms. "I see." Extra ration cards flapped into her palm. She fingered her crucifix pendant. "Yes, I do have a guest room. I will take them in."

Her attention fastened upon an elegant shield pin glinting on the woman's lapel. Later that afternoon, Klaus returned home. He attended classes at Schwandorf's *Oberschule*—middle school—and devoted his spare time to volunteer work. An identical pin adorned his uniform collar.

Helene despised party entanglements, for it meant that she had to monitor every word uttered beneath this roof. Each time her eldest stepped outside their house, the party dominated his young life, and she keenly remembered the consequences of parental protest. Slicing potatoes for a stew that night, her eyes gravitated toward his collar. Klaus grinned as he prattled about his day. He had biked around Schwandorf delivering messages, then spent an hour chatting with girls who shared a shift in the government office where he volunteered. She prodded him about the office director. What was he like? Did they talk? How often, and about what—

"Mutti, stop."

She slowed her chopping.

"This is the one place I can go where nobody talks about war, or pulls me into some big fight. That is not bad, is it?"

Helene remembered a child shaking his fist at the world's harshness. Much to her satisfaction, he had found himself again. It had been ages since she had seen him smile.

A potato slowly gave way beneath her knife. Two paths had woven together in the Framework and the implications vexed her, yet motherly intuition compelled her to trust this change in Klaus. She felt *goodness* at work. Her son had a choice. He could seek company and acceptance among Hitler Youth members or charity workers. Given those options, she preferred the latter.

After *der Krieg* invaded homes throughout the Oberpfalz, it entrenched itself into daily life. Food rations dwindled, whittling diets to a meager 1,000 calories per day. For every material item imaginable, shortages abounded. While serving customers in the Gindele bakery, Helene cradled bread in her hands.

"Norbert, are you putting stones in the dough of your bread? This loaf feels like a rock."

The baker hauled out another batch. "Stones? No. It is a new recipe, courtesy of Adolf." He raised his head in a surly manner. "It seems that the wheat supply in Germany is getting low. To assure our Final Victory, we have been ordered to make sacrifices and use different ingredients, such as they are." He scoffed and backed against the kitchen door. "One might as well stuff a potato down one's gullet for all the flour that is in there."

The widow shook her head.

"Maria. Yelena!"

Both women looked toward the parlor entrance. "Zizi!" they greeted cheerfully.

Another soul uprooted by *dem Krieg*, he had become a weekly fixture in their bakery. Zizi sidled up to the counter and introduced new laborers, clapping them on their backs, chortling with the joviality of a man in a beer hall. A gaunt Pole presented an empty ration book in trembling hands. Maria's scissors snipped slowly, carefully, and Helene reached for his bread bag without a word. Wispy breathing gusted in her ear. She turned.

"Hans? What is it, child?"

Her youngest leaned close. He had turned ten, the age when German boys joined the Hitler Youth. Hans accompanied her here during the summer months and she prevailed upon him to paste customer stamps to reports for the Office of Nutrition. This un-assuming public service provided enough justification for Norbert to thunder from his kitchen and drive away Hitler Youth leaders who prowled in, demanding that Hans participate in activities beyond compulsory roll calls.

"Mutti," her son whispered, "why does that funny man call you 'Yelena?'"

She laughed. "Oh. Don't mind him, *mein Kleiner*. He is just a silly old friend."

Maria folded her arms upon the serving table and engaged the Russian in conversation, asking what he intended to do after the war. Zizi mused.

"After war. Hm . . . I think. I think I stay here."

"I thought you would return home to Russia," Maria said.

"Back? To Russia? To *Stalin*?" His expression soured. "No."

"How come?" Hans piped. "Why don't you like Russia?"

"A boy." Zizi gasped. "Yelena, your boy?"

"Yes," she said. "This is my youngest."

A stream of Russian followed, and in customary fashion, Zizi offered a gangly hand. Hans flinched, mimicking, perplexed. He understood right arms raised at an angle, but handshakes baffled him. The laborer laughed and clasped his small hand. "Good boy! Good." Zizi's German had improved over the years. A rolling drawl colored broken phrases, yet he projected the confidence of a native speaker and expected listeners to take him seriously.

"Russia. I return? No. In Russia, if one likes Stalin—ah, Stalin, Stalin!" Zizi's lean arms thrust up in feigned praise. "You know? As if Stalin is like God! Yes? This man, he will live. But if one does not like Stalin, will he be tomorrow living?" Zizi's head shook. "To say the wrong word is death. I do not like Stalin. No. When I come on the train to this town, my father, my brother. Where are they? I know not." He trailed off, looking lost and mournful. Helene studied his candle-wax features and melted in sorrow.

"What happened to them, Zizi?"

"A man. He says my father spreads lies about Stalin. My father? He is not stupid. My brother. He fights police. He is stupid. He is gone. My father is gone. Are they in the *gulag*? I think, yes."

"What is this 'gulag?'" Helene asked.

"*Gulag*. Like this." Zizi gestured in a way that suggested shackles. "One does not come back from *gulag*, Yelena."

"Oh. Like 'KZ,'" she said, pronouncing the two letters with distaste. A KZ—short for *Konzentrationslager*—was the worst of all prisons, reserved for political dissidents.

"Yes. Like KZ. One day, no Stalin? I go back to Russia. Today? No. In Schwarzenfeld, I have work. It is heavy work. I have hunger a lot. Yes. But I am strong, I am good worker, I have food, I have friends, so here I stay. This is all right?"

Maria brightened. "Why, of course you can stay! You would be missed, Zizi."

He bid them farewell with a lopsided grin. Helene shook her head, then turned to their next customer. A refugee woman sauntered up to the serving table. She wore her brunette tresses in an elaborate twist and her hat was angled fashionably, imparting such refinement that they suspected the woman was Frau von Something. Helene envisioned her at parties, her siren lips smiling at officers in uniform, smoke curling from a cigarette in her manicured hand. The widow smoothed a dowdy dress and tried to forget how bland she looked with her wheat-blond locks pulled back into a bun, the efficient, yet rustic mode of Bavarian country women.

"No cinemas," she heard the refugee mourning to her daughter. "No theaters. Barnyard animals running loose on the roads." Her cynical eyes followed Zizi. "They let the vermin roam free, too. I thought there were laws against that."

"Zizi is not vermin," Helene retorted. "He is a Russian laborer. They are permitted freedom in Schwarzenfeld because it is better for them."

If their customer felt any remorse, she failed to show it. "He is an *Untermensch* and a Russian. They are killing our men on the front every day! That makes him twice the enemy."

Helene shoved aside bread, feeling an irresistible compulsion to serve up a piece of her mind instead. Maria touched her arm, easing her.

"Oh, Zizi is not an enemy to anyone," the baker's wife assured their customer. "He is welcome here, just like you are. How can we help you today?"

The refugee woman snorted and pinched her bread bag in an uplifted hand. Helene sighed in exasperation and glanced to her left. Hans finished pasting stamps to one report sheet and paused before starting another. He struck up a conversation with their customer's daughter, a pert, freckle-faced *Mädchen* about his age.

"How come no one in this town keeps buckets by the door?" the girl asked him.

"Buckets? What for?" Hans frowned.

"At home, they told us to keep a bucket of sand and a bucket of water by our apartment door, in case there was a fire. There were lots of fires where we were."

"Where do you come from?"

"Berlin," the girl said. "Well the buckets were dumb. I mean, it is not as if water or sand will help when you come crawling from your shelter and the building is burnt to the ground."

"Yea, I guess," Hans said in a feathery voice.

"Where is your *Luftschutzkeller*?" the girl asked.

"Huh?"

A pause. "What do you do when the sirens go off? Where do you run for shelter?"

Hans shrugged. "We, ah. We don't get sirens here."

The girl stared speculatively. "Do you know what Christmas trees are?"

"Christmas trees?" Hans' voice rose to a squeal. "Of course! Everyone knows what Christmas trees are. We put one up in our parlor every December!"

The refugee woman tossed her head back in throaty laughter.

"I was talking about bombs," the girl muttered.

"Bombs?" Helene said, not caring anymore if these city people considered them ignorant country mice. "Why on earth would you call them 'Christmas trees'?"

"Oh, they are not the bombs, exactly." Their customer stirred the air with silken fingers. "They are markers that are dropped by the bombers before an attack. We saw them every night in Berlin. You would understand if you saw one. The beacons are green. When they fall, they hang in the air and slowly fan out. The shape looks just like a Christmas tree when the candles are lit. When one sees those in the sky, one runs for the *Luftschutzkeller*." She beckoned her daughter. "Come Hilde, we are leaving."

The door jingled behind them. Helene plunked back heavily in her chair, her hands falling loose in her lap, cupping thoughts. "Christmas trees."

"Mutti, where is our shelter?" Hans quavered.

For his sake, she pulled herself from a pit of fear. "Oh. Don't worry yourself, child. There is nothing to bomb in Schwarzenfeld, only cows and potatoes. We are safe in this town."

———

Even this early, free will had been twisting the Framework, Helene reflected. Thus far, the errant crossings merely scraped the boundaries of her life, and those of her friends. Then a new problem arose and catastrophe began to take shape. In May, Fr. Viktor developed a nagging cough.

"It's just a scratchy throat," he insisted when they gathered in Norbert and Maria's sitting room. "I'm fine. Stop worrying."

His illness hardly surprised Helene. The weather vacillated between cool nights that misted the ground with dew and afternoon warmth that drove her to open windows. Although she had faith in Fr. Paul's ability to keep that flower sacristy heated, she knew he found it difficult to maintain a consistent temperature. If only Herr Seiz had confiscated another building for the Hamburg children. If only its new occupants had sought a different location to carry on their mysterious work. If only the Provinsche had gone to a doctor. If only . . . If only . . .

Weeks passed. They hoped that the summer warmth might speed Fr. Viktor's recovery, but to their dismay, he trudged into the Gindele house on a Saturday in mid-June, a fist pulled tight to his mouth. "Fine, fine," he gagged, though he sounded far from it. Maria bolted into the kitchen to fetch a glass of water.

Helene pressed her palm against the Provinsche's damp brow. Bloodshot eyes rolled up. He grunted in defiance. *Stubborn mule.* Yet, she smiled. Even in this miserable state he projected enough strength to tether their yearning for an authoritative father figure.

"You have a fever, Pater. A high one."

Norbert vanished from the sitting room and strode back, a coat draped over his arm. "No, we are not having another week of this. You need a doctor."

"Pete's sake," he hacked. "I'm fine!"

Maria offered a glass of water and crouched, lifting a beatific smile to him. "Pater. You have a mission in Germany. Take care of yourself, so you can fulfill it."

Fr. Viktor heaved a sigh that caught in his throat and set off another fit. "Guess I'm outvoted," he muttered.

"Indeed," Fr. Paul agreed.

Norbert took that response as the clearest sign of consent they would wrangle from their indomitable pater provincial. The baker strutted down the Hauptstrasse. Helene expected him to fetch the town doctor—a man who prominently displayed Hitler's portrait in his parlor, but a doctor nonetheless. He returned forty minutes later with Herr Gietl's canvas-covered wagon. "Oh God, Norbert," Helene groaned. The paters departed for Schwarzenfeld's train station and headed for the closest civilian hospital in Amberg.

———

On Sunday morning Helene genuflected near her usual pew in the Miesbergkirche and waited for services to begin. Her shoulders sank. She saw no sign of the Provinsche.

Fr. Paul said Mass.

"As some of you know, the pater provincial is in hospital," he announced. "The doctors have informed me that he has a severe respiratory infection. Surely this is not good news, and such a thing is not tolerated well by a man of his years. But, the doctors assure me that he will make a full recovery. For his well-being, he will remain in hospital for the next four weeks. Let us pray on his behalf."

Throughout the sanctuary, heads bowed above clasped hands. He would return. Helene felt a gripping certainty. At seventy-one, Fr. Viktor possessed the hale constitution of a fifty-year-old man, a testament to the peace that reigned in a monk's life. Health aside, however, their revered pater had weathered one trial after another in Germany. The Framework brought him to Schwarzenfeld for a purpose. Heaven would not take their Provinsche from them now.

At the altar, Fr. Paul led a prayer. The widow studied him, this mild priest swathed in white vestments. He was the quiet pater with a velvet voice, the man who folded his hands in ethereal calm and hovered at Fr. Viktor's side, ever dutiful, content to support him. It struck her as an act of courage, volunteering to remain in that sacristy. She fiercely admired him for that.

"Amen," Fr. Paul finished. Parishioners echoed the word in response. The Austrian priest unfolded a square piece of paper.

Helene knitted her brow in curiosity.

"Dear friends," he said, "I have another announcement to share with you this morning. While we have many a reason for fear today, it seems that we have a reason to rejoice also. You may remember the novices and priests who lived in our Miesbergkloster, before the war. One of them is serving the Reich in Italy. He wrote of events that he has witnessed in that country. I had short notice to prepare a sermon. So, I will read this letter. It is a rather extraordinary one." Paper crinkled. Fr. Paul adjusted his spectacles.

"Lieber Papa." He broke into a smile. "'Papa' is what all of our novices call Pater Viktor. He is, of course, the leader of our province, and each member of our congregation in Germany and Austria looks to him as sons look to a father."

Naturally, Helene thought.

"Lieber Papa," Fr. Paul read with perfunctory swiftness. "My heartfelt greetings to you and Pater Paul, my sympathies for all that you endure, I will remember you in my prayers." He slowed, his tone turning earnest.

"I told you that our regiment is stationed in the Lombardy region of Italy, in the province of Bergamo. We have astonishing news to report from this place."

Helene focused intently. She thought Fr. Paul as serene as an Alpine meadow at dawn, yet the Austrian priest flicked paper, adjusted his spectacles, straightened pages a second time.

"Apparitions of the Blessed Virgin are appearing in a village not far from us. This has been reported in Italian newspapers. *I have seen a sign from the Virgin with my own eyes!*"

A unified gasp tore through the sanctuary.

The widow straightened in her pew.

"A friend and I received furlough to see the vision ourselves," Fr. Paul continued, the words pouring forth in a rush, "and so on May 31, we were witnesses to a sight. It was exactly 6:00 p.m. when circles were seen moving around the sun. Light shone from the sky in rays of many colors: gold, green, red, blue. The event itself lasted only five minutes, but it soon began again. My comrade and I saw this happen exactly three times. I tell you, Papa," Fr. Paul's breath caught, "I tell you, I spoke with some witnesses who said that they doubted Christ before this event. I located them afterwards. They doubted Him no longer."

Whispers resounded below a vast ceiling. Stunned by the impropriety, Helene whipped a finger to her lips and joined old women demanding silence in the church sanctuary. The Gindeles kept their heads, at least. She leaned for a view of her closest friends seated in a pew across the aisle. Head bowed, Norbert fingered his rosary. Maria clutched a handkerchief. Shining trails spilled down the woman's cheeks.

Helene swiveled and glared.

Officer Dobler planted himself in the left rear pew like a menacing lump of muscle, observing.

"But Papa, this is not the reason why I have written you today. There is more."

The widow swung back to Fr. Paul.

"The words of our Blessed Mother are heard by a child in the village of Bonate," he hastened, "and She spoke to the girl on this occasion. She said, 'Another miracle will occur on July 13, and this will be a sign of joy to the whole world!'"

Helene pondered the prediction and heard a flurry of whispers behind her. These people so grieved by the absence of husbands, sons, and farmhands, disgusted by scientists doing God knows what in Pater Viktor's monastery, flummoxed by foreigners on the streets, irritated by strangers flooding their houses, and terrified by stories of Christmas trees all reached an identical conclusion. "*Der Krieg*," voices hissed behind her. "The war is ending!" No one questioned whether the sign portended victory or defeat for Germany. Helene didn't care either. Instead, she ached for simple pleasures forbidden in wartime: shops with shelves that spilled fruit; radios and papers that announced dull news rather than war reports, and above all, a world where her boys reached military age in peace.

God Himself is ending this war, she thought, her heart daring to hope. *Is it true?*

"Papa," Fr. Paul finished, "I pray for a day when I return, and find that sacred Germany is ruled by God alone. Let us pray that this day is not far away. Yours in Christ Crucified, Br. Konrad, C.P."

———

At daybreak on Monday morning Helene staggered half-asleep toward work at the Gindele bakery. A woman raced down the Bahnhofstrasse, panting, a hand clapped to her heaving bosom. "Frau Heidl! Frau Heidl!"

Helene braced herself for news of a fire consuming the Rathaus or reports of a townsman killed at the front. A copy of Br. Konrad's letter flapped into the widow's hand. The crone whispered a theory on the meaning of the Virgin's prediction.

Helene gasped. "What? You cannot be serious!"

The older woman nodded. Her black-bead eyes caught sight of Frau Obendorfer strolling toward the meat market. Stubby legs hobbled away.

Helene rushed to the Gindele bakery.

"*Gruess Gott.*" The widow scrubbed her hands in the kitchen. "Norbert?" He was occupied in his oven room. She tore an apron from the wall and raced into the parlor. "Maria? Maria! Have you heard what people are saying about that sign from the Virgin Mary? The one from the letter that Pater Paul read at Mass? Can you believe it? I heard it from Frau Gietl, who heard it from Frau Baumann, and she heard it from Frau Schmid. They are flying down the Hauptstrasse, talking to anyone who will listen, and they are distributing copies of that letter everywhere. I almost died from shock! Although," Helene paused. "Well, one cannot deny that a sign of joy like *that* would end this war—and in an earthly and practical way."

Helene reached for a customer's ration card, expecting her friend to blithely dismiss gossip as a sin, but a venial one that God forgave easily enough. She looked over.

The baker's wife was praying harder than ever before.

CHAPTER NINE

FAITH AND DOUBT

JULY 13, 1944

Six years before the war started, Papa trudged across Depression-era Germany in search of work, and during that journey, he encountered the worst storm he had ever witnessed in his life. He squinted up from a meadow, watching clouds roil across a sky that made him wonder if Judgment Day had arrived. Lightning erupted with a crash that shook the hills. Stags fled for the forest, rabbits scrambled into holes, and sparrows fluttered to trees that tipped and swayed like drunken men, but Papa prayed Our Fathers and Hail Marys until the downpour eased into a trickling calm and the tempest surrendered to a vast mountain peace. Every animal in creation fled for cover, but faith had served as his shelter.

In 1944, Klaus plodded against the hardships of wartime life, a storm more ominous than the one his father faced, for this one raged without end and it blew away all sense of normality. Strangers flooded his house. At night, all five of them slept in the guest room and he, a light sleeper, tossed and turned at their droning snores. At fourteen, he found himself swept into Schwarzenfeld's senior Hitler Youth group. During field exercises his troop leader thrust a Mauser Gewehr 98 rifle into his hands and commanded him to shoot human silhouettes standing helpless from a distance of fifty meters. He swallowed hard, taking cold comfort in a realization that the bullet pierced only straw and wood.

Amid the howling windstorm, Mutti and Hans fled to Herr Gindele's house and the Miesbergkirche sanctuary. Religion served as their shelter. Three afternoons a week, Klaus donned the black corduroy shorts and brown shirt of a Hitler Youth, leapt upon a bicycle that Mutti snatched through happy circumstance on the black market, and after a twenty-minute ride down southbound roads he slowed, breathless, before a sandstone building nested deep within Schwandorf. A door was propped open to alleviate the summer heat. A sign on the wall bore a familiar, three-letter rune. He strolled inside.

"Klaus is here!" Two girls with sapphire eyes and auburn braids announced his arrival in sing-song tones. They wore the starched white shirts, black neck ties, and knee-length skirts of the female Hitler Youth branch.

"Klaus, these boxes just arrived. Will you open them for us? Please?" The eldest, a blithe spirit about his age, stuck out her lower lip. Wooden crates towered in a shadowy corner.

"Sure," he said. "What is inside?"

"No idea." The girls cupped their chins in velvet hands while he probed at a lid. They always flitted about like pixies, challenging him, pointing at blankets stowed on high shelves or handing him donation canisters that refused to open, then they would step back, all twinkles and grins, observing. When he started this job a month ago he had regarded them with a leery eye, fearing that they were hatching pranks against him, but he managed to fulfill their requests without incident. They simply derived giddy pleasure from his contests of manly strength.

Latches sealed the crate. He grunted, flexing his muscles, basking in chimelike laughter prompted by his antics. A woman signing papers at the front desk turned to watch. Refugee mothers strained for a view of mysterious boxes like children ogling a sack of Christmas presents. They knew that the contents would be distributed to them just moments after the crate wheezed open.

"Oh. There are shoes inside," Klaus said.

The three of them proceeded to count, mindful of accuracy.

Footsteps echoed in a hallway, the thunder of authority striding across its domain. Klaus offered a flawless greeting and stood at attention, his feet parted in military precision.

"Would you like a report, Herr Amtsleiter?"

This occasion hardly demanded militant comportment, for the NSV office director wore gray suit pants and a simple dress shirt, not a party uniform decked with war medals and the badges of a county-level political leader. Muffled giggles burst behind Klaus, tickling his spine with the knowledge that girls watched him from across the room. Herr Amtsleiter Seiz flicked a shrewd glance at them, head shaking, then his attention slid back to Klaus. They stood nearly at equal height now. An approving smile creased the older man's features; his easy stance firmed into a bearing worthy of a German commander. "Proceed, please, *Genosse* Heidl." He still spoke to Klaus in the manner of an adult addressing a child, yet plainly he also considered him a comrade.

The boy felt his chest puffing.

"Yes, sir, Herr Amtsleiter. We have counted ten crates, all containing women's and children's shoes. There appear to be fifty pairs in each one, so there are two hundred pairs total, I think—but we will confirm this with a precise count." Klaus nodded assurance.

"Two hundred pairs?" Seiz turned, pondering the crates. "And these just arrived?"

"Yes, sir."

"Well. Your efficiency is commendable, if you came up with an estimate that quickly."

"Oh, it was easy," Klaus said. "They are organized already."

"Organized? Show me, please."

Klaus tugged at a crate and stepped aside dutifully while Herr Amtsleiter inspected its contents. Given Seiz's standards, he expected that this tidy arrangement would please him to no end, but instead the man hovered, his lips pursed.

"You are correct. They are organized precisely. Even the mates are tied at the laces." He fished out slippers the color of pink roses and cradled them in an uplifted palm. They fit so perfectly in his hand that Klaus mistook them for doll shoes until he noticed faint scuffing on the toes and heels. A refugee mother craned her neck for a better view and cooed in adoration, though Herr Amtsleiter stood oblivious. His brow twitched, smoothed, then tightened again, as if absurd ideas welled up from the dark of his mind and he kept wringing them out again. Klaus edged toward the eldest of the two girls, leaning close enough to breathe in the warm nutmeg scent of her hair. "What is wrong?" he asked.

"Normally things in crates arrive tangled up," she whispered, "and we spend a day sorting everything out."

"Sometimes we will get donations collected by soldiers on a raiding mission," Seiz elaborated, overhearing them. "But this. I have never seen this before. Clearly there was a process behind it. Two hundred pairs." He held the shoes to his chest. A finger absently stroked petal-pink leather. "Are there labels on these boxes?" he asked. Klaus searched, then shook his head. "From where did they come? Who was here when they arrived?" A questioning glance darted between the girls.

The eldest fingered a long braid. "They were just left by the door, so we brought them inside. Is something wrong?"

Klaus drummed his fingertips against the crate. A leisurely Mozart concerto poured from the round maw of a radio. The music ceased for a war report. Frau Seiz whisked by on her way to the storage room and rolled a switch to silence.

"*Vati?*" the girl prompted. "Daddy?"

"You had shoes just like this when you were a baby," Seiz murmured. The charity worker flashed a smile at his eldest daughter. "But I prefer to know who is giving us donations. Who would have time to organize two hundred pairs of shoes?"

"Where are you going?"

"To make a call." Seiz strode away, slippers in hand. "Get an exact count of these shoes and report to me. After that, you may distribute them as needed."

Klaus and the girls watched his door thump shut. They blinked at deep, shadowy crates, then at each other.

"*Vati,*" the youngest girl groaned. "He is never happy until he knows everything. At least we don't have to spend all day sorting. I think it is nice that someone did it for us."

"Yea," Klaus said. *Vati.* Seiz's daughters imbued such blossom delicacy in the word that they managed to sound endearing rather than childish. They numbered among the few children in Germany who had a father in their lives, and he envied them. They radiated the contentment of girls untouched by the troubled world: they found all the stability they needed at home. He would give anything to feel so safe and self-assured. *Vati.* The daughters heaped shoes upon the oak floor. For their sake, Klaus hoped Herr Amtsleiter would never be called to the front.

"There must be an explanation," the eldest girl insisted. "Maybe someone did it as a surprise for us."

"Or perhaps it was a punishment." Unenthused with the task at hand, her little sister kicked at a box.

"They have punishments in the army," Klaus said. "These supplies came from a raiding mission, right? Well, my papa was in the army, and he said that if a soldier did something bad, like get drunk and chase women in a town that was occupied, he could be given a boring assignment, you know, as a . . . punishment."

He surveyed two innocents who slowed in their movements. For a moment he imagined himself striding up to their father next week and finding the man scowling at him for spreading rumors about the German army and corrupting his daughters' minds.

"Do you think that is it?" the older girl said.

Klaus shrugged. "I guess."

"I think that is possible. Don't you?" Her eyebrows raised in eager surmise, the girl turned to her little sister. "The army was punishing drunken, women-chasing men. They learned their lesson, and we got sorted shoes. It all makes sense." She frowned. "Why are you upset?"

"All your talking made me lose count!" her sister whined.

The older girl clicked her tongue. "You know what *Vati* says. Put them in groups of ten, then count the tens. That way you never have to start over."

Klaus pulled a shoe crate. "Hah. That is smart." The girls were not offended by his mindless prattle, and that set him at ease.

He peered at Herr Amtsleiter's door. A veteran of the first Great War, the charity worker knew the army's disciplinary practices, and yet he still chose to pick up a telephone. "Hm." Klaus reached for children's shoes. "*Eins, zwei, drei . . .*" A phone rang. Frau Seiz greeted the caller in Hitler's name. ". . . *acht, neun, zehn.*" Klaus finished three boxes while Herr Amtsleiter's daughters counted the remaining seven. The telephone clattered down. Frau Seiz's auburn head was shaking.

"If trouble is going to occur anywhere in the Oberpfalz," she muttered, "I swear it is always in Schwarzenfeld."

The seeds of curiosity in Klaus' mind sprouted into fear.

The rumor. Not that.

Herr Amtsleiter shot from his office and marched toward the filing cabinets. Anticipating his need, his wife held up a file. The shoes were counted, confirming two hundred pairs. Klaus struck the dutiful pose of an adjutant begging to report. For the moment, both adults ignored him.

"I don't understand," Frau Seiz was saying. "How could eighty refugees show up in Schwarzenfeld, just like that? We have people watching the roads."

"No one has been watching the *eastern* roads," Seiz said. "Now Schwarzenfeld is swarming with people. Bürgermeister Braun is out of town today and his office is refusing to do anything about the problem until someone gives them orders."

Klaus scraped a sleeve over his brow. "Oh, good." A dilemma surfaced, not that dreadful rumor flying around town, but another that was familiar and equally problematic. "Refugees." He doubted Herr Amtsleiter intended to waste another second worrying over mystery donations. They seemed like such a trifling matter.

"These refugees," Frau Seiz said. "Who are they?"

"Germans who settled out east. They are fleeing the Russians."

"Look at this place." His wife pointed to urchins at play, scampering around mothers who bickered over donated clothing. "We cannot find enough food and shelter and volunteers to handle these people from the north. How can we take more from the east?" She huffed. "Running from the Russians. That is a false report. The army is holding firm, they say."

Sharp-faceted eyes shifted toward the woman. Seiz and his wife locked gazes in the manner of adults who easily read each other's faces and tossed aside a need for explanations. Papa and Mutti had interacted like that, Klaus remembered with an ache. *The army is holding firm.* A classroom war report flared through his mind. His instructor at school had scrawled a livid white zigzag upon the blackboard, representing the eastern front where their army engaged Russian forces, then delicately he had drawn a second line behind it, a perfect vertical depicting Germany's strategy of holding firm. "How ingenious, this tactic!" the teacher had enthused, for defending that flattened line required fewer men and conserved the army's strained supplies, improving odds of victory for Führer and fatherland. Klaus twisted his mouth at this happy news, for it was clear to him that the line swept back toward Germany.

Seiz heaved open a weighty book listing vacancies in the districts he managed. Pages flapped sharply at his touch.

"There are rooms available for precisely ninety refugees in Schwarzenfeld. We can house them—if these numbers are correct. But someone must go there and straighten out this mess."

Frau Seiz shook her head at Klaus. "Wilhelm, tell that soldier of yours to stand at ease before he strains something."

"What? Oh. He is disciplined. The Hitler Youth is obviously doing its job." Seiz turned to Klaus, thoroughly indulgent. "Well. It seems that us men have a mission ahead of us, *Genosse* Heidl. Prepare to move out on my command."

The boy tingled with elation. They were men embarking on a mission—for real! The charity worker strode forward, then he paused. Slippers in hand, he studied an orphan huddled in a corner, sucking a knuckle for comfort. Watching Seiz kneel before her, Klaus halted and retreated to a respectful distance. He could never imagine Officer Dobler or his Hitler Youth troop leader humbling themselves before children. The charity worker smoothed back curls dangling in the girl's face, murmured greetings in balmy High German, then attempted phrases from other dialects, all of which sounded vaguely foreign to Klaus. After five tries, she lit up. "A Saxon child," Seiz concluded. "You are far from home." The girl's cerulean eyes studied the shoes, then bounded up to the man helping her step into them. A dainty arm slid around his neck for support. Klaus watched nimble fingers ease leather around tiny feet.

"Looks like they fit," he said.

"Yes, perfectly." Seiz rose again, smiling. The orphan trotted in circles, then gasped. "Oho!" Tiny hands flapped like a fledgling about to take flight. "Hah." Klaus chuckled. He glanced back to the man beside him and fell somber. The charity worker's expression slackened to a dead stare fixating on pale pink shoes.

———

At half past 2:00 p.m. Klaus mounted his bicycle, Seiz hauled a box with twenty pairs of children's shoes beneath his arm, and together they braved the summer heat, taking a brisk walk downtown. A building the shade of sun-warmed sand loomed ahead. The *Bahnhof*—train station—spanned an entire city block. While Seiz flashed government permits at a ticket booth, Klaus pedaled past women crowding the station hall, and minded children chasing each other around their mothers' legs. Blankets lay strewn over benches. It occurred to him that refugees lived here.

A light breeze blew through open windows. He propped up his bike and hung outside, gazing north toward home. Eleven railroad lines stretched from the hazy emerald hills. They rushed up like a vast iron river, then flowed past a knot of city residences before they curved south, out of sight, toward Regensburg. This train station served as a regional railroad center: every train that crossed the Oberpfalz rumbled through Schwandorf.

Warm winds ruffled Klaus' sandy hair, then they gusted inside the station. Behind him, a banner hung from thin cords. Black letters rippled on its flapping canvas.

"'Wheels Must Roll for Victory,'" he read aloud. "What is that supposed to mean?"

Footsteps clapped behind him. "It means that all civilians should restrict frivolous travel as much as possible. The trains are needed to move troops and supplies to the east." Seiz tucked papers and tickets into a hip pocket. Outside his office, he dropped from High German to the cordial ease of their native dialect.

"We cannot get a car to Schwarzenfeld, huh?" Klaus responded in kind. He had been hoping for a ride.

"I doubt that even a Kreisleiter could get a car these days." Mutual regret tinged the charity worker's words. "Every drop of fuel is being saved for the war effort. One must have a frightening level of authority in the party to have such a luxury."

They had ten minutes to spare before the train arrived. Seiz dropped the shoe box near a wall decked with NSV posters. Refugee mothers trickled in and pored through its contents without inquiring whether they were entitled. They knew that any box bearing the three-letter rune contained donations for them. Seiz plunked down in a convenient chair near NSV tables and propped his feet upon a storage crate. Klaus pulled up another chair nearby.

"Look at these people," the charity worker mused, and Klaus obeyed. "For one minute, picture yourself in their place. They barely escape the bombings with their lives. The attacks destroy their homes, taking every possession. They are left only with the clothes on their backs. They travel on wagons, or on foot, for hundreds of kilometers in this heat, with little to drink and nothing to eat for several days at a time. For many, this is only one stop on a very long road. Can you imagine living like that?"

"We have five people living in our guest room," Klaus said. "Is it like that everywhere?"

Seiz nodded. "In my house I have six refugees in addition to myself and my family, and we do not have a large home. This is far from ideal, especially for my wife and daughters. I am sick of settling arguments." He let his voice drop to a confessional tone that the boy strained to hear above an ambient din.

"I realize that everyone is making sacrifices. It is this way all over Germany, my young friend. The NSV was never prepared to provide for this many refugees. Hm. The greatest social welfare organization in the world is caught without a proper contingency plan. This is unbelievable to me!" He drew his chin back in dismay. "People pour into my districts like water over a fall, and I am simply expected to provide for them. Whether the shelter is available, or the food supply can be logistically stretched to feed another mouth, this seems to matter not at all."

"I know." Klaus understood the need to whisper. A stark truth permeated the muggy air. The Wheels for Victory banner and the sight of people sleeping on benches hinted at its gravity, but neither of them dared to speak of it. He studied Seiz, reading his tense expression, the exhausted sag of his shoulders, and rumor of sleepless nights in the darkness beneath his sunken eyes. It dawned upon Klaus that the leader he held in sterling regard spoke to him openly, judging him worthy to hear adult burdens.

His jaw slackening at realizations, the fourteen-year-old strained for a manly bearing.

Seiz swallowed and drew a fragile breath, watching swastika banners fretting on the wall. "But, we have orders. Yes?" He nodded firmly at his own declaration. "We must have faith that our leaders are doing what is best. If we do our duty, then all will be well."

"Can I ask you something?" Klaus said.

"Of course. *Bitte*—please."

The charity worker propped his chin against a fist. The boy reflected upon a desperate hour when Officer Dobler and Headmaster Schmitt cornered him for information on Mutti.

"On that day, my teacher said it was my duty to say everything that I knew, and that meant snitching on my mother."

"And what did you do?"

"I, ah," Klaus shrugged, "I totally lied. I blamed Herr Gindele. I didn't even know if he was involved, but it seemed likely."

Seiz tipped his head back slowly, as if pairing memories with explanations.

"It didn't help anyway," Klaus continued. "Lying, I mean. But my mother was in trouble. I did not do my duty, but did I do the wrong thing, really? Even you helped her. You and the Provinsche. She told me so."

"Yes, this is true." Seiz eyed him sidelong. "I remind you that orders are given by our superiors, and we follow them. This country would be in a state of complete anarchy if one could pick and choose the orders he wants to obey."

Klaus flinched and inspected the dirt crusting his shoes. "Yes, sir." He felt a dreadful pang of confusion.

"But . . . my own mother was a woman exceptionally devoted to her children. No sacrifice was too great for her. Not even her own dignity. I could never have forgiven myself if I betrayed her."

The boy looked up. "So, you would have done the same if you had been in my place?"

"I think," Seiz brooded, his fingers interlaced and pulling in opposite directions. "I think it is understandable, what you did. But this answer," he stared, his voice low, "it is not to be repeated, nor used to justify insubordination, is that clear?"

"Yes, sir—*jawohl*," Klaus vowed. He decided to venture another question. "Our teacher said another thing also."

"Mm? And what was that?"

"He said there is no such thing as compassion. He used nature as an example. Flies caught in spider's webs and hawks catching mice. He said the world is just like that."

"Did he," Seiz said flatly.

"You are a party member, right?"

"*Natürlich.*"

"And you believe in National Socialism."

"I believe that it has done good things for our people."

"But this charity stuff. Everything you do is about helping weak people. Right?"

"Everything I do is for the People's Community only," Seiz corrected. "My orders are very strict on this point."

Mutti would disapprove of that part, Klaus knew, though it was a statement of duty, not hate like he heard from his teachers. "At school, they say that compassion makes Germans weak," the boy continued. "And my Hitler Youth leader says that the Führer wants us to be 'brutal and dominating.' If one is weak, then it is better for the whole if he dies off."

He held a breath, fearing he had verged on impertinence. To his relief, Seiz chuckled.

"Poor Klaus. Your mother teaches you Catholic principles, you receive National Socialist instruction at school, and then you get something in between from me. You must be terribly confused."

Hearing the easy warmth flowing in Herr Amtsleiter's voice, Klaus relaxed. Station workers trudged by. The boy rested an arm upon an upraised knee, listening.

"Your teacher is a . . . he is a very narrow-minded man," Seiz began. "I agree with him about nature. Predators kill to survive, and compassion for weakness is not possible. In nature, a weak member of a population will die." Klaus nodded. "But," the charity worker raised a finger, "he oversimplifies by saying that these natural laws alone govern human life, and this is because we possess superior intelligence." He tapped a temple. "This means we have a social conscience. We have the ability to empathize with suffering when we see it in our community, and we can envision the good that comes from supporting our people. But, note that I say *ability*. Some people observe suffering, yet they fail to see it."

"How can they miss something so obvious?" Klaus asked.

Sapphire eyes darted toward the shoe box, then moved everywhere else in thought. "Perhaps, simply, they fear what they will find, if they look too deep."

"So, good things like compassion come from intelligence," Klaus pondered. "Yea. I like that. My mother and the Provinsche say that it comes only from God."

"And what do you think about that?" Seiz asked.

"I used to believe in that stuff," Klaus said. "I was even an altar boy at the Miesbergkirche." Seiz read his face intently. Refugee children scampered past unnoticed.

The boy dug at his fingernails. "When Papa went to war, I searched the Bible for verses that promised something. 'Ask and you shall receive, knock and the door will open,' and 'pray in secret, and God will reward you openly.' Every night, I snuck up to the attic and prayed. I never missed a night while Papa was gone. Never. I even knocked on the attic door, in case it meant something. Stupid. Kids do stupid things sometimes. Hah."

His wan laugh died alone. The station rippled around them, and yet silence broadened like an ocean, leaving him shipwrecked upon a shoal of bereavement. He visited this forlorn place every day after Papa's death and never invited another soul to tread upon its shores. Not until now. It was sacred ground. He continued speaking to his hands.

"All the boys I know, they get into fights for fun. My teachers and troop leaders just talk about how great the war is, or how much they hate people. My mother does nothing but fuss over me. Mothers do that, I guess. My grandfather falls asleep when I try to talk to him. And Hans, well, he is little. Sometimes a man needs somebody who just understands. You know? Somebody who listens without fretting, and tells him if he is doing all right, when the rest of the world is being so hard on him. For me, that was Papa. He was, um. He was my best friend. And I needed him home." Klaus breathed deep without looking up. Silence surged in waves ponderous enough to swallow him whole.

"I thought if I prayed hard enough, when Papa was in battle, my faith would make bullets bounce right off him. Every night, I prayed in secret like it was up to me to save him. Then it happened. We got a real knock on the door. And then. Then I learned the truth. If all that praying and asking and knocking could not bring him back, then God does not exist."

He sniffed and scratched his cheek, proud of himself for pouring out that story without crumpling into childish tears. A locomotive thundered through the station. Refugees fished shoes from the crate. At first Klaus thought that Seiz had abandoned him and rowed off to a remote shore haunted by his own troubles—or perhaps he intended to chasten him for his despicable lack of enthusiasm over the war. Finally, he peeked up and discovered that the charity worker remained with him the entire time. His eyes were steady and clear, emphatically present.

"I am so sorry, my young friend. Nothing hollows a boy like the death of a father he loves. Nothing. This pain I know personally, and I understand what you are going through: all the agonies of self-doubt. You are growing into a fine young man, and you have a good heart. *This* is what is important. Do not worry yourself."

Klaus absorbed that. *Herr Amtsleiter says I am fine.* His teachers would disagree, but he no longer cared. A vast, healing peace swelled within him. "Did you ever believe?"

"In God, you mean?" Seiz said. "I did, once."

"What changed things for you?"

"I went to a rally."

"Like one of the rallies in Nürnberg?" Klaus leaned closer.

"Mm-hm."

"What was it like?"

"What was it like?" The man heaved a windy sigh, as if Klaus had asked him to reveal the meaning of life. He straightened. "The square was filled with Germans. Thousands of Germans. One felt as if all of Germany was standing with him. And after one had lived through a time of such poverty and despair, well. It felt as if we had risen, finally, to a place of greatness above the ashes of the first war." A dreamy quality pervaded his words. Klaus was captivated.

"Everyone had hope. Standing there in the square, one could feel this sense of . . . of destiny in the air. And the frenzy! People shouting. Shrieking, until they grew hoarse. And the pageantry. Fanfares. Music. Banners in the wind. Then the Führer spoke." Seiz plunked back. "For those of us who had lost our fathers in the first Great War—and there were many—it felt like we had a leader who would protect us, and fight everything that stirred such fear."

Klaus nodded and hugged an upraised knee. He understood exactly what he meant.

"A long time ago I found meaning in life from religion, but," Seiz shook his head. "One rally. That was all it took. The Führer changed my mind about all that."

The boy imagined flags rippling in the wind, clarions blaring in cerulean skies, the beguiling sensation of national unity. It was a stirring vision. Seiz retreated into memories for a long moment, then his attention drifted and riveted on children's shoes heaped in a box. The euphoria in his face suddenly slid away, replaced by a desperate vacancy.

"Herr Amtsleiter?" Klaus called him three times.

"Hm?"

"The train is here."

"Oh. Why didn't you say something?"

Klaus frowned. "Are you all right?" He looked toward the crate. "Did you find out where they were from? The shoes, I mean."

"*Nein.*" Seiz shook his head. "No one would say."

Klaus studied him. He seemed strangely remote. The impression unnerved him. "But why are you so worried about them?"

The charity worker sharpened to attention. He hauled himself up. "We have a train to catch. Let's go. *Schnell!*"

———

They found a nightmare brewing in Schwarzenfeld. Bürgermeister Braun's office had initially reported eighty refugees requiring food and housing, but an hour after they made the call, a second convoy had surged in from the east. Gendarmes arrived at a new tally: 175 refugees swarmed the country roads.

Seiz stormed from the town hall and smacked his fist against the door. Ten police officers jumped. Klaus stood statue-still while his leader paced back and forth, pinching skin between his brows. A low voice whipped orders. Four policemen selected refugees for housing assignments while the remaining six trudged off toward farms around town. If farmers balked at the idea of transporting refugees to neighboring hamlets, then gendarmes were authorized to confiscate their wagons and perform that task themselves.

Klaus hopped on his bike, helping Seiz coordinate. During missions like this a leader depended completely upon his adjutant. The boy tore off at a frantic pace, delivered messages, then raced back to Seiz, restive, panting, ready to shove off again at a moment's notice. He found it hard to breathe: a tempest brewed in the skies above Schwarzenfeld, but the weather was the least of their worries. Refugee women from the cities were fluttering up to Seiz.

"This place where I am ordered to stay is a farm. I am from Frankfurt, *mein Herr*, do I look like the kind of woman who is suited for farm life? You must find me another place. And where is the *Kino* around here? With this circus of yours going on, I simply must have a diversion to calm my nerves."

Klaus groaned. There was a *Kino*—a cinema—in Schwandorf, but it was a frivolous trip for sure.

"Fräulein, get back into that house," Seiz demanded, pointing.

The refugee's jaw dropped. Another woman stomped up. "I am looking for the man in charge here. Is that you?"

"It is my misfortune to be so," he muttered.

"This farmer says if I stay in his house, then I must milk his cows every morning. I would rather go back where the bombs are than touch a filthy animal in a place like *that* with my bare hands!" Delicate features curdled in disgust.

An old man hobbled up. Klaus recognized Herr Obendorfer. "I am eighty-two years old, *mein Herr!*" The farmer held out arthritic hands with knotty joints. "My sons are all in Russia. I have a 40-acre farm that I must tend myself, and if I fail at this, there is less food to go around! It is not as if I am asking her to shovel manure."

Seiz regarded them both with a burned out glare. He refused to grant a housing reassignment and ordered Herr Obendorfer to find another task the woman found tolerable. She glowered, far from satisfied, though two police officers plodded over and tugged attention away from her. A gendarme spoke in tentative tones. Seiz stood poised in fatalistic expectation.

"What now?"

"*Das tut mir leid,* Herr Amtsleiter, but there is something you should know. We are expecting a religious riot any minute."

Klaus blew a sigh through gathered lips. Papers fluttered in the breeze.

"This note is being distributed all over town. It is a copy of a letter that was read during Mass at that church up there." The officer gestured toward a hilltop steeple. "The Catholics say that the war is about to end, but that is not the real trouble. The people here are spreading a rumor."

"What rumor?"

He cupped Seiz's ear, whispering words of incendiary gossip. Klaus stiffened as paper crumpled in an angry fist. The NSV director wandered aimlessly, hands on his hips.

"Which Passionist read this at the pulpit? Was it the old man?"

"It could not have been him," Klaus blurted. "My mother said that the Provinsche has been in hospital for the past three weeks."

Seiz swung around. "You know about this rumor? You will tell me everything you know, young man. Right now!"

Klaus withered at the implications of spilling information to a party member, yet everything he had lost when Papa died was *here* in this man, the one who sheltered him beneath an enfolding wing when every other authority figure would shove him naked into a brutal storm. Remembering that fact, his hesitation vanished. Entrusting his heart and mind to a leader, he poured out a fountain of knowledge until every fact and trembling suspicion that trickled from Schwarzenfeld's rumor mill lay bare before him.

They halted on a street corner where Schwarzenfeld's Hauptstrasse sprang in a T from the Ambergerstrasse. Thunder pulled their attention east, toward a sleek iron bridge that spanned the Naab River's iridescent flow. A motor rumbled in the murky summer heat, growing louder, clearer.

A Mercedes. It soared into view with murderous grace. Its black-silver blur held bystanders spellbound until it rolled around the Hauptstrasse corner, vanishing. Klaus gasped. Seiz swore and cupped his mouth, though the boy knew his dismay had nothing to do with remorse for cursing in a teenager's presence. They faced each other, both remembering a discussion about automobiles, fuel rations, and the war effort.

Seiz ripped another copy of the note from police officers discussing the prediction. He stalked off. Klaus charged after him the way he would follow his father into unknown peril.

"Go back to the Rathaus and stay there," Seiz commanded. "That is an order!"

Klaus froze, his heart pounding. "*Jawohl!*"

CHAPTER TEN

THE SIGN

JULY 13, 1944

Fr. Viktor ascended from sleep and drew a thick gravel breath, flinching. Silver blurred before his eyes, an oval medal. Entangled in waking dreams, he thought Fr. Paul stood at his bedside and presented a get-well gift from anxious parishioners, perhaps a devotional token depicting the Blessed Virgin.

His vision cleared enough to identify symbols gleaming in crisp relief. A hazy insignia sharpened into focus—not the Marian icon he had expected, but a rigid-winged eagle clutching a wreathed swastika in its talons. Jolted awake, he shot a leery look at his visitors, three men dressed in tailored black and gray. It dawned on him that he had gazed upon a *Dienstmarke.* Plain-clothed German police flashed these warrant disks as a means of professional identification, a practice that reminded him of sheriffs displaying badges back home in America. Meaty hands turned the medal and he recoiled, reading an omen inscribed upon its flipside: *Geheime Staatspolizei.* Secret state police.

Gestapo.

"Pater Koch. Get dressed. You are coming with us."

He hauled himself up. The room listed and his joints ached, as if three weeks' bed rest had turned his limbs into lead.

Gestapo officers permitted him only five minutes to change. They dragged him toward a street curb, forcing him to lumber along, still looping rosary beads upon his belt. A Mercedes prowled up from a deserted alley.

"What's this about?" Fr. Viktor demanded, straining for calm. "Where are you taking me?" Schwarzenfeld, they announced, and they implied that he would learn why soon enough. The first officer grinned, and in an icy tone, offered him the hospitality of a ride home. "This is a friendly public service, huh? Right."

My God. What in the hell do they want with me?

An American had entrenched himself on German soil and the Gestapo intended to wrench an explanation from him, he figured. And what would he say when he couldn't explain it to himself? He was rooted here. Faith told him that a higher power willed it so. Yet, if German officials branded him a spy, no law in the Reich obligated the State to prove his guilt.

The Mercedes roared across the Naab River bridge and waded into a human flood that inundated Schwarzenfeld's streets. Refugee women and children crowded his window. A waif cupped the glass and peered inside as if gawking at a lurid public spectacle. Fr. Viktor closed his eyes, hissed through gritted teeth. Rosary beads warmed between his fingers. Free will ran wild today, like a wayward horse. He prayed that Fr. Paul remained safe in their sacristy.

"Stop here," an officer demanded.

The Mercedes lurched to a halt before their destination—not home, not his church. He peered outside to find Schwarzenfeld's police station looming before him.

Gestapo agents ushered him along winding hallways toward a numbing unknown. Doors moaned shut. He had been flung into Dobler's office. The town police chief hastened out, granting a stranger the use of his desk.

"Father Koch? Heil Hitler. You found the ride home pleasant, I hope? I speak English. We can speak English, if you prefer."

Fr. Viktor flinched at a sharp iron voice speaking in his native tongue. He considered debating that point about arriving home, but decided against it.

"Does this please you, Father? Does speaking English make you feel at home? Or, do you prefer speaking *auf Deutsch?*"

Easing back in a cushioned chair, the Gestapo leader lifted a face like carved marble and ran a hand over blond hair that swept primly from a high and narrow brow. No introduction was forthcoming: as a rule, the Secret Police never revealed their names. A question hovered. German. English. What did he prefer? Fevered breath warmed Fr. Viktor's lips while he pondered a rush of sentiment.

"Father?"

"I'm a German citizen." Prudence compelled him to clutch at the language. "I speak German and English fluently, I really don't have a preference."

Papers shifted and hissed in the Gestapo leader's grasp. The man read documents obtained from Schwarzenfeld's registration office. Fr. Viktor raised his chin, feeling wary.

"You were born in the United States, and you have citizenship in the Reich," a voice persisted in razor English. "Your native place:

Sharon, Pennsylvania, USA. You are the third child and eldest son of German immigrants Nikolaus and Viktoria Elser Koch. You have pure German blood. This is good." His inquisitor studied him for a probing moment.

"I have always wanted to visit America, Father. Perhaps after this war ends, I shall. Is there any place that you recommend?"

Fr. Viktor's limbs sagged like rope. A high-backed wooden chair faced the desk. He regarded it with longing.

"Look," he said, collapsing into weary English, "I've just been pulled out of the hospital, I'm not well."

A sigh resounded against wood-paneled walls decked with party mementos. "Well. How disappointing. If it pleases you, then we shall turn from pleasantries to business." Papers clapped straight against the desk. The Gestapo leader smiled. "Pleasantries before business. That is the way of Americans, yes? It is the reverse for us Germans, and therefore much more to my liking. I shall ask you about America later, perhaps."

Fr. Viktor wondered if he would live to visit his brother's house on Jefferson Avenue and light a cigar while recounting his interrogation by the Secret Police. He watched the Gestapo leader pluck an envelope from a pile on the desk.

"Do you get many letters from priests who are serving in the German army?"

"Yeah, I have them—" The provincial broke off, blasting a cough into his fist. "Mm. 'Scuse me. I have them write me to provide a sign of life from the front." He pointed to the high-backed chair. "Do you mind if I sit?"

"Have you seen this letter?"

"What letter?"

"It is addressed to you. 'Lieber Papa.'"

To his surprise, the Gestapo leader clamped the paper between his fingertips and rose to deliver it himself. A fine suit rustled softly around a tall, muscular frame; a stringent odor of polish wafted up from shoes so lustrous that they must have been whisked from a shoemaker's store only days or weeks before. Fr. Viktor glanced toward the high-backed chair and pursed his lips. Certainly courtesy to elders transcended cultures, and a well-kept, educated German knew enough to offer him a seat.

"This letter. It's from one of our Passionist brethren on the front." He read an agile script spelling out news of Marian apparitions. "No, I haven't seen this one."

"But your 'fellow-brother' visited you in the hospital. Is this not true? Did he not bring letters to lift your spirits?"

"'Fellow-brother.'" The phrase was a direct translation of *Mitbruder*, a word steeped in religious connotation. "Oh. Paul, you mean. He visited, but I don't recall him reading letters. I slept most of the time he was there. Did I mention I was sick?"

"Read it aloud. Now."

Fr. Viktor drew a hand over his eyes. A feverish heat pulsed beneath the lids. He flapped the paper straight. "Lieber Papa—"

"No no no, we are speaking English now! You will read it in English, Father."

He heard the groan of his molars grinding together. Translating Br. Konrad's letter served no purpose, other than emphasizing a fact that made him feel naked in this room. "Dear Dad." While Fr. Viktor deciphered sentences in stop-start bursts, the Gestapo leader paced, checked a clock, flicked his hand, and rubbed knuckles as if they pained him, though the provincial was only dimly aware of his restless movements. Years had passed since he had last conversed in English. He heard himself speaking, and although the fluid voice belonged to him, its flow felt erratic, the words churned out of order and poured into a linguistic form that felt confining, unnatural. How awkward, finding verbs nested between a subject and complete, predicating thought in contexts where German grammar moved them to the tail of a sentence. The Gestapo leader stopped pacing. Fr. Viktor sighed, feeling wan and weary.

"You ordered this letter to be read at the pulpit, Father?" his interrogator asked.

"I told you, I didn't know it existed." His unshaven features crimped. "Wait. It was read at the pulpit?"

"Would you read it?"

"Are you asking me to?"

"Would you?"

"I don't know. Maybe." Fr. Viktor perused the letter again. During his first reading, he had fixated so intently upon translation that the words cascaded through his mind without leaving a residue of meaning. This man intended to trap him. Given one missed fact, one ill-considered response, he would find himself ensnared. "Yeah, I might. I'd amend the words a bit."

"And why is that?"

"Signs can be anything. The apparition Herself left the matter open to interpretation. That part at the end that Konrad wrote, 'I will be praying for a day when sacred Germany is ruled by God alone.' That could be a little touchy." The provincial looked away, thinking, *Amen to that, Konrad.*

"And what 'interpretation' would you draw from this prediction, Father?"

"It's ah, it's real hard to say." A chair tempted him. "Look, I'm taking a seat—"

"YOU WILL STAY WHERE YOU ARE!"

Fr. Viktor flailed against the door. A stir of breath snagged his attention. That gasp, clear as day, came not from him, nor from the Gestapo leader, unless this man possessed a strange ability to breathe and bellow at the same time. Goose bumps prickled his skin as he glanced at the high-backed chair.

It's the fever. Your imagination is playing tricks on you. You heard nothing.

"Again." The Gestapo leader kissed a red knuckle on his right hand, his face easing back into marble gentility. "What conclusion would you draw?"

Fr. Viktor eyed him sidelong. "It's, ah. If it's a sign of joy to the world, it's going to be something everyone wants." He grunted. "I can think of one sign I'd like to see."

"Our Führer getting shot dead?" the Gestapo leader said.

The provincial's jaw plunged.

"Could it be our Führer getting a bullet in the head?" his interrogator persisted.

"I was thinking the end of the war myself." It shocked him to hear a party faithful suggest an attack against Hitler.

"Are you aware that this letter is being distributed all over this town, and people are spreading a rumor predicting the assassination of our Führer?"

Fr. Viktor went numb.

"You are an enemy in Germany! Did you order this letter to be read at the pulpit? Were you sent here to spy on us and breed discontent? Is that why you are hiding in that sacristy?"

"Pete's sake!" Without thinking, the provincial slid back into speaking German. "Look. I'm a German citizen, and I'm here on a mission. I've been in the hospital for three weeks, I had no idea this letter was written, and I certainly didn't order it to be read during

Mass." He rubbed an aching brow, feeling haunted. "Right now, I'm old, I'm sick, and I'm tired. Okay? If you want to make me feel 'at home,' I need to sit down—if that isn't too much trouble!"

He pulled a bulldog face and felt his bone marrow curdling at the consequences of this brazen display.

The Gestapo leader surveyed him, his head high, eyes turning to slits. "So far, your story checks out, Father. So far." He halted and pointed at the chair, switching to German.

"You. On your feet!"

Silence. Stillness. Fr. Viktor swallowed in a raw, dusty throat. *Oh my God, I'm trapped in a room with a mad devil.*

A pale hand clutched an armrest. Fr. Viktor stared. The chair had an occupant. Out spilled an eavesdropper who sat bound and gagged by ignorance of English, overhearing their conversation without understanding a word. The captive groaned, hauling himself to his feet. Blood coursed from a battered nose. Quaking fingers lifted spectacles to a bruised face. In spite of his deplorable state, the man stood upright and folded his hands with a serenity that brought Fr. Viktor to tears.

"God Almighty. Paul!" He bit a curled finger.

The Gestapo leader rubbed a knuckle. "Tell him what you confessed to me. *Jetzt!* Now!"

Fr. Paul struggled to articulate with a swollen lip. "Viktor. I read Konrad's letter, during Mass. I had no sermon . . . I was going to tell you later . . . about the letter."

"This rumor about the Führer's death," the Gestapo barked. "Who started it?"

"I do not know. It seems . . . I gave the townspeople this impression when I . . . when I read the letter." Fr. Paul sniffed through blood. "I am sorry. I will take the punishment for this . . . for this grievous sin upon myself."

"Wait, wait, wait. Everybody wait." Fr. Viktor heard the blood-rush of a racing heart. He yearned for a name to invoke—a cardinal, a bishop—but the Church left them to confront the State alone, and their mother province lay beyond a bitter ocean. At this moment he could do nothing but pray to a power working through the Framework. Only He could turn this around.

"Listen. I'm the leader of my province, and that means I'm responsible for my priests and followers. Right?"

"Naturally," the Gestapo leader concurred. "We in the party believe this as well."

"All right, then." Fr. Viktor considered his fellow Passionist, then continued in English. "If someone's getting punished for this, you're taking me."

The interrogator's refined features smoothed in deliberation. "Fine. I will take you both," he concluded in German.

Fr. Paul gasped. "*Nein.*"

"Wait! Trade! I meant a—" Fr. Viktor broke into a coughing fit.

"I know what you meant." The leader roared a command to fellow Gestapo lurking outside. The door groaned open.

"March the paters through the streets," he ordered. "We are going to give the religious fanatics in this town a sign that they will never forget."

———

A bruised sky. A monstrous alley. Shrieks rose up from a human sea parting in horror. Sandaled feet swung in and out of view, left, right, left, right, the toes swelling ripe and round and red with blood, each step eliciting grunts of weariness, groans of pain. Dust prickled a mouth parched by fever, and grit scraped loose and dry over a thick tongue. Each detail rushed full upon Fr. Viktor's senses, the sights, the screams, the raw sensations swirling and blurring in a carnival of torment, all while he prayed over and over, *oh my Jesus help us.* A burden crushed his left shoulder, a load so ponderous he found it easy to imagine how Christ felt while staggering beneath the weight of worldly sin. He paused, chest heaving. Fr. Paul stumbled. His right arm reached limply around the provincial's shoulders and his free hand cupped a battered rib. Jeers plunged down from above: Fr. Viktor squinted up through a haze to find Herr Schmitt, the school headmaster, shaking a fist.

The Gestapo leader strolled backward, appraising reactions from Catholics who leaned out high windows and blanched at the spectacle below.

"Do you see this? Do you see? This is what happens to traitors who start rumors about the murder of our Führer!"

"Come on now," Fr. Viktor groaned to Fr. Paul, "lean on me, my friend. We'll get through this somehow." He doubted that the Austrian priest had heard a single word. He immersed himself in slurred prayer:

"... *Heilige Maria, Mutter Gottes ... bitte für uns Sünder ... jetzt und in der Stunde unseres Todes ...*"

Fr. Viktor joined in, reciting the same prayer in German until a nagging fear of forgetting his English compelled him to switch languages. "Holy Mary, Mother of God, pray for us sinners now and at the hour of our death."

Fr. Paul collapsed. They both spilled onto a dusty road. The provincial watched spectacles flutter end over end, and winced as a heel hammered the lenses into powder. A stone face glowered from a menacing height.

"Get up, both of you!" the Gestapo leader demanded.

Teeth gritted, Fr. Viktor rolled upright. His fellow religious lay prostrate, his hand probing for the pulverized glasses. He considered helping, then finally withered in despair. *What's the point?*

Their tormentor halted, his attention suddenly drawn across the street. Norbert and Maria's bakery towered before them. The door jingled open and a hush fell over bystanders while a gangly figure stalked out, an "R" patch blazing bright upon his sleeve. Fr. Viktor caught glimpses of candle-wax features stretched in an oblivious grin. The laborer was nodding, laughing, slapping a knee in hearty guffaw, his face still turned toward a parlor where Helene and Maria bid him a blithe *auf Wiedersehen*.

"What is this?" The Gestapo leader wrenched a ration card and bread sack from the Russian's grip. "What is this!"

The leader's white marble hands seized in spasms, tearing bread, sending blue-white flakes of stamps fluttering to the ground. Zizi cowered.

A pistol flashed beneath a suit jacket.

A unified gasp tore from refugee women pulling children into a bosom, from Catholics leaning out windows, from Fr. Viktor reeling in horror while a gray arm rose in dream-slow motion and a pistol swung from a white, trembling fist to smack the laborer. Crimson ribbons lashed the air, hovering for a nightmare instant before spraying an ivy door. Wails of agony rose like spires toward a black and blue sky. The Russian's skull thunked against a wall, leaving smears. He balled up to protect himself from battering feet.

"How . . . dare . . . you . . . you animal!" the Gestapo leader grunted in exertion. "Stealing food from a German shop!"

"Mother of God. Leave him alone!" Fr. Viktor clambered on his knees, forgetting Fr. Paul for the moment.

A blood-spattered door whacked open. The noise jolted bystanders who mistook it for a gunshot. Helene, Maria, and Norbert poured outside in panic.

Norbert thrashed out of his apron. "What are you doing? This man is not stealing food! *Mein Gott!* He is allowed."

"What do you mean he is allowed? He is a Russian." Panting, the Gestapo leader turned to survey Schwarzenfeld's streets. Zizi shrank away and huddled into a battered knot upon the roadside. "Slavs. There are Slavs walking free. There are *Untermenschen* loose among Germans!" A cloud of Poles drifted past the meat market, their knuckles whitening around sacks that swung heavy with bread and sausage. They recoiled from a stone face flushing to a ruby blaze. "These rats should be locked in barracks behind barbed wire! Their German masters are supposed to be providing room and board. Are you people completely ignorant of our racial laws?" The Gestapo leader swung in fury. "Why was *this* not reported to us?"

Pale faces gazed down from high windows. Schwarzenfelders traded glances with neighbors. No one had ever questioned the sight of foreign laborers ambling freely around town.

Officer Dobler trailed the procession. Shoulders hunched, the police chief retreated into a throng of refugees. Fr. Viktor recalled seeing his dark, stony presence hunkered in a rear pew, his attendance at Mass so sterling it left no doubt who phoned the Gestapo office in Nürnberg after Fr. Paul read Br. Konrad's letter.

"What is happening?" Norbert demanded. "What are you doing to the paters?"

"They have started rumors about the death of our Führer. As you can see, they are paying the price for this action."

The baker's jaw dropped, but before he belted out a word, the Gestapo leader whirled. "You! Stop right there. Get up!"

Maria had reached for the Russian sobbing in a bloody heap. She realized that the command was intended for her and fled into her husband's arms.

"Yes. Get away from him. German women have no business being near these animals."

Norbert's face soured. "Talk about animals. I will tell you who is the animal—"

"Norbert, be careful not to say something we'll all regret." Fr. Viktor nudged his head toward a pistol clenched in the Gestapo leader's hand.

The baker's face contorted in grief. "Pater!"

A whimper tugged their attention to Fr. Paul. He pawed at the roadway and discovered his spectacles.

Fr. Viktor felt his teeth grinding into powder. The people of Schwarzenfeld looked to him for leadership, and that fact wrenched him to his feet. He raised his hands in a calming gesture. "Hey. You like speaking English? Then let's talk in English, you and me. Nobody else will understand." Clouds loomed in an iron sky. A gale carried the raw mingling scents of meadow grasses, barnyard animals, and forthcoming rain. Back home in Sharon when the day turned this blustery, his Koch relatives bolted for storm cellars. An impending speech wove first in German, then it unraveled upon the loom of his consciousness to fit patterns from a past life, a far shore, one that felt more distant than ever before.

He swept a palm toward Zizi. "Listen. This situation with the foreign laborers. This is the way it is in Schwarzenfeld. The owner of the ceramics shop gives them ration cards and lets them get their own food and clothes. Put yourself in their place, just for a moment. They've got one hell of a hard life, and they deserve to be treated with dignity." He shrugged. "What's the harm in that?"

Silk lips pursed into a quivering line. A knuckle whitened around a trigger.

Zizi stopped sniveling and twitched still.

"Say another word and this bullet goes into his head. What the hell do you know? You are a foreigner here. Shut up!"

Fr. Viktor clamped his mouth shut so quickly that pain flashed in his molars. *The light of the body is the eye.* He searched for a gleam in the Gestapo leader, some sign of a mind that remembered how bruised muscle throbbed, how terror twisted the gut, but he read only dark detachment from the human race, a void where hatred held unchallenged dominion. For all his refinement, this creature was a putrid husk. Pride had turned his soul barren long ago.

A motor rumbled behind them. Fr. Paul wobbled upright. Both Passionists froze. Fear tore the breath from their lungs. A Mercedes rolled up.

"Enough of this nonsense," the Gestapo leader muttered. "Take the priests."

"No!" Norbert howled. Maria and Helene clapped hands to their mouths. Cries erupted from high windows.

"*Mein Herr.* A word with you, if you please."

Refugees swiveled, searching for a voice that sliced the din in High German and followed up with a Hitler salute. A human sea shifted currents and a figure surged up from the waves.

"Holy Moses," Fr. Viktor said.

"Finally, someone in this dirt-road village shows respect for our Führer." The Gestapo leader turned. "Who are you?"

"Wilhelm Seiz, Kreisamtsleiter of the Schwandorf NSV. I would ask with whom I am speaking, but I suspect that I will get a *Dienstmarke.* Correct?"

The Gestapo leader swaggered, his lip curled. "An Amtsleiter. An Amtsleiter from Party Welfare has come to talk." The comment prompted incredulous snorts from his comrades. "And ah, what 'charitable errand' brings you here, Herr Amtsleiter?"

"This is no errand of charity," Seiz said, "I know these priests, and I know something also about this rumor."

While Seiz spilled out a story in exacting detail, Fr. Viktor peered at Helene. The widow scraped a thumbnail between her teeth, and within her aquamarine eyes he read suspicions balanced between fear and hope.

The provincial turned back to observe two party members. Head raised at a dominating angle, the Gestapo leader sized up the NSV director, a mere civil servant. He frowned upon office attire lightly frayed at the seams, upon shoes coated in dust, the leather creased by a dogged march from one calamity to another. Seiz likely wore that same pair while confiscating the Miesberg monastery three years earlier, Fr. Viktor reflected. The fast-talking civil servant engaged the Gestapo officer in a spirit of brotherhood, ignoring Italian finery.

"When one manages a social office, one understands the ways of a small town. Listen." A note flapped in Seiz's hands as he began to read. "Br. Konrad says, 'I myself will be praying for a day when sacred Germany is ruled by God alone.'" The civil servant shook his head. "If you are looking for someone to accuse, then point a finger down the road and take your pick. Every Catholic gossiper ran from that church with the same foolish idea."

"There," Fr. Viktor said, "you've got the word of another party member. This whole thing's a misunderstanding. Let us go."

The Gestapo leader gestured toward Zizi, now a heap sniveling in a bloody pool. "Did you know that these pigs are running loose?"

Seiz absorbed the sight of a Slav's pain. He flinched and shifted away quickly. "No." A hawkish presence was watching him. "No. I am from Schwandorf, I know nothing about that."

Fr. Viktor firmed his lips.

"Pater Böhminghaus has admitted guilt for inciting the town," the Gestapo leader deigned to explain. "Pater Koch is an American living in Germany for reasons that I find suspicious. He himself has asked to be held accountable with his *Mitbruder*."

Seiz shot Fr. Viktor an irritated look from the corner of an eye, then shifted weight from one weary shoe to the other.

"If an enemy invites me to put him in prison, Herr Amtsleiter, this is a request that I am not going to refuse." Laughter rippled up from officers prowling around the Mercedes.

"Pater Koch is a German citizen, and his situation is completely understandable. Do you see that building there?" Seiz swept a finger toward the hilltop monastery and then explained its history. "The pater is living there to protest his eviction. He is a spiritual leader who is respected by the people here."

"He is a father to us!" Helene burst.

"He and the paters have done nothing but good for this town!" Norbert bellowed. "That monastery saved us all from poverty!" Leery and baffled, he squinted in Seiz's direction.

"You cannot take our Provinsche and Pater Paul from us!" an old crone shouted from a high window. She tucked herself out of sight and evaded Gestapo men scanning the crowds. "You just wait and see if the party gets anything from us after this, Herr Amtsleiter. We will give you stones for *Eintopfsonntag*. Stones, I tell you!" She referred to a program that asked housewives to avoid making elaborate suppers on the first Sunday of each month and prepare a simple stew that required fewer rations. Leftover stamps were then donated to Party Welfare. The NSV depended upon them to scrape together soup kitchens for refugees.

Fr. Viktor nodded in comprehension. "Hm." Parishioners leaned outside and traded glances with their neighbors. Behind each face he discerned the same message. *Boycott the collections! Give the party nothing!*

Seiz swiveled to face Fr. Viktor. A sharp gaze conveyed fear and a plea. Without a single word spoken between them, they understood each other.

"Are you attempting to interfere with us, Herr Amtsleiter?" The Gestapo leader drew his words out like a blade.

"No. I am an expert advisor to the Reich, I am simply offering my assistance to you." Seiz leaned closer. "And now, I wish to advise you on another matter of concern."

The Gestapo leader turned to his men. "Do you hear that? Party Welfare wants to advise us." He then snarled loud enough for the entire crowd to hear. "I don't want your advice. Why don't you go to a street corner, shake those idiotic little red cans of yours, and *mind your own goddamn business!*"

A muscle twitched between Seiz's cheekbone and jaw. He flushed, aware of a hundred eyes watching him. At last, his gaze fell to those high-polished shoes.

Fr. Viktor ground his teeth on the civil servant's behalf.

"The party has seen already how a public relations flap with the Catholic population will draw attention to a town," Seiz said, collecting himself with admirable dignity. "The Oberpfalz is seventy percent Catholic. If this situation is not handled carefully, we will have one here." He pointed toward the Miesbergkloster.

"The NSV had that building, as I have said. I was ordered to leave under conditions of absolute secrecy. I suspect our leaders will be grateful if things are kept quiet in Schwarzenfeld, and the people up there can continue their work without a religious riot drawing attention to their presence. But, you have no need to accept my word only, if this is not enough. Where is . . . ah." Seiz swung toward the crowd. "There. Schwarzenfeld's *Ortsgruppenleiter.*" He beckoned a dour man. "Tell him!"

The town's leading party member cringed at the demands placed upon him. He stepped forward grudgingly. "Herr Amtsleiter Seiz is correct: the old man is revered in the Oberpfalz. He has never caused any trouble. Pater Paul is the one who started this today."

Fr. Viktor looked to his fellow Passionist. Stillness fell over creation. *The party always punishes disobedience.*

"Wait!"

The Gestapo leader raised a hand to block his protest. He turned back to Seiz and glared. "Did Gauleiter Wächtler share information with you about that monastery?"

"With me?" Seiz said. "Of course not. It is clear that the people up there are doing something to support the war effort."

Fr. Viktor felt a year drag by in a minute. His fellow religious lifted a face that shook him. Beneath blood and bruises shone the smile of a lamb.

"Viktor." Fr. Paul mumbled with a swollen lip. "Our sufferings. They pave our way . . . to Heaven . . . with gold. Remember?"

Panicked, he floundered into English. "Listen—"

Again, the hand.

The Gestapo leader spoke in a low, chilling tone. "You party members in this town. You are all on report for your complete failure to enforce our racial laws. You are imbeciles if you cannot keep order over peasants with pitchforks. And you, Herr Amtsleiter Wilhelm Seiz." A finger whipped sharp. "Whatever you think you know. You know nothing. If you breathe a word about your suspicions, I will hear about it. And I will come back for you, your wife, your children, and everyone that you tell."

Seiz visibly wavered. Fr. Viktor felt his own heart stop for a beat. A cold gaze shot toward two Passionists awaiting judgment.

"We don't need the old man. Arrest Pater Böhminghaus."

———

Muscular hands shoved Fr. Paul into the Mercedes. Doors slammed with a terrible finality, jolting Fr. Viktor into a fit that turned his voice raspy, but his protests accomplished nothing. Gestapo men faced the windshield. His fellow religious slumped in a back seat, docile as a lamb. "Paul." Serene fingers flattened against a window. Through a hot blur, Fr. Viktor watched his own hand touch glass, his own hand covering a tranquil palm, his own hand groping helpless when an engine sputtered to life. "Paul?" The Mercedes' roar blasted a hole in his soul that would never be filled the same way again.

The rumbling of an engine died on the wind and left Fr. Viktor listening to the fevered rush of his breath.

"Paul!"

Lightning flared. Sorrow dripped from a leaden sky.

Wagons somberly creaked up the Hauptstrasse. Gendarmes stirred, remembering that refugees awaited housing. Oblivious to his surroundings, Fr. Viktor looked down. "Oh." Broken lenses shimmered at his feet. He picked up slivers and dropped them into a reverent palm while Catholics showered apologies. Norbert. Herr Gietl. Herr Obendorfer. His trembling fingers pinched, dropped, pinched, dropped while rain fell faster and men yanked his sleeves. "No!" he bellowed. "I'm not leaving him. I'm not leaving Paul lying here on the road!"

A yelp lashed the air: Maria and Helene hauled Zizi to his feet and hastened him into the bakery. Bystanders swung toward the commotion, except for Seiz. The charity worker kept his back turned until Helene peered out, tense and pale, clutching a bloody door. They locked gazes for a long, breathless moment, then quietly Seiz invited her to retrieve Klaus at the Rathaus. He swiveled back.

"Pater?"

Fr. Viktor realized that wagons were stopped in the road, refugees stood sulking in a downpour, and police begged him to move. A stranger's hands swept shards onto a kerchief. They showed sufficient respect, so he stopped shooing them away. Looking up, he found the charity worker offering him a bundle.

Parishioners gathered around, all wet and shaken. "Go home," Fr. Viktor told them. He ached for solitude, yet shuddered at the thought of returning to his sacristy alone. "It's all right. Go home." He yearned to meditate while sensations remained fresh in his mind—the march, the sickness, the insane weight crushing his shoulder, and grief as deep as a sepulchre tomb, a presence that was ancient, yet raw as an open wound. Helene and Maria recognized Him in a Slav. The sower shed tears of pride, watching seeds of Passionist theology flourish in black soil. Norbert poured out a roadway confession on behalf of their parish. "I know. I blame the Gestapo, not you people. It's all right." Catholic interpretation of Br. Konrad's letter arose from disgust with an oppressive regime, and the American could only sympathize with parishioners who seethed under its yoke.

Norbert and Seiz debated what to do with Fr. Viktor. They started to snipe at each other, but he was too dazed to care.

Blessedly, younger arms ushered him out of the storm, into a door recess. For an hour he stared at rain falling gray and whispery upon country roads.

"Pater. Pater, are you still unwell? If you wish to return to the hospital, I will make arrangements personally."

He sat hunkered upon the front step of Schwarzenfeld's police station. Summer showers eased to a murmur and a voice trickled down in warm droplets. Seiz crouched on his haunches, tugging at a soaked shirt. He had been slogging around town, housing refugees.

"Pater. I am heartily sorry for the way that things have turned out today," the charity worker said.

Fr. Viktor sighed. He cradled Fr. Paul's glasses in his hands.

"We are not in a place where one can do and say whatever he damned well pleases," Seiz said bitterly. "We must remember this. It is appalling that people must be beaten and arrested as a reminder." He pinched skin between his brows.

"I wasn't here," Fr. Viktor said, "but I know Paul didn't mean to stir up anyone. That's got to count for something."

Seiz drew a breath, let it go.

"I'll get Faulhaber," Fr. Viktor persisted. "Or someone in the Church. Someone." His voice felt fragile, like a scrape of bible pages.

"Your Cardinal Faulhaber could not stop the confiscation of your monastery, and this case is more serious," Seiz reminded him.

A wagon of refugees creaked by. Down the road, Norbert and Maria dipped sponges into a bucket and rinsed blood from their door. The baker eyed Fr. Viktor, as if ensuring that he was safe. The provincial gripped spectacle frames, remembering the eagle shining bright and deadly on a *Dienstmarke*. Seiz prodded him again, asking if he needed hospital care, and he shook his head. If the Catholic Church could not help him pry Fr. Paul from the talons of a hostile State, he had no idea where to turn.

Fr. Viktor watched refugee children bound into a wagon with the resilience that only youth could muster in the darkest of times. A waif kicked her legs over the edge. She let loose a cry. Her left slipper. The tiny shoe smacked a house, barely missing a window, then it plummeted into a heap on the roadside. Plaintive wailing went unheeded by refugees absorbed in their own troubles, but Seiz burst into a chuckle and retrieved it for her. The charity worker clambered into the wagon, pulling up a bedraggled woman and a one-armed man, a veteran discharged from the front. Fr. Viktor observed him in silence. Seiz remained blind to Christ's face, perhaps, but he fully processed the cold, leaden fact of human suffering. When the man strode back, he stopped short, as if stricken by an afterthought. Fr. Viktor studied a soul entangled in thorns.

"You know, I'm the one who's been dragged from the hospital, but you look more sick and shaken than I do. What's wrong?"

Seiz swallowed hard, watching the urchin who had kicked off her shoe. He turned away quickly. "It is no concern of yours."

A watchband counted seconds on the charity worker's wrist. Fr. Viktor read him intently, sensing an erratic tick in the wine-venom machine.

"Just stop your people from boycotting collections. It is not the party that suffers when my collection cans are empty. It is those people." Seiz pointed toward refugees. "It is galling to me, being trapped in the middle of these disputes."

"I see," Fr. Viktor said. The Reich allowed few avenues to express dissent, and it dawned upon him that this inroad ultimately brought about more harm than good. He nodded, yet the shadows only deepened in Seiz's face.

"Is it something more than fear of a boycott?" he asked. Seiz's eyes followed children swinging their feet. "Is it the monastery? Do you know more than you've let on?"

"Of course not. I know nothing more about it than you do."

"Then what is it?"

A huff. "Pater. I am *nothing*. Don't you understand? I am a civil servant who begs for the poor. No one tells me anything! I have no information. Only suspicions."

"What suspicions?"

The charity worker sighed sharply, looked down the road.

"Listen, my friend," Fr. Viktor said, "I've been a priest for fifty years. I've seen a lot of frightened and burdened people. You've got a look on your face I've never seen before in my life."

Tolling shimmered from a hilltop steeple: it was 6:00 p.m. A clean-shaven chin jerked in thought. "I am showing you far more consideration than usual, but I would hardly call us friends, Pater."

"Yeah, we've got a history all right. But I'm willing to put that behind us, if you are." He ran a finger over twisted spectacles, then sniffled, tucking grief into a pocket. As a Passionist, he gravitated to pain. Restlessness drew him like a magnet.

"You know, we've got this saying back in the States: 'Misery loves company.' Lord knows I'm miserable after this day, and you. You look like a man who has opened his eyes and seen something horrible beyond description."

Seiz loitered within earshot and pretended not to hear. Fr. Viktor continued speaking in a voice that carried through brambles. "Herr Seiz. If you need to keep a secret, then confide in me. If we call it a confession, I'm sworn to silence." Horses neighed, pulling a final wagon down the Hauptstrasse. "Tell me. What's shaken your faith?"

Tolling bells fell silent. The charity worker drew a labored breath. The man looked pale and tormented.

"I will never lose faith in Germany, Pater. Save the preaching for your parishioners."

Seiz strode off with an *auf Wiedersehen.* Fr. Viktor watched him stalk through long shadows cast by a row of houses. Darkness swallowed him one moment, then he trudged, head bowed, into sunlight. Extremes washed over him, dark, light, dark, light, never a gray instant between them. Fr. Viktor could not bear to sit and watch in silence. He had seen enough tragedy for one day.

"*Mein Herr!*" he called into the wind. "How much time do you spend looking at those pictures and letters on your office walls? How often must you walk your 'stations' and remind yourself of the good you've done, so you can forget the things that haunt you?"

The fallen Catholic froze as if the words were a rope jerking taut and holding him fast. He refrained from turning.

Fr. Viktor mustered himself. "A National Socialist charity worker. A party faithful—and a humanitarian? I can't even begin to imagine the twisted world they've got you trapped in. This People's Community of yours. If National Socialism really united all Germans in common blood and destiny, don't you think that Gestapo man would have shown courtesy to another German, regardless of class?"

The charity worker sagged.

An ache swelled within Fr. Viktor. "Herr Seiz. Listen to a friend who will tell you the truth, no matter how repugnant you might find it. You're blindly following a Führer who's misleading you in a most despicable manner—"

"What is this?" Seiz wheeled. "This is heresy! Your Pater Böhminghaus was arrested for less than this. Are you mad?"

"—and you know how *wrong* things are," Fr. Viktor persisted, tearing at thorns. "If you really shared the values of the party, you wouldn't stand in silence while two German women helped a Slav. And what about those laborers? You knew those people were walking freely around here, you've always known!"

"I warn you, old man, I will report you, and you will be sitting in that prison cell right beside Pater Paul!"

"If you're in conflict, take it as a sign: you're on the wrong road in life, but you can turn around. Not even you are forsaken. Your Father will take you back!"

"I can call those Gestapo right back here!"

"I know you can!"

Silence clenched the roadway.

Fr. Viktor confronted Seiz without a flutter of fear. He could see a mind limbering up behind a depleted and desperate face.

"You think I am conflicted?" Seiz said. "*Ich?* Then look within yourself, Pater, because you are more conflicted than me. You have fought hard to stay in Germany. Why?"

"I have a mission," Fr. Viktor said. "Today it includes saving a soul from himself."

"A mission. But what if it is not a mission that is holding you here? What if it is your own free will? Not God's. Yours."

Fr. Viktor grunted. "You would say that."

"You were not born here, but your parents were German. Your blood is pure." Seiz's eyes slivered in surmise. "Deep down in a way you cannot explain to yourself, do you feel rooted in Germany? Is this why you refuse to return to America?"

The provincial swallowed muggy air, then looked toward his hilltop church. "Okay. This discussion is going nowhere. Good day."

He lumbered off. A carpet of maturing wheat undulated at the Miesberg's base, and a rough dirt path wound sinuously up its slope, functioning both as an access route for farmers and a shortcut to church. Fr. Viktor trudged up an incline slickened by rain. A wiry coil of nerves sprung behind him.

"What is wrong, Pater?" Seiz demanded. "Is it you who needs to 'see a sign,' as you call it? You, *der befreundete Feind*—the 'friendly enemy!' When you stand on German soil and speak the tongue your fathers spoke for centuries, what burns in your blood? When you are in the presence of Germans—even when you are with me—what do you feel in your soul?" Breath lashed his ear, whispering words that turned him gray. "Do you call me 'friend' because you feel a spiritual bond with another member of your race?"

The Miesbergkirche soared up from a grassy hilltop like a safe haven. Fr. Viktor reeled into the vestibule. A voice thundered in the marble hollow, shaking him to the marrow.

"Pater. Listen to a friend who will make you see the truth. Can you look me in the eye and say that I am wrong?"

Seiz gripped the doorway. Sunlight poured in shafts behind his extended arms. Shadows swathed his face. Fr. Viktor met a stare that was like an iron press, crushing him to pulp.

The party member nodded.

"You see? It is not a mission from God that holds you here. It is your own doing. When you draw your last breath on this earth, it will be in Germany. I know, because I am a German. And so are you. The allure of blood and soil cannot be denied."

The gaze holding Fr. Viktor captive slid away like a knife. Footsteps padded over the courtyard. Once they faded, the provincial breathed against an ache in his chest. Weary and haggard, he retreated to his sacristy.

CHAPTER ELEVEN

WHERE IS GOD?

April 17, 1945

At 4:00 a.m. a chorus of screams shivered up from the Bahnhof-strasse. Wrenched from the oblivion of sleep, Helene lugged herself out of bed and fumbled at her window. Light seared her bleary eyes. The widow sucked air through gritted teeth.

What on earth?

She ventured a second look. A stream of sparks poured down from silver clouds, shining brightly, like a thousand candles glowing in darkness. The green lights fanned slowly in a shape that resembled a Christmas tree.

Neighbors fled down the country road. Shrieks splintered the black air. A siren wailed to life in the cold, dark night.

"Klaus! Hans!"

She ran. Still in her nightgown. No time to change.

"Klaus! Hans! Wake up, wake up!" Helene shook their arms, legs, shoulders, anything to wrench them awake. They tottered around. She thrust them into the hall.

Refugees rushed up from her parlor like ghosts. They had shoved back the drapes and recoiled from the sight of deadly angels swirling down, sparking hysteria on the earth below.

A refugee from Hamburg pelted questions. The woman slept fully clothed. She had lived through this nightmare before. An air raid shelter?

"Not in this house," Helene quavered. "Town, town, in town." She shook all over. She couldn't stop shaking. No one in Schwarzenfeld had thought to prepare a shelter.

"Shoes! Coats!" The widow yanked her jacket from a hook. No time to think. Or breathe. Just move. Sirens tore the air, a banshee howl. Klaus and Hans obeyed without a word.

The attack began the instant they fled their house.

A single blast. Fierce. Deafening. Then an unbroken string of detonations followed like God hammering the earth. Winds roared from the east. Helene's hair whipped her face, blocking her vision, though she gripped both boys and dared not let go. "Mutti!" Hans wide awake now, bawling. "Mutti what do we *do* where are we going Mutti!" Helene running in the dark. Hens clucking and thrashing in a neighbor's coop. A horse shrieking in the road. Three hundred kilograms of animal muscle reared against a wagon. Refugees spilled out, a convoy from the east, fleeing the Russian army. *Cows. Potatoes. Four in the morning.* Never thought it would happen in a mud-road village like Schwarzenfeld. Helene spat out strands, tossed her head, felt the cross pendant around her neck fly up and snag her hair, felt her mind freeze amid howls and screams and black obscenities from a human herd running senseless. "Mutti!"

The wheels of a mind stricken by terror jerked into motion. Shelter. Where? Helene recalled bulletins pinned to message boards in the Miesbergkirche vestibule, announcements about a cellar beneath the hill's grassy heights. The Bauer family stored beer kegs there during the summer months to keep them cool. Town officials had designated it as a shelter.

Her hands clinging like talons, she gripped sleeves, checked her sons, Hans and Klaus, both here, both alive, Hans bawling, Klaus dragging, straining to look for bombers roaring above. "No, don't look—go go go!" He didn't hear. She felt her vocal cords tightening, lungs heaving, the words tearing raw from her throat, but heard nothing herself, the plea lost in a shrill deadly symphony whistling down from mad blackness, all while her heels pounded dirt, left, right, left, right, felt nothing, feet cold, legs numb, but still attached, still moving, still carrying her in the heart-pounding night toward the Miesberg.

An iron door in the hillside. Groaning open. Arms pulling her inside. Blackness swallowed her. Safe, safe . . . safe.

Helene wept.

"Come here! Oh, my boys." She pulled Klaus and Hans close. They surrendered and hugged her back, far too shaken to whine over a public display of motherly affection.

Deep in the cave's gullet a child vomited. A snowy Labrador barked. Refugee women sobbed. "There. Now you country people know what is happening to us in the cities!"

"It is the British, probably," a Berlin refugee declared with grim authority. "The British strike at night and the Amis strike by day."

"Did you hear about what happened in Dresden?" a third voice wafted up. "The bombing was so intense, some people melted where they stood. Their bones had to be scraped from the pavement."

Helene swayed in the dark. "Oh, help . . ." Klaus and Hans caught her. The world pulled away slowly, like waves slipping from a far beach. Rosary beads rattled nearby.

"Pater?" Dunked in calamity, she floundered back to sounds from the comforting familiar. "Pater Viktor, is that you?" She worried about him. All of his followers did. The old man lived alone in that miniscule sacristy. Fr. Paul's whereabouts still remained a frightening unknown. To Helene's relief, a familiar figure swam into focus and peered at her with fatherly concern. "Yes, I am all right. I just need to sit here with my boys. Norbert, Maria, Dean Spangler. Did they make it?" Fr. Viktor pointed: a wild-haired man heaved the door wide, his teeth gritted below a black mustache; at his feet, a woman embraced a mound of weepy girls. Above the ringing in her ears, Helene heard Dean Spangler trumpeting an Our Father. "Oh, God, what is happening to us?" She hoped Zizi and his fellow laborers found shelter.

"That sounds damned close, but they are not bombing here," Norbert said. "The horizon south of us is burning. The target must be Schwandorf."

A thump shook the cave. Wooden beams creaked. Dirt hissed from the ceiling.

"Schwandorf?" Klaus struggled to his feet.

Helene sighed, grateful that the bombs weren't falling upon them. Then she recoiled from a dreadful realization. Fr. Viktor turned swiftly to Norbert.

"Schwandorf. You're sure?"

Klaus scrambled to the door. Norbert pushed it open, and together they looked out, their faces lined in the eerie green glow of bombing markers.

"It is not Schwandorf," Klaus insisted. "The wind is blowing the fire that way. The bombs are falling between us and Schwandorf."

"There is nothing but potato fields between us and Schwandorf," Norbert said. "Do you think they would waste bombs on that?"

Klaus deliberated, indignant.

"They might."

"But there is that train station over there!" the baker objected. He observed the look washing over Klaus' face and then softened his tone. "I am sorry, boy, but it is a tactic of warfare: disable the enemy by crippling his ability to move troops and supplies to the front. The British want to stop those 'wheels rolling for victory.'"

Another string of bombs fell, their throbs evenly spaced like a chain of beads, *boom, boom, boom, boom,* the pounding dull, unreal, distant, sinister.

Klaus' head turned in tight, panicked motions.

Helene met Fr. Viktor's stare.

"Do you hear that?" The Berlin refugee jabbed a thumb over his shoulder. "That is a carpet bombing. That town will be dust by tomorrow." The man slumped, his head shaking.

Fifteen minutes later, Helene curled her nose against a reek of sweat and vomit. "It stopped," she gasped. "Is it over? The bombing? Tell me it is over." Refugees warned that another bombing raid might erupt any moment and these people, so bitterly experienced in war, assured her that any creature possessing an ounce of sense would remain entrenched in this foul hole until the air wardens sounded the 'all clear.' Hans whimpered. "Mutti?" Helene pulled him close. Together, mother and son listened to alarms in the shattered dark, their pitch falling softer, deeper, until moribund wails died somewhere above the ruins burning eight kilometers away, and that slow, bending moan struck them as the most haunted sound they had heard in the living world. Helene had an absurd mental image of Death gathering souls the way Hans collected pebbles in the street, stooping occasionally and loafing about, humming sweetly.

Her eldest collapsed upon the straw-covered floor. "Are you all right?" She watched his shadow huddle up and rock slowly. "Klaus?"

"Is he crying?" Hans asked. "He is crying, I think."

Rosary beads rattled in the dark. "I think right now would be a good time to pray," an accented voice said.

"What for?" Sniffling ripped through the cave. "Don't tell me that praying will save anybody, because I know better!"

"Klaus," Helene scolded.

"No, I won't promise that, son." In the wake of a bombing, Fr. Viktor's tranquil tone struck the widow as surreal.

Norbert wedged the door, inviting night winds to dispel the fetid air, and moonlight stretched in a velvety blue swath upon their Provinsche. He sat cross-legged, turning earnest while he studied a young face quivering in tears. "Well, you've grown," he said. Helene shifted uncomfortably, realizing that ages had passed since her eldest last attended church, though Fr. Viktor uttered no word of blame. Instead, the old man concentrated upon the unbearable specter of a child's grief.

"You know, you remind me of somebody I once knew back in the States. In fact, his name was Klaus, too."

"Uh-huh. Yea."

"I'm serious."

"But that cannot be true," the boy insisted. "If he was an *Ameri-kaner*, then his name could not be Klaus. That is a German name."

Fr. Viktor paused and immersed himself in thought. When he spoke, his voice was thick with his round, downy accent. "Yeah, it's a German name, all right. But America's a country of immigrants, you see. People come from all over the world. In Sharon where Klaus and I grew up, many people were German—either a native who had stepped off the boat, or a child of one."

Helene fingered her crucifix pendant. It shocked her to find that it remained fastened around her neck after that harrowing dash. She heard gray movements in darkness as people turned to listen. The Gindele daughters huddled against Maria. *We all feel like shaken children right now,* the widow thought. Stillness fell over a cavern silvered by moonlight.

"I remember when this boy Klaus was—oh, how old was he?" Fr. Viktor smoothed a hand over his unshaven chin. "Seven, I think. He was seven years old, and his mother was pregnant. Klaus had two older sisters and two younger brothers, so this newcomer was the sixth child in the family. His mother gave birth to the baby. A boy." A smile washed over weathered features. It suddenly ebbed. "But, the infant was weak. It died six hours after it was born."

Norbert clicked his tongue in sorrow. "Oh, how tragic," Maria sighed, holding her daughters closer.

"Taking in a sight like that," the provincial brooded, "that tiny, precious child lying in a coffin, you wonder how such a thing could happen in a world with God. But it did. And it was only the beginning of the sorrows that Klaus and his family faced."

"What happened?" Minding her nightgown, Helene pulled her knees to her chest. It was a relief to hear a voice in the sepulchral silence, assuring Death that it had nothing to reap here.

"A month after the baby died, there was an outbreak of typhoid at the coal mine where Klaus' father worked, and he trudged home one day, burning up with fever. Have you ever seen anyone with typhoid fever?"

Fr. Viktor directed that question at Klaus. Silence stretched so long that the boy finally blinked up from a hangnail and shook his head. "No. Believe me, you don't want to. It's one of the most horrid things you'll ever see. It starts with a rash. At first, the victim spends all his time in the outhouse. The disease cleans him out. Then the fever rises so high, he lays there delirious, his eyelids fluttering. The stench of sickness fills the house, until the walls seem to drip with it." The flow of Fr. Viktor's river voice swelled with memory.

"This Klaus in America. He had a special bond with his dad. A very strong bond. He was the eldest son in the family, so he was named after him, in German tradition. I remember when his father was fading fast, that boy walked twice a day, morning and night, to this little stone church that was just down the road: St. Rose of Lima. Day after day, I watched him make promises to God. 'Father,'" the old man winced in the vise of memory, "'Father, save my dad, save him and I swear on all that's holy, I'll never sin again. I'll be so perfect, You won't be able to tell me apart from Your own Son.'" Quiet deepened in the cavern. Helene's eyes shut. Her fingers tightened around the cross pendant.

"Klaus walked home, absolutely certain that everything would be set right. But when he got back, he found his mother on the porch, weeping so hard it seemed she would split apart. He learned that his father had died . . . even as he was praying."

Hans wiped tears. Klaus turned burning eyes to the door and watched fire consume southern skies. If anyone else recounted this horrible story, Helene would have begged for the telling to cease, but the old man was as dear as a father, and she understood what he hoped to accomplish.

"And even *that* wasn't the end," Fr. Viktor continued to Helene's dismay. "Three months later, Klaus' paternal grandmother—she'd come over from Germany with them—she woke up one morning, she couldn't get out of bed, or speak a word. The family prayed until it seemed their fingers would rub the paint off their rosaries. But within days, she too was lost."

The Berlin refugee stirred, the one who recognized the sound of a carpet bombing. "Well, that is a heap of misfortune."

Helene remembered the crowd. She squinted toward knots of Catholics, clusters of refugees, an occasional party member soured by a defeat they all acknowledged as inevitable. Paula Dirrigl knelt in a spot that permitted her to lip read. Their Provinsche relayed a story of American suffering—*enemy* suffering—yet no one stopped to ponder that. They sat rapt, each man, woman, and child relating intimately to the pain. Fr. Viktor turned to the refugee.

"Yeah. This kid was seven years old, and just like that, he was raising his two brothers, Peter and Albert. He had to tend their cuts and scrapes, pack their lunches, nurse them through measles, defend them from schoolyard bullies. Walked away with a black eye a couple times, too. Though rest assured," Fr. Viktor shook a finger, "those bullies got what *they* deserved." Smiles flickered around the cavern. "After school, he and his sisters managed the farm. They barely saw their mother. Six days out of seven, that poor woman worked as a seamstress. She had five kids to support, all on her own."

Helene glanced around the cavern, trading looks with other German widows. They all empathized with that.

Fr. Viktor reflected on heavy memories and bowed his head. "It was a hard life. Even in America, the land of plenty. Klaus was in despair. He once said that, if his dad died while he was making the most heartfelt prayer of his life, there was no God."

"Yea?" Klaus said. "Well, that Klaus was right."

"You think so?" Fr. Viktor said.

"I know so." The boy's eyes flared with the inferno of a child's fury. "Where was God when his papa was sick? Where was He when mine was shot? And where is He now when the bombs are falling in Schwandorf!"

"Klaus!" Helene hissed.

Fr. Viktor raised a calming hand. "I know someone in Schwandorf. Seems like you do, too. I'm worried for him."

The boy eyed him warily. "You mean that?"

"Of course I do."

"But why? He is your enemy."

"We've had a difference of opinion at times," the provincial admitted. "But we're not enemies. I've seen *good* work through him. I want to see him redeemed. It's important to me."

Helene watched the old sage study her son, reading him the way one read pages in a book. Klaus frowned, deciding what to make of his words. The boy blinked at the stone floor. "He is . . . it is hard to describe. He is strict, but lenient. He is demanding, but also the kindest person I know. My teachers and troop leaders say I should be fierce and brutal, but he doesn't say that. He says that I am a fine young man with a good heart, that *this* is what is important. He says Papa would be proud. And he is proud of me, too. From the moment we met, he has been like a father to me." Bathed by firelight, Klaus' face warped in the heat of grief. "If he is dead, this is so unfair!"

Fr. Viktor listened intently. At length, he nodded.

"You got charity from him. Good. That's very good. I'm glad to hear that."

Klaus buried his face in his hands, and the provincial turned mournful. They looked like a matched set, Helene thought: young and old, doubt-ridden and faithful, one scarred by grief, the other healed by a bond with the infinite.

"Oh, son," Fr. Viktor sighed. "During moments like this, we're tempted to think of God as a wishing well, and our prayers as gold coins. The more we pray, the more we deserve an answer. Right? It doesn't work that way because that's not what prayer is about."

"Then it is pointless!" A sobbing voice blurted. "All that Bible stuff. 'Ask and you shall receive.' It is a lie!"

"No, it's not," the old man assured. "You see, the point of prayer isn't to make God change your troubles. The point of prayer is to change *you*."

Klaus sniffled and held still. "As I told my friend in America, prayer—real prayer—is a *bonding*," the provincial revealed in hushed awe. "It's a communion with all that is good in this universe. That grace gives us the courage to fight evil. And when evil overwhelms us, as it's doing now? Prayer gives us the strength to endure." The old man gazed toward distant flames. "We can pray for others and give them strength. If our friend in Schwandorf is still alive, he'll need strength to climb out of the ruins and find his way back to us. If he perished, then he'll need strength to stand before his Maker."

Helene studied her eldest. He cradled a shield pin in his palm and watched moonlight dance over its engraved contours.

"I'll tell you another thing, son. Even now—although it's hard to see during times like this—even now God is working through our troubles. He *will* provide."

A young face lifted up. "Not always. My prayer for Papa was not answered."

"Not the way you wanted, no," Fr. Viktor said gently. "Free will intervened, and the answer you wanted isn't possible anymore. But from what you told me, there was an answer to your prayer. It just happened in a way you weren't expecting."

Klaus straightened. Bewilderment tightened the pert line of his lips. Slowly, slowly . . . he turned toward Schwandorf.

People stirred throughout the cellar. Pale light swelled from the eastern hills; the Miesbergkirche bell tower tolled from afar. Dour-faced refugees stood up, stretched their legs, and bid each other

Guten Morgen. This was a normal day for them. Helene imagined it: Christmas trees lighting the sky night after night, the wraith-wail of sirens screeching in the cold dark, the insane dashes for shelter. It appalled her to think of this as *her* new normal.

Shivering at that thought, she looked up. Dean Spangler was wandering over. He rested his arms upon a beer barrel and angled his plumed white head.

"This American friend, this Klaus," he rumbled softly to Fr. Viktor. "After the sorrows he faced, did he regain his faith?"

The provincial sat in thought, an elbow propped upon an upraised knee. "It took a while for him to grow out of that spiritual adolescence, but eventually, he did."

"How, Pater?"

He rested his head back, reflecting. "I think it happened when a missionary visited St. Rose. This priest connected suffering with the Presence in a way that helped him make sense of everything."

Curiosity emboldened Helene. "This missionary. Was he a Passionist?"

"In fact, he was," he replied with a cryptic smile.

"Did this Klaus come to Germany?" Norbert asked.

"Oh, yes," Fr. Viktor enthused. "He was *drawn* here. When he joined the Passionists and learned that they were starting a province, he had to go. The compulsion was overwhelming." For a moment he seemed darkly pensive. Or perhaps it was just the angle of the light bathing his face. Helene couldn't tell.

"Your name—Viktor," she prodded. "Were you born with it?"

His secretive smile returned. "No. In the order we take a new name, as a rule. It means that we've forsaken a world of material possessions and started another life in the service of Christ."

"Who are you?" Helene challenged.

Fr. Viktor chuckled.

"My birth name is Nikolaus Koch. I was named after my father, and his father, according to German tradition. But in my youth, everyone called me by my nickname."

Helene grinned. Everyone in the cavern did. They had known from the start.

A long-awaited alarm beckoned inhabitants throughout the countryside. It prompted them to emerge from shelter. First Norbert, Maria, and their daughters staggered out, followed by Fr. Viktor. Helene gathered her sons and bolstered herself. She wondered what calamities awaited them in the coming days.

CHAPTER TWELVE

THE FACE OF EVIL

APRIL 19, 1945

"Hey. Are you asleep on your feet? Wake up! What sloppy posture. Stand up straight and don't make me kick your butt."

Klaus languidly confronted the Hitler Youth leader barking at him. He had been staring at a train that nudged up to Schwarzenfeld's lonely railway station.

The troop leader loomed nose to nose. "*Jawohl.*" Klaus puffed his chest to match boys lined up beside him, but once their leader stomped off to howl at another kid, he fell loose and lethargic again. The train pointed south. He envisioned it thundering through the velvet night, only to learn that Schwandorf's decimation lay ahead. Now it stood upon a track to nowhere, struggling to look brave despite the darkness inside. Klaus commiserated with its sorrows and felt lukewarm gratitude to the Hitler Youth for distracting him from his own. Schwarzenfeld's troop leaders had summoned every boy in town: full-fledged Hitler Youth, diminutive Jungvolk, even refugee children who recoiled from a menacing display of authority, baffled why they deserved to be wrenched outside on this dismal morning. Bracing for war, administrators closed the town school; Klaus doubted that his middle school in Schwandorf remained standing. Their leader stomped down the line, relishing his uninhibited access to each boy. An identical scene played out all around town. They constituted one team in five.

"*Achtung!*"

Carrion crows stopped foraging and squawked toward a crimson dawn. A line of young masculinity quivered to attention.

"You will spread out, so when you stretch your arms, you just barely touch the fingers of the man on your right and your left!"

At Klaus' side, Hans yawned and rubbed his eye. Confusion rippled down the line, then the boys obeyed.

"Do you see that out there? The papers?"

Tall grasses undulated around the train station. Klaus looked up to find white leaflets fluttering in the breeze.

"The 'gangsters' flew over last night and dropped these from their planes," the troop leader bellowed. "No one in town must see them. They are undermining our will to fight by writing lies! When I give the command, you will pick up every leaflet in your path. Do not read them. That is an order! You will turn them in to me when you are done. Ready? March!"

They trudged forward. The grass was fallow, touched by frost, and the leaflets remained stuck where they had fallen.

A breeze wafted up from the south, stirring posters tacked to the train station's weathered edifice. Klaus read a slogan painted in blood red strokes: *Um Freiheit und Leben: Volkssturm!* "For Freedom and Life: People's Storm!" The letters blazed above and below a depiction of two men gripping rifles, one a youth suited in party brown, the other a grandfather with a salt-and-pepper mustache. Hitler had issued the order last October: *All men on the home front between sixteen and sixty must form a militia and defend Germany!*

Gunshots rumbled from a wooded glen. Twenty boys clutched papers, their breath held in fear, until silence stretched long enough to dismiss gunfire as militiamen preparing for battle. War, fifteen-year-old Klaus brooded. Their world teetered upon a precipice and he stood upon the brink, his mind devoid of dreams, for here was the maw, the horrid mouth that devoured Papa and consumed his safe haven in one impossible swallow.

Reaching for a leaflet, he mulled. This morning he had slogged outside and Mutti had bustled out to deliver a coat he had forgotten. "Klaus, it is freezing!" she had rebuked. He had numbly watched refugee wagons shudder past their house while she bundled him up.

"Dear boy, you are really starting to make me worry. I have not seen you in such a state since your father died."

"Mutti, do you . . . do you believe that stuff the Provinsche says? You know. All that talk about God answering prayers in unexpected ways?"

Her chilled fingers had tested his brow. "Yes, I do."

"Can God work through anyone? I mean *anyone.*"

He held a breath while the sunlit pools of her eyes probed his. "I don't know, child," she said. "I prefer to think so."

Klaus had intended to tug this thread and unravel the answer to a question that perplexed him since they had emerged from the bomb shelter, but then his Hitler Youth leader had grunted impatiently from the roadside. After ordering him and Hans to return directly home, Mutti had leaned out the door, fingering her cross pendant as she watched him plod away.

"Hey. Klaus?"

His brother jabbed his shoulder.

"What?"

"That troop leader is coming, don't stand around like that."

He fumbled for a leaflet. The teenage overlord scowled at a pitiful collection of papers in his clutch, then stalked away. Klaus longed to swing a kick at him, but other Hitler Youth boys loitered nearby. They burned with enough fervor to snitch.

A miserable face gazed out from a window in the train. The boy flinched at wretchedness that exceeded his own.

"This is dumb," Hans whined. "We do not need leaflets to tell us that the Amis are coming." A pause. "It will be the Amis. Right?"

"I think so," Klaus said.

"Not the Russians?" His brother's mouth twitched in anxiety.

"No. I think they are up in the north, around Berlin." He slid a sidelong look. "What do you know about the Russians?"

"I know that women are afraid of them. Mutti will not say why. Do you know?"

Klaus turned to the windswept grasses. "Maybe. I talked to some women refugees at the NSV. They had escaped the Russians. They had seen bad things."

"Like what?" Hans drew close.

"They saw Russian soldiers killing people. They said they saw German women being stripped naked and nailed to barn doors. The Russians have been leaving behind entire villages full of attacked women." Klaus shivered and clutched his woolen coat while remembering the expression those refugees wore. Their faces were so bleak and shattered they reminded him of broken porcelain dolls. The word *Vergewaltigung* had baffled him at first, but then he had observed a girl clamping her legs so tight that her knees trembled, and she had folded her hands in her lap, positioning them in such a guarded manner. He had absorbed enough obscene banter from older Hitler Youth troopers to surmise what it meant, and avoided mentioning that part to his eleven-year-old brother. Hans' milky features turned sour.

"Don't worry. The reports on the radio say the Russians are far away." Klaus felt a rush of relief for Mutti's sake. It terrified him, the thought of her suffering through *Vergewaltigung*.

The pert line of Hans' lips curdled further. "But what about the Amis? The troop leader calls them 'gangsters.' What are gangsters?"

"Are you sure you want to know?"

"Yea."

Klaus glanced at the train. That disconcerting face scarred with lines and pits of anguish retreated from the window. "All right. But don't tell Mutti I told you this, you will get me into the devil's kitchen." His brother nodded anxiously.

"'Gangsters' are criminals who get paid for murder," he said. Hans recoiled. "They sneak up on a man in dark places and shoot him, and dump his body in a river, or some hole where nobody will ever find him."

"Dump him? Like in the Naab River?" Hans squealed. Klaus whipped a finger to his lips. "That is horrible! Who told you that?"

"Refugees from the cities. They are always talking about films, just like Headmaster Schmitt. I guess if one lives in the city, one goes constantly to the cinema." Klaus sniffed against the cold, scratched his nose with a sleeve. "There were a lot of films that came over from America—before the war, I think. Some are about gangsters who run around cities like Chicago, shooting people up." He frowned at his brother. "Better pick up something before you get into trouble." Hans chased a leaflet tumbling in the breeze.

"The newsreels have speeches by the Führer. He says that America is full of gangsters and they are coming to shoot us all, so the militia has got to shoot them first."

Hans twisted his mouth, deliberating. "If America is full of gangsters, then how come the Provinsche never talks about them? He lived in America for fifty years!"

"I don't know. It is just what I heard."

"You know what? I think that stuff about the Amis is just talk. The Amis are going to be just like the Provinsche."

Klaus longed to share that hope, yet he found it impossible to dismiss an ominous fact. "The Provinsche is not a soldier trained to kill Germans."

"The Amis are free people," Hans continued cheerfully. "That is what Mutti says. When they come, nobody will get into trouble for dumb things, like reading letters in church, or reading leaflets. I bet they will let us put our crosses in school—"

Spring winds rustled grasses.

"Hans?" Klaus said.

A leaflet dangled between his brother's slim fingers. "I read something about white flags. It was an accident, I swear."

"Yea. The Amis are telling us what to do."

"You *read* it? But we have orders!" Hans gawked and spun around to survey the field. "Klaus? What does it say?"

"Shh! Stupid order." His mentor would condone this as one of those squirrelly instances of understandable insubordination. The Amis had printed the message in German, ensuring that civilians would read it. Across the field, their troop leader harangued a fat, sobbing kid for overlooking a leaflet. "They say we are supposed to stay in our homes and hang white flags outside our windows. If we do that, and if nobody shoots at them, then nobody will get hurt."

"But what if we don't have white flags at home?" Hans' chestnut eyes flew wide.

"I don't know. Maybe we use Mutti's dish towels."

A gunshot echoed from the forest glen. Both brothers peered at the leaflet, then shared a stare.

"Hans," Klaus said, "don't worry. No matter what happens, I will take care of you and Mutti. All right?"

The maw gaped before them. He felt its breath gusting like a bitter and putrid wind. He was fifteen and he had no idea how he would protect anyone when the inferno of war came raging into their lives, but Papa offered reassurance during moments like this. So did Herr Amtsleiter Seiz. Apprehension ebbed from Hans' face.

"Hans? Um. Can I ask you something?" Klaus fidgeted. "You remember that stuff the Provinsche said about prayers? What if. Well, is it—?" He wriggled, his attention sliding back to the train. "Oh, never mind, this is stupid."

"What?"

"God cannot work through someone who doesn't believe in all that religion stuff. Can He? I mean, to answer a prayer."

Hans bobbed his head back and forth, considering. "What if He can? What if He is just that powerful?"

Klaus fingered a pin adorning his coat collar. He turned south, where smoke curled above the ruins of Schwandorf.

"I think He is so powerful and His ways are so mysterious, He can work through anyone," his brother piped. "You know what? He is working through you."

Klaus swung back to him.

"What do you mean?"

"I prayed for Papa because I didn't want to live without a father. My prayer was answered, just in a different way." Hans stooped to collect a leaflet. He smiled up. "You look after me, just like Papa did. When I look for an example of what a man should be, I look to you, because you are tough and all, but you are kind at the same time, just like he was. God could not answer the prayer the way I hoped, but He is answering the *need* behind my prayer. And to do that, He is working through you."

Klaus held a breath until his chest ached. "Um. You missed a leaflet. Better get it before that troop leader yells."

Hans scampered. Klaus felt a lemon sun waxing full upon his face and his thoughts swept back to that secret shore where he grieved daily over Papa's death. A realization washed up amid cold, flinty rocks. "*Nein!*" He cast it away, but a split second later it drifted back, refusing to be dismissed. Hans grinned, his dimpled face aglow in a shiny veneration Klaus had failed to notice before. Fear and grief plunked into the pit of his stomach like leaden weights, but he hauled himself up. Death swallowed Papa whole, maybe Herr Amtsleiter as well. Leutnant Heidl was no longer just a follower. Today he was a leader. A younger presence drew strength from him, just as he had sought it from his father and mentor, and they would expect better from the boy they had nurtured gently beneath their iron wings.

The thump of boots tugged his attention. A cluster of officers disembarked from the train and exchanged salutes with the station-master. Klaus observed them in glances: crisp overcoats. Gray caps, black banding beneath peaked crowns. Sunlight glinted upon silver ornaments. Cap insignias intrigued him. The one that graced Papa's had been ornate, a delicate swastika fringed by oak leaves, but the emblems mounted upon these officers' caps were austere clumps of metal. Looking closer, he made out the symbol: a *Totenkopf*, a death's-head skull. They were SS officers. He shivered, feeling a strange and sudden chill.

"I wonder where this train is from and where it was going?" Hans pondered.

"I don't know." Klaus breathed in the scent of damp grasses. The Miesbergkirche bell tolled the hour: 8:00 a.m. "It cannot go farther south, that is certain."

"It is all shot up," Hans said.

"Huh?"

"The train is shot up. See?"

"Oh." Bullet holes perforated the cars. "It must be taking our soldiers to the east," Klaus said. "Our enemies must have shot at it to stop reinforcements from reaching the front."

"There must be a whole army inside. Look at the boxcars. *Eins, zwei, drei,*" Hans' finger bounced. "Twenty-three. Did you see the men in there? They look miserable."

"You would too, if you were being sent to war." Klaus poked bullet holes and waited for that soldier to approach the window again. He wanted to hear about the sorrows etched in his face.

He whirled at a strange impression that a line of sparrows had leapt into flight behind him. "What was that?"

The sky tore open. It screamed above him.

"Hans! RUN!"

Boys scattered. Hans fled. Papers flew. Klaus' mind blanked, but his body knew what to do. Panic induced an astounding transformation. It changed him from a sinewy boy to a human bullet, a projectile that bit the air and sprouted legs thrusting out and down and back and out and down and back as fast as joints and muscles and shivery tendons permitted and his hands were two giant clamps squeezing speed into a racing bloodstream, all while a behemoth drummer pounded the train, *rat-tat-tat, rat-tat-tat, rat-tat-tat-tat-tat-tat!* The sky roared. Brutal winds lashed sandy hair. His heart, his heart! He slowed almost to a stop, nearly wheeled at a sickening notion that the organ catapulted from his rib cage and he would have to teeter around bullets while straining to find it. Then, *oh, good, there it is,* still thumping beneath a wool coat, its feral beat leaving him lightheaded, breathless. Hans dove into a grassy thicket. Klaus thudded beside him. Weeds and sticks enfolded them like a quivering nest.

"Stay down!"

"*Jawohl,*" Hans whimpered.

Klaus hugged him tight. If stray bullets zipped from the blue, at least his little brother would remain unharmed. Safe for the moment, he craned his neck to peer skyward.

"There are airplanes. Two of them." Small and agile, they soared with deadly grace. "The planes have stars and stripes on them. That means Amis, right?"

"But they cannot be here already," Hans protested, "we don't have our flags out yet!"

Klaus' gaze plummeted to a doomed convoy. A plane opened fire. The boxcars shuddered. The boxcars belted a ripply scream. SS officers hunched, ducking bullets, heaving open doors.

"They are coming. They are coming out!"

He braced himself for the heart-stopping sight of German soldiers surging forth in a gray-green tide, their guns raised to return a barrage of death. When the train's passengers thrashed into daylight, his jaw fell.

"Oh, no."

American planes bucked and trembled, as if the pilots were weaving a tapestry of curses in their cockpits. Their guns fell silent.

Hans gasped. "Klaus. This train is not carrying soldiers!"

"Yea, I see that." He felt just as shocked as the Amis.

"They are wearing striped uniforms and star badges. Who are those people?"

"Get down."

"I want to know what is going on!" Hans squawked.

"No, you don't."

"Is that shooting?"

"Of course it is shooting."

"Who is shooting? Not the planes. They stopped!"

"Stay down, you hear? If someone sees that brown hair of yours in this field, they might pull a trigger."

Klaus gulped and lifted a sandy head above dry grasses. He felt no inclination to witness more carnage, but a younger presence reminded him that he was Leutnant Heidl, and a true leader remained aware of his situation, sniffing out danger, protecting his men. *What happened to the leaflet collectors?* Papers littered the field. They had fled when planes roared out of the mad blue, he figured.

Ami pilots circled overhead. They were trying to fathom this flood of men in stripes and golden stars. Klaus recoiled. Bony phantoms filled the field, the same specters of living death that once haunted his childhood nightmares and sent him bolting to Mutti and Papa's room in the black night, but he saw the way these men huddled against the train, and he read such terror in their faces that he wilted in pity. He doubted they feared the Americans—despite the strafing that shredded a boxcar, five prisoners waved striped caps in the delirious manner of men greeting saviors—but the majority cowered, their tension beyond his understanding.

What are they afraid of? he wondered.

Klaus watched a prisoner crouching the way he would before a foot race, his knees bent, his mind focused. The man leapt. Then another. SS guards shouted. An SS man leveled a pistol. "Oh!" Klaus cupped back a cry. Escapees tumbled into loose, rubbery heaps, but that failed to satisfy the guard. He stomped over and shot bullets into corpses to ensure that they lay dead.

"What is happening?" Hans pleaded. "Who is shooting?"

Klaus' voice refused to work. He found it impossible to believe what he had just witnessed, let alone explain it.

Airy buzzing heightened to a pitch that reminded him of enraged bees. The Amis dove. The Amis swept low. The Amis were firing again. Another teeth-rattling *rat-tat-tat-tat-tat* burst from torn skies, but this time pilots directed hot, heavy fire upon the train engine. Klaus ducked. Hans covered his ears. Shots ricocheted, whizzing overhead, plucking trees, slicing branches, until at last the deafening orchestra of drumming lead and violin bullets erupted in cataclysm. Hans screeched. Metal shards flipped end over end, hurtling through the dappled sky until gravity remembered itself and they thunked down, shocking the silent ground.

American planes rumbled away. The attack began and ended so swiftly that the air wardens had no time to sound an alarm.

Spring winds hissed through swaying maples. Klaus stiffened at the broadening silence. A distant voice shouted in High German:

"On your feet, you rats!"

Hans' face ripened into tears. "Is that our troop leader?"

"No." Klaus clung to the ground. "It is an SS man. Stay down."

His brother's apple face squeezed out of shape. Leutnant Heidl thought of his mentor. Now he understood why Seiz declared a good heart as the best of virtues.

"Hans, I know you are scared. I am also. But nobody will hurt you. I am in charge, and I will get us out of this."

A sniffle. "All right." Dark eyes glimmered above a wavery smile. "The train is all busted. What are they going to do?"

"I have no idea." Klaus cocked an ear. "Wait. Something is happening."

"Line up!" One SS guard bellowed across the field. "Line up. If a man is too injured to walk, he will be shot."

"Klaus, can we get out of here?" Hans whined.

"We cannot be seen, that is certain." His mind felt like a roaring gale, his thoughts loose leaves blasted in all directions. *Why would they shoot men who cannot walk?* His jaw dropped at the sight of a legion that stretched beyond view.

"The men are getting up. The SS are making them stand in formation. There must be hundreds of them, Hans."

A bang galloped over the windblown fields. Klaus met his brother's owlish stare and refused to look elsewhere.

Thunder. It shocked a hazy sky. It stilled the winds. Baffled the hills. A carrion crow perched in a stark maple. It cawed toward the fields. "No, don't shoot—" Screams clawed at Klaus' spine. A plea for mercy shivered in his skull. "I walk. Look—" He envisioned pistols rising, smoke curling from hot metal, but at that point his imagination turned impish, swapping the bodies of prisoners with the straw bags that his Hitler Youth leader propped up across a shooting range before target practice. Screams leapt in a bizarre language. Hans' pupils reflected Klaus' face in detail, showing a mouth working in tiny movements, counting thunder, "ten, fifteen, twenty!" and the higher that toll climbed, the tighter he clung to visions of SS officers shooting burlap bags, for he could not believe the reality unfolding in his train station, his Schwarzenfeld, his Germany. He was Leutnant Heidl, a mere boy accompanied by an adjutant, but they could no longer hunker in the grass, listening to this symphony of torment.

"Come on Hans. If we crawl, perhaps we can leave unseen. We will go to the police and see if we can get help."

———

Bedlam erupted along the Hauptstrasse at noon. Helene met the black marble gaze of a Polish laborer holding his bread bag wide. She shot a glance in Maria's direction.

"You don't suppose the Amis are here?" the widow said.

Maria pulled a hand to her cheek. "Oh, heavens. But, the wardens would sound the alarm, I should think. Don't you?"

Helene shrugged, not knowing what to expect when an army invaded one's town. Their Polish customer hugged his bread sack, turning. Customers swiveled warily toward the parlor door. Men bellowed orders from the Bahnhofstrasse, their words grayed by distance, yet loud enough for Helene to detect raw panic. If the Amis had arrived she would have to race home. She shuddered at the possibility of finding her boys still out and about and then traipsing through unknown perils to find them.

Maria withered. "That does not sound good."

"It sounds like the police are clearing the streets." Helene leapt to her feet. "I think something is happening."

Maria's shoes clapped across the parlor floor. "Norbert!" Pans clattered from the kitchen where her husband and four daughters were rolling out the next bake.

"Move aside!" Helene cried. She bumped shoulders on her way to the windows. "*Bitte!* Please! Move aside. Let me through!" Familiar patrons crowded her, mostly Polish and Russian *Fremd-arbeiter* emerging fresh from their morning labors in the factories. Despite Gestapo orders, they still ambled freely into the bakery, ration stamps in hand. Russian laborers nodded hasty greetings to Helene, stepping aside, permitting her room to open the blinds. Zizi stomped up. Frantic refugee women squawked questions, begging to know what transpired outside.

"I have no idea what is going on," Helene hissed in frustration. "People are moving off the Hauptstrasse, they are blocking the window, I cannot see a thing!"

"Yelena," Zizi said. "You are all fear."

"Of course I am all fear, I have no idea what is happening, I am scared out of my wits!"

"No worry. Zizi will go see."

She turned to him. "You remember, Yelena?" The Russian pointed at a pink scar that marred his nose, an indelible reminder of the Gestapo encounter. "You and Maria help Zizi, and now Zizi, he will help you. No worry." He rocked on his heels and regarded the German woman with a lopsided smile.

"I go now."

"*Danke*, Zizi," she breathed. "*Danke schön.*" Helene admonished herself for snapping at him. A refugee woman's features slid into sheer incredulity. "He is our friend." The widow shook her head when German customers exchanged bewildered looks. She understood their shock. It was an extraordinary friendship, given the state of their world.

A heartbeat later, Zizi burst back into the parlor. "Yelena," he panted. "There are men. Many men outside."

She gasped. "Amis?"

"No. Not soldiers. They are here, coming. You come see." He clasped her wrist. "You will come look, now!"

Helene vacillated between compliance and an impulse to race straight home. "All right. Just one look, then I must leave to check on my boys."

Daylight sliced down between plaster houses in long white shafts. The widow squinted, and when her sight cleared, the spectacle confronting her seared into living memory. She paled at a dreadful certainty that Hell's gates swung wide at the train station and every soul condemned to suffer eternal damnation lurched up the Bahnhofstrasse. They surged forth like a slow-moving river, their heads shaven, eyes bleak, sunken, bereft of hope. A man collapsed into a heap. "Let me die," he moaned, "let me die!" But fellow prisoners hauled him to his feet. A multitude marching from torment into torment, they plodded up the road until it veered into the Hauptstrasse, then they turned southeast, staggering toward the Naab River bridge. A chorus of murmurs and shrieks filled narrow caverns between houses. Frau Schmitt, wife of the school headmaster, collected a bawling grandchild and slammed her door. Herr Gietl hobbled to the roadside, pointing. "Look! *Juden.* They are *Juden!*" A wasted visage lifted to Helene. The widow felt time itself falling away, and she heard a voice thundering to her across the ages:

My God, my God, why have you forsaken me?

"Oh, Jesus!" She cupped her mouth. A battered specter of Christ wore a golden star, and He was turning to her, imploring.

Bürgermeister Braun and Officer Dobler stalked up the Bahnhofstrasse. They edged through, immersed in discussion:

". . . a report of shooting," the police chief stammered, "so I expected bodies. One, two, ten, but there must be more than one hundred dead lying in that train station! The Americans are nearly here, Herr Bürgermeister. What would you have me do?"

Helene stood bloodless, not knowing what appalled her more: the report of a massacre or their blindness to pain.

Motion stirred. Zizi. Norbert. Maria collapsed against her husband's shoulder. A moment stretched before he noticed and drew his wife close. Zizi of all people remained collected enough to discern Russians trudging past them. He prattled in his native tongue. To Helene's astonishment, prisoners turned and responded in the confiding manner of men who recognized a countryman. They carried on a conversation in bursts.

"Many here are Ukrainian, some Poles, a few Germans," he drawled grimly. "All Jews. They come from *gulag* in Germany. What you call 'KZ.'" His accent thickened his pronunciation of the two German letters.

"A *Konzentrationslager*." Norbert seethed like a kettle that threatened to boil over. "What KZ, Zizi? Where are they from?"

"Flossenbürg." The town lay about sixty kilometers north of Schwarzenfeld.

Helene met the baker's stunned gaze.

The laborer spoke bursts of Russian, then angled his head, listening. "They say . . . they say Amis were coming to their camp. They were close, they heard guns. The guards put them on train so enemies could not set them free. The train was shot by planes. Three times was attacked. And now is," he groped for words, "is broken. They are walking now."

"Where are they going?" Helene asked.

"They do not know. They say it does not matter." His voice faltered. "They know they die before they get there."

Maria sobbed on Norbert's shoulder. "Can they escape?" the baker asked.

The Russian questioned prisoners. "Some have tried. The death-heads, they kill fifteen Jews for each that runs."

Guards and commanding officers stalked up the roadway like dread shadows. Pistols and rifles in hand, they ordered Schwarzenfelders to step back. Norbert's face shifted into a mask of revulsion.

"SS. Ohh," he hissed, his head shaking, "Hell cannot burn hot enough for those *Schweinehunde*."

"Norbert," Helene said. "Look."

Prisoners lifted fingers to their mouths in a pitiful gesture. The Pole Helene served five minutes earlier tore his loaf and secreted chunks into grasping hands.

"They have got nothing to eat and nothing to drink since they got on the train," Zizi reported. "This was five days past."

"Maria." Norbert stirred. "Come, *mein Schatz*. We must work quickly." He shot a look to Helene. "Our normal customers will have to tighten their belts."

She caught the gist. "Yes, all right. You go get the bread, I will distribute it."

Norbert nodded. "Zizi?" The Russian swiveled. "You and these Poles better get back inside. I don't need to tell you what those SS will do if they see you standing here."

They departed. The widow leaned one shoulder against the ivy-fringed door and felt a hot sting welling in her eyes. "Flossenbürg." Until today, no Schwarzenfelder questioned what occurred beyond the barbed wire shroud of a concentration camp. They were prisons, and that forbidding fact dissuaded them from pondering further. She wept, haunted by questions, fearing the implications for her homeland, her Germany, and the river kept flowing. A stream of men and stripes and tattered stars plodded by, drawing their fingers to parched lips. A cadaverous inmate with hollow eyes and gaunt cheeks stared at her, the features elongated, distinctly Russian. She wondered if this explained why the Red Army performed abominable acts of hatred against German women and children.

What will the Amis think after they see this?

It occurred to her that someone should summon Fr. Viktor. *Later, fetch him later.* What could he do anyway, when he was holed up in that church? After absorbing eight years of his ministry, she knew what he would tell his parishioners.

Doors moaned open all along the Hauptstrasse. Women emerged, cupping potatoes or bread bits in their palms. Helene dug a thumbnail between her teeth, watching. Housewives crept toward inmates, their arms outstretched in a tenuous, flighty posture. "You there!" Pistol in hand, an SS officer drove them back. "Get back in your homes! No one feeds the prisoners."

"Oh, God." Helene's hand dropped to the crucifix jingling at her throat. She felt a desperate urge to try.

Norbert and Maria's eldest daughter bustled from the bakery. "Mother keeps crying," the girl grunted, lugging a basket and water bucket, "and father is shouting to himself. I have never seen them in such a state."

Helene froze. One of the guards. He was prowling toward her, a rifle slung over his shoulder. "Jesus, be with me." She kissed her cross pendant and gripped the bread basket.

"What are you doing?"

She drew a breath at the rifle, tore her gaze from the rifle, forced herself to ignore pale fingers cradling the rifle, as if through sheer will she could wish away this implement of coercion and death.

"What does it look like? We are feeding your prisoners. These people are starving, can you not see that! Let them go!"

Beneath his felt cap the guard narrowed eyes like chips of sky. "No." His filthy hand plucked a slice of bread, turning it in cynical examination. "But since you have taken the trouble to bring this out, you will feed us Germans."

Guards thickened around Helene and the widow clutched wicker until her bones quaked. "What do you have for us?" they said. Their faces rolled plump beneath stubble. She fought sickness while listening to smacking lips, nasal inhalations between bites, the crinkle of tongues rolling in dry mouths, and the thick, sick, gluttonous sound of tissues contracting during a swallow. "Water? Over here, girl!" Each guard groped for a second slice, then a third, all while Jews staggered behind them, starving, pleading, dying, and Helene bit back a shriek, hoping against hope that her cooperation might buy her one chance, just one desperate chance to reach men in pain. "Don't tell your father about this," the widow quavered to Norbert's daughter. The girl's doe-brown eyes flashed wide.

Crumbs snowed into an empty basket, and Helene gestured. The Gindele daughter whisked back into the bakery.

"You call that bread?" The guard's head lolled back. "More like potatoes masquerading as a loaf. The skins are even baked in."

The ivy door swung open. The Gindele daughter upturned a bag. Fresh slices cascaded down with a hot whisper. Helene held the basket, her grip steady and determined.

"You men are fed. Now we are feeding the prisoners."

"Why would an Aryan woman like you care about the vermin of an inferior race? They are a pestilence to our people. A burden."

"I am a Catholic woman, *mein Herr.* God works through me to help all who suffer in this world, no matter who they are."

"No. Save your bread for German customers." The SS guard turned away.

"This bread is sliced!" She shouted after him. "The bread is sliced, it cannot be sold!" Her persistence tethered his attention and wrangled it back. "The ration laws are specific about the ingredients that must be in each loaf. Now that it is sliced, we can no longer tell if we are doling out precise rations." She surveyed him, weighing the effect of an entirely different appeal. "It is practical. You see? The bread is useless. You might as well let us feed your prisoners."

The guard smirked. "My wife is soft-hearted, like you. She would sooner feed the rats that chew holes in our pantry floor than set traps to kill them."

Helene swallowed a rise of vomit while imagining herself married to this man. She would dine upon hemlock if she were that woman, and leave hearty portions for a hungry spouse.

"You there, girl," he said. Norbert and Maria's daughter lifted her chin, her eyes averted. "You tell the people in there to stop slicing bread. *Jetzt*—now!" A filthy hand pilfered another serving, flicked away crumbs, then shook a finger.

"Distribute what has been cut already. But that is all. Do you understand?"

Helene glared.

"Of course."

After issuing commands, the SS guard stalked off. The widow braced herself. They would stampede their way to this basket, these prisoners. Their starvation entitled them to descend upon her like wolves. She stood in jaw-dropping dismay while men lined up, meek as children fearing the wrath of an oppressive parent, and they filed up one at a time in such tentative fashion that it wrung her heart. Bony fingers trembled into the basket. Broomstick wrists protruded from frayed sleeves. The sight made her face bloom and twist in a mortifying spectacle, but Helene let her tears flow unhindered before the Jews. When she shuffled off her mortal coil and approached Heaven's gate on a road paved with gold stones, these people would soar straight to God's throne, their passage assured by agony beyond her blackest dreams.

A prisoner hobbled up, his mouth puckering in misery. "The last thing I had to eat was a handful of grain," he warbled. "That was five days ago!"

"Listen," she sobbed. "I know how hard it is to believe this. But God sees you. He does. He is with you in your suffering."

Haggard wells of misery shifted up, overwhelming her with the anguish of a dying man entombed in a tormented world. "Well. At least this gives me a little hope. For today." He plucked a bread slice. "For this, I thank you." He vanished into the river of stars.

A break developed in the death march, and the Hauptstrasse cleared enough for her to catch a glimpse of bystanders fringing the street. She gasped.

"Klaus. Hans! Oh my God, where have you been?"

They lugged themselves over with the raw, wept-out look of children who had absorbed far too much hell for their tender years. Helene passed the bread basket to Norbert and Maria's daughter. She kissed Hans' hair, breathing in its sweaty ginger scent, and smoothed the locks of her eldest while he droned through a horrific narrative of their morning.

"We told the police about the shooting," Klaus said, "but there was so much confusion, I don't think anyone did anything."

They had attempted to help, and its futility grieved them. The authorities would never intervene, not under these circumstances. "Oh, my boys." Helene embraced her sons. "I am so sorry."

Klaus gloomed at prisoners. "Is there anything we can do?"

"You wish to help?" Motherly pride bloomed amid Helene's tears. Hans picked up his head and nodded. "The Gindele girls are going to bring out buckets of water with ladles. Why don't you boys help them?" They agreed. "And, Klaus?"

"Yea?" He turned.

"Remember that question you asked?" Helene said. "I think the answer is before you, my dear boy. If God could work through anyone, then surely these men would not be suffering so terribly. He can work only through a heart that is capable of love."

Klaus sank into reflection, his fingers stroking a shield pin. She sensed weighty cogitations behind that young face, fresh thoughts taking root. Helene said a prayer for him, then another for the river of souls marching toward death, and finally, one for Schwarzenfeld.

CHAPTER THIRTEEN

THE AMERICAN ARRIVAL

April 22, 1945

"There was a pounding on my door. When I opened it, they were there, Pater. I was afraid for my life."

On Sunday morning Fr. Viktor bowed his head in the gloom of the Miesbergkirche confessional. A whisper shuddered through an iron lattice separating priest from penitent.

"Who was there?"

"The SS men. Officer Dobler had brought them. Even Dobler's eyes were wide in fear. The leader said, 'Come with us, and bring your wagon.' Then he asked me, 'Do you lime your fields?' I said yes. 'Bring all the lime that you have,' he said."

The provincial's brow furrowed. *Lime?* In Schwarzenfeld, farmers scattered limestone powder over their fields to reduce soil acidity and ensure proper crop growth. *Why lime?*

"Go on," Fr. Viktor said.

"They were SS. What could I do except obey? They led me to the train station. *Mein Gott,* it looked like the floor of Hell. So many bodies littered the field, I nearly crushed them beneath my wagon." His parishioner shifted on a bench in the two-hundred-year-old confessional. Fr. Viktor sat riveted, his stomach in knots. "Three other farmers rolled up in their wagons. We just looked at each other in horror. The prisoners. The ones who were still alive, able-bodied. They started—they loaded the dead into our wagons. Oh, God!"

"All right," Fr. Viktor eased. His nose twitched at a pale odor of sweat amidst fragrant and aging oak. "When was this?"

"Friday. It was, eh. It was at 11:00 in the morning. Just before the last of the prisoners was marched through town."

"I see."

"This is unbearable. It feels like a sin to be involved."

"I understand."

"Even this small thing they demanded of me."

"I know. Go on."

"Yes, Pater." The farmer strained to collect himself. "While the bodies were being loaded, the SS men and Bürgermeister Braun were talking. They had to be buried quickly, he said. The gang—I mean, the Amis," the farmer amended. "They are almost here! I heard the SS leader tell the mayor that the prisoners would look to the dead, but a place had to be found for their remains. A suitable place. That is what he said. 'Suitable!' Then, the leader, he got into the wagon, beside me. He told me . . ."

"What did he tell you?"

"He told me where to take the bodies."

"Where did you take them?"

When his parishioner blurted the answer, Fr. Viktor stared at sallow daylight seeping beneath the confessional door.

"Pater?"

Fr. Viktor found his voice in darkness. The man had complied out of mortal fear, and he wept with such remorse that the provincial offered absolution to ease a perturbed soul.

"Listen. I realize this is a dangerous thing to say, but about the Americans. Don't believe everything you hear. They want peace." He seethed at inflammatory rants that kindled German media. Hitler stopped at nothing to stiffen resistance against his countrymen.

"Yes, it is dangerous. If Braun or Officer Dobler knew what you just said, then both of us could be shot, Pater."

"I have no doubt." He kneaded a temple.

"But Pater?"

"Yeah."

A whisper gusted through the lattice. "They will hear nothing from me. This I promise."

"Go in peace," Fr. Viktor said. Once the farmer departed, he let his brow sink into weathered hands. "Oh my Jesus." Stories of men in torment chilled him, but that was only the beginning. "The lime." Aside from its agricultural uses, powdered lime inhibited bacterial growth and masked odors. He recalled torrid summer days in his boyhood when he had pinched his nostrils and shook a tinful into the pit of a family outhouse.

Darkness fell in velvet swaths. He strained to see beyond it and read shadows aligning in the Framework. Last Friday, a fist had tapped his sacristy door and Paula Dirrigl's maid bustled inside, a basket in hand. After delivering lunch, the young woman, an incorrigible gossip, tugged a chair across the dingy room. "Like a bunch of stirred-up bees we all are," she had burred in her local dialect. "One would think that somebody stirred up a beehive, Pater, and we are shaken up inside, not knowing what to do!" But they had known what to do. They had needed no prompting. Helene and the Gindeles had distributed a day's worth of bread before SS men shut down their roadside stand in wrath. Three Jews had crept into barns around town, and frightened, harried farmers secretly cared for them. A fourth had ducked into the *Gasthof Bauer,* Schwarzenfeld's guesthouse, where his presence wrenched a crowded barroom to silence. Herr Bauer, the innkeeper, had ushered him to a table, served him a bowl of soup, and pushed a wall of bewildered guests to a respectful distance. They had obeyed, except for one German refugee woman who felt inspired. She had wrapped her arm around the Jew in motherly fashion and implored him to eat a little slower. Her name was Rosa Semff.

Fr. Viktor's eyes teared in grief for victims of brutality. His parishioners had reacted the same way. He had trained them to view life through the prism of Christ's Passion. When the Americans arrived, they would stumble upon the remains of a massacre. The Schwarzenfelders would desperately need him to explain what had transpired and identify the men responsible. *But the "suitable place." My God. How do I explain that?*

———

The confession revealed one impending disaster to Fr. Viktor. While Catholics hastened to Mass at noon, new crises brewed in town. A mob swelled and choked the Hauptstrasse. Horses screeched at frantic whips. Wagons shuddered, speeding refugees away from Russian hordes that marched only forty miles east of Schwarzenfeld.

In the midst of hysteria an infant squalled. Its fist-clenching wail soared above a second human wave limping up the Deiselkühner Weg road from the south. Their faces were grimy, bloody, peppered with burns and lacerations.

"We have come from Schwandorf!" A wretched woman in a scorched overcoat and shredded stockings floundered up the roadway. "*Hilfe!* Help, please! We are survivors from the bombing. We have only the clothes on our backs. We have children who have eaten nothing in four days. Nor have I myself. Can you find it within yourselves to be charitable with your supplies? *Bitte!*" She mustered her languishing strength and waved at wagons, but their occupants pretended not to hear.

At Schwarzenfeld's Rathaus, Bürgermeister Braun slammed down his phone and shoved his way toward the Naab River bridge. The wretched woman lunged after him. She muttered her party affiliation and neglected to hail Hitler. "Herr Bürgermeister. There you are. I have been ordered to advise you. We have been waiting for relief in Schwandorf. Nothing has come. More survivors are on the way. My husband will arrive with them soon. We require food, water. Shelter. Even barns will—*mein Herr.* Are you listening? Stop, will you! Please, I beg you. Stop—" She halted in the road and sank to her bruised and bloody knees. "Ohh God! What is *wrong* with you people? If there is a God, help us!"

A brawl erupted between a refugee and looters plundering his cart. Gunshots rang out. Braun stomped off, oblivious, consumed by yet another emergency more dire than this one.

Three olive-green trucks plowed through bedlam unnoticed. They were *Holzbrenners.* He discerned that much from the pungency wringing tears from his eyes. Their engines had been converted to run on fumes from burning wood, virtually the only fuel attainable in this decimated country. SS men dressed in greatcoats and sleek boots leapt out. They clotted around the Naab River bridge, scrutinizing its iron beams.

Swastika-stamped papers slid into Braun's hands. The mayor read words aloud to himself and turned pale:

". . . American armored units sighted in Amberg. Orders are to deny them a crossing over the Naab River and slow the invasion. The town is to be defended. Citizens flying white flags to be shot as traitors. *Volkssturm* to be summoned . . ."

They barked salutes in reverence to Hitler. SS men hauled out crates. Braun ogled their cargo: a stash of automatic rifles, tank-obliterating *panzerfausts*, and waxy, brown sticks bearing an ominous label—*DYNAMIT*.

At the Miesbergkirche altar Fr. Viktor lifted a *paten*, a plate holding Eucharist hosts during a prayer that transubstantiated bread and wine into the body and blood of Christ. While horror slept on Schwarzenfeld's borders and SS men strung detonation cables around bridge abutments, he chanted urgently in Latin:

"*Líbera nos, quæsumus Dómine, ab ómnibus malis prætéritis, præséntibus, et futúris.* Deliver us, we beseech Thee, O Lord, from all evils past, present, and those to come . . . through Thy mercy, let us be free from sin, and protected from danger."

Fr. Viktor swallowed a wafer that tasted of dread and human torment, dry and bleak and bitter. His hands trembled as he drank deep from a chalice.

There were moments when the world spun hopelessly out of control and the soul searched desperately for answers, for higher meaning, for an indication that God still played a cosmic chess match, trying to maneuver around evil. *This is one of those times.* He knew how to proceed when American forces rolled in and the dust settled. He would explain the suitable place and encourage them to hunt down SS men marching Jews into a dark, desolate unknown. With any luck, these doomed men would lift their eyes to American liberators by morning and discover that they had a new lease on life. But these were straightforward problems. First, he would have to answer another question for his countrymen.

Why is an American citizen living behind German lines?

Fr. Viktor pinched a round, white wafer between his thumb and forefinger. "*Corpus Christi*, Body of Christ." Parishioners herded around the communion rail, a practice specific to German pilgrimage churches. In all other parishes where he had celebrated Mass, the faithful lined up in single or double lines before their priest. "*Corpus Christi.*" He slid a host upon the tongue of a weeping Paula Dirrigl. "*Corpus Christi.*" Norbert approached the altar in a state of inner torment. "*Corpus Christi.*" Maria bit back a sob and accepted a wafer. "*Corpus Christi.*"

Helene swept forward, so earnest and dear. At this dark hour, she alone was incandescent, kindled by a light that stunned him. Then she moved aside. "*Corpus—*"

Klaus stood before him, hands cupped for a host. He wore a black suit that once belonged to his father; a shield pin gleamed upon his lapel. "*Corpus Christi.*"

The boy padded back to his pew and knelt in prayer, hoisting all fears into God's hands.

The provincial's features burst in unalloyed joy. *My Germans.* Oh, he loved these people. Gazing upon them from the altar, he felt paternal devotion burn in his heart and rush through his veins, but therein lay the problem. How could he tell the difference between love rooted in a sacred mission, and one sprouting from an affinity for the country that nurtured his mother, his father, and every ancestor that came before them? What if God had woven a different destiny for him back in America, a design that unraveled the instant he had stubbornly entrenched himself in that minuscule sacristy? Seiz had argued the case with terrible certainty, and surely Grennan would agree. After the Miesbergkloster eviction, his father superior wrote him from Pittsburgh. He failed to see any reason justifying his decision to remain in Germany.

What if my presence here is not part of a mission from God? What if I've been following a path of my choosing this whole time?

Rain pelted the windows. Then a dull popping echoed outside. It came from the northwest, the direction of Amberg.

A scout plane raged overhead.

Dean Spangler ducked behind the communion rail. Screams shook the pews.

"Go in peace! Run for shelter. Hurry!" Fr. Viktor's dismissal triggered a stampede.

Alone in the emphatic emptiness of his church, he flung off gold-threaded vestments he had donned for Mass and wrestled back into Passionist garb. An urge to pray the rosary gripped him. "In the name of the Father, the Son, the Holy Spirit . . ."

A hammering heart deafened him to the rest of his prayer. He could feel mayhem outside.

At last, the Americans had arrived.

———

The air observer roared overhead at 2:00 p.m. The guns probing Schwarzenfeld's borders fell quiet. An iron silence persisted until 6:00, when a massive explosion jolted the town. That, Fr. Viktor assumed, was the Naab River bridge.

A peculiar sound made his breath still. At first he dismissed it as a bull lowing from a distant barnyard. Then it broke off with a metallic wheeze.

The church doors loomed before him like a gate between the untroubled life of a village monk and a surreal dimension of service far beyond anything he had experienced in fifty years of priesthood. He bolted outside.

Panicked gasps. Beads jingling. The acrid odor of smoke tinged the air. His boots splashed rain pools in a hazy courtyard.

Thunder shook the hill. An elephantine mass of army-green steel vaulted up to the Miesberg's crown. Then a second lunged into view. Three more. Five tanks converged upon him.

"Don't shoot! For God's sake. This town will surrender peacefully! These people are not your enemies!" He tore a kerchief from the pocket of a black overcoat and waved it frantically.

A helmet-covered silhouette shot up from the front tank.

"Colonel!" A voice bawled over the word-swallowing drone of diesel engines. "Hey. We got a Kraut here who speaks English!" The soldier whirled back. "Whadda ya mean, 'not enemies,' Father? This town's crawlin' with Nazis! And where the hell are the white flags?"

The romping flow of American English stirred an impulse to laugh and cry a river of tears, but Fr. Viktor focused.

"You're facing a crew of *Wehrmacht*, at most. Maybe SS. Don't pass judgment over this town because of them. They don't represent the people here." Sensing party intervention in the absence of flags, he reiterated peaceful intentions on Schwarzenfeld's behalf. "And by the way, I'll have you know you're on American property and speaking to an American citizen."

More helmets shot up against the stark sky. Diesel engines rumbled in consideration.

Three soldiers clambered down from their high perches on mammoth machines. Dressed neck to foot in brooding khaki, they stalked up, militant, vigilant, their stubble-covered faces so rigid that it made his spine stiffen. They radiated the aura of men who ducked bullets every day while riding on an adrenaline rush, chewing Doublemint to take off the edge. Reading its toll on them, Fr. Viktor heaved a breath, let it out slowly. His visitors warily surveyed the church tower; he raised open palms in peace, assuring their safety, but they weren't about to take him at his word. Rifles in hand, they ushered him into the courtyard, where the encircling plaster wall shielded them from the roar of idling Shermans.

"This here's American property, sir?" the first soldier asked, a twenty-something, given the supple skin around his hawkish eyes.

"That's right."

"And you're an American, sir?"

"That's what I said."

"Who won the last World Series?"

He angled his head. "I'm sorry?"

"Who's Dorothy Gale, sir, and what's the name of her dog?" the second soldier asked, equally young and deadly earnest.

A wind shook rain from the branches of budding maples.

"You ever heard of *The Wizard of Oz*, sir?"

Fr. Viktor flinched at tanks crowding the church gates. "The, ah, *The Wizard of*. . .? It's a children's book. I've never read it."

"Uh-huh."

The two young militants froze over with icy suspicion. The third American—a man nearing middle-age, given the faint lines etched around his breezy blue eyes and sculpted mouth—stood at a remove, assessing exchanges.

"Why are you asking these questions?" Fr. Viktor demanded.

"Sir. We get Nazi spies comin' out of the blue every day, posing as Americans, so they can penetrate our lines and blow our units to Hell. And you can't even answer a simple question from the States. Why should we believe you?"

He gulped at the sight of hands tightening around rifles. "Hey. We've started off on the wrong foot here. I'm sure this is, ah—yeah. Let's start over." This was going worse than he had expected. He rubbed his face with clammy hands, fumbled through an explanation of his mission, then pulled a paper from his coat pocket.

"Okay. Okay. Look here. See? This is my birth record. I was born in a town called Sharon. It's in Pennsylvania, about an hour northwest of Pittsburgh. Surely you've heard of—"

"Yeah, all Krauts have got flawless paperwork," the first soldier said without giving the birth certificate a glance. "You tell us, Father. What are the odds of finding an American in a dirt patch like this?"

"It's unlikely, I understand that. But it's true."

"You say you're Nikolaus, ah . . ." The second soldier frowned at his last name: *Koch*. "Is that Kotch? Koe? Koke?"

"You pronounce it like the English word *cook*." His teeth ground in annoyance. The Germans enunciated his name fluidly, but those four letters gave Americans no end of trouble. "Yes, 'Koch' is a German name. Lots of Americans have German roots."

"Colonel," the first soldier said, glaring at Fr. Viktor, "you want us to take him in for questioning?"

Blue eyes shifted in deliberation below an olive helmet. "I do find it hard to believe that the Germans are just gonna let an American roam free." He took the birth certificate from Fr. Viktor's outstretched hand.

"I've got, ah. What's the word? Forgive me. I've been speaking German for—" Oh, damn. His nerves. Fr. Viktor kneaded his brow, straining to crush forgotten knowledge back into memory. "It's called, ah. Twice? No—*dual* citizenship! That's it." He withered at an absurd notion that his freedom rested upon knowing the name of a fictional woman's dog.

"Okay, look. I'm sure everything I'm telling you sounds far-fetched, and if I were in your shoes, I'd be real skeptical too. There's a lot about this 'dirt patch' that's unusual for a German town. Now, I'm sorry I don't know this Dorothy, or her dog, but if you're going to quiz me, you better reach back to facts long before your time, boys, because I left the States when movies were silent and folks were up in arms about Prohibition, and I bet you have to open a history book to know what that was about. All I know is I'm sick to death of this war, and I'm damned glad to see it over!" He pulled a bulldog scowl.

Both soldiers awaited their commander's decision.

"Sir?"

The colonel sniffed, shrugged. "He seems American enough to me. I've got a crotchety old neighbor just like him back home in Syracuse. And, ah," the man leaned toward younger comrades, "*The Wizard of Oz* was a book before it was a movie." Handing the birth certificate back to Fr. Viktor, he shared a martyred look between elders reminded of their age. He then swiveled toward the tanks. "Do you see white flags?"

A soldier lifted binoculars. "Yeah, they're comin' out now." Schwarzenfeld's citizens took a chance, figuring that the party could no longer terrorize them with threats of shootings.

The colonel nodded. "I tell you, Father. A little burg like this, firing at us? Normally we'd shell it to the ground and move on. We don't risk American lives over desperate Nazis. But you say it's just one SS detachment, and the town won't give us trouble?"

"That's right," Fr. Viktor confirmed.

The colonel nodded. "Good. I'll take your word for it."

Fr. Viktor stowed his birth certificate back into a pocket and patted his brow with the kerchief. He had been pulled through a wringer just saying hello, and worse lay ahead. At least this colonel had enough wisdom to assess a situation before passing judgment. He led the tank unit that encircled his hilltop church. Fr. Viktor engaged him in conversation. Schwarzenfeld's liberators hailed from the Eleventh Armored Division of the United States Third Army, commanded by General George S. Patton.

The colonel's easy, soft-spoken manner engendered trust, and the provincial stuck close to him. Together they strode along the Miesberg's crown and gazed upon a town in the throes of liberation. Figures squirmed within the coffin-sized spaces between houses. *Schwandorfers*, the provincial realized. They had scattered from the streets once a herd of gray-green mammoths lumbered down Schwarzenfeld's Hauptstrasse. He turned left—south—toward the Naab River. To his shock, the bridge stretched calmly over glistening waters; a black murk billowed from a barn instead. That, he deduced, was the explosion he had heard.

"What happened there?" he asked.

"We've been engaging the SS all day," the colonel said, tugging off his helmet with marvelous calm. "They're blowing every bridge on this river, slowing our advance. That one there," he pointed to the Naab bridge, "they have it wired up with enough demolition to blow it clear to Berlin—preferably with us on it. Seems the fellas who were supposed to ignite it had wet matches. Thank God for the rain." He smoothed away drops falling upon his rust-colored hair. "When they couldn't detonate it, they retreated to that barn there and tried to make a last stand. That's where we stopped 'em."

Curiosity tugged Fr. Viktor. "Did your men encounter any local militia?"

The colonel shook his head.

"Good." Schwarzenfeld's militia refrained from an attack. They had ignored Hitler's orders and taken the word of an American. He felt a rush of satisfaction.

"Is this your place, Father?"

He turned. All these years he had dreamed of this moment, and when it finally arrived, he had given no thought to his Miesberg-kloster. "Oh. Yeah! The church is mine. The monastery is, too. It was taken by the party four years ago."

"Oh. Huh. You want it back?"

In spite of his troubles, the provincial grinned. "You bet I do. But you might want to have a look around. They've got a group of scientists in there doing God knows what."

The colonel whistled, pointed, sent a squad hustling into the monastery, then loitered about, pensively chewing Doublemint. Fr. Viktor stood in awe. This man waved his hand and a Framework path tugged out of alignment by Seiz had been set right. It seemed like magic. He yearned to accompany that scout team and discover the things that gestated in the belly of his monastery, but another matter demanded his attention.

"Colonel," he murmured darkly. "There's something else you should know."

The provincial told him about the death march. He quoted body counts reported by farmers—one hundred dead, perhaps twice that number. The colonel merely nodded. This man had staggered away from engagements where blood coursed in rivers and victims numbered in the thousands. Yet, when Fr. Viktor identified the suitable place, this war-hardened soldier swung to him, his features split between revulsion and disbelief.

"Few people in town have reason to go there, to that place," Fr. Viktor said. "The SS would probably be halfway across Germany before anyone realized that a grave was there. But I think it's clear they call the location 'suitable' for another reason entirely."

"Jesus Christ," the colonel breathed, his voice hushed in horror. For all they had endured, the Eleventh Armored had never experienced any evils that compared to the suitable place.

"You want to get the men responsible? Just send your boys down that road." The provincial swung a finger toward the Hauptstrasse. "You have tanks, you'll overtake them in no time. And I pray you do, because they've got more prisoners."

"Yeah. We're going after them, all right. We'll find them. This division leaves first thing tomorrow morning. I'll see to it."

"Okay." Fr. Viktor bit his lip and nodded. He had hoped for immediate action, but he could not tell the American army what to do. Liberation awaited prisoners on the march. He took solace in that certainty.

He pondered what the colonel just told him. "Wait. You just got here, and you say you're *all* leaving?"

"Well, this is a sweep-and-clean operation, Father. See, the armor sweeps in, takes out all resistance, enforces martial law, then the doughs—the infantry—they take over, and we move on. The spearhead rarely stays in one place longer than a few hours. That's the way Patton wants it: we move fast. Your occupying force will be coming in at, oh, 07:00, maybe eight-ish? They'll decide how to resolve your 'suitable place.'"

"Eight-ish. All right." A German would quote an exact hour and fly into a huff if comrades showed up even a minute late. Fr. Viktor felt a twinge of irritation himself. He would have to lay all the facts out for another commander, and he had no clear idea when to meet this man.

"Father, I've got a problem. I have to communicate the terms of surrender to the people here, and I don't speak a word of German. It's been a pain managing on my own. I'll tell you, it would be great if I could work through you."

The feeling's mutual. Fr. Viktor liked this colonel. He was a rock of calm self-possession, exactly what he needed to resolve Schwarzenfeld's predicament, but this thread did not weave into that design. The provincial meditated.

"An American surrendering a German town to Americans. I think a German should be involved. But not the mayor. He's a *Gold-ener*—a Nazi." He was picking up on American lingo.

"Well, all right." The colonel nodded. "You know of a German who'll cooperate with us? Preferably one who isn't a Nazi. Or is that like trying to find a saint in Hell, Father?"

Fr. Viktor smiled. "Not at all. I know just the man you want."

————

Their entrance was worthy of a riot of drums, blazing clarions, and a hymn of shattering beauty. Struck breathless at a street corner, Fr. Viktor watched them rumble up the Hauptstrasse, Sherman after Sherman, the tank commanders and gunners riding out in the open, their bodies swaying with the motion of iron mammoths veering toward an outlying road or farm field. The faces beneath olive-green helmets were young, yet bitterly experienced. The Eleventh Armored had landed in Liverpool eight months ago, he learned. They had suffered a bloody christening to warfare in Bastogne, a campaign that Americans dubbed the "Battle of the Bulge." They had endured it all, these men, the sight of grenades ripping comrades to shreds, the chill of winter battle, the terror of climbing into a patched-up tank still reeking of death from the last crew to plunge her behind German lines. Moved to tears, Fr. Viktor shook his head. They were fine boys, and he lamented only the lack of a sign to let them know that a countryman stood here, awed by all they had suffered to liberate a continent in chains.

Fr. Viktor climbed into the passenger's seat of a jeep. That vehicle unnerved him. "What in blazes do you hold onto?" No door kept him from tumbling out to the street, no handles provided relief for a passenger jostled about. The jeep lunged ahead and he kept a white-knuckled grip on the seat. His free hand lifted a bullhorn.

"*ACHTUNG*," he announced *auf Deutsch*. "ATTENTION: MARTIAL LAW IS IN EFFECT. NO GERMAN IS PERMITTED ON THE STREETS. LEAVE AT ONCE!"

He heard pleas in German. A frantic woman: "Where do we go? Where do we—" A man roared in vein-popping ferocity: "Stay away from my family!" A hysterical wife: "My husband! Don't take my—" Americans arrested German men of military age. They could be enemy soldiers on furlough or SS officers. Both were subject to immediate apprehension. *Who was taken?* Fr. Viktor twisted, searching. He grimaced. Too many refugees swamped the roads, too much exhaust stung his eyes.

A blur tugged his attention to the town elementary school. Left to fend for themselves, Schwandorfers pounded their way inside. That stark, eggshell-white building might house two hundred survivors, but a thousand more stood begging in the muddy cold. *Where will they go?* They had stumbled six miles for help, only to be driven away to another town where the process would repeat itself. Fr. Viktor groaned, hoisting up a bullhorn that felt made of lead. "ATTENTION, YOU MUST LEAVE . . ."

By 8:00 p.m. the streets loomed clear. The jeep swept past an intersection where the Bahnhofstrasse branched off the Hauptstrasse. Fr. Viktor barked in German to his driver, unthinking. Then he remembered himself.

"Stop the jeep!"

The vehicle wheezed to a halt. Five bedraggled men barricaded Norbert and Maria's door. An American soldier reached for a rifle.

"What's going on here?" the provincial demanded first in English, then in German.

A lanky creature prattled to the soldier. "Hey! American, you see this?" A bony finger gestured to a crimson shoulder badge. "I am Russian. *Russian!* We are comrades, you and I." Zizi pumped the soldier's hand hard enough to shake tendons from the bone. "American, you listen to your comrade Ziziswili: *here there are good people living.* You got no trouble here."

"Hey, Father!" the soldier said. "Tell this guy to get outta here before I shoot his ass!"

"Pater! Come here." Zizi huddled with a conspiratorial air. "How does one say in his words: *Hier gute Menschen?*"

The provincial clapped Zizi's arm in fellowship. The men guarding Norbert and Maria's house were laborers, patrons of the bakery. He translated. The soldier lowered his weapon.

An ivy door flung open. Norbert strode out, still dressed in the suit he had worn to church. The instant he recognized Fr. Viktor and Zizi he wilted in relief.

"Good people living here," Zizi wailed in English. He pointed at Norbert. "Good man!"

The provincial smiled. *Good man, indeed.* Norbert had even refused to join the militia, a fact that subjected him to countless vexations at Dobler's hands. Maria crept to her husband's side, absorbing the news that Fr. Viktor had to report.

"The Americans are declaring a curfew," he informed them in a rush. "Germans are only allowed on the streets between 8:00 and 10:00—that's morning and night, four hours total. All shopping and personal business must be conducted during those hours. Anyone who has a gun, or camera, or binoculars, anything that might be used as a weapon or for surveillance, it has to be surrendered at the Rathaus. We've got to call everyone to the town square, so they can hear these terms. I would appreciate your help, my friend."

"Of course, Pater," Norbert said. "I will do anything you ask."

"Here."

"What is that?"

Fr. Viktor tied a white cotton strip on Norbert's right sleeve. "A man with this armband can walk free at any hour. They're meant for facilitators in this process. For translators—or, for a representative. Someone who might become mayor, eventually."

"Me? A Bürgermeister?" Norbert's eyes swept up to his wife. Maria whispered his name, her gentle mouth quivering between a smile and an anxious wince.

"Can you manage the bakery, Frau Gindele?" Fr. Viktor asked.

"There is nothing to manage, Pater," she said. "We emptied our stores when the Jews came through. We have only twenty-two loaves that we could not distribute. With this going on, who knows when more supplies will be coming?"

He nodded. They were adrift in chaos and only heaven knew when peace would sweep them back toward a normal shore.

"Pater," Norbert said. "The Amis. Do they know?"

"Do they know what, my friend?" Fr. Viktor asked, fastening the armband with a pin.

The baker's voice dropped to a whisper. "This morning, Pater, I talked to some farmers before Mass. I asked if they could deliver potatoes. They said they could not deliver a thing to me, until their wagons were washed down with lye."

They shared a stare. Behind them, Zizi shouted at passing jeeps and belted out the extent of his English vocabulary.

"Pater. If you had seen those Jews, you would know they had no strength to bury bodies. The dead must be close by." Norbert swallowed, his Adam's apple bobbing. "The Amis. Do they know?"

Fr. Viktor handed him a bullhorn. "We're going to take things one step at a time."

The baker nodded. "Yes, Pater."

The jeep lunged forward in the dark and carried Norbert down the Hauptstrasse. The provincial kneaded a weary brow.

At 10:00 p.m. the Americans granted Fr. Viktor full run of his Miesbergkloster—except for the cellar. They cordoned that off until Army Intelligence arrived to pore over its contents. He did not know what plans his mysterious tenants had hatched down there, but he no longer cared. The American arrival stopped their efforts, and that knowledge satisfied him. Spent and pale, he staggered into his monastery with a shocking lack of ceremony. The suitable place remained unresolved, and that thought made him collapse into a chair, staring at shadows.

Father, have You led me here? Or has my own free will brought me to a juncture beyond Your reach? How is a soul in the Framework to know the difference?

A knight on the cosmic chessboard, he waited to feel a vibration from beyond, a sign that God moved him toward a checkmate against evil, but he sensed nothing, nothing, no flutter of intuition, just a tide of silence that rushed dark and heavy toward a terrible dawn.

At 6:00 a.m. sharp, Fr. Viktor said Mass in solitude. He had just shrugged into a long black overcoat, preparing to depart for the town hall, when a fist hammered the monastery door.

"Good morning." He presumed a need to speak English. It was only half-past seven. The curfew prevented German citizens from walking free at this hour.

"You're the American priest?"

Three strangers in uniforms and army-green helmets lurked upon his doorstep. The provincial stiffened at a gravel voice.

"Yeah."

"You're coming with us, Father. Now."

CHAPTER FOURTEEN

THE ULTIMATUM

APRIL 23, 1945

The Americans swept him to a place where corpses stared at an austere sky, their jaws sagging in a shriek heard only by the dead.

Fr. Viktor staggered. The fetid reek hit him first. It rolled up the field to assault him, choking his throat, searing his nostrils, wrenching tears from clear blue eyes widened in shock. The SS had spread lime powder to suppress a funk and obscure their handiwork, but nature had intervened: two days' steady rain had washed away every trace. Human wreckage surrounded him, a sea of men with shaven heads, their skulls smashed by bullets. Shoved off a wagon and left for the flies, they lay twisted in grotesque repose, at least one hundred bodies by his swift estimate. A seeping putrefaction eroded facial features beyond recognition, but the expressions remained clear enough to haunt him. They had met death in a state of terror.

Fr. Viktor fell to his knees, his face seizing in grief over war, over hate, over victims of brutality beyond belief, and the sins kept trembling through the Framework, the scarlet totality adding itself hour by hour, day after day. Yet another fact rushed up to batter him with waves of despair. This was far from a proper graveyard.

A suitable place.

Disposed wooden crates rotted in a sandpit. A chair thrust its broken legs in the air like a stag struck dead. Ash heaps scattered in a cold wind, possibly the remains of swastika-stamped papers, uniforms, and memorabilia discarded by party zealots before Americans discovered them decorating a study or office.

On the fringes of his consciousness he heard boots crunch over brittle grass. A young infantryman vomited. "Jesus Christ." He scraped his mouth with a sleeve. "I tell ya, Father. Now I get it. Now I understand why they shipped our sorry asses over here to kill these evil Huns."

A stocky, grizzled man stomped up. "You speak the guttural pidgin these barbarians use?" he demanded in a gravel voice.

Fr. Viktor licked a dry lip. A stench of death permeated the air so heavily that he tasted the tartness of decayed flesh.

"Father?"

"Yes, I do," he rasped.

"Good. 'Cause we're rounding up these murderous fuckers, and you're going to translate everything I tell them, word for word."

Fr. Viktor nodded. Americans lashed questions while the dead watched, the dead listened, the dead shrieked a soundless keening that shook the stars. "No," he heard himself respond in a strange, husky voice. "No, I didn't see the death march." Rumpled khaki uniforms towered above him. The soldiers who wore them were young, yet deadly earnest, aged by the macabre carnival of war. They desperately needed a shave. These men hailed from a regiment in the

Twenty-sixth Infantry Division. He had learned that much during a brusque introduction at his monastery door. "No, it was the Death's Heads who killed these men. Yes, some farmers transported bodies. They were coerced, afraid for their lives. No, I can't say who, it's a matter of confession."

The grizzled officer glaring down a chiseled nose was the regiment commander. He breathed windily through flaring nostrils. His ruddy Irish features pulled taut in a scowl.

"Let me get this straight, Father. You got a hundred men lyin' here, shot through the head and left to rot in the goddamned dump. By your own admission the locals moved these bodies, and you're telling me that this town is *innocent?*"

"That's exactly what I'm saying."

His countrymen peered at him. The commander clamped a cigar in a tight, bitter mouth and stormed off, a smoke cloud roiling behind him.

Throughout the field, soldiers crept around corpses. Fr. Viktor heard crude, oily English flow from men of war. "Butcherin' Nazis. I been sayin' it since the Bulge. These Germans are all fuckin' butchers." "You see how bony these guys are? What did those Kraut bastards do to them . . . ?" "At first I just wanted to shoot these sonsabitches and go home. Now I really wanna kill 'em."

"It's Hitler's *zealots* who did this, gentlemen," Fr. Viktor bellowed, struggling to his feet. "Not all Germans are Nazis. There are even party members who would find this sight despicable. Take it from me, I know these people! I've been in this country since Hitler launched his revolution in a beer hall."

American men stared at him. They stalked back to their jeeps.

A fine sweat beaded the provincial's brow. He scraped at it and examined jittery fingers, half-expecting to find himself sweating blood from every pore.

———

A jeep propelled him across town. The muddy Hauptstrasse splashed beneath its roaring wheels. His hopes of sowing amity between Americans and Germans tumbled away and behind, dying beneath a shroud of diesel fumes.

Dear God, what lies ahead?

His driver slid furtive glances at him. So did two hawkish GIs who ushered him along the corridors of an occupied town hall. They gestured to a seat in a murky conference room, then offered coffee, rations, cigarettes—even a cigar. Fr. Viktor declined. His countrymen awaited instructions, he gathered, and in the meantime, he spent a tedious afternoon translating aloud, reading documents, orders, and miscellany plucked from German POWs, several of whom had been denounced. They were sifting for intelligence, he realized. During each breathless pause, he sensed American men turning somber, exhaling smoke, their eyes narrowing at him.

Hairs stiffened at the nape of his neck. *You'd be just as leery, old man, if you stood in their combat boots.* Fr. Viktor attempted to assuage their suspicions with unstinting cooperation.

He tried a lamp switch to no avail. The skirmish yesterday between the Eleventh Armored and desperate SS men decimated a utility pole, leaving Schwarzenfeld bereft of electricity.

Hissing through gritted teeth, he tugged at shades covering a musty window. Trucks, jeeps, and tanks choked the streets, an army-green river of rumbling iron. The curfew kept civilians out of the way while Patton's Third Army surged deep into Germany. GIs clutched rifles and prowled along alleys where children usually played *Himmel und Hölle*—Heaven and Hell—or hopscotch, as they called it back home. The memory of laughter haunted every street corner. A militant presence made the air turn thin, cold, steely.

He mulled over a command to "translate for murderers." *So that armored division must be dragging those SS men here.* The notion offered consolation. If justice swung down upon Hitler's faithful like a hammer and the Americans forced them to exhume corpses with their bare hands, he would step aside, letting it fall. He drifted through prayer for men dead and dying, for those doomed to suffer righteously, then at 7:30 p.m., the thump of footfalls roused him.

"Here." An officer flung a folder upon the conference room table. "We got these off the bastards who are on grave detail."

This time no one requested translation. Curiosity tugged Fr. Viktor. While Americans bantered, he opened the folder and pored through its contents. *What's this?* He had expected to read papers with orders, the brutal directives of the SS, but this file contained little more than oddments from lives planted firmly on the German home front—hunting licenses, personal identification, black-white portraits of wives and children.

His attention fastened upon a slip belonging to an associate of the German Red Cross.

"Hey!" He waved the card. "This fellow here. Where is he?"

Americans loitering around the town hall stirred in bafflement as he hustled out, the rosary clattering from his leather belt.

Outside the town hall he found a street flooded with men in Bavarian garb—flat caps, wool jackets, breeches that fell in weary folds above knee-high boots. He recognized faces in his midst: Herr Gietl, Herr Obendorfer, farmers, carpenters, police officers, all old, all men. Schwarzenfeld's entire adult male population had congregated out here. *What's going on?* The sight confounded him.

A smaller assemblage of German men stood mute and morose under the guard of American MPs, military police. He turned that way. Braun stood in line, along with Officer Dobler, Headmaster

Schmitt, the town doctor, and twenty other Schwarzenfelders—all party members, now prisoners of war.

"Pater," one POW called hoarsely.

An MP grabbed the prisoner who spoke and scraped a pistol against his temple. "You so much as breathe, you Nazi bastard," the American gritted, "I'll blow you straight to Hell."

"All right, that's enough!" Fr. Viktor barked. Dobler and Braun stiffened in shock, watching him pry the soldier and POW apart. "Back off! For Pete's sake, does he look capable of putting up a fight?" Gaunt and disheveled, the prisoner collapsed into a heap.

The MP caught sight of Fr. Viktor's cassock and swaggered back. *Good*, the provincial thought. A priest's command elicited obedience from Americans. He would remember that.

He eased a hand on the prisoner's shoulder. A shock of oily hair spilled over a high forehead. A filthy face prickled by a week's stubble turned up to confront him. Exhaustion bruised the hollows around sapphire eyes.

"*Wasser*," Seiz pleaded. *Water*.

Fr. Viktor asked the MP for his flask, then rushed it into Seiz's grasp. Americans bristled in protest, but the provincial shot a bulldog glare. In this context more than any other, God raged for recognition of suffering.

"You're alive." He winced at a white shirt stained gray, at grit dusting black street garb. "What are you doing here?"

The charity worker scraped his mouth with a filthy sleeve. "Schwandorf is a desert of death. During the attack, a wind blew the bombs from their targets and they hit the residential area hardest. Half the city is *gone*, Pater. Simply . . . gone. The injured are too many to count. The dead? I lost count after two thousand. We have no supplies. There was no relief coming. I thought I could get help here.

Then, I run straight into the Amis!" He wiped his nose, checked for blood. "Anna, my daughters. I don't know where they are. Have you seen them?" Fr. Viktor closed his eyes in sorrow, head shaking. Seiz cursed and raked a hand through stringy hair.

"*Warum—*" The provincial broke off, grimacing. *Remember your English.* "Why have these men been brought here?"

An MP snorted. "They're Nazis, Father. Every one."

Fr. Viktor angled his head. "How do you know they're Nazis?"

"Sir? They've been denounced. This one who asked for water? If he had a gun, trust me, he'd thank you by blowin' your brains out. We seen 'em do it to our guys at the Bulge." The MP spat at Seiz as if he were a loathsome composite of every German who had gunned down an American in the Ardennes.

Fr. Viktor drew a strained breath, feeling crushed by suffering and death pressing all around him. The Jews. The Americans. The Germans. Pain, pain, and more pain. He had never felt the presence of Christ so keenly.

"Listen, son. I grieve for you and your comrades. I'm a Pennsylvania man myself, and you're all my countrymen. I know this fellow. He's no saint, that's for sure. But he isn't a killer either. He's a charity worker."

"A Nazi charity worker?" The MP scoffed in disbelief. "Well, I don't care what he is, he's a Nazi. You saw what he and his kind did in that dump. They're payin' for it."

"He's got nothing to do with that grave. He's just survived a bombing, can't you tell?" Fr. Viktor shook his head. "I don't understand. Why are all the men in town standing out here? Where are those SS officers? I thought—"

Running feet pounded dirt roads. He turned. Norbert jogged down an alley connecting the Hauptstrasse and town square. The baker halted, breathless, pointing out the white band on his sleeve to MPs. He observed Seiz's presence without surprise, Fr. Viktor noted.

"Pater, the Amis," Norbert panted. "I have been going house to house with them. They are taking our men. They are dragging them from their homes. Their German is terrible, but I am not mistaken. Pater, they are going to shoot *Schwarzenfelders* in retaliation for that mass grave!"

"Mass grave." Seiz choked on water, hearing it referenced in German for the first time. "What mass grave?"

Fr. Viktor met Norbert's gaze. The provincial looked down the road, then heaved a sigh. Rumors flew wild at a time like this. "No. No, that can't be right. I'll find out what's going on."

Tolling boomed from a hilltop steeple: 8:00 p.m. The curfew lifted; Schwarzenfeld's streets loomed clear of traffic. Calamity brewed along the Hauptstrasse, not from an army truck delivering SS men, but an incoming tide of German women, all frantic, panicked. They needed to gather foodstuffs during this fleeting interlude, but instead they flooded the town square, looking for their husbands. "Norbert!" Maria cried. Helene accompanied her, followed by Klaus and Hans. Both boys shied away from gun-toting soldiers and pulled their mother between them. Three bedraggled refugees edged past unnoticed. Fr. Viktor recognized Anna Seiz and her daughters. They had battled the masses and found shelter in the town school. He felt a rush of relief on Seiz's behalf. "Wilhelm!" Frau Seiz screamed.

Klaus overheard. His sandy-blond head turned in a frenzy, then he caught sight of his mentor and cried out in tearful relief.

A horn bleated. A jeep plowed through the masses. Standing erect from the passenger's seat, the infantry commander peered down at Germans. Fr. Viktor drew a breath, let it seep out. This officer with the gravel voice unnerved him: he had a granite mind, every thought carved in stone, unchangeable. He reminded Fr. Viktor of another Irishman, old Stanislaus Grennan, the father superior who condemned his German mission as a fool's errand and remained blind to every triumph that hinted otherwise.

Translate for murderers.

Fr. Viktor saw no SS here, only Norbert, Maria, Helene, her boys, Seiz, his family, and a town square flooded with German parishioners and refugees.

"Colonel?" He edged his way to the jeep. "I've got a parishioner here saying something about *shooting*. Where are the SS men? I thought—"

"Not now, Father." A meaty hand shoved away his protests. "You tell these goddamn bastards what I say." He lifted his head to address the crowd.

"Listen up! You see that road leading from your town?" He pointed toward the Naab River bridge, where SS men had death-marched their Jewish prisoners out of Schwarzenfeld. "I've been told that, for the next twenty miles, that road is *littered* with bodies."

Fr. Viktor's arms fell limp at his sides. Watching his reaction, Norbert blanched. A muscle flexed between Seiz's jaw and cheek.

The commander bellowed in English while Fr. Viktor struggled to keep up. As he translated news trickling down the ranks of the American army, a river of memories rushed through his mind: the eviction, the crucifix affair, the petition, a refugee influx, the Gestapo incident, Fr. Paul's arrest, Schwandorf, all those Saturday gatherings over coffee and cake in between. And this whole time, factories processed human herds by the trainload, asphyxiated them with corrosive fumes, burned the evidence, then belched out mountains of ash, hills of bone. Schmitt, Dobler, and Braun remained impassive. *They don't believe.* Fr. Viktor paced, trying to fathom it. The notion seemed too preposterous for a sane man to grasp, the barbarism so outrageous that it vaulted into a realm of implausibility. Then his attention shifted toward Seiz.

He stopped short.

Frowning down at the roadway, Seiz had the appearance of a man dredging a muddled brain for a memory that could reconcile Auschwitz against stratum upon stratum of lies and rumor and bankrupt ideals building up over twelve years' time. He sagged, his haggard features sliding into that unnerving expression that Fr. Viktor remembered observing after Fr. Paul's arrest.

His own doubts withered and died away.

Norbert tugged off a flat cap and scraped at tears. Helene, Maria, and Anna Seiz cupped their mouths. Klaus, Hans, and every other youngster stood quiet as mice. Fr. Viktor read the Germans, engraving this cold, hard moment into memory. There was a visceral chill, envisioning yourself stretching awake to the dawn, bustling into line at the meat market, or hauling yourself through daily monotony behind a desk while the men who governed your country carried out an agenda of mass murder unseen, unheard, unknown, and reflecting back, it dawned upon you that the signs had been there all along, lurking on the fringes of your harried life. In every believer he perceived humiliation bearing down like an iron, a heat that seared the heart, scorching the spirit. He pondered the spectacular oddity that he, an American, endured it with them.

"And what do we find here!" the commander railed. "A mass grave of Jews left to rot in the dump. You Nazis. You who stand there and claim ignorance. You who followed along with it all, including that order to lay human remains out with the ashes of your trash. *You* are the trash." His mouth curled as he glowered at Norbert Gindele. "People like you disgust me."

Fr. Viktor flinched at Norbert and Maria, at Helene clutching a scarf against the gray chill of dusk. The priest frowned at his own weathered hands. They were shaking.

"Colonel. Sir. I understand your rage over this news, over that mass grave, the war. But you don't know these people. You can't judge them by the sins of—"

"This regiment has orders." The commander descended from the jeep and stalked around, his voice lilting in a militant cadence. "If our American boys encounter atrocities, *you* are going to bury the bodies. We are here to make sure that *you* atone for *your* crimes. If you fail to do this, you will suffer the consequences, and they *will* be dire." Aware of lingering silence, the commander turned.

"Translate!" he demanded.

Fr. Viktor stared.

The whisper of boots reminded him that soldiers skulked about, rifles slung over their shoulders. He could feel their minds playing a rolling reel of brutalities at German hands.

Military police had divided Schwarzenfeld's men into two groups: one with his parishioners—*his* Germans—and the other with party members, all POWs. "Those of you who are prisoners of war," Fr. Viktor said, straining to focus on a torrent of English. "These trucks will take you to the mass grave." He pointed at two olive-green hulks lurking in shadow. "You're going to dig the bodies from the dump. You're going to wash them clean. The townspeople will donate clothing. You're going to clothe the dead and prepare them for burial. The rest of you," he turned to the crowd of arthritic Catholic men. "These other trucks just pulling in will take you to the cemetery, where you'll dig a trench for a grave."

Radiating satisfaction, the commander lifted a chiseled jaw. Dismay rippled up from the Schwarzenfelders.

"Pater, why must *we* do this?" they asked.

"Hey!" Fr. Viktor snapped his fingers until a hush fell. "Hey, listen. The least we can do is restore the dignity of these victims, if only in death. In God's eyes, it's an act of charity."

Seiz read him narrowly, perhaps attempting to discern whether he meant it, or if he simply manipulated Germans into performing a grisly task under duress.

Fr. Viktor shot the party member a sharp look.

"We need caskets," he continued translating with a sense of suspended reality. "All the men are digging graves and exhuming bodies. There's no one left to make caskets . . . except women and children." He doubted that any of them had swung a hammer in their lives, but the scarf-covered heads nodded without protest. Fr. Viktor expected no less from Germans enmeshed in crisis.

An old man flew into panic. The provincial recognized Herr Josef Schmid, the owner of a carpentry shop. "Pater, the electricity is off all over town. The saws in my place are electric! Aside from this, there is a shortage of supplies, as with everything in Germany. My work has stopped because it is impossible to get nails. Surely it is the same in the other shops." He looked to fellow carpentry owners Herr Baumann and Herr Rieder. Their gray heads nodded.

"So, we've got no electricity to run the saws, and no nails." Fr. Viktor felt his molars grinding together. He translated revelations for the commander, but it failed to move him. The man stood like a khaki mountain. He didn't even flinch.

"But there are nails," Hans said. "I have seen them!"

"Where, *mein Kleiner?*" Helene prodded.

"In Herr Gietl's barn, Mutti. He pulls them out of the shoes of his horses, and leaves them lying around. They are bent up and all, but we can pound them straight."

"But those are horseshoe nails. Would those work?" She turned to Fr. Viktor, as if he would know. He shrugged. A nail was a nail.

The provincial continued translating. "Once the dead are put into coffins, and the grave trench is finished, we're holding a Christian funeral." Sudden questions flooded his mind: what were the implications of burying Jews in a Catholic ceremony? The commander didn't concern himself with that detail. Dean Spangler might assist in the planning. He would ask him to write the sermon, at least. "Everyone's expected to attend the funeral. We," Fr. Viktor paused to listen, "we've got twenty-four hours to get everything done. Twenty-four." He swallowed, wondering how many bodies lay in that grave. One day hardly seemed adequate. "If we fail to get everything done in time . . . if we—"

He wheeled, hearing a jolting statement in English.

"Wait. That's a *real* order?"

"Oh, yes, Father." Ruddy Irish features burned with an intensity that made his blood curdle. "Yes, it is. If this isn't done in twenty-four hours, I will give that order. Believe me, the Germans themselves wouldn't be this gracious. They'd do it now."

Fr. Viktor wandered aimlessly and rubbed a temple. Norbert and Seiz read his face. They turned wide-eyed.

"Colonel. I agree that these victims need a decent burial, and the party members should be involved. They need to see what their government has done—"

"What *they* have done."

"—I can see why you feel justified assigning collective blame for these sins, these atrocities, but you don't know *these* people—"

"It's you who don't know them, Father. You." A thick finger jabbed at him. "I'm sure they're pious in the pews, but you don't know what we've seen out there in the battlefield. *They are demons!*"

"A proper burial is the moral thing to do," he overrode, "but this threat of yours, this ultimatum? No sir, I see no purpose in that, no purpose at—"

"Finish the translation!"

"Some men here despise the party as much as you do! And others here are refugees. Refugees! They came from a bombing. They have nothing to do with this!"

"FINISH IT!"

Fr. Viktor vaguely noted the Germans turning pale while he stood toe-to-toe with military authority. The commander crimsoned like a coal catching flame.

"*You can't punish these people for the sins of a country!*" The provincial bellowed. "That's exactly what you're doing here, and I refuse to—"

"You won't—fine! I'll give that order now." The commander snapped his fingers. "Get these men lined up!"

Guns rose. Fr. Viktor whirled. Seiz gasped. He stared into the maw of a rifle. "*Nein!*" his wife shrieked. Braun and Dobler and Schmitt stiffened. Norbert shrank from a gun. Maria wept. Helene yanked Klaus and Hans behind her.

"All right!" Fr. Viktor tossed up shaky hands. "All right, fine. I'll translate." GIs eased quivering fingers away from triggers. He collected himself beneath a falling veil of darkness.

"We've, ah. We have orders." Dazed with disbelief, he nodded at his own statement. "The, um. The victims must be pulled from the dump. They must be washed. Clothed in donated clothing. Caskets must be made, a grave trench dug, a funeral held." He blinked at the ground. "If we fail to finish everything in twenty-four hours, every adult male standing here . . . every German man between sixteen and sixty will be shot to death."

Americans heard the wailing that followed, but they didn't comprehend *Hochdeutsch*. They stood unmoved. Maria crossed herself. "Hail Mary full of grace . . ."

Seiz's daughters convulsed in tears. Their mother tumbled into hysterics. "*Nein!*" she wailed. "Don't shoot my husband, don't kill my husband! Ohhh no, don't make me a widow!" Helene reached out to her.

"Frau Seiz," Fr. Viktor said gently. "You and your daughters are refugees. You don't have to participate in this."

"Are you insane?" she cried. "I will not sit in that schoolhouse like an idiot and wait for your gangsters to shoot Wilhelm! The girls and I are going with Frau Heidl."

Fr. Viktor scraped a palm down his face. *That damned propaganda.* This declaration fanned the flames of paranoia. He considered ordering her to stay in the schoolhouse, but thought better of it. This town needed all the help it could get. *Twenty-four hours.* Americans threatened to shoot German civilians. Americans. He ached to find himself shaking awake in his sacristy, but the air chilled his face, a gritty dirt road stretched cold and hard beneath his boots, and diesel fumes seared his nostrils too keenly for this moment to be the product of feverish dreams. Seiz traded helpless glances with his wife. Soldiers prodded him at gunpoint like farmers subduing an obstinate steer, and the charity worker looked to Fr. Viktor with an expectant air. The priest drew a breath, preparing to defend a wayward son, but an impulse held him back. Instead, he stood grief-stricken, watching MPs bully the man into a truck.

Norbert offered a kerchief to Seiz's daughters. The baker offered condolences. Fr. Viktor heard a tone in his voice that sounded like remorse.

An argument erupted between Helene and Klaus.

"No, child. Absolutely not!"

"But Mutti."

"What on earth are you thinking? This is not the time to declare yourself a man."

"But look at all those old men." Klaus pointed at farmers hobbling into a truck bound for Schwarzenfeld's cemetery. "They move even slower than Grandpa Heidl. How are they going to dig a grave trench?"

Helene's pale wheat features pulled taut in dismay. "No! You are fifteen, thank God you are fifteen! You are staying with me."

"Mutti, I have to go help!"

"You *will* help, dear boy." She cupped his cheek in her palm. "You will help me and Hans with the coffins, as the Provinsche said."

"Yea, help with the coffins," Hans encouraged.

"There are lots of children to help there," Klaus protested. "They need more young people to dig that trench. If they don't get it dug in time—"

"Young man!" Seiz shouted from the truck about to haul POWs to the mass grave. "You will stay with your mother. Do you hear me?"

Confident that the charity worker's command settled this matter, Helene tossed him a look of gratitude.

Fr. Viktor's gaze traveled from Klaus to Seiz in a direct line, as if following an invisible thread. Beneath the uncompromising demand for obedience he read a current flowing swift and deep, an energy that was unmistakably paternal.

Klaus' chest heaved in panic. He licked his upper lip, bit the lower one, blinked at his mentor, then at trench diggers. Trucks lurched into motion.

"Klaus!" Helene screamed.

Fr. Viktor shot around. By the time he realized what had transpired, the muddy olive truck carrying trench diggers was already pulling away, spewing exhaust, with Klaus bolting, groping for a hand, then surrendering to the old men who hoisted him up. His small face shrank into a dot as he observed the shock in his wake. Helene moaned in terror.

Seiz looked stunned.

"You call yourself an American, Father?" A gravel voice demanded. "I think you're sympathizing with the wrong side."

A furnace of fury burned in him. "Can't you see you're about to commit an atrocity yourself? They can't possibly get this done in twenty-four hours!"

"Didn't you see that grave? Didn't you hear what I said about the camps? These people are *evil*. How can you side with them?"

The man of granite thoughts stood bewildered. The sower met his eyes and beheld a sight worse than darkness: an inferno blazed in this man's soul and there was nothing holy in the fire that raged within. It chilled him to witness that in an American. Fr. Viktor shook his head, feeling torn between mission and mother country. Gasping in the vacuum of pain between both sides, he prayed that a higher wisdom guided him now.

"I don't want to take sides," he said, "but I will. I won't forsake my followers, even if they are the enemy. I tell you now, Colonel, if you give that order, then you're no better than the Nazis you've come here to kill."

"And you, Father. You're just as guilty as the Germans you protect." Bitter lips curled around a cigar and blew out a stream of smoke. "May God have mercy on your soul. If I were Him, I'd throw you into the hottest corner of Hell."

———

Two convoys of trucks roared along Schwarzenfeld's rain-soaked roads. The first raged south toward a field of death, and the second thundered west up the Ambergerstrasse, where ancient spruces veiled a cemetery in shadow. Three weeks before American occupiers arrived, groundskeepers had extended the graveyard another forty meters, and they had marked the enclosure by improvising a barrier of wooden planks. From a distance Klaus thought it resembled the flimsy matchstick fences Hans fashioned around the graves of toy soldiers. Given the gaps that stretched between each post, it looked incapable of holding a lazy cow, let alone men condemned to die, but after the Amis shoved him inside, he realized that they had addressed that problem. Angry snarls of barbed wire bristled between each post. A gate yawned wide, but soldiers stood by, ensuring that no German escaped his fate.

He swallowed hard at an impression of being caged.

A soldier thrust a muddy shovel into his hands. Voices shouted English; fingers pointed at stony ground. He began digging.

While he hacked away at the dirt, Klaus surveyed his fellow trench diggers. They snorted at him. *Stupid kid,* that's what their expressions conveyed, but he didn't care. Pebbles and roots sang against his shovel. He dug faster, harder, deeper. Normally he would comfort himself by imagining this predicament as another installment of Leutnant Heidl's missions, but those were childish things, and he had rushed headlong into manhood today.

Vater unser im Himmel, geheiligt werde dein Name. Klaus prayed an Our Father. He needed strength to find Herr Amtsleiter and explain why he had jumped on that truck.

Fr. Viktor stomped into their cage every two hours. He would shake a finger at the Amis, then sullenly they tossed canteens to the trench diggers.

Night fell fast and thick. At 10:30 p.m. the Amis permitted Herr Gindele's daughters to distribute bread. The girls allowed two slices per man, rationing it out until circumstances allowed Schwarzenfeld's bakeries to replenish their depleted supplies. On a normal day, unbuttered potato bread tasted as bleak as a dry sponge, but after hours of grueling labor it made Klaus' stomach rumble in anticipation. He traded bashful smiles with the girls as they slipped their offerings into his hands.

A soldier ushered German men to a shadowy corner of the enclosure. That was their toilet, Klaus gathered.

Exhaustion seeped into his bones. He curled up beneath his wool jacket and slept fitfully. The prod of a gun barrel woke him.

The Miesbergkirche bell tolled out four somber tones.

A starry expanse opened above Klaus and voices swirled down like fragments of dreams. Regaining consciousness in the cold nightmare trench, he swung upright, gritting his teeth against a spasm in his back. Ami guards swaggered by. Wriggling tickled his scalp, a sensation of beetles crawling through sweaty hair. He scratched madly, then froze.

Real voices rolled across the field. German voices.

Klaus perched himself upon a knee-high ledge and peered over mounds of black earth. During the past hour a violet glow had stretched high above haunting pines. Phantomlike figures trudged in their shadow: POWs from the mass grave. He strained to make out faces in vain. Herr Amtsleiter could have been any one of them. They lumbered two at a time, each pair holding a litter between them, and stooping, they let a corpse roll gently upon stony ground. A row of dead lay in the moonlight, perhaps twenty men.

A group of prisoners clustered around a body. They gingerly peeled a shirt from its bony rib cage and yanked its pants down to the ankles. The sight made Klaus squirm in rage. *Hey! Why are you doing that?* Then they flung buckets of water and he sank on his haunches, recalling American orders to wash the dead. Corpses stretched before him like naked sticks, their stomachs tumescent in death's bloat, their heads and loins completely hairless. That was unnatural. He had grown old enough to know. It dawned upon him that they had been forced to shave all over, and that realization made him wilt in despair. It felt personal, knowing that his people had treated these men in a despicable manner. It seemed a savage betrayal to Germany itself.

Night winds blew a reek into his face. He gagged. POWs stripping the dead doubled over in vomiting fits. Elderly Catholics shoveled and wept in prayer. *Heilige Maria, Mutter Gottes, bitte für uns Sünder, jetzt und in der Stunde unseres Todes . . .*

Thank God Hans and Mutti were working in a carpentry shop. He hoped his brother managed to gather nails and wondered how many coffins they had finished.

Moonlight darkened above him. A soldier howled in English. He tumbled into the pit and continued digging.

Amis marched POWs back toward the mass grave. At 5:00 a.m. a fresh group of prisoners trudged into the pen.

Klaus slithered back up to the ledge. His scrutinizing gaze fastened upon a lean figure lurching through the gate. The man's size and shape sparked familiarity, but shadows obscured his face. An Ami handed the prisoner a bucket while another shoved him toward the disrobed dead. Guards waited for him to pour, but he stood limp and agape.

Shouts rose. Guns cocked.

Klaus whimpered. "No, don't make them shoot, don't make them, don't make them, oh God just move, please?"

A soldier jabbed the prisoner's ribs. He stifled a grunt and tipped his bucket. Klaus withered in relief.

A wagon rolled into the hazy cemetery, its bed spilling a fountain of arms and legs. POWs stalked off to collect another body. Guards milled around for a minute, then they strolled away, leaving the bucket holder standing alone to commune with death. A mixture of mud and vomit caked his knee-high boots. Klaus heard a shaky exhalation, followed by sniffling. This prisoner grieved, as if remembering every rumor he had heard, every suspicion dismissed. Today, Klaus had an inkling of what those were. Over the years he had done no different.

The boy lumbered on squatting legs, keeping a shovel in his clutch in case circumstances forced him to dive back into the trench. He darted from soil heap to soil heap, staying low so the Amis wouldn't notice him. "*Hallo?*" A pail slid from the bucket holder's grasp. It rolled with a tinny clattering. "Herr Amtsleiter. Is that you?" Moonlight reduced the figure to a silhouette, but it was him. It had to be. Corpses stretched in a gruesome row, yet if a mountain of dead separated them, Klaus would scale it, and if a river bled between them he would plunge toward the flinty shore, all in hopes of seeing Herr Amtsleiter's face and hearing his voice and seizing this one terrible chance to tell him why he had braved death's maw.

Klaus spied a barren space between bodies, one just wide enough to crawl through without disturbing the dead.

Goosebumps flushed his skin. His quaking knee moved up. Then his trembling hand. The other knee. A whisper spooked him. *What is that?* Rotted faces gaped in an eternal shriek. Something buzzed his ear. An insect. Flies. That's what he had heard.

The quickening gale of his own breath deafened him, but still he crawled on. He focused so intently on reaching the bucket holder that a group of POWs slogged by unnoticed. Icy fingers clutched his suspender, brushing his cheek.

"What are you doing there?" a voice demanded in German.

A screech pierced the blackness.

Klaus flailed. Amis wheeled. Guns cocked. Death clattered into empty chambers. He fled to the trench, the wail still blaring from the mad square of his mouth. He waited for a *rat-tat-tat* of bullets. His heart slapped his breastbone, pounding out the seconds. *Eins! Zwei! Drei!* Fear. Darkness. Silence. Nothing.

He peeked out.

Amis cursed and swung around in search of a target. German men clung to the ground. They spat strings of obscenities laced with the word *Junge*, boy.

"Stupid!" Klaus smacked his brow. "Stupid, stupid, stupid!" He yearned to burrow under a dirt heap and die.

The bucket holder lay in sight. Bloodshot eyes gleamed behind filthy strings of hair. They fixed upon him like daggers.

"Have you gone mad? Don't you dare leave that trench, young man, or you will be digging bodies at that grave—and you will obey, if you know what is good for you!"

Klaus snapped to attention. "Yes, sir! Sorry! I am sorry. Are you all right?"

The ragged head sank, but that might have resulted from shock, rather than an intention to offer reassurance.

A cloud engulfed the moon and Klaus groped for words in the dark. The man who blazed into his life tough as leather and strong as Krupp steel lay before him, a fragile shell sinking from darkness into blacker fathoms far beyond his ability to shine comforting light.

Amis headed in their direction. Circumstances permitted only moments to say what beat so forcefully in his heart.

"I am sorry I didn't follow your order to stay with my mother. I could not. I had to be here, where my help matters."

"Why?"

"You know that prayer I told you about? It was answered."

A wind hissed through pines. He heard approaching boots crunch over gravel.

"Klaus," Seiz said. "Your father is dead."

"Yea. Um." A whimper caught in his throat. The darkness smothered him, yet he pushed on. "God could not bring my Papa home, that is true. But He answered. You see, He is working through someone who has become a second father to me. It must have been almost impossible to answer this prayer, because He knew I was in too much pain to follow a religious man, and there are a lot of people He cannot work through. I realized that when those SS men came through town. And that is why I didn't obey. I cannot let my second father die."

A scoff. "That old man convinced you of this."

"No. You did."

Silence stretched so long that Klaus fled into childish habits and picked a fingernail. A lump swelled in his throat.

"I know," he said painfully. "You don't believe in that stuff."

"Klaus," the broken man quavered as the guards wrenched him away, "I don't believe in anything anymore."

CHAPTER FIFTEEN

A TOWN IN CRISIS

APRIL 24, 1945

At 8:00 a.m., twenty bandits skulked from the Schmid carpentry shop and ventured into the bitter morning. The Miesbergkirche bell tower tolled. Its knell incited panic. Time was an overlord in Schwarzenfeld, each moment lashing like a whip.

Fr. Viktor slowed on the Ambergerstrasse as the raiders lurked into view. They chewed fingernails down to raw nubs. They sucked thumbs for solace. They gnawed braids to stave off hunger. He bared his head and pulled a black fedora against his heart. These bandits were all twelve years old and younger.

"Hurry, come *on!*" Hans bounded to the lead, his plea shocking the silent street. "We have to get more nails, even if we have to go into houses and take stuff apart this time. If we don't find enough, people will die—like my brother and my grandfather."

Fr. Viktor brooded over the sight of refugee girls tottering around ruts left by trucks. He read tulip faces drained of joy and color. These innocents understood death. This war had wrenched their fathers and neighbors away in grim seconds and bloody moments, and here in the realm of the gritty surreal he grieved, watching them stumble beneath the full comprehension of a brother's peril, or that of a grandfather, an uncle, a family friend.

His left eyelid spasmed from sleep deprivation. Blisters swelled on his feet, but he kept on going, kept on plodding through a war zone between conscience and country. A stark white building loomed before him: the Schmid carpentry shop. He rushed inside.

This carpentry stood far from death's gorge-raising stench, yet the air was far from sweet. Seventy women swarmed around ten work tables; a briny odor of sweat and tears saturated the cramped wooden room. He found old Herr Schmid hunkered on a bench. The shop proprietor seemed fit for nothing beyond listless staring. Frazzled apprentices rushed from station to station, ensuring that the women were measuring boards properly. The *thunk thunk thunk* of hammers pounded Fr. Viktor's eardrums.

Imagine having to make coffins to save your husband or father or son. What would run through your mind?

He pondered the emotional magnitude of that concept and felt a rise in his throat. These women were wan, their faces tarnished by fear, and each bared her teeth in anguish as she imagined her spouse or child lying dead in the coffin she made with blistered hands.

A *wham* deafened the room. Seiz's eldest daughter shrieked wretchedly and unleashed her fury upon a nail. Helene rushed from a crowd to embrace the girl and stroke her hair.

Unreal. This is unreal. Fr. Viktor understood the need to grant victims a proper burial. *But this?* Americans coerced an entire town with fear of death. The realization sickened him.

"Frau Heidl," Fr. Viktor beckoned. She had been helping him keep track of progress here. Neither of them wanted to distract the apprentices. The widow caught sight of the provincial and held up a hand, bidding him to wait for a moment. Across the room Paula Dirrigl propped her elbows upon a sawhorse and her maid stood nearby, offering a kerchief.

"Paula?" Helene crouched, ensuring that the deaf woman read her lips. "Paula, dear, keep working. Every coffin brings us closer to saving your husband—child!" A teenage girl flinched up, yet another refugee swept into this maelstrom of the macabre. "Child, mind that hammer. Tap *slowly* like the men said, or you will hit your fingers." The widow massaged her left thumb. "Anna." She eased down beside Frau Seiz, addressing her by her first name, while the charity worker rocked herself. Germans tended to let formalities slide during emergencies, Fr. Viktor knew, yet signs of a lasting bond shone between both women. Anna Seiz clung to Helene's hand the way she might grip a lifeline unfurling into a chasm.

"Pater." Thick-heeled shoes clomped over. "Oh, this noise. Come!" Helene strode toward the door.

"Frau Heidl," he greeted in haste. "Did the boards arrive?"

"The what?"

"The *wood*."

Helene pointed at a stack of pearly white planks in the aisle between tables. "Good," Fr. Viktor said. It was their lone stroke of luck in this crisis. The Baumann carpentry had a warehouse brimming with Black Forest pine already sawed into boards.

Helene huddled in the door recess. "And Klaus. Have you seen him? Is he—oh, it is freezing!" She darted back into the workroom and yanked out a wool coat, one that didn't even belong to her. "What is that child wearing? I cannot remember. Is he dressed? I mean, is he warm enough? Do the Amis know that he is fifteen?"

"He's *fine*," the provincial eased. He studied a drawn face, the wheat strands spilling in sheaves from their pins. His lips firmed in concern. "Just take a deep breath. Okay?"

"Yes, Pater." The widow pulled on the coat and obeyed.

"Don't worry, I'm watching over Klaus. And yes, I've informed the guards of his age. They say he's old enough to dig, so they're keeping him in the cemetery. Despite the circumstances, that boy's been a real help."

"Well, that is good," she said. "The, ah. The coffins. How many do we make?"

"How many do you have?"

"Twelve."

"Twelve?" Fr. Viktor bit loose skin off his lower lip. "All right." The Baumann and Rieder carpentries reported ten and twelve respectively, thirty-four caskets total. He had been waiting for dawn to obtain an accurate body count.

"We're still working with an estimate of one hundred corpses. I think each carpentry should expect to make thirty-three coffins, at least. Perhaps thirty-four."

"Thirty-what?" Helene said. Hammering slowed in the shop. "And the time is—it is 8:00. We are halfway through this, we should have, there should be, what? Seventeen by now?"

"You're behind," Fr. Viktor conceded in a steady voice, "but you've been learning, you're getting proficient. You can catch up."

"Thirty-four coffins. We are behind by five. Oh God." Helene shivered. "Suppose we fall short—we will try not to. But if there are not enough coffins . . . what will you do?"

Two houses away, Hans was yowling to fellow bandits. Fr. Viktor gazed at a roadway deeply scarred by tire tracks and felt dread seeping into his core. "Well, it's obvious I'll have to confront that commander again."

A delicate jingling mingled with hammers as Helene fingered the cross pendant at her throat. "I am sorry, Pater. I cannot imagine approaching that man and speaking for us Germans."

"If it comes to that, pray for me," he urged softly.

Helene offered an anxious nod.

In the carpentry, news of the quota spread like a contagion and shrieks rose, the sound of fear in the nerve-shredding extreme.

Fr. Viktor's jaw slackened.

"*ACHTUNG!*" Helene's voice echoed through the workroom. "Attention!" Shoulders squared, she marched past tables of wives and mothers until she stood at the front of the shop. Women froze. Even old man Schmid straightened.

"I know how you feel," the widow said. "My eldest son—my first baby!—is out there, digging graves with your men. I know the agony of loss. This war has stolen the love of my life from me. But I know another thing also. This ache we feel here," she hammered her heart, "this need to make something good happen, this is what God works through. And because of it, I HAVE HOPE! So the tears stop now, because we will not be defeated by despair! For the next twelve hours we will come together, and we will trust in Him to carry us through this day. All of us!"

Fr. Viktor stepped back in awe. Oh, this mighty daughter. He wondered if she realized how brightly she dazzled, how everyone *leaned* on her, surrendered to her, she this magnificent pillar of hope. Still, he rushed from the Schmid carpentry without illusions. At this moment, all hope for this town rested on faith.

———

He hastened to Dean Spangler's parsonage. His fellow clergyman hunkered in candlelight; a persisting power outage denied him any other source of illumination. One hand scrawled out a homily while the other gripped a lock of white hair. "Writing this sermon demands no physical strain," he rumbled morosely, "but it is quite laborious. It seems correct to draw parallels between Christ's Passion and Jewish suffering, but the crucifixion is a contentious matter for the people we are burying. And given what has happened in Germany, how does one say an uplifting word about the passing of Jews into eternal life? This will sound obscene!"

Fr. Viktor sympathized, but the Americans insisted upon a Christian funeral with a proper homily. He advised Spangler and departed, encountering Norbert on the Hauptstrasse by chance. The man nodded in a daze. He faced a real prospect of meeting his maker and his soul was not at peace. Fr. Viktor wished that circumstances allowed time for pastoral care. Instead they discussed concerns that no Schwarzenfelder had stopped to think about food, and this crisis subjected every citizen to grueling labor. Even if hope sustained this town, hunger and exhaustion would seal the fate of its men.

"Yes, Pater." Norbert rushed off to coordinate Schwarzenfeld's four bakeries, carrying unspoken burdens with him.

A familiar intersection stretched before Fr. Viktor, the spot where Gestapo agents hauled away Fr. Paul. Now more than ever, he longed for the company of his fellow religious and wondered if he was still alive.

Norbert's slate gray house towered above a yawning intersection. A kitchen window revealed Maria and her daughters bustling about, preparing a batch of bread. A memory surfaced: Zizi and his fellow laborers standing before an ivy-fringed door like a human barricade. *Here there are good people living!* Fr. Viktor recalled refugee stories of the Russian advance, the stories vivid and chilling. They had described Red soldiers unleashing a vengeance-stoked orgy upon German womanhood, committing acts that made him beg for the tale to cease; yet only thirty miles away, Zizi, a Russian, defended a former German soldier and a house full of Bavarian women. Considering that he was a forced laborer, this made the incident even more remarkable.

"Hm." The provincial shook his head. Schwarzenfeld was still a town in Hitler's Germany, and zealots like Schmitt and Dobler and Braun called it home: in all fairness, he acknowledged that. And yet, a garden of conscience flourished here. The implications of sowing Passionist theology on German soil stunned him.

"But how do I convince that commander?" Alone with the road, he kneaded his brow with cold hands. "Father. Germany is overshadowed by war and mass murder. How do I draw breath to speak? What can I say to change a skeptical mind?"

He reflected upon advice that Christ offered His disciples in the event that they face a trial: *Take no thought of what ye shall say, for it shall be given to you in that same hour. It is not ye that speak, but the spirit of the Father that speaketh in you.*

Fr. Viktor found it damned hard to follow that advice when one hundred lives hung in the balance.

A jeep slowed at his call. It propelled him across town to a purgatory where the air throbbed with pain.

The broomstick bodies. The gaping mouths. Silent shrieks howled amid the foulest curses ever uttered in German and English. "Oh my God." Fr. Viktor lifted a kerchief to his nose. In this tortured place, each sight and cry and fetid odor made him reel. He watched two men bend to lift a corpse and then retch from the stench of death. In obvious exhaustion, they slid on their own vomit.

Fr. Viktor's attention traveled the clearing and fastened upon boxes and pails heaped upon a table. "Hey. Hey!" He waved down two guards. "Do you see that? Are you blind!"

The MPs stalked over.

"Sir?"

"This bread, these buckets of water. We brought provisions for these men six hours ago. Has it been sitting here all night?"

The first soldier gawked. "Father. Have you looked out there? Do you think these Nazis gave those victims any food?"

"Sir," the other broke in, "we've got orders from our C.O., he says these guys are gettin' the same treatment given to those Jews."

Fr. Viktor gritted his teeth. He pulled the kerchief from his face. "You've got orders from your commanding officer?"

"Sir? Yes, sir."

"I get mine from the Man up there," he jerked a thumb skyward, "and guess what? He outranks you, your commanding officer, the commander in chief back in D.C., not to mention everyone else in the American Army combined. Now you give these men a break, dammit, and you distribute that food and water!"

Both soldiers glared at him coldly, blackly. The first flicked ashes from a cigarette. He waved to fellow MPs and ordered a respite.

Fr. Viktor stomped off. American men absorbed horror and it pushed them down that dark alley of the psyche where God and the soul parted company, but he refused to stand by, letting them commit an atrocity themselves. Chiseled faces and war-hardened stares glinted beneath army-green helmets.

They think I'm insane.

A hilltop church tower announced time's passage: 10:00 a.m. He beckoned soldiers and focused upon a task at hand.

"You need to know how many bodies are out there, Father? Well, seventy-five's what I reported to headquarters." Another GI interjected: "Seventy-five? You sure? I coulda sworn the colonel said one hundred." "No way," a third said, "I talked to a fella from the Signal Corps, he said there were three hundred." "Listen, Father, make those Nazis count."

He grunted, his head shaking. "Yeah, I'm asking the wrong people." Military police prodded Germans away from the grave, so he headed that way, minding his step across a sea of sin and human flotsam. The POWs slogged by with the haunted stoicism of men who expected an execution any moment. They slumped in relief once their captors hauled out bread and ladled water from pails. "Good. All right, you. Come here." Fr. Viktor waved down a soldier. "You see that prisoner there? That shaggy thing that hasn't shaved in a week. Yeah, him. Bring him over here." MPs jabbed the German without mercy, though the man staggered along, silent and docile, entombed so deep in himself the provincial felt a spasm of grief. Then bloodshot eyes shifted up, catching sight of him.

"*You!*" Seiz shrieked. Veins pulsed in his temples. "I stop your arrest over that petition. I stand up for you when the Gestapo are about to haul you away. And what do you do for me?" Prickly features quivered, biting back tears. "This is because of that monastery. Is it not? You despicable, vengeful, pious—"

"I need a body count," Fr. Viktor announced in German.

Seiz blinked. The provincial raised a hand, calming Americans reaching for weapons. "I need a count—an accurate one—or there's gonna be hell to pay in ten hours."

"What?" Seiz wheezed. "Make these Amis do it."

"They're not giving me precise figures."

"Hm. Oh, really. Is the task too daunting when the number exceeds what they can count on their fingers and toes? Or are they just waiting for the chance to shoot Germans?" Seiz wheeled toward a soldier and weighed the hate in his eyes. "Well, what are you waiting for? Do it. Shoot me, damn you! Shoot! SHOOT!"

The soldier failed to make out a word, but he discerned Seiz's intent. A deadly metallic *click* jolted Fr. Viktor.

"Son!" he blurted. "You pull that trigger and I'm writin' *The Washington Post*, *The New York Times*, and the *Chicago Tribune*, and I'll make sure they hear all about our men shooting German POWs. That violates the rules of war, and if it's comin' from an American priest, I think they'll believe me."

The soldier cursed in earnest, lowering his gun.

"Ah, God almighty." Fr. Viktor gripped a flutter in his chest. Americans peered at him, wary of the improvement in his English. Hearing their inflections had brought it all back. He grabbed Seiz by the collar. "Now, listen!" The charity worker grimaced as if his breath stank, and it held true on both sides. The provincial fasted, subsisting only upon Communion, the body and blood of Christ, and Seiz had been vomiting up everything but his boots.

"Listen," he hissed in the German's ear, sparing them both, "your wife and daughters are making coffins to save your hide, and there's a kid in the cemetery who would be overcome with grief if he had to bury your bones—and he's in danger, just like you."

"I don't give a—"

"Oh, that's bull!" Fr. Viktor scowled. "Don't you give me that."

"God *damn* you! This is intolerable! If you had any idea what I have been through. Just let them shoot. God! Let the Amis shoot! I feel dead already."

Fr. Viktor imagined himself in this wretch's shoes, fleeing the molar-rattling punishment of carpet bombs only to plunge into this hell. "You're nailed to a cross," he said softly. "I know. You're beaten and betrayed, despised by the world. You are in great pain. Now, look at those corpses. Look!" Seiz lifted his ragged head. "Realize that you're not alone. Blood and soil isn't what binds you to a greater whole. Suffering is! I beg you to think about how you feel when you look out there. I beg you to realize what that feeling *is*, what it means! I beg you, because you're headed for a place worse than this, and if you are lost forever—if *you* are lost—it will torment my soul until the end of time." Fr. Viktor meant it. Against all reason, this vagrant of sin and eternal night scraped crevices of his heart that only his own brothers had touched.

The charity worker collapsed. Fr. Viktor's fingers relaxed, letting the man gently sink upon tortured ground.

"One hundred and forty," Seiz said.

"I'm sorry?"

"One hundred forty." Seiz lifted eerie eyes drugged by exhaustion. "Tell your carpentries to make this many coffins."

He had counted. *Good God.* He had already counted. Fr. Viktor lifted a ghastly grin to the sky. Then the smile plummeted.

"One hundred forty. You're sure?"

"No," Seiz admitted. "Corpses are being moved from place to place. Several have been taken to the graveyard already. It was dark when I was there. But if you manage to get one hundred and forty coffins, I think that you will have enough."

"I need an exact count," Fr. Viktor said. "As quick as you can."

"Yes, Pater."

Schwarzenfeld's Catholics uttered those words without a thought, but from this wayward soul it was a first. The man crumpled in despair. Fr. Viktor rested a hand on his shoulder.

At 6:00 p.m. the Rathaus door groaned open. The provincial caught his reflection in a dusty window and saw his haggard face, the eyes round and red and sunken, yet he felt energized by realizations. It dawned upon him that all preparation for this hour had been woven into his experiences day by day, one moment at a time, over the past four years. *Your Father knows what you need, ere you ask Him.* Staring into that pane, he caught glimpses of Helene, Klaus, Norbert, Maria, Seiz, all the others. Their lives coursed through his veins and whispered in the rush of his pulse: *Pater, Pater, Pater.*

The provincial marched on. He was cast-iron determination and free speech. He was fatherland and mother country. *Fight fire with fire.* All along he had attributed that strategy to his own ingenuity, but it was as ancient as Moses. A higher power had worked through a prince of Egypt to liberate His chosen from the pharaoh. He had poured divinity into flesh to reconcile worldly sin. He had pushed a party member to frustrate the Reich, ensuring that a German-American strode down this hall today. *Pater, Pater, Pater.* Now God made him a blaze raging toward an inferno. And it all turned upon faith.

———

"I'm here to plead on behalf of Schwarzenfeld," he announced.

One olive helmet and two combat boots settled upon a desk in Braun's old office. The grizzled army officer plucked a cigar from a leather case. He clipped its tapered end in an unhurried manner, then lazily he flicked a lighter. Three aides tamped out cigarettes and whisked matches to the ends of fresh Lucky Strikes.

"We've got exactly one hundred forty dead to bury," Fr. Viktor reported in urgent tones. "Only forty coffins are ready, only half the bodies have been tended, and that grave trench is barely three feet deep. On top of that, we're still trying to find clothes for the dead. Your ultimatum won't be fulfilled in the time that remains."

The commander exhaled a stream of fragrant smoke. "On the second day of the Bulge, Fr. Koch, Battery B in the 285th—that's a field artillery battalion—they were given orders to move from Schevenhutte to St. Vith in the Ardennes. On the way to St. Vith, they came to a crossing of five roads southeast of a little Belgian town. Some burg called Malmédy. They were ambushed by lead elements of the Sixth Panzer Army. The reports say they came up against the First SS Panzer Division. Hitler's finest."

Fr. Viktor flinched against smoke. He gripped threads of thinning patience. This story drifted out of nowhere, but he sensed meaning behind it, and he could predict how it ended. He recalled Norbert weeping behind the lattice of his confessional, his hands tearing at his hair as he enumerated the atrocities this division had committed in Poland. Hitler declared the First SS Panzer his elite because of its spectacular brutality.

"The SS opened fire. Our boys fired back, but they never had a chance. It was clear they were outgunned, so they surrendered. The SS herded 'em behind a café. One hundred and twenty Americans, all prisoners of war, unarmed. The Germans pulled out machine guns. I saw the results myself, a few days later." The commander puffed on his cigar, letting smoke stream from his nostrils. "Seventy-two lay dead in the snow. Barely a third of them escaped and survived to tell the tale."

Fr. Viktor swallowed in a dry throat. "And that's what you intend to do here?"

Ice-ringed pupils shifted up to engage him. "After the horrors I've seen in this war? After finding that grave—in a goddamn *dump*? I'm convinced that Judgment Day has come for Germany, and God has made this army an instrument of His vengeance."

Fr. Viktor shivered. He had encountered uncompromising men before—Braun, Dobler, the Gestapo—but nothing chilled him like an American using the Almighty as a pawn in dark reasoning.

"You know, I've got you figured out, Father." The commander reached for a folder. "I've been wondering, 'Why would you be here in Germany?' We found your records in the town hall. They were enlightening." Thick fingers leisurely turned pages of the provincial's life. "Here you are, a man of German blood, with citizenship in the Reich. You've been here for, what, twenty-three years? It's natural that you have an affinity. But here's the thing. It's possible to sympathize with the wrong people and let them muddle your thinking. I suspect that's the case here."

"I'll admit I've given that some thought," Fr. Viktor conceded. "Someone posed the question to me before, and I examined my conscience. But I swear to you, Colonel, that's not why I stayed. I'm certain." He let urgency pour back into his voice.

"If you're serious about executing the Germans out there, then I beg you to hear everything I have to say. I've listened to you. Now hear me out. Please."

A clock ticked on the wall. Aides looked to their commander. The grizzled officer checked the time and rubbed a sculpted chin.

"You want to preach? I'll give you five minutes. Explain it to me, Father. How can an American side with Germans against his own country, and in good conscience?"

Fr. Viktor read faces around the stark, smoky office. At best his countrymen deemed him misguided; at worst they suspected him a minion of evil incarnate. Beyond the expectancy that permeated this murky room he felt a deeper silence, the sensation of a million dead listening from the edge of Eternity, all wondering why one Bavarian village should be spared the cup they had been forced to drink in one unfathomable swallow. And yet, a bright conviction lined every thought crossing his mind: *My cause is righteous.* The priest drew a breath and prayed that Americans would listen.

"Whatever you've seen in this war," he heard his voice tremble into a void of blood and tears. "Whatever you've heard about German atrocities. I'm not here to contest any of it. Germany *as a nation* will have many crimes to answer for. It's inevitable that she will bear a devastating cross of shame and reparation, and the men responsible will surely be brought to justice—in this life, or the next."

The commander drew on his cigar. A spiral of smoke rose in the stillness.

"I'm not speaking for Germany, or for all Germans. I can't." Fr. Viktor swung his hands in futility. "It would be naïve to think I could, and foolish to try. I wasn't in all of Germany. I was *here*, in Schwarzenfeld. And I've been in this country for a long time, but I can't tell you what the average German is like, because those people out there are not average Germans. They've been depending upon an American to set their moral compass—and a Passionist! You can't say that about any other town in the Reich. And these people . . ." Fr. Viktor felt a tidal wave building inside. *Pater. Pater! PATER!*

"Gentlemen, I wish you knew *them*," he thundered. "I wish you'd been here when the Nazis evicted my brethren, and they protected us. I wish you'd been here when they found the gumption to circulate a petition over crosses being removed from the school, and the consequences were ruinous. I wish you'd been here when they reveled in rumors of Hitler's death, and one of my priests was beaten and arrested by Gestapo. I have no idea where he is! It terrifies me to wonder. And I wish you'd been at the Gindele bakery during that death march, when the workers rushed to provide bread to the Jews. I ask you. Do these sound like people who should be defined by the same hatred and loyalty you've encountered on the battlefield?"

Fr. Viktor surveyed faces that were mute, ungiving. He found it impossible to read them when the fate of one hundred Germans hung upon his every word.

"And I wish you knew some of the others," he pressed on. "The party humanitarian walking a tightrope between conscience and obedience. The Hitler Youth boy soured against National Socialism by the war. I wish you knew them, because if you did, you'd realize that you can't paint every single German with the same brush stroke you'd use to color a guard in the camps, or fanatics performing acts of brutality on the front. These people are not as black and white as you think."

Fr. Viktor paused, waiting for inspiration. He found it in Irish features that darkened in granite reproach.

"You want to condemn the Schwarzenfelders—and me—for our ignorance." Inhaling air thick with the musk of cigar smoke, he pondered that prospect. "The Reich made no secrets about the existence of the camps, but I swear to you, we never knew what occurred behind their walls. Our attention was consumed by the oppression and hardships we faced every day. What will God say to that? I don't know." He shook his head. "When I meet Christ face to face, if He says, 'I was forsaken by Germany, and you, Viktor, you and your flock will suffer hellfire for My plight,' I'll accept His judgment, and it will be *righteous*." The provincial drew himself up.

"What I will not abide is the self-righteous condemnation of strangers who appoint themselves our judges, jury, and executioners. That, gentlemen, is tyranny. I had to endure it from the Reich but I will not tolerate it from my countrymen. We're *Americans*, by God! Let's follow the principles that make our nation a beacon of truth and justice to this world. This town is on trial. You need a witness for Schwarzenfeld? I am their witness. Put me on the stand! You want to be our jury? I pray you hold each man accountable, not for the sins of his country, but for *his own actions*, as we would in the States. And remember: God is watching. Not just the Germans. But you as well."

His red-rimmed eyes swept the room, his molten gaze a warning. "Spare this town, I beg you. Stop this execution. Leave judgment to a higher power."

————

The Miesbergkirche bell tower throbbed eight times over Schwarzenfeld. A pall fell thick over the beleaguered village.

In the Schmid carpentry shop, seventy drained and disheveled women stared while each bell beat them like a rebuke. Twenty-two coffins haunted the yard outside. Fr. Viktor had amended their quota to forty-seven caskets and their time had run out.

All eyes swept to the woman who had kept them soaring high on impossible hope. Helene wilted on a workbench, her back facing them. They watched her brush wood shavings from a coffin, the motions so slow and tender they passed for a motherly caress.

The door groaned open. Two American infantrymen thumped into the workshop. They didn't bother knocking. Not anymore.

Old man Schmid squinted up through a haze of age and fatigue. The sight of soldiers made him throw his back against the wall. Hans had been assisting him. He cowered at his side.

Winds moaned through an open door. Sobs shook the room. Every woman expected gunshots any second.

Cold realizations wrenched Helene to her feet. "Herr Schmid," she said to the old carpenter. "Don't move. You stay there."

She strode up to the Amis.

"Um. We are not finished." The widow felt an eyelid trembling in spasms. "I am sorry."

A soldier spoke, elongating his words like a man addressing a dimwit child. She made out one inevitable reference: *Nazi*. The rest struck her ear as gibberish. Given that patchy stubble on his jawline and the velvety hands curling around his rifle, he had barely crossed the threshold of manhood. If he were a German, she would demand the respect due to an elder, but this boy clutched a weapon and his comrades intended to kill her child.

Another American stomped in, no more communicative than his younger comrade. He pointed toward a stack of coffins.

"Yes, I know," Helene snapped, "we are not finished! We just need more time. Time?" She pointed to a wall clock, feeling as inept as Zizi begging for bread. "Time! You understand time? Give us more time. Please!"

They turned wary. Her word *Zeit* bore no resemblance to their word for "time."

Where is the Provinsche? Helene hoped—she prayed—that he made this same appeal to men taking aim at the breast of her firstborn child.

The Amis turned to Herr Schmid. The old man looked up and cowered. Helene felt a pang of desperation, one that sank deeper and keener than the ache that had made her confront SS guards outside the Gindele bakery.

"Don't look at him, look at me." She yanked their attention back. "Where is my son? *Sohn?* You understand this word? *Mein SOHN.* His name is Klaus. Let me see him!"

"Frau Heidl," the old man creaked in a wicker voice, "I think that you had better not aggravate them."

"Don't touch my son," she rumbled in an intense voice. "Don't you touch my son, don't do it, *don't you shoot my child!*"

Helene's anger jolted American men. They lifted rifles. "Klaus! *Mein Sohn. Mein Kind.* He grew in here." She clutched her womb. "I remember how it felt when he kicked. If you kill him, that bullet kills me. Listen! If my words mean nothing to you then hear *me* listen to *me* hear the *pain and fear in me* because they need no translation. They are not German things or American things they are *human* things!" Her voice strained in throaty octaves of terror. "I know you are not evil. I know in places that your hatred makes you forget, something sacred is raging inside, and it is telling you how wrong this is! Please! Spare our men! Spare my son! Ohhhh God! If You hear me—this is one golden stone I cannot take!"

Helene was no longer a woman, but a howling whirlwind. Behind her, frantic wives and daughters blanched. Hans shriveled into a screeching ball. She heard Frau Seiz sobbing in fear and calling her name, empathizing with a fellow mother.

The Amis moved toward Herr Schmid. "*Nein!*" The widow blocked them, fought them. "*Nein*, don't, don't—*nein . . .*!"

A black blur shot out of nowhere. It thrust itself between Helene and the Americans. It shoved the soldiers back, speaking the gibberish they understood, then it stunned the hollow of the shop in accented German.

"We've got another twenty-four hours! We've got another day. Klaus is alive, Frau Heidl. No one will harm your son."

Her knees buckled. The world turned into blurs and shadows and an old man shepherding her to a bench. While she rocked herself and gripped the reins of maternal fury, he made his rounds, assuring every woman in the room that he had just seen a father or grandfather or husband who remained alive and well.

Fr. Viktor knelt before Helene. Her face was red and stretched and ugly, but the provincial beamed, as if he had never beheld a creature more beautiful than her.

"I'm sorry it came down to the wire like this, Frau Heidl," he said. "It took forever for that commander to make up his mind."

This American. Why are you here, protecting Germans? No lights circled the sun, no bushes burned, no biblical figures materialized before her eyes. Yet a miracle graced this dirt-road village, a riot of goodness that dazzled in the blackest hour, and it was as true and dear and real as the hands taking hers, warming them gently. Years ago, she thought that God had forsaken her. This old Passionist served as her wellspring of hope.

She would never doubt God again.

———

Fr. Viktor slogged from the Schmid carpentry shop. A pile of coffins rose chest-high beneath the boughs of a sleepy maple. He folded his arms upon the topmost casket and indulged in a moment's rest.

Giggling bobbed on a wind. He blinked across the street, his chin resting upon a fist. Five children clotted around an American soldier. The winsome, unshaven thirty-something knelt down and chuckled while distributing Hershey's chocolates and Wrigley's gum, neither of which these urchins had experienced under the harsh realities of Nazi Germany. The American grinned, watching their dough-soft features stretch in delight. Doublemint required a little explanation, though. The children gulped it down like bread and sausage on a dinner plate.

"No, don't swallow," Fr. Viktor instructed in German, "you chew it. Chew, chew, chew." The children donned bewildered expressions. He smiled at the soldier. "These kids were raised on a ration system," he explained by way of apology. "If you put it in your mouth, it's food to them."

There were no hard feelings, only laughter and a second offering. Fr. Viktor smiled. Of all the things he had witnessed this day, this month, this year, nothing evoked tears like this moment. It assured him that hatred between nations was a transient reality, one destined to pass in the eternal ebb and flow of God's time.

A voice called his name on a wind, echoing out of a dream. "Viktor? Viktor!"

A hand shook his shoulder. *Tired. Haven't slept in two days. Seventy-one years old. Feel about two hundred right now. This had better be good.*

A GI roused him, a man with an olive face and a Brooklyn accent that rolled like amber grain.

"Father? Hey, we got some fellas here who say they know you, and ah, they look like your sort: they got the robes and beads and all that? So we let 'em through. I sure hope you know 'em, sir, 'cause if you don't, my C.O.'s gonna kick my ass into next week."

He massaged bleary eyes. Black robes drifted into focus. Medals adorned weather-stained cassocks. Crosses crowned heart-shaped emblems.

"Oh, Lord. Yeah, I do know them." He straightened, recognizing Br. Bernard, the religious who spilled mass wine during a harried departure from the Miesbergkloster. Fourteen more Passionists trailed behind him, all priests and brothers from Maria Schutz, the monastery in Austria.

"Pater Viktor!" Br. Bernard spread his arms in mourning. "The Russians have our monastery in Austria. It is now in the middle of a war zone. We could stay no longer. The only thing left standing is the statue of our Lady!"

The provincial clapped Bernard's arm. They would have time to celebrate and grieve their losses later. "You came to the right place. I've got the Miesbergkloster back—most of it." His brethren pelted him with questions. "It'll take some time to explain, and we have other matters to worry about. This town's in a real fix. Do any of you know carpentry?"

"Eh, we are servants of a carpenter, we can muddle through." Br. Bernard shrugged, as if that fact alone made them qualified. Fr. Viktor grinned, head shaking. "But during our journey, we were joined by someone who is gifted." The brother gestured behind him.

"Viktor."

The provincial gaped.

"Paul?"

His brethren stepped aside to reveal a priest with a broad, serene face.

"Paul!" Fr. Viktor cried. Faint scars marred his cheeks. Mud still dusted his black robes. "Paul! Thank St. Paul of the Cross and all the saints!" The provincial embraced him. "Where have you been?"

"I am safe," the Austrian priest assured, squinting. "I am very thankful that I am no longer in a prison cell. I need glasses. And what is happening? Why do you need carpenters?"

"Don't worry, your spares are in the sacristy," Fr. Viktor said. The Passionists had returned to Schwarzenfeld just in time, and threads of fate aligned to haul a town from the mire of crisis. "Come on, everyone, let's stop at the monastery. We'll trade stories along the way and sing a *Te Deum* of praise to God later. Right now, we've got a town to save."

CHAPTER SIXTEEN

INTO THINE HANDS

APRIL 25, 1945

At dawn a POW in Schwarzenfeld's cemetery turned a bucket into a makeshift seat. He wilted before a row of corpses and sat in morose contemplation.

Fr. Viktor observed with deepening concern from across the barbed wire enclosure. The prisoner yearned for isolation, he gathered, and selected a spot where military police felt little inclination to disturb him. So much activity teemed around the guards that they hardly noticed or cared. The weary sigh of shovels rose from a neck-deep trench where farmers continued digging. A wagon train rolled up a dusty road, their beds groaning beneath stacks of coffins. The sight of an endless procession thudded heavily into Fr. Viktor's soul. POWs bore caskets upon litters, making their way toward a gate that was difficult to access from the road. They plodded circuitously around headstones until Br. Bernard slid down from a wagon, pointed out that the fence rose only chest-high, and suggested that it might be more efficient to hoist caskets over the barrier. Fr. Viktor translated, and the guards agreed. Together, they watched Braun, Schmitt, and Dobler catching coffins. The provincial frowned, hearing their prattle.

". . . the rallies. Remember when . . .?" "We came close in '42. We almost had it. The world was nearly ours." "These Jews. If the Amis care so much, why do *they* not bury them?" They gathered a corpse with crawly hesitation and lowered it into a coffin.

A glint snared the provincial's attention, a flash of metal reflecting sunlight. It dangled from Dobler's pocket.

Norbert strode up with a box of vests and suit pants donated from a local clothier. He swaggered up to the barbed wire enclosure.

"Ay, Dobler!" he crowed. "Is that a rosary? So, you are a devout Catholic now, eh? Well, they will have to nail your sorry ass to a cross before I believe that one. What a pity we had to use the wood and nails for something else."

MPs looked to Fr. Viktor for a translation. He shook his head. *What does Dobler expect to gain from this farce? Benign treatment?* The Americans were not fools. Neither was God.

Norbert edged through a crowd of POWs, weaving his way into the enclosure. For a long moment he stood bareheaded, his cap to his breast, as Fr. Viktor led a prayer for victims of brutality in Schwarzenfeld and beyond. The sun gleamed behind pines, casting garish ribbons across a field of dead. The baker stood half in light, half in shadow.

"Pater, these Amis," he whispered as if the confessional's lattice separated them. "When this regiment arrived, they pulled me aside. They showed me papers from the men they had captured. They asked, 'Nazi?' And I answered with zeal." Fr. Viktor nodded.

"I have no regrets over *them*." Norbert pointed at Dobler, Schmitt, and Braun. "In another case I am conflicted." He gestured toward the man who hunched in shadows, communing with death.

"I was right to denounce him," Norbert continued. "But, I saw his wife going hysterical, and his daughters in tears. That was damned hard to watch. Even Leni's boy leapt on a prisoner truck because of him. They are all suffering now. I ask myself, 'Was I driven by the Lord's will, or only by my own?' How is one to tell?" Feathery brows stitched together in anguish.

Fr. Viktor rested a hand upon his shoulder. "My good Herr Gindele. It's not always as clear as we'd like it to be, is it?"

"No."

"What's done is done, for good or ill. The man is a prisoner. We'll let a higher power work through it."

"Yes, Pater." Norbert meditated. "I will pray for his salvation— just as I pray for my own, and the safe return of my son." The baker slid his cap on and departed.

Fr. Viktor shuffled across the enclosure on achy feet. Passion- ists and charity workers, he mulled. They absorbed worldly suffering in their bones, and this man had spent an unsettling amount of time meditating on death.

"Herr Seiz?" He waved a hand before the charity worker's eyes and a creepy feeling shivered through him. Seiz was a vacancy behind his own face. The provincial wondered how many Germans would return from war like this, his Passionist brethren among them. Gazing upon a wretch drained of wine and venom and the very juice of life, he sensed his purpose sharpen into focus. At last he knew why fate had flung him into a paternal role at age seven, and then rooted him here in a land of lost sons to weather some of the most devastating events in this country's history. He stood amazed. The incredible ways of God. He could not fathom those factors coming together by chance alone.

"Come on, son," Fr. Viktor said softly, "let's get away from this." The charity worker was too weak to walk. He hauled him toward a breezy pine and slid him down against its bole. "Easy, now. Easy." Briefly, he departed to collect bread and water and speak to American MPs.

"I couldn't say this before, there wasn't time," the provincial said, returning to Seiz. "But I could have sung a *Te Deum* to Heaven when I saw you alive. I have no appetite for vengeance. The matter of the Miesbergkloster was forgiven and forgotten years ago."

Fr. Viktor set out a plate with bread and two canteens. He plucked off his fedora and perched himself on a stump, sitting face to face, the same way he had engaged his own brothers a life-age ago in Sharon. But they had never looked this seared. He continued talking in a slow, easy tone.

"You know. Schwandorf gets . . . annihilated. By sheer chance, a train is stopped in the station of an obscure town because the bombing prevents it from going farther. The SS leave a horrific grave. The American Army arrives, and catastrophic events follow. I've talked with a few soldiers. They're getting reports of graves from here to Neunburg vorm Wald. This same situation is playing out in other towns. Civilians being compelled to bury the dead. But this is the only place—the only one—where the commander made an ultimatum. And in this exact spot, this dirt-road village in the back of beyond, there's an American who can speak for you all. One who stayed because of faith." Hooves clopped along the dusty roadway. Another wagon wheezed by. "I think even you, my cynical friend, have to admit that the odds of these events aligning so perfectly are slim and none. But it's happening. We're witnesses."

He watched Seiz closely. Sunken eyes refrained from meeting his, but they blinked wearily and the pupils roved, chasing thoughts.

"I guess what I'm saying is this. Even now, during the darkest of times—and I've never seen them darker—even now, there are ancient forces in the Framework of this universe that align purely for good. These occurrences may seem like coincidences driven by human actions, but they're more than that." He angled his head. "I'm sorry. Did you say something?"

"Is that Pater Böhminghaus?" Seiz asked in a broken whisper.

Beyond the barbed wire enclosure, Fr. Paul slid down from a wagon. He helped Norbert and a band of farmers unload coffins.

"Paul? Yeah. He returned."

"Where was he?"

"They took him to a prison south of Schwandorf. Not a camp. He says they've been making him chop wood. After the bombing, they gave him his robes and opened the door. He's been making his way here ever since." Fr. Viktor uncapped both canteens and nudged one in Seiz's direction. "Maybe your intervention planted enough doubt in that Gestapo leader to spare him the worst of fates."

"He had exceptional fortune," the charity worker breathed.

Sapphire eyes swam up from a canteen with gratitude; Fr. Viktor nodded. Seiz avoided the bread. *Still nauseated,* the provincial discerned. Pickaxes clinked, breaking up rocks in the trench, and farmers groaned, hoisting coffins.

"Your reasoning, Pater," a voice scraped faintly over the ambient noise. "You speak of unlikely facts rather than mindless doctrine. You have not mentioned God once. This I respect. Yes, it is inexplicable, the way these events came together so precisely. But you are wrong in believing that the force in this 'Framework' is God. Look at those bodies. There is no God."

"A charity worker can never say that."

Seiz huffed.

"*Nächstenliebe*," Fr. Viktor said. "Charity. 'Neighbor-love' is a perfect description because that's exactly what it is: love. And it's not just any love. It's the wine of God's concern for all life. There is no higher virtue in Heaven. You can't pour yourself out to fill the needs of others and deny His existence at the same time."

"If there is a God, and He is goodness itself, then explain this to me. Assuming that He sees all pain, and all life is precious to Him—you agree with this?"

"I do."

"Assuming that, why is He capable of saving one village in an extraordinary way, yet incapable of saving a multitude in the concentration camps? If He is all-knowing, then why did He not stop Hitler from ascending to power and deceiving Germany?"

Fr. Viktor sipped water. He meditated upon a pale, tattered figure lying drenched in the shadow of pine boughs.

"You have no explanation, Pater?"

"Herr Seiz. I'm trying to sustain you on all the peace I can give, and there's none to be found in the answer."

"You know what I think? You have fear that I am going to tear apart the theories that make you a man of faith."

"Oh, really," the provincial said.

"If you will not allow your beliefs to be challenged, then don't say another word. It is impossible for me to have a meaningful conversation with you."

Fr. Viktor harbored fears, but not the ones Seiz thought. An impulse told him to leave this discussion for a time when traumatic experiences stopped hammering the man's mind. Then a realization struck the provincial. *He's a POW. Once the Americans take him away,*

I might not see him again for years—if ever. After Wilhelm Seiz had vowed loyalty to Hitler, who else would bother stomping through the wreckage of the wine-venom machine to haul him out?

"All right." Fr. Viktor dragged a hand from brow to chin and stroked sandpaper stubble. He could not forsake this man and let him wither in the ruins of the Reich. "You demand my thoughts? You've got them. But first, give me yours. Let's start with that look on your face."

"What look?" Seiz hedged.

"You know what I mean," he pursued. "That look you had when Paul was arrested. The same one I see now."

"How does this relate to my questions?"

"Bear with me. What's that look about?"

The wretch shifted in shadows, turned from his probing gaze, and looked toward coffins towering upon wagons.

"I knew something."

"You knew something. Okay. That's a start. So, tell me. What did you know?"

"What did I know. I knew the procedures of the NSV. That is what I knew. The rest—it was simple arithmetic."

The sun filtered through branches, casting a filigree of light and shadow below. Details shook loose like pebbles: the crates at Seiz's door; the shoes ordered perfectly, the pink slippers that made him sick, for they reminded him of his daughters. "Go on," Fr. Viktor said. The story poured out in a landslide: the doubts that this largesse resulted from raiding missions, the fears sparked by rumors, the calls to superiors who exhorted obedience to Reich and Führer. "Go on."

"When supplies are distributed it is not the country areas, but the cities that receive them first," Seiz said in a confessional whisper. "They are devastated, the need is greater there. The cities: Berlin.

Dresden. Hamburg, Frankfurt, Köln, München. There are more, but let us take these ones, these six. There are millions of Germans there. Millions. Let us assume two million per city. This is not precise, but it simplifies the mathematics. Also, it is impossible for the NSV to provide for all who are in need. It is likely that they provided for one percent: twenty thousand per city." Fr. Viktor felt his own features slump into that telling expression.

"If the NSV could provide two hundred pairs of shoes to Schwandorf, a town in the 'back of beyond,' as you describe this part of Germany, how many went to the cities that I mentioned? And how many more were distributed throughout the Greater German Reich?" Seiz leaned back into darkness again. "You call charity the highest of virtues? I know it only as the gravest of sins. So, we come back to my question. If there is a God, why did He do nothing?"

"Did you tell anyone?" Fr. Viktor said faintly.

A scoff. "How can you ask me that? What proof did I have? Have you forgotten what the Gestapo told me when they dragged Pater Paul through the street? If I breathed a word of my suspicions, the man would kill me, my family, and everyone that I told."

"That was about the monastery."

"You are wiser than that, Pater. It counted for everything."

"You could have told me. We had a moment alone on that day, you and I."

"And what would you have done?" Seiz challenged.

"I would have made the Church aware, at least. I certainly would have tried like hell to get a message to the States."

"Hm. Right. Then your shoes and mine would have been distributed by the NSV in some other district."

"Maybe they wouldn't have found out."

"They are Gestapo, they find out everything! Do you think that you were not being watched on that hill?"

"Of course I knew, I had the chief of police sitting in my pew every day. Why? Why didn't you tell me?"

"Because." Seiz looked away. "Because . . . I wanted to tell you—desperately so! But . . . I could not bring myself to believe . . . I could not."

"Well, there you have it: the answer to your question."

The charity worker's brow knit. Fr. Viktor maintained a paternal tone.

"Take the things that paralyzed you. Your fear, your loyalty, your reluctance to believe. Multiply that by one hundred million Germans. Add a million more who were immobile pillars of hatred. Perhaps it goes beyond that. How many world leaders saw Hitler for what he was, and stood still until the first tanks rolled into Poland?" Remembering his own prayers for America to remain uninvolved, the provincial mulled over coffin-filled wagons. "It's not the Maker who fails to stop evil. It's us. When too many people freeze of their own free will, even He—the Almighty Himself—can do nothing."

Shovels whispered from the trench. Seiz recoiled. "You would have asked me to risk my life and yours, and the lives of everyone you contacted—and those of my wife and daughters?"

"I would have asked you to have *faith*," Fr. Viktor said. The charity worker gingerly kneaded a temple. "When I was about to be arrested over that petition, and when the Gestapo nearly hauled me away, could you have foreseen the need to have an American here today? Could you have foreseen Paul coming back?"

"I swear to you," Seiz retorted huskily, "most people who are arrested by Gestapo are not as fortunate as your Pater Paul!"

"Yes, you're correct. I'll admit that," the provincial conceded. "But you *can't possibly know* what lies ahead, or imagine how God will work through you—or protect you—if only you follow your conscience in times of fear and doubt. It's all a matter of faith."

Seiz huddled in shadow and Fr. Viktor felt a throb of grief. As he had feared, the trauma of indoctrination, a bombing, a mass grave, and guilt compounded upon a shattered psyche.

"I know where you are right now," the provincial said. "It's a dark place, and you've been misled for so long, you don't know what's right, or who to trust. But you're not lost. That voice you hear inside, the one that's making you sick with remorse. It's sacred. Listen to it. Let it be the light that guides you from darkness."

"There is no way through this. There is no hope."

"Of course there is."

"Why should I have hope?" Seiz demanded. "I am a prisoner, and we are again living in defeat! My family is homeless. I don't know if I will see them again. What dangers will my girls face on the streets? What despicable things will my wife have to do to survive? Pater, I don't know what to do!" Fr. Viktor understood his despair. The man's mother and sister had prostituted themselves to endure the aftermath of the first Great War.

"I know what you'll do," he said. "For once, you're going to trust me completely, and you'll do what I say." The ragged shadow rested fingertips upon his eyelids.

"I've told the guards you're too ill to do any good out there. You're going to eat, then rest for a while, and get your strength back. After this funeral, you will leave with the Americans. You'll give them your full cooperation, come what may."

"My family."

"Helene Heidl's taking them in," Fr. Viktor announced. "She feels it's unfair that you all should give so much to the refugees of Germany, and yet receive nothing when you become refugees yourselves. And, she's grateful for your interventions on Klaus' behalf."

Seiz lowered the hand covering his face. "If there was space in that house, I would have filled it with a refugee already."

"She's moving the boys into her room. You're going to let us care for them, and you're not going to worry over their welfare."

"She is . . . you would all make a sacrifice like that. For me and my family? Why?"

"They're acts of good people working in the Framework." He smiled when that gave the man a moment of pause.

"Finally—and most important. You're going to let it all go. All the fear, the pain, the rage, and despair. After you unfetter yourself from those burdens, you'll surrender to your Father. And no matter how dark things get, you'll trust in Him to carry you through." Seiz drew a hand to his forehead, as if he had been ordered to jump from a cliff and expect to fly.

"The world has failed you, my friend. It's time to find your faith again. At this moment, He's the only hope you've got left."

———

That afternoon, five hundred Germans congregated inside the barbed wire enclosure where 140 coffins lay arranged in triple rows. Trench diggers climbed mountainous soil heaps and peered down at the scene below. The grizzled commander glared down from a jeep. He and his regiment observed from the yard of a nearby chapel, their POWs close behind, under guard. They watched the townspeople stare at coffins and cup their mouths in dismay. Fr. Viktor surveyed the Germans: Norbert wore a crisp suit, projecting the dignity of a would-be mayor; Helene frantically searched the crowd, then pulled a hand to her heart, catching sight of Klaus; Maria, Frau Seiz, and a throng of girls looked wan in the stark sunlight; to his shock, the Berlin scientists occupying his monastery had donned their finery and paid their respects.

Three escapees from the Flossenbürg death march emerged from hiding, each swathed in donated street garb too voluminous for their frail bodies. They said *Kaddish*, their prayer for the departed. Fr. Viktor heard exaltation in the lithe Yiddish words and reflected upon a statement the Jews made while confronting him about funeral arrangements.

"We must say *Kaddish*. Now more than ever, we must. It is our way of letting God know that, despite our loss, despite what has been done to us, we praise His name."

The provincial shook his head, his mouth a taut, quivering line. *My Lord. That's grace,* he thought.

He glanced down at coffins stripped of crosses at the Jews' request. A German refugee girl in braided pigtails and a plaid skirt had overheard their conversation. The thought of coffins without decoration saddened her. She had pointed at a garden thriving with spring ivy and suggested they adorn caskets with greenery instead. A band of children picked vines, making sure that sprays of greenery adorned every casket.

Swathed in the robes and chaste white surplice of an altar boy, Hans rushed a paper into his hands. Dean Spangler slid him a look. Fr. Viktor sniffled. "Right. The homily." He had given his fellow clergyman no mean task. American men and three Flossen-bürg survivors stood by, listening intently, making him aware of raw emotions that throbbed like bleeding wounds.

"Lord Jesus," he read aloud in English as Spangler preached conscientiously in deep, somber German. "After Your disciple Peter denied You three times, You came to him, and three times You asked, 'Do you love Me, Peter?' In doing this, You showed Your compassion for the penitent heart, Your yearning for reconciliation in the face of sin, and Your need for obedience to Your will. Father, despite the evil that ruled this land, there is many a servant in Schwarzenfeld who remained true to You. If You ask, 'Do you love Me, Germany?' gladly we would respond on behalf of our fatherland, 'Yes, Lord, we love You.' But Father, it is becoming clear that there are not enough hours in a day, nor days in a month, nor years in a human life to answer for every evil in this war. And so, in the days ahead, we can only have faith in Your mercy, find strength in Your love, and with hopeful hearts, we deliver Germany . . . into Thine hands."

The American commander dismissed trench diggers and issued orders for a bulldozer to complete the burial. Klaus skittered down from a dirt heap, bounding into the arms of his mother.

"Oh, my boy, my boy! My sweet boy!" Helene sobbed and laughed in relief. Hans rushed over to join in a family embrace.

Frau Seiz and her daughters swam through a crowd like fish straining against a current, and they begged Fr. Viktor for one last moment with a husband and father. MPs refused, until he compelled them to think of their wives back home. They produced the charity worker. The provincial felt a wrench, watching Seiz whisper tenderly into the ear of a weeping woman, and plant kisses upon the faces of two daughters who could endure a carpet bombing, but not this parting. Fr. Viktor willed himself to remain a fountain of calm.

"Klaus," Seiz beckoned.

The boy whirled around and edged through a crowd. His lively features creased in shock as he drew near. "You look terrible."

"I have been through some terrible things," the charity worker admitted in a fragile voice. "This 'second father' concept. I don't know if God is behind this. I did not have any conscious intention of playing such a role, it was just duty. I was simply looking after the welfare of a child in grief. But the way I care about you now. This is no longer duty. You are like a son to me." He touched the boy's shoulder, a thumb sliding gently. "So, no more formalities between us. From now on, you may call me Wilhelm, if you wish."

Klaus' mouth worked, but no words came. He could only nod.

"Your father would be proud. You handled yourself in this crisis as a man would—except for that scream." They both laughed. "But he would be proud of you. *I* am proud."

"I don't care if you believe in God or not," Klaus said, hauling his voice from the pit of his being, "I am praying for you every day."

Seiz stared beneath his brows. "Then listen to me—and listen well. You cannot save me. This is not up to you."

"Yes, sir."

"Nor was it your job to save your father."

"Yes, sir, I know. I will pray to give you strength."

"Then we shall pray for each other with this hope. Yes?" Seiz said. Klaus nodded. The charity worker glanced at two daughters who stood weeping. "Protect them for me. That will give me strength also. Promise."

Klaus swallowed hard. "I will, Wilhelm. I swear."

Americans prodded POWs into a truck bound for the nearest camp. The charity worker boarded and mouthed a *'Dankeschön'* to Helene, who nodded back. His attention drifted toward a stricken wife and daughters, but it didn't settle there. Fr. Viktor found Seiz turning his way again. The man filled his lungs, released a soul-cleansing breath, then slid a meaningful look in his direction. The provincial nodded. He knew what it meant.

The muddy olive carrier lurched forward. Weary eyes remained fixed on him until the truck vanished beneath a thin veil of exhaust. His heart pounded. He wondered if he could ever return to Peter and Albert and describe what he felt: the soaring joy of a mission fulfilled, the marrow-deep relief of knowing this catastrophe ended without a bullet fired, the ache to believe that a wayward son now walked a road to redemption. *Have I saved him?* He prayed it was so.

He fled to one thought like a refuge: *Schwarzenfeld is safe.* He would wake tomorrow to a country plagued by defunct currency, postwar uncertainties, and scarce food supplies. His parishioners would have to process a horrific national legacy and they would clamber up the Miesberg's slope, seeking his guidance. *But Schwarzenfeld is safe.* He let peace wash through his veins. Footsteps padded to his side.

"Hello there, Klaus," Fr. Viktor greeted.

Clear blue eyes swept over to him. He read it at once: this boy had been shielded by charity. Love and hope flourished in the garden of his heart, and faith was on the mend.

"Will everything be all right now?" Klaus asked. "With the Amis, I mean."

"I think so," Fr. Viktor said.

"And Wilhelm," Klaus ventured. "Will he come back?"

He sighed. "Oh, son. This is one of those times when we can only trust in the Framework. We'll put him in God's hands. We'll put it all in God's hands."

Funeral ceremony, April 25, 1945. Approximately 500 citizens of Schwarzenfeld gather for a service conducted by Fr. Viktor and Dean Josef Spangler.
Source: NARA Signal Corps Photos, 111-SC-265456

AUTHOR IN THE CONFESSIONAL

The Sower of Black Field is based upon the true story of Fr. Viktor Koch, C.P., and his experiences in Nazi Germany. He is my paternal grandfather's uncle.

Readers will be quick to pose inevitable questions. How did I learn this story? More importantly, what elements are based on fact, and what has been embellished by fiction? I'm honor-bound to enter the confessional, identify points where I applied creative license, and leave judgment to the reader.

This was not a story passed down through the generations. In fact, the Kochs didn't even learn it from Fr. Viktor. In 1947, he made one last visit to his family in Sharon, Pennsylvania, but neglected to mention the day he confronted an enraged American commander and spoke for Germans under harrowing circumstances. I attribute this to the revelation of the Holocaust, which would have been fresh in his relatives' minds. Given the horrors of Auschwitz, my great-granduncle may have feared that the idea of protecting Germans would spark disbelief and contempt, even from the people he loved most. Thus, when he died in Schwarzenfeld on December 15, 1955, at age eighty-three, surrounded by parishioners and Passionists who revered him, virtually no one outside the Bavarian town knew of the role he played in its salvation.

In 1997, an American World War II veteran named Ed Pancoast traveled to Europe with his wife Eunice. They visited with longtime friend Zita Mueller, a German woman who constructed coffins during the forty-eight-hour ultimatum. Throughout the years, Ed, Eunice, and Zita avoided discussing the war out of courtesy, but on that occasion, Zita broke the long silence. Eager to learn more about the heroic American priest who dared to defend a German town from his own countrymen, Ed returned home to Maryland and began an exhaustive search for our family. Thus, the story reached us through sheer coincidence.

Once I discovered that my great-granduncle had saved a Bavarian town from Patton's Third Army, it was not the ancestral connection that inspired me to start writing, but the tide of veneration flowing from the people that he had protected. They honor him for more reasons than one. After preventing American forces from inflicting reprisals upon Schwarzenfeld, he helped them emotionally and spiritually cope with the trauma they sustained during the forty-eight-hour incident. He pleaded for the release of German soldiers held in Allied POW camps—particularly if the prisoners and their families were conscientious objectors of Nazism. In addition, he arranged the delivery of care packages to Schwarzenfeld, and ran donation drives in the U.S., imploring American Catholics to donate money and goods to war-torn Germany. In 1946 the town council declared him an *Ehrenbürger*—an honorary citizen. When they constructed a new thoroughfare in the 1970s, they named it Viktor-Koch-Strasse. In 1995, they affixed a plaque to the Miesbergkirche commemorating his intercession on Schwarzenfeld's behalf. Every ten years they hold seminars, ceremonies, and exhibitions in his memory. Their reverence of him is boundless—and timeless. Eighty years later he is still their Provinsche. I am grateful to Nikolaus "Klaus" Kainz, Herta "Hedy" Arata, and Bettina McClain, the German friends and eyewitnesses who critiqued and corrected me during the writing process. As my own admiration swelled for Fr. Viktor and his followers, their objectivity kept me grounded.

The laboratory operating in the monastery cellar is also based on fact. As Fr. Viktor suspected, the Continental European Research Institute for East Areas was a cover name. In actuality, his tenants hailed from the *Elektronen und Ionenforschungsinstitut* (Electron and Ion Research Institute) for the Technical University in Berlin. Dr. Alexander Nikuradse, a Russian immigrant, led the research team. Rumors flew on the wind in Schwarzenfeld. The townspeople speculated that Dr. Nikuradse and his staff were developing atomic weapons for Germany, a theory that was promptly refuted after the war. According to reports written by the U.S. Counterintelligence Corps (CIC), Dr. Nikuradse's research focused on the effect of electrical charges on various metals. He was attempting to devise technology that would allow the Luftwaffe to evade Allied radar. After a brief incarceration, Dr. Nikuradse was permitted to continue working in the monastery basement until 1953—with Fr. Viktor's permission—but the nature of his work changed. The Americans prevailed upon him to develop ways to turn the rubble of Germany into adequate building material.

The Flossenbürg Death March is also taken from the pages of history. The concentration camp was situated in the northern part of the Oberpfalz, about thirteen miles east of the Czech border and forty miles north of Schwarzenfeld. Before its liberation in April 1945, over 96,000 prisoners passed through its confines. Nearly 30,000 people died there, including Dietrich Bonhöffer, a German Lutheran theologian who supported the conspiracy to assassinate Adolf Hitler. On a frigid spring day in mid-April 1945, as Allied forces drew closer to Flossenbürg, SS guards forced approximately 16,000 Jewish inmates to board trains that were bound for Dachau. According to records from the International Tracing Service, these convoys scattered throughout the Bavarian countryside, and all of them dissolved into nightmare marches that left roads littered with dead. Prisoners were frequently shot for falling behind, or attempting escape. The transport that American pilots crippled in Schwarzenfeld's train station carried 750 Jews, including the victims who were executed after the Allied attack. In the early hours of April 23, 1945, the U.S. Eleventh Armored Division liberated prisoners who had survived the march out of Schwarzenfeld. By that point, over half of the Jews in the convoy had died. Their SS captors were swiftly apprehended as prisoners of war, and in 1947 they were brought to justice by a U.S. military tribunal.

Did American pilots really fire on a train of Flossenbürg prisoners? Tragically, yes. This has been verified by accounts from Jewish eyewitnesses. The Allies assumed that any convoy crossing German territory would be carrying troops and ammunition to the enemy front, and pilots were given orders to stop them in their tracks. The concentration camps were still a rumor floating down the ranks. It had never occurred to them that these trains might be carrying prisoners.

Is the forty-eight-hour ultimatum true? Again, yes. I did invent the scene in which all characters gathered at the town square and

Fr. Viktor translated the order. In reality, newly appointed German officials went door to door, announcing the order to bury the dead and the circumstances that would ensue if Schwarzenfelders failed to comply. Dr. Christopher E. Mauriello, Director for the Center on Holocaust and Genocidal Studies at Salem State University in Salem, Massachusetts, can corroborate my research. He has conducted extensive investigations into cases where U.S. troops forced German civilians to confront the atrocities of the Nazi regime and accept collective responsibility for them. The Flossenbürg Death March left mass graves throughout Bavaria, and there are at least seventy other towns where U.S. troops compelled German civilians to bury victims. However, Schwarzenfeld is the only known instance where an American commander imposed a time limit and threatened to kill civilians if they failed to meet the deadline. I encourage readers to seek out Dr. Mauriello's book, *Forced Confrontation: The Politics of Dead Bodies in Germany at the End of World War II*. He provides a comprehensive overview of the "forced confrontation" incident in Schwarzenfeld.

The story of a death march escapee greeted with a bowl of soup at the *Gasthof Bauer* originated from Herta "Hedy" Arata. A teenager at the time, young Hedy arrived with the *Elektronen und Ionenforschungsinstitut* in 1944 and worked in the monastery as a secretary. A native of Berlin, she traveled back to her hometown and brought her mother Rosa Semff to Schwarzenfeld just hours before the Russian invasion. Both women were present at the *Gasthof Bauer* when the escapee stumbled into the barroom. The touching reaction of Herr Bauer—and Hedy's own mother—is relayed briefly in chapter thirteen.

The Heidls are a fictitious family. Helene is based on Frau Barbara Friese, a woman who worked as a maid for the Gindeles during the 1940s. While interviewing her in 2005, I listened in awe as she told me about the petition incident and the experience of feeding Jews stumbling past the Gindele bakery. The impassioned plea, "Can't you see these people are starving? Let them go!" are her words. The exact details of her encounter with guards driving the Flossenbürg Death March are unknown. In the book, the encounter is presented with maximum tension in mind.

The character of Klaus was born from correspondence with the aforementioned Klaus Kainz, a former Hitler Youth who hails from Pfaffenberg, Germany. He joined the Jungvolk with vim and vigor and began to despise both the youth group and the party.

In 2005, I had the great fortune of interviewing Liebharda Gindele and Josefine Gindele Vogel, and through their stories I became acquainted with their father and mother, Norbert and Maria Gindele. The scenes in which Maria secretly distributed bread to Russian and Polish laborers is based on fact. Liebharda confirmed that her father fought early in the war, but she knew nothing about his experiences on the front, so I created a backstory—grounded in research—that explained his deep-seated antipathy for Reich and party, and his motivations for supporting a disparaged people. When Schwarzenfeld held its first free election in 1946, the townspeople elected Norbert Gindele as mayor, a position he held for twenty years. He, too, was declared an *Ehrenbürger*. Norbert died in 1976 at age seventy-seven. To this day, he remains one of the town's most revered historical figures. Norbert and Maria's son was drafted not in 1941, but in 1944. I changed the timing because it provided a tantalizing opportunity to demonstrate the unity between front and *Heimat*—home front—during the "Mother's Revolt." Young Norbert never returned from the war. He was declared missing in action on the Russian front.

Frau Paula Dirrigl and her maid Fräulein Anna Thanner are historical figures. They graciously prepared and delivered food to the Passionists throughout the duration of their eviction from the Miesbergkloster. Similarly, Fr. Paul Böhminghaus, C.P. is also a real person. I learned about his arrest in a correspondence that Fr. Viktor penned to the Passionist father general in Rome. The scene where Gestapo agents marched Fr. Paul through the streets is based on a true story, though I inserted Fr. Viktor and Seiz for dramatic effect. Fr. Paul's imprisonment lasted only six months, and he was released without a trial. I have never been able to find the letter that resulted in his arrest, nor identify its author.

I should mention Zizi. He is as real as I can make him: only his name is fictitious. Even his cry on behalf of the Gindeles—*here there are good people living!*—is historical. The idea of Poles and Russians roaming freely around town is controversial. Dr. Mauriello believes that some may have been Jews, and this level of freedom would have been unprecedented. As a rule, factory owners were obligated to provide room and board for workers and keep them segregated from the German population. According to my research, the breach of protocol in Schwarzenfeld is confirmed by several independent sources in the town itself.

The names of several antagonists have been changed. It is not my intention to protect them. I'm keenly aware that they may have relatives in Schwarzenfeld, many of whom were born after these events unfolded, and I'm certain they're already haunted by the long shadows of history. I have no desire to offer up reminders that make their lives difficult.

The novel's catalyst demanded the most creative energy from the author. I found him in the Miesbergkloster chronicle. History records that a Kreisamtsleiter Seiz penned letters to Fr. Viktor proposing that he sell the monastery for use in the NSV's 'Children to the Countryside' program. The historical NSV leader made an appearance during Gauleiter Wächtler's initial visit, and he appeared again during the monastery eviction. After surrendering the Miesbergkloster keys to authorities in 1943, he wandered out of the history books, but I couldn't let him exit the stage. I was far too smitten with the idea of exploring the schism of good and evil that existed within the character. History gave me the character of Amtsleiter Seiz, but I never did learn his first name. Wilhelm the charity worker is my creation.

A historical fiction writer delves into research to inject context into her work. Thus, I must give credit where it's due. The sitting room conversation on the Mother's Revolt in chapter five originated from material found in *Popular Opinion and Political Dissent in the Third Reich* by Sir Ian Kershaw.

I am indebted to Mayor Manfred Rodde for graciously welcoming the Koch family to Schwarzenfeld in 2005. I also wish to thank the Schwarzenfelders who shared their stories, especially Liebharda and Josefine Gindele, Zita and Karlhans Müller, Peter Bartmann, Irmi Ehrenreich, Rita Wittleben, Barbara Freise, Anton Obendorfer, Hans and Anna Gietl, Max Rentsch Grünweiler, Josef Schießl, Hans Hartinger, Josef Schmid, as well as many others who approached me during my visit and spoke into my tape recorder without identifying themselves. I'm grateful to American friends who reviewed this book in its manuscript phase—Jim Cirigliano; Bill Thompson, III; and Julie Zickefoose. No writer can succeed without constructive feedback. Theirs was gold.

I owe a special debt of thanks to the Passionist community for its prayers and unwavering encouragement. Fr. Rob Carbonneau, C.P. Ph.D., director of the Passionist Archives, was my invaluable guide on this journey into the world of historical research. One of Fr. Viktor's successors, Fr. Gregor Lenzen, C.P., offered steadfast support from the start.

I'm also grateful for the tireless support of my family, especially my mother Rosemary, brother Sean, and father Gary. They accompanied me on every trip from the Passionist Archives to Schwarzenfeld, and my father stood by my side throughout the entire research and writing process.

Last, but certainly not least, I wish to thank Ed, Eunice, and Zita for their courage in remembering the dark and gritty past. Without them, this book would not exist, and if you are reading it now, then Ed's dream to convey Fr. Viktor's story to the masses has been realized. Rest in peace, Ed.

———

The plaque that Schwarzenfelders affixed to the facade of the Miesberg church during the 50th anniversary ceremony is depicted on page 341. Its engraved text reads as follows:

In gratitude to honorary citizen Fr. Viktor Koch C.P., Provincial of the Passionists. Through personal engagement and civil courage, he prevented in April 1945 an act of retribution by U.S. troops upon the population of Schwarzenfeld.

IN DANKBARKEIT DEM EHRENBÜRGER
H.H. PATER VIKTOR KOCH C.P.
PROVINZIAL DER PASSIONISTEN
DURCH PERSÖNLICHEN EINSATZ UND ZIVILCOURAGE
VERHINDERTE ER IM APRIL 1945
EINEN VERGELTUNGSSCHLAG DER US-TRUPPEN
AN DER BEVÖLKERUNG DES MARKTES SCHWARZENFELD.
SCHWARZENFELD, APRIL 1995
MARKT SCHWARZENFELD